No Greater Crown

Part V of
The Autobiography of
Empress Alexandra

by

Kathleen McKenna Hewtson

ISBN-10:   1720161283

ISBN-13   978-1720161288

'No Greater Crown: Part 5 of The Autobiography of Empress Alexandra' is published by Taylor Street Publishing and is the copyright of the author, Kathleen McKenna Hewtson, 2018.

Dedication

This book, Part V of The Autobiography of Empress Alexandra (yikes), is dedicated first of all to my patient readers.

I'd like to apologize as well for it being Part V and not the final book. The thing is, I couldn't do it; there's too much to tell and I can't stand not telling it, so one more time and then, honest, I'll say goodbye to this astounding Russian family, a family like any other and like no other on earth, and therein lies the profound fascination that lots of us feel for them.

Alix was a very difficult woman, but after all these years she feels like a friend too, one I would have spent a lot of time rolling my eyes at. I guess that makes me Anya, but, like Anya, I too have written about her and it's been an honor and a pleasure and a nightmare.

Who writes six volumes? What kind of idiot ...?

Well, I didn't know what I was getting into, and once in, it's hard to leave, so here I stay.

Moving on, as always, this is for Tim, my great love, husband, companion, editor extraordinaire, and for the city I love so much and love to write in, if not about, ah San Francisco!

To my wonderful, long-suffering family, thank you, Carolyn and Steve, and Barb, and Sally and Philip for everything, always.

Last, but not least by a long shot, to my beautiful and astounding friend Belle Avery. What a woman! She can wrestle prehistoric sharks into movie theaters and could probably make pigs fly too. You'd have been a great Empress, lady, and I love you.

"Commend me to his majesty and tell him that he has been ever constant in his career of advancing me. From a private gentlewoman he made me a marchioness. From a marchioness he made me a queen; and now that he has no higher degree of honor left, he gives my innocence the crown of martyrdom as a saint in heaven."

Quote attributed to Anne Boleyn.

Chapter 1

How much betrayal will break love? Does love grow stronger over time? Can an old love, one between two people who have lived soul-to-soul together for a long time, bear more than a young, untested love? Or does time, that old enemy of youth and beauty and hope, make the heart smaller, less able to expand and thus forgive?

"Germany has declared war upon Russia. We are going to war."

With these few words and the foolish actions and pride that inspired them, Nicky ended everything.

I think, in fact, that is exactly what I said, or certainly something like it. "It's all up now."

And then, with Anya holding my hand, I cried as I had never cried before.

How far it went and how fast – the madness that claimed all of Europe – is what may be more interesting to some who will come after me and study it than the fact of the war itself.

Once, when I was in England as a wee childy, out with my sister Irene while visiting Grandmamma at Balmoral, a storm blew up seemingly from nowhere; the sky had been clear moments earlier.

An old gardener, who was standing nearby, scratched his head and said to us, "That came out of the blue, didn't it, girls?"

Funny, isn't it, how these things stay with us?

But as regards the war, that was the truest of true things to say about it, for it did come out of the blue in a most literal sense; for that's what the summer of 1914 began as, the longest, hottest summer in living memory. The sun shone uncharacteristically hard over Europe, and maybe we all should have known that it wasn't the strange and wonderful blessing that it seemed to be, but a warning, a sign that, since it was all so bright and clear, we should have looked harder and basked less in its beauty.

I think now that Nicky knew war was coming all the time; maybe he even wanted it. Why that would be so, I do not know, but then no woman ever knows why men seek what they consider to be the glory and honor of war. We women know, and have always known, that neither glory nor honor is to be had in war. Wars bring only suffering beyond imagination, and loss.

I say that Nicky knew the war was coming because I am gifted, like many people, with great hindsight, and with that hindsight one can examine situations more clearly and see the hidden motivations tucked behind seemingly innocent situations.

The possibility of Olga marrying was the first of the signs I missed that summer. When Nicky came to me with a half-smile and a letter in his hand, I had been sitting outside on our loggia at our palace in Livadia.

It was early spring and glorious. We had in actuality spent the better part of a year there. Then, when October arrived and Nicky idly commented that we must plan our return to Tsarskoe Selo, he raised the matter in a questioning tone.

We were outside and it was early evening, and the scents were heavenly, and the sky over the sea was just turning lavender.

I responded by smiling at him.

"Oh, but Nicky, it's so lovely here and the children are so happy. And I always feel better in Livadia."

"So linger a while, so fair thou art," Nicky quoted, raising my right hand to his lips and meeting my eyes. "Is that what you were going to say, Sunny?"

I leaned in so that he could kiss my lips, and we lingered outside that late afternoon while he read me a funny letter from my cousin Missy, now married to the Crown Prince of Rumania.

Missy, whom I remained fond of despite her being the ghastly Ducky's younger sister, had invited us all to come and visit her. Unsaid, was that she had a marriageable son, Prince Carol, and we had many marriageable grand duchesses, although she did mention her "longing to meet your sweet eldest, your Olga, most particularly."

Nicky observed that I didn't seem overly upset by the invitation, nodded to himself, and said no more about it, moving on to say that, if I was happy to remain in Livadia, he saw no reason to "scurry back to that swamp of a capital," mentioning only that we would, of course, have to return in time for Irinia and Felix's wedding.

I had my own thoughts on those particular nuptials, but stayed my tongue, not wishing to argue. For, if Nicky was in the mood to indulge my dearest wish to remain exactly where we were, I didn't wish to muddy such tranquil waters. Besides, I could not stop that ghastly wedding, and Xenia and Sandro – Irinia's parents, who could have done so, had failed to listen to me on the subject of what a misalliance it was destined to be.

This was hardly surprising, I suppose, as not a soul in that wretched town paid any attention to what I said or how I felt about matters, this despite my being their Empress and having given them an heir for Russia.

How they all hated me despite my best efforts, all of them – Nicky's dreadful family, the so-called nobility, the ministers, the wretched Duma – and how, in return, I hated the capital and everyone accommodated there.

So, stay in Livadia we did, on and on, and when Christmas approached, we shrugged off the rituals in Petersburg and celebrated my first and only green Christmas, so-called because of the lack of snow, only to discover that I didn't mind it at all, although Baby was a bit fretful about it.

"It just doesn't seem right, does it, Mama? All green like summer when it's Christmas."

I petted his glossy little head and looked about us. My new palace was a series of open loggias that could be reached from every ground floor room. There were splashing fountains and, even now in December, I could enjoy roses and jasmine and lilac, not sent to me from greenhouses but grown right here before me.

"Don't you like it here, darling?" I asked.

He nodded.

"Oh, I do, Mama. I like it better here than any place in the world. It just seems funny, that's all, like maybe we should have gone back just for Christmas, and then come back here." Brightening with his idea, he finished enthusiastically, "We could come back and live here all year except for Christmas, couldn't we?"

"But not at Christmas?" I queried, amused.

He frowned and started speaking slowly.

"No, I … I mean … I don't know. You know, because …"

"Because …?" I prompted gently. "Is it because you are worried that Father Christmas won't be able to find you here, Baby? For, you see, you shouldn't worry about that."

"Oh, Mama, I haven't believed in Father Christmas for ages," he said indignantly, as though he were a man of twenty,

I bit my lip to keep myself from laughing.

Mollified, he added pompously, "Anastasia explained all about Father Christmas to me last week."

I rose abruptly and buried my face in a Wisteria vine to suppress my amusement.

"Mama, what are you doing?" he asked, annoyed.

Choking with laughter, I gasped out that I was checking the vine for bugs.

"Why are your shoulders shaking? You aren't crying, are you? Oh dear, did you still believe in Father Christmas? Didn't anyone ever tell you before?"

It seemed forever before I could manage to stop gasping from the most uncontrollable fit of giggles I had suffered since girlhood.

At last, when I was able to straighten myself up and return to my chair, I wiped my streaming eyes and, still short of breath, addressed his worried little face, a face I just barely managed to keep from covering with kisses.

"It's all right, darling. I did, of course, suspect he might not be real, but naturally, having you confirm it is a bit of a shock."

He nodded solemnly and reached over and patted my knee.

"I know, Mama. I was quite upset myself. In fact, I wondered if she was telling me a fib, just to upset me. You know how she can be ..." I managed a nod. "But then I went to Olga and she said it was most probably true what Anastasia had told me, although M. Gilliard said he wasn't quite sure ..."

I looked down and spoke to my lap as I said, "Yes, well Monsieur Gilliard is Swiss, and they set great store by Father Christmas as they live amid so much snow." Realizing that was one of the most evasive answers I had ever given to one of my children, I tried again. "Baby, if you don't believe in Father Christmas any longer, and if this is your favorite place on earth, why were you talking about going back to Tsarskoe Selo for Christmas?"

He frowned, looked away, and then mumbled something I didn't catch.

I moved closer to him and tilted up his chin.

"What is it, agoo wee one? You can tell Mama. Is there something you want but haven't told Papa and me about yet?"

He shook his head and looked at me with great sorrowful eyes.

"No, Mama. What I want isn't something you or Papa can get for me. It's just ..." He shrugged and then with a catch in his throat said, "... it's God and, well, Baby Jesus too. Christmas is a good time to talk to them, isn't it?"

"Anytime is a good time to talk to them, precious. It's why we pray."

"No, but it's especially good now because this is when Jesus was born and I want ..." He began to become tearful, but whether in frustration or because of something deeper I could not tell.

I held out my arms and he threw himself against me with his hot little face at my neck.

He choked out what he wanted and the hearing of it nearly killed me. He was frightened that if he didn't have Father Grigory with him at the sacred time of Christ's birth to help make "God hear him," he would have to wait another year to ask Jesus to make him well again, and help him to stand and walk like he used to.

All I could do was murmur mama-isms. "He hears you always, Baby. Father Grigory prays for you every day. He prays for all of us. Your leg is straightening. It will all be all right. Everything will be fine. Don't worry, my darling."

Chapter 2

We did stay through Christmas in Livadia that year, for our first and only time. It was so lovely this green Christmas, and Baby seemed to enjoy it as much as, if not more than, the rest of the children. He certainly shouted the loudest of all of them in sheer glee at the utter novelty of bathing outside during wintertime in the fine, round, saltwater bathing pool that Nicky had ordered to be constructed on the grounds. He had arranged this before our new white palace had even been thought of, following the near-drowning of Anastasia when she was taken by a rogue wave when she was very little.

Baby, of course, knew none of that. To him it had always been there, and he, brown as a berry, and healthy – oh, he was healthy, with only a tiny bend in one leg to remind us of those terrible days at Spala – swam and splashed and showed none of the fears he had voiced to me earlier.

Our whole family, in fact, was in excellent health and spirits, although it couldn't really last, as I had to caution Nicky when he told me that it was as though I was my old self again.

"You see, Nicky dearest, my heart is so terribly damaged that times such as these can only be viewed as small miracles. I was just speaking to Anya about it this morning, before your little tennis game with her, and she said she wasn't a bit surprised that I had been so well of late."

Nicky inclined his head non-committedly.

"Oh, and why is that, Sunny?"

"It is as I suspected. She has been writing regularly to Father Grigory and he has written to her as well."

"I see, and …?"

"And, Nicky, he has informed her that he has been exhausting himself in Pokrovskoe, doing nothing but praying for my health, and that he fears, should he stop for even a moment, it will all go away. I cannot expect him, or even wish him, to pray for me all the time as he has so many others who need his healing prayers as well. Indeed, I told Anya so." Nicky leaned back, stretched himself out and yawned ostentatiously. "Forgive me, Nicky, if I'm boring you," I continued. "Certainly it cannot be my mentioning of Anya that bores you so, as you spend such a great deal of time with her. I can only assume that it is the mention of Our Friend that causes you to yawn so, or," I felt my throat tighten, "is it simply that you find me tedious?"

Nicky leaned forward and reached for my hand, which I pulled back.

Sighing as if it was all too much for him, he stood up and lit a cigarette.

"No, Sunny, you never bore me, and I don't quite know what you mean by mentioning the time I spend with Anya since you demand that she tag along with us on every possible occasion. And she herself is rather insistent that I play tennis with her, which is, I can assure you, quite an undertaking."

This made me curious.

"Why is that?" I asked, trying not to let him see that I was diverted, but I was, and pleasantly so, for he and Anya had been playing tennis every morning.

17

Sometimes watching their silly running back and forth from my lonely balcony, I had felt ... oh, ridiculous things, emotions that Nicky's words could easily erase before these tiny things I had begun to wonder about were no longer quite such small concerns.

Nicky, sensing my change of mood, eagerly said, "She's really a dreadful player, you know. If she weren't so deuced cheerful and amusing, I'd really have to ..."

He broke off at the look on my face.

"*Deuced cheerful and amusing*, Nicky? Why, that must be a pleasant change for you."

"Alix, what are you saying?"

He spread his hands in a show of helplessness.

I spoke to his hands, for I was oddly frightened of what I might see on his face just then. I shrugged and tried to explain myself, but it was difficult to explain to Nicky something I was so unsure of myself and so much wanted not to have confirmed. Three people spending a lot of time together; the wife is care-worn and sick; the girl companion to his ailing wife is younger, more physically energetic and eager to please, keen to establish her own place in his heart; the husband compares the two women and finds the forbidden one more congenial; then the husband becomes tempted by what would be forbidden to other men, but he is the Tsar of all the Russias after all; he is allowed to do anything he wishes. It happens. It had happened with Nicky's grandfather.

"I ... I don't know exactly what I'm saying, Nicky, but look," I pointed to his crossed ankles, "even now you're wearing some of those silly socks she bought you."

18

I tried to say more. I wanted to tell him how it felt to see them laughing together, and I wanted to ask him if Olga had been telling the truth when she had asked me why Anya's foot "kept rubbing Papa's foot under the table at luncheon today," 'today' now being yesterday.

I wanted in fact to say things about Anya that I wasn't certain I meant. Didn't he think she was fat and stupid, and that she chewed her food half-in and half-out of her mouth like a great big cow? And if she had indeed played some sort of disgusting footsy game with him, wasn't he repulsed?

But then, if I said any of that, I might have to ask him if I was still beautiful to him, if when he looked at me he still saw the young princess that he had loved so much, or if he, too, was beginning to see the failed Empress that the rest of the world saw, and if seeing me as they did, then was he seeking a newer and pleasanter view?

I couldn't ask any of that because Nicky could fail me at times when I needed his reassurances the most. It might be better to …

"Sunny …?" Nicky interrupted my ponderings.

"What?" I answered stupidly.

"Is there something about Anya and my behavior that is upsetting you?"

That seemed a strange way of addressing the problem and I looked at him, this time in the face.

"How ridiculous, Nicky! Should there be?"

He got to his feet, stretched again – nervously? – and wouldn't meet my eyes.

"No, obviously not. So, did you want to tell me more about her and Father Grigory, because if not, I have to …" He trailed off. I turned away and twirled my hand around dismissively. I didn't need to see his face to know if he had understood me as he announced somewhat defensively, "I have to answer a letter to young Yusupov."

"What in the world are you writing to Felix about?" I asked. "I hope you are suggesting that he cancel his wedding. I don't wish to see him and his entire, ridiculous, jumped-up family become our relations. Yes, good idea. Do write to him, Nicky, and tell him that you cannot approve of his marriage to your niece after all. I assume that is what you are going to say, is it not?"

"No, you know that is not what I am going to say. I gave my permission to them a long time ago and the wedding will undoubtedly take place. Xenia and Sandro, as Irinia's parents, have given their permission too."

"But you are the Tsar."

"And Mama has personally approved the wedding after speaking to Felix at length," he continued.

As always, what could I – only his wife, merely Russia's Empress – say to such an irrefutable statement as, "Mama has personally approved the wedding"?

In all truth, I didn't much care. I had little use for Xenia and Sandro these days. If they wished to throw away their only daughter onto an ambitious commoner of compromised reputation, then who was I to question them? Their daughter was a simpering little thing who managed confoundingly to be both too worldly and too shallow at the same time, and I was somewhat relieved that her marriage would place her outside my own girls' immediate circle, for Maria had long hero-worshipped her cousin Irinia and I did not like their association.

20

I was merely letting Olga's report of Anya's revolting flirtation with Nicky at luncheon the previous day affect my mood and starting arguments about matters I had little interest in.

Understanding this about myself, I said nothing beyond, "Yes, well then, I suppose it's a *fait accompli*. Listen, Nicky, I'm feeling tired and think I would like to rest. You go and write your letter now."

This left him nonplussed, because, as I knew to my own sorrow, it was unlike me to let a matter go unresolved in my favor once I had raised it. Still, he was so obviously relieved at his reprieve that he tried eagerly to reengage me.

"Well, all right, darling, you rest. I am indeed keen to reply to Felix's letter. Do you want to know what it is really about?"

I shook my head, showing neither an interest nor lack of it in what Nicky was proposing.

Nicky continued hopefully. "It's quite funny, really. You see, I wrote to Xenia and commanded her to ask the children what they wanted for a wedding present."

"They are hardly children if they are to be married, are they, Nicky?" I caviled.

Nicky shrugged in half-agreement with me. "No, I suppose not. After all, that's what marriage is, isn't it, Alicky, the very death of childhood and innocence?" Before I could answer, if I could have done so, he continued. "Anyway, I asked Xenia to ask them, and I received a quite nice letter from young Felix, thanking me for thinking of them, and saying that really they didn't need anything that he could think of."

"Rather an understatement, given the Yusupovs' wealth, don't you think, Nicky?"

Ignoring my little pinpricks again, he finished with, "But what he would like is to be able to use the imperial box at the Mariinsky when he and Irinia are in town. I thought it was a rather charming request, so I am writing to give them my permission, although, of course, we'll be delivering them a real gift as well. By the way, darling, you said you wanted to be the one to choose it. Won't you tell me what our present is to be?"

I gave him an enigmatic smile and shook my finger at him.

"Oh no. It's a surprise. But I promise you it's most suitable, even extravagant. The family will be speaking of our gift for years to come."

He looked at me worriedly and shrugged.

"Oh well, I suppose it will be fine, although it's not one of your vases, is it, darling?"

"Nicky!"

"You know that I love them, Sunny. Consider how many I have of them even in my study here. It's just that nearly everyone we know has so many of your beautiful vases already, and I thought ... well, I thought maybe there should be something different for the young pair."

He fell silent and I felt an agitation building up inside me at the callous injustice of his thoughts. He was referring to all the lovingly hand-painted vases I had made as gifts for people over the years, personal gifts, not things bought with no thought or feeling behind them. But I knew, oh yes I knew, that my little vases had become yet another way to poke fun at me, and that, worse, they were despised by all those who had received

22

them. It seemed so cruel of Nicky to mention them. If only he had known what I had in mind, he would have been forced to swallow his words and beg for my forgiveness ...

But he didn't, and I didn't want him to know, so I attempted a smile and spoke steadily.

"Of course I know how much you love them, Nicky. But no, it's something else entirely. Well, you'll see ... Oh, and darling, if you run into Anya on your way to your letter writing, could you ask her to join me for tea?"

He looked at me with a puzzled expression, or, as I thought more likely, with a dull anger disguised as puzzlement.

"If I run into her, of course I'll tell her, Sunny, but there's no reason I should do so. Wouldn't you think she'd be more likely to be found in her rooms, or maybe in the gardens with the children?"

I eyed him carefully but he appeared to be genuinely innocent of any knowledge of Anya's whereabouts. Relieved, I smiled at him, genuinely this time.

"You are right, darling. I'll just ring for Maria to go and find her. Forget I asked it of you, will you?"

He looked as though he might be wishing to come closer and kiss me, so I closed my eyes in anticipation of it and opened them only when I heard his footsteps fading away.

Sighing at the ordeal I had just faced and at what I feared might prove a much greater one ahead of me, I rose and rang to summon Maria.

Chapter 3

I had intended to use Anya and my *tête à tête* somehow to prod her into explaining to me what Olga had witnessed at that luncheon, but nothing ever went quite to plan around Anya, and this time was no exception, as she managed to wrong-foot me the moment she bustled onto the balcony where I had ordered tea to be served.

She was unkempt, for one thing, her face all red and perspiring, and her shirtwaist untucked, and, for no reason I could imagine, she was carrying a tennis racquet.

The funny thing about Anya was that one might almost consider all this to have been a deliberate ruse, her way of constantly distracting my attention and engaging me, amusing me, as no other person alive could, but of course nothing about Anya was ever deliberate or thought out, which is why I had trusted her – and yearned to do so again – as I had trusted no one else.

So I had to ask her, "Anya, I see you have brought your tennis racquet to tea. Is that to swat away flies and mosquitoes, or to thrash one the servants for some grievous lapse or other, perhaps to punish them for bringing the wrong kind of cake?"

The joke of my remark, for I was already in a better mood, was that, by immutable Romanov family lore, we were always served the exact same cakes for tea every day, however much I tried to persuade them to throw all caution to the wind and attempt the occasional variation, and so I was anticipating that Anya would issue a companionable harrumphing sound in recognition of our mutual frustration with the impenetrable *status quo*.

Instead, she scowled at me, sat down in a great red mound of frumpiness, and objected, "Well, no, I haven't done that since I was a little girl. Why would you ask me that?"

Stifling a grin and trying to remember why I needed to speak to her, I merely shook my head and motioned to the footmen to set out the tea. I then waited until we were alone again to resume speaking, and then had to wait still longer until Anya's mouth was quite empty so that she should not be tempted to spray me with seed cake as she spoke.

However, it was Anya who spoke first, and in doing so did nothing to allay my growing fears.

"I'm just carrying about my tennis racquet in case Ni... His Majesty ... has a spare moment for another game. He does so like to play with me."

She announced this piece of self-congratulatory nonsense in an unsettling mix of coquettishness and complacency, and then, horribly, licked her lips clean of cake remnants and gave off the most dreadfully smug expression.

I was too appalled at her presumption to summon the will to respond to her provocation, but this did not seem to bother Anya, for, with growing self-assurance, she continued, "Yes, I think everyone is noticing how refreshed and contented His Majesty is these days, although, naturally, I cannot take even the slightest credit for that. How could a few silly games make such a difference to His Majesty's state of health and happiness?"

"*Silly games*, Anya?" I inquired.

I could not tell from her jaunty explanation whether she had missed the underlying tone of menace in my voice, as she eyed me suspiciously for a moment but also continued our conversation seemingly untroubled by my querulous exclamation as she popped some more cake into her mouth, chewed it so that a cascade of crumbs fell through her open lips (which she brushed away with a little embarrassed giggle), and finally shrugged dismissively.

"Well yes, in that most people don't consider tennis to be an important game, although personally I find it most entertaining when I am playing with His Majesty."

"Is that the only game you are playing, Anya?" I asked sharply, now sounding more like the Empress I was, addressing the remiss servant I suspected her of being.

Anya straightened, slowly set down her cup and plate, and stared at me in a manner I can only describe as more put-upon than apologetic.

"What are you asking me, Alix?"

I was utterly taken aback, for there was this woman facing me, in all temerity, through narrowed, shrewd eyes, with an expression on her face that resembled much more that of my relentlessly hounding mother-in-law than my naïve and clumsy Anya. Oddly, I even felt afraid of her for a moment before collecting myself.

Afraid of Anya? How ridiculous!

I sat up straighter in my chair and decided to return matters to their natural course by reminding Anya of the code of behavior expected of a commoner in her dealings with her Empress, be she a regular companion to that empress or no. No doubt it was all just a misunderstanding, but Anya's newfound attitude of barely-concealed disrespect towards me could not be permitted to continue.

However, before I could dress her down properly, she smiled at me and said, "Never mind. Actually, I wanted to ask you something today, you and His Majesty, although I can ask His Majesty later, I suppose."

I could not believe what I was hearing.

"You will not ask His Majesty one thing, Anya!" I commanded her at the top of my voice.

Anya looked at me calmly before selecting a biscuit from the plate and examining it closely. Then, instead of cramming it into her mouth in its entirety, as she usually did, she took a delicate bite from it and set it back down on her plate, wiping her hands on her napkin in a precise, even finicky, gesture.

"I see. Well, aren't we in a funny mood today?" she declared, and before I could respond to this outrageous remark by shrieking at her further, or by fainting from the sudden attack of heart pain I was experiencing, or possibly by tossing my tea right into her great fat face, she finished by saying, "You see, I would like to marry Dmitri," and raising her hand to cut off my involuntary exclamation of shock, she went on. "Oh, I know what you are going to say – things you have already said."

I think my eyes must have bulged almost out of my sockets at that. Was she saying what I thought she was saying: that she was determined to become a member of the imperial family one way or another, and that she was going to do it either by luring Nicky away from me or by being offered a suitable alternative, such as Dmitri? Had she gone out of her mind? But what else could she have been suggesting by suddenly bringing up her desire to marry Dmitri again? Hadn't we been over this ground several times already?

I could not see how what she was doing was anything other than nakedly threatening me – give me Dmitri or I will take Nicky! Now she was going to explain to me why she could have Dmitri, reasons I could lay before Nicky to get her off my back and to get her to leave Nicky alone. The nerve of the woman! To think I had ever trusted her. To think how tolerant I had been of this silly, conniving, manipulative little girl from nowhere!

Anya proceeded exactly as I had feared.

"Firstly, you will argue that he's a member of the imperial family and has to marry a princess. But I know he wanted to marry Irinia, and yet she's marrying Felix instead. Felix is a terrible sodomite and not remotely royal, so does that not make me a far better candidate for Dmitri than Felix is for Irinia, if you think about it?"

I had to fight off a fit of dizziness as she paused to raise another objection she was going to counter. This was all going terribly awry.

"You also told me that Dmitri might marry Olga, but I know you will not allow that marriage to take place because you don't like him anymore, and His Majesty told me over tennis this morning that you are taking Olga to Rumania to see about her marrying Prince Carol."

A red mist descended in front of my eyes as, despite the seismic shaking in my legs, I managed to rise to my feet.

For the first time since entering my rooms that day, Anya looked startled.

"Alix?"

I raised a trembling hand, while using my other trembling hand to hold myself upright.

"Anya, you will never marry Dmitri and nor can you ever marry into the imperial family at any level. You are not of noble birth and moreover you are divorced. What can you be thinking?

Anya pounded her hand on her lap to interrupt me.

"You and His Majesty let Nikolasha marry a divorced woman, and he is a member of the imperial family. And I am of nobler birth than almost anyone. I'm a descendant of Emperor Paul."

She just wouldn't stop! And while she kept referring only to marrying Dimitri, all I could hear her saying while she stared me directly in the eye with an unheard of insolence was, 'It's Dmitri or Nicky, Alix. You choose!'

"Quiet!" I screeched. "You be quiet! This exchange will never happen again. In fact, I think, Anya, that you should plan to spend less time with our family altogether from here on, for clearly our kindness to you has gone completely to your head. Furthermore, how *dare* you discuss private family matters, such as Olga's marital future, with His Majesty? You are not one of us, Anya, and you never will be."

Anya tilted her head up at me – not rising, not crying, and apparently not remotely alarmed by my threat.

"Are you being so cruel and awful to me today," she inquired, "because I want to marry Dmitri or because His Majesty told me something before he told you?"

"You, you …you cannot know what … what Nicky and I … what His Majesty and I … discuss."

Apparently determined to rattle me, to push me beyond measure, almost beyond reason, Anya picked up another small cake, swallowed it in one bite, and sighed heavily in the direction of an invisible person of her imagination positioned somewhere across the room, as though I were so mad and such a trial that her patience was wearing thin.

"I happen to know that His Majesty told me before you, because he said he was telling me before you. And you should sit down before you take a fall. Should I fetch Dr. Botkin?"

"Anya," I began speaking very slowly, trying desperately to master myself, "why in the world do you think that His Majesty would discuss something so private and important with you before speaking about it to me?"

I hoped she hadn't heard the fear in my voice.

She lifted a shoulder, dropped it, spread out her hands, and raised her eyes to heaven, all, I imagine, to indicate her inability to think of any reason for Nicky's extraordinary behavior. Then, as if inspired, she said earnestly, "Well, of course, I couldn't speculate, but maybe he was excited about it and wasn't certain you would be out of bed yet. It wasn't even gone noon when he told me, so that must be it, don't you think so? Yes, that must be it. After all, you are more often than not asleep or having trouble with your heart at that hour, and he wouldn't want to disturb you, would he? We both know how considerate he can be."

I badly wanted to remain standing, but my poor weak legs and my overworked heart did not allow me to do so, therefore, shakily, but still managing to fend off Anya's unwanted assistance with a forbidding glower, I lowered myself back into my chair.

Then, trying not to gasp for breath, for this was an Anya whom I did not know or understand, and one whom I felt I should not show any weakness in front of, I managed to say, "You'll need to leave me now, Anya. I must rest. In fact, I'll need you to prepare yourself to leave Livadia altogether. His Majesty and I only have a few days remaining here ourselves, and I find that I wish to be left alone to enjoy being with my family for a while." I cut her off with a smile before she could protest my decision. "One other thing, Anya ..."

I raised a finger which I was gratified to see was no longer shaking. Indeed, I was suddenly feeling altogether better. Power over oneself, and in my case power over all, could, I had found, be a restorative. It was one I made use of all too seldom. I needed to correct that, especially with Anya.

Anya had gone pale and was visibly trembling from her chins to her toes.

I smiled again.

"In view of your concerns over Felix's character, I think it would not be appropriate for you to attend his wedding to her *Imperial Highness* Princess Irinia," I said, placing an emphasis on Irinia's title.

Anya, who had developed an unbecoming purple hue as I spoke, was literally spitting in outraged innocence. I turned my head to avoid having her spittle land across my face.

"But I was invited to the wedding ... and I ... I don't want to go back to town. Why can't I stay here? And how will I go? Are you going to send me home on The Standart and then have it come back for you, because that doesn't seem sensible."

"Of course that would not be sensible, Anya. Besides, The Standart is only for our use," I replied. "No, you will have to take the train back to town. I'll arrange a car to run you to Sebastapol."

"Oh no, I can't possibly take the train. I'll be hot," she protested, frantically fanning herself to remind me that she had a tendency towards becoming overheated, but only serving to underline why she had to go, and the sooner the better.

"Anya, my dear ..." I began, adopting an air of restrained patience because it was very important to me that she not know I was worried. Appearing worried in front of Anya would betray weakness on my part; worse, appearing worried in front of myself would validate my silly, no doubt groundless fears, although Anya's behavior towards me over the last few minutes had made me seriously question how groundless they really were. Still, groundless or not, Anya needed to go, at least for now. "... You will not be any warmer on the train than you are running about under a hot sun playing tennis with His Majesty, so I am confident that you will be fine. Now you should go and instruct your maids to begin packing for you."

Then we had one of those moments, Anya and I, the sort that always made me wonder, before I managed to shake off the thought, whether Anya was rather more cunning than I gave her credit for. For now, instead of bursting into tears or making protestations, as she inevitably did when faced with not getting her own way – Anya was such a child sometimes, or pretended to be – she merely looked at me with a calmness bordering on arrogance, and said in a light tone, "I see, then. Well, all right. I would like to go back to town. I have missed my family, and, naturally, I'll wish to spend some time with Father Grigory to tell him all about our visit here and how everyone is doing." She rose with a great deal more grace than she usually did and smoothed her ghastly skirt with an exaggerated gesture of propriety. "I have to agree that it really is time I left."

I was so taken aback by her response, and then suddenly doubtful about my decision, that I instantly sought to modify my position as to whether she should leave us or not.

"Anya, maybe I am wrong. Maybe you'd like to stay on a bit longer …"

Anya smiled straight into my eyes and gave a sneaky little laugh. "No, I think I'll leave you all to your last few days together here."

Then she was gone, even without seeking my permission to make her final departure. She must have ordered her maids to pack for her with great haste, too, because, when she did not appear at tea time, I sent for her, only to be told that, "Mrs. Vyroubova left for Sebastopol an hour ago."

Adding to my discomfiture, every face at the table turned towards me in confusion, and Nicky said, "That is odd, isn't it, Sunny. Is she ill?"

Before I could answer him, Olga seized the opportunity to announce emphatically, "Good, I'm glad she's gone."

Tatiana looked at her sister in shock.

"I'm not. It will be strange here without Anya. Can't you call her back, Mama?" to which Olga said coldly, "You don't even really like her, Tatiana. You only pretend to because Mama likes her. Only yesterday you said –"

"Girls, enough!" Nicky interrupted with sudden irritation.

Tatiana ignored him and, red of face, turned on her sister. "You're a liar. You're the one I wish was gone. Fortunately, you will indeed be gone soon enough."

Baby, who was very fond of Olga, looked alarmed and said, "What does Tati mean, Mama? Olga isn't going anywhere, is she?"

I shot a look at Nicky, inviting his help, but as always in any situation where help was needed, he resorted to staring absent-mindedly into his soup plate in order to ignore the whole affair. Regrettably, neither Olga nor Anastasia followed his lead.

Grinning, Anastasia said to her brother, "Oh, they're trying to find someone to marry Old Big Head, and we're all being taken off somewhere to try to talk some silly prince into taking her off our hands, which makes me glad because then maybe Maria can move into her and Tati's room and I can have one to myself," with the result that both Olga and Baby got even more upset, to be followed a few moments later by Maria.

Then everyone began talking at once. Tearfully, Maria asked Anastasia why she wanted her to move out

34

of their room, Anastasia replying that she was quite sick of Maria's snoring and chewing at her toenails. This was news to me, but before I could address it, Olga demanded loudly to know, "What on earth are you lot talking about? I'm not marrying anybody just yet, am I, Papa?" and Tatiana shouted at Anastasia to demand where she had heard about this, to which Anastasia cheerfully answered by disclosing that she had eavesdropped on Papa and Anya's conversation of the day before.

It was left to me to end all the arguing by standing up and abruptly leaving the room without addressing another word to any of them, while Nicky later commented that he at least had had the fortitude to stay behind to try to calm everyone down, "And really, Sunny darling, our children do rather get beside themselves, do they not, and somebody has to settle matters."

"They are certainly highly spirited," I replied and took the opportunity to add, "Olga is getting decidedly out of hand, I have to say. I was most shocked at her lack of manners, giving opinions on something she knows absolutely nothing about, and so rudely too. You must have been quite shocked yourself, Nicky. And did you know that she disliked poor Anya so?"

I was now thoroughly regretting my decision to send Anya away. I missed her already and I was fast realizing that I had reacted far too hastily to something I might only have been imagining. I had also had an inspiration which had instantly soothed my troubled mind: Anya was the one person in Russia more hated by absolutely everyone than I was, so verily I had nothing to fear from that quarter.

Nicky, who had always been terribly fond of Olga, immediately came to her defense. "Darling, in all fairness, do you not think that it was Tatiana who spoke out of turn?" he said, knowing full well how equally close Tatiana and I were. "And where is Anya? What could have been so urgent that she was obliged run off back to town without so much as saying goodbye to me ... to us? I thought she meant to sail back with us for the wedding."

Seeing a chance to get myself off the hook for this whole situation, I shook my head ruefully and said, "It seems, darling, that Anya still takes it somewhat amiss that Dmitri once wished to marry Irinia rather than her. She also harbors a strong dislike of Felix." I shrugged. "How tactless and outspoken she can be at times! So I suggested to her that it might be more appropriate for her to go on ahead to Petersburg. Nor did I want her speaking in front of the girlies about her silly infatuation for Dmitri, which, as it happens, given the girls' outbursts at luncheon, is probably for the best. Obviously Anastasia overheard you and Anya discussing why we are going to Rumania this spring."

Nicky chuckled. "A wise decision, Sunny my precious one. And maybe it is for the best in many ways."

"What do you mean by that, Nicky?" I asked sharply.

He looked at me, puzzled, or seeming to be puzzled anyway.

"I didn't mean anything by it, darling, just that you were right, as always. Whatever would I do without you?"

I accepted what he said because I did not want to know if he was telling me the truth about something I did not want to know anything about at all in the first place.

Chapter 4

Despite our reluctance to leave the beautiful and peace-filled haven of Livadia, we all enjoyed our rare deep-winter cruise back to Petersburg, although Nicky became visibly subdued as we neared the capital and began to catch up with the remnants of the usual brutal Russian winter, a dark season the first part of which we had for once managed to avoid.

I joined him on deck during our approach to land, and found him smoking and staring morosely at the small ice cutters busying themselves around us as they carved out a path for us towards the dock. I placed my hand against his back and rubbed it in small circles.

He turned his head towards me and tried to smile.

"Sunny darling, here we are then, back safely."

"But you are sad, aren't you, my Nicky. Why ...? I mean, heaven knows I loathe these endless winters, but we're traveling again soon, and there's that ridiculous wedding where you get to give the bride away, which will, I think," I smiled more widely, "be good practice for a papa with four beautiful girlies."

He nodded distractedly and waved his hand towards the nearing shore.

"Yes, and I am indeed looking forward to the wedding. As you know, I do not share your feelings about its being a misalliance. No, it is just ..." He stopped. "Look at them, Sunny, look at all of those men just standing about, hovering, lying in wait for me."

Confused, I grasped his chin and studied his face in concern. "Who, Nicky, the stevedores?"

"No," he growled, "the ministers."

Quite alarmed by his vehemence, I stepped back.

"Look at them, Alicky, all gathered there in their black coats, like crows waiting to pick my bones. I can almost hear them, can't you? 'Oh, Sire. Oh, Your Majesty, the Duma ... the *zemstvos* ... the strikes ... strikes here, strikes there ... and the Jews are at it again ... and this grand duke wants this, and that grand duke wants that ...' And there will be a thousand telegrams waiting to be answered. 'Oh, Sire. Oh, Your Majesty, you have been gone so long ... What are we to do here ... and here ... and here?' God, Alicky, I just cannot bear for it all to start up again!"

He bowed his head against the icy railing and shuddered, while I looked around nervously in case someone might have overheard him and be tempted to repeat this intemperate tirade of his to others. Fortunately, the officers all seemed totally preoccupied with the business of preparing to dock our ship, so if they had overheard him, they gave no indication of having done so.

While I was somewhat at a loss at Nicky's explosion of emotions, there was certainly much truth in what he said as it was traditional for Nicky's ministers and various members of his family to gather at the Winter Palace to greet us on our return, and I knew that this would inevitably entail many tedious rounds of toasts and tea that would test my endurance every bit as much as his, and most likely considerably more.

After all, it was normally I who moaned to Nicky about having to greet people, as I was usually thoroughly exhausted by then and didn't see why we simply could not board our train and go straight home to Tsarskoe Selo without all this silly fuss. Indeed, I had largely trimmed the whole ridiculous charade down to a minimum, demanding that it last no more than half-an-hour, no matter what, but now eyeing Nicky doubtfully, I worried that even that might prove too much for him.

How unfortunate it was that we didn't have Count Fredericks with us for the occasion, but he didn't like to be away from his wife and children for too long. Most selfish of him, I thought at that instant, for he was so good at being a soothing presence and knowing just what to say and do in awkward situations. I therefore resolved to summon Father Grigory to us the minute we got back to Tsarskoe Selo, as clearly Nicky was having some sort of spiritual crisis, which, considering that we'd been in Livadia resting for months, was surprising. Yes, Father Grigory would, as always, know just what prayers and words were needed, although I had been planning to wait a while before summoning him to our presence in order to forestall another round of relentless gossip.

At this instant, however, I was the only one who could calm Nicky down before our landing, there being nobody else on hand to help me, and I didn't like the idea of letting people see him in his current agitated state, especially not my ghastly mother-in-law who I knew would be waiting to welcome her darling one home. So I cast about me for a way to end this most inconvenient of moods, and then, realizing what was best to be done, I called an officer over to me.

"Find the captain, young man, and please tell him to announce as we dock that His Majesty and I will be delayed from disembarking for an hour."

He looked at me as if about to question my decision, as we were mere minutes away from arrival, but catching the sternness in my expression, he bowed and said, "It shall be done, Your Majesty."

At that, I took Nicky by the hand. "Darling, will you do me the honor of accompanying me to our cabin?"

He looked at me, still unsettled in anticipation of his forthcoming ordeal, and impatiently shook his head.

"Sunny, we have to disembark in a moment, and I'll need to say a few words, and I don't have time right now, darling."

I placed his hand against my neck and, leaning in very close, whispered in a way that he could not mistake my meaning, "You do, my precious one – you do have time for this."

It was remarked upon later how exceptionally charming Nicky had been that afternoon, although I fear the children made a rather poor impression as I had forgotten to give orders that they should precede us off The Standart and go on to the Winter Palace ahead of us. They were therefore forced to hang around, clicking their heels and with nothing to do, until we were ready to disembark, and this made them rather sulky, but overall I think our homecoming was perfectly splendid.

Chapter 5

It was surprisingly pleasant to find ourselves back in our dear little nest at Tsarskoe Selo, despite the bitter January cold and the persistent darkness, and after two days I summoned Father Grigory to join me for breakfast.

I hadn't seen Father Grigory for months, and although I often wrote to him from Livadia, it was understood that my letters would not be returned. It wasn't necessarily that Father Grigory was illiterate, for Anya said that he could often be found scribbling words onto scraps of paper, or maybe she said that he would direct others to write things down for him, I can't remember. I do know that he could print his own name, but, I had never myself seen him write anything down, so I was never offended by his silence. Besides, both Nicky and I did receive telegrams from him now and then, often causing Nicky to remark in an amused tone that they were the oddest telegrams he had ever received from anyone anywhere. I chose to ignore such scruples as I felt that Father Grigory's mind and heart were so elevated that it was terribly difficult for him to communicate with those of us not in constant communication with Our Savior.

For example, the previous July he had sent me a telegram announcing, "The vine is ripe, the mind is ripe, but all will wither before harvest."

For my part, I struggled vainly for hours, even days, to understand what he meant by this, but Nicky merely snorted and said, "Sunny, I believe that Father Grigory is finally showing an interest in wine and how it is made, and is just reflecting, in his usual muddled manner, on how the successful harvesting of the grapes can be such a precarious business."

These were the sorts of dismissive and slyly debunking remarks that Nicky often made about Father Grigory and his pronouncements, which served only to remind me that in so many ways Nicky's heart and mind were still closed off to the great blessings of retaining this holy man at our side.

While I let such concerns pass, as a devoted wife and mother I continued to ask for Father Grigory's particular prayers and blessings upon my two dearest ones, Nicky and Baby, which was why I was anxious to see him that morning, beyond having simply missed him, for, with the wedding looming in less than a month, I feared that Baby might somehow harm himself.

I say this because it seemed that ill fortune particularly dogged us right before any public appearance involving Baby. The anticipation of such events made him frantic, and us too, as tongues at court would invariably be set to wagging if Baby did not make an appearance on such occasions, and it was even worse when Baby begged to be allowed to attend and had to be carried around in the arms of a Cossack. For then, not only did those in the highest of places question his health, but so also did the ordinary people who took every opportunity to gather together to watch us as we passed.

I knew that Father Grigory would be in a particularly fine mood that morning as, during my telephone call inviting him to come to Tsarskoe Selo, I had said that he need not consult the train schedules on this occasion but should rather simply get himself ready and go outside his apartment to discover something that would come as a great surprise to him.

I was expecting him to be pleased and intrigued by my suggestion, but in fact his first reaction was one of suspicion. It seems that peasants are not particularly fond of surprises.

"To a peasant, Mama," he said, "hearing that something is happening we do not know about means that our hut has burned down, or that our crops have failed, or, as was the case during the last war, that it is time for us to go off to some terrible place and face the enemy's guns like cannon-fodder." He warmed to his theme. "Yes, I think it is best for poor Grigory to have no surprises, but thank you, Mama, for thinking of a worthless fellow such as me."

He was so delightful in his funny, whimsical ways that I chortled at him and replied that I thought he might find what was outside more to his liking than a burned hut, and that, at any rate, "it's a direct order from His Majesty and me that you step outside now. So it must be done, Father Grigory!"

"I don't want to, Mama," he grumbled stubbornly.

Angered by his refusal to enjoy our wordplay, I ended up ruining the surprise by saying sharply, "His Majesty and I have bought you a car. We have also supplied you with a driver who will be available to you at all times, and both of them are awaiting you outside your apartment, Father Grigory. Please forgive us if this is an unwanted gift. We were hoping that you'd be pleased."

44

"I would have been very pleased indeed, Mama, if you had just said, 'Father Grigory, Papa and I have bought you a car. It's outside now,' but since you chose instead to make me wonder if my family in Pokrovskoe had all died, or maybe had an even worse fate befall them, I am now only a little happy … and relieved, too."

I found myself torn between expressing to him my exasperation at his ingratitude for our kindness, and my need to get off the phone as quickly as possible and go downstairs to share the great joke of it all with Nicky. I chose the latter, wishing Father Grigory an enjoyable first trip in his new automobile.

Nicky was always overjoyed at any opportunity to be drawn away from the mountains of paperwork that always awaited him when he had been away, if only for a moment, and he did indeed laugh heartily, almost until he choked, at Father Grigory's tale of people bearing gifts towards peasants.

Wiping his eyes, he chuckled, saying, "Isn't it marvelous, Sunny darling, the innocence of the *moujiks*? They really are children, aren't they?" I nodded happily, for I agreed with him, and then he added more thoughtfully, "I wish more people could understand them as we do. They are just children who need us to care for them. These liberal monsters who speak of more freedoms for the people, who call for an end to the Autocracy, to us, to all of our kind throughout the world, they do not understand them even slightly. Without our care for them, our peasants would perish in a day. I do not do this for myself. I do it only from my sense of duty and from my great love for my people – all of my people. And yet so little do they appreciate it!"

I nodded in fervent agreement, for who had ever worked harder or sacrificed more than Nicky had for his people, with the sole exception of Our Lord and Savior Jesus Christ? At this thought, I shuddered in superstitious horror, for, like Jesus, Nicky was hated by many who should have revered him; and unlike Jesus, Nicky could not ask that this bitter cup be taken from him.

My gloomy thoughts were mercifully cut short by the announcement that Father Grigory had arrived at the palace. Nicky smiled but jumped to his feet quickly, explaining that, much as he wished to join us, he had dozens of idiotic ministers waiting to bedevil him, so, with a hurried kiss, he dashed off, only to encounter Father Grigory in the doorway of my boudoir.

"Papa!" I heard Father Grigory joyfully exclaim. Nicky muttered something I couldn't catch and then Father Grigory, who, it must be admitted had a rather carrying voice, replied, "Yes, that is so, but there are still many things I must discuss with you. Do not worry whether I might be busy. I will come to your study after I leave Mama."

So it was that Father Grigory found me trying to stifle my amusement as he entered.

"Why, Mama," he said happily, "you are looking so well and so filled with the joy of God today. Or maybe you are just glad to see old Father Grigory again, yes?"

I rearranged my face into a more solemn expression and held out my hand for him to kiss, which he ignored, instead leaning over to kiss me on my cheek, which I didn't like at all, although I didn't bother to remonstrate with him about it. I had long ago resigned myself to the

46

fact that Father Grigory, as the holy man that he was, tended to ignore social niceties, and those included all elements of court etiquette. The saints, as I had explained to Nicky once, kissed everybody indiscriminately, regardless of their social status, or lack of it.

Seating himself immediately and grabbing at some cakes I had ordered to be set out, Father Grigory started to speak before I even had a chance to invite him to do so, and with his mouth still full of cake. "Poor Anyushka is most upset with you, Mama," he said, "and I am too. But you needn't worry, for I shall set all to rights between you. Friends must not be unfriendly towards each other, for if so, then they are not friends. You understand?"

"She has complained of me to you?" I exclaimed indignantly.

He nodded, wiped his mouth, and seized another cake, reminding me so much of Anya as he did so.

"Of course she has, Mama, to me and I imagine to everyone else she has spoken to since you sent her packing back to town. She is very upset, and as you know," he shrugged, "our Anyushka is not one to keep her troubles to herself."

Coldly angry now, I snapped back, "That may be so, Father Grigory, but I prefer to keep my husband to myself, and Anya overstepped her bounds by a great deal on this occasion, taking shocking advantage of my great kindness and condescension toward her."

Father Grigory appeared neither surprised nor dismayed by my words. He sighed instead.

"Mama, I am not just a *starets*, I am also a man and a husband too, and I am sometimes also the greatest sinner God has ever allowed to draw breath. All of these things have made me see that we have all, at times, faltered greatly on the road to heaven, a road on which the Devil has strewn many a rock for us to trip over, as we do. But are a man's falls of more importance to God than his rising up again?" Before I could answer that question, if it was a question, he stared at the ceiling, still chewing on his cake openmouthed so that I had to look away, and continued ruminatively, "Poor Anyushka is as frail as any of us, and not bright, but she offers something better to you and Papa than that. So you must put all this out of your head and forgive and forget, and be friends again, you see?"

I shook my head to indicate that, no, I did not see, and remarked somewhat curtly, "It is all very well and good your knowing about sin and forgiveness, Father, as do I, as do all people who call themselves Christians, but I fail to see how Anya contemplating breaking the commandment that 'thou shall not commit adultery' means that she offers something better to me. What exactly might that better be and why do you care about it one way or the other? In short, what business is it of yours?"

"Why, Mama," he laughed as if addressing something that was impossible to comprehend, "are you mad at poor Father Grigory? No, you cannot be." He paused. " It is not my business, except that where there is one Russian on our soil who is sad, I must bleed for him. Only you and Papa can save Mother Russia and its people from sadness, and if you yourselves are sad, then how can you do that?"

Confused now, I protested, "I am not sad, Father Grigory, so unless when you speak of one Russian's sadness you mean Anya's, I fail to see what you are referring to."

"You are sad without Anya, or you soon will be. Despite her silliness and failures, she is a loyal and loving friend to you, Mama. Do you have so many such friends around you that you can afford to lose even one? No, I see you do not. So you will be sad, and then Papa will be sad too, and then he will worry about you and not the Russian people, so all will suffer merely because Anya is silly. But we already knew this about her, and silliness is not evil. Forgetting what matters most, however, is."

No one alive, not even my own husband, the Emperor of all the Russias, would have been able to speak to me like that and ever be forgiven, but Father Grigory was the sole reason my precious son was alive, and I knew that if Alexei should die, I should too. I knew it, and I knew now from his boldness that Father Grigory knew it, and was relishing the power it gave him. This was what Nicky feared, and why he had tried to keep his distance from him, but he was as silly as Father Grigory described Anya as being to think he could. For I needed Father Grigory to live, and Nicky could not live without me, and so here we were, trapped by what we needed, and controlled by this man, a man I hoped was indeed a holy one, but one who at times, like now, I was reduced to doubting, much as I might deny it.

In the end, of course, all I could do was to exhort Father Grigory vehemently to explain to Anya that she must never again test my kindness by showing an inappropriately amorous interest in Nicky, and that she must especially refrain from ever playing foot games with him under the table again. If she agreed to this, I said, she would be allowed back to court daily for tea and companionship, but I would much prefer her not to insist upon staying all evening, every evening. Moreover, no matter what, she would not be invited to accompany our family to the wedding of Irinia and Felix. I also told him that I expected to receive a fervent apology from her for so far overreaching herself and abusing our friendship.

Oddly, he did not seem as pleased as he should have been by my easy capitulation, saying only that he would try his best, but that he found, "the minds of ladies harder to puzzle out than the ways of Our Creator."

I decided I'd had enough of this rigmarole and called for someone to bring Baby to me so that Father Grigory could check him over and thus reassure me of his continuing good health. He did so, and blessed him, and asked him questions about his leg – the one that still was not straight – and then the three of us prayed, but he did not give me the unqualified assurance that I wanted to hear (no, needed to hear), that Baby had outgrown all attacks, saying only that such matters were in God's hands.

How I restrained myself from snarling back, however foolish he might consider me, that I knew that much already. I did know that, but God's hands had not always proven gentle with my boy, which was why Nicky and I tolerated this sometimes infuriating madman in our midst.

I banished this thought immediately, knowing I must not even let myself think these things, for Father Grigory had once told us that if Nicky and I lost faith in him, we would lose everything, and since in truth Nicky had no faith in him, it all rested upon my shoulders to save us, to save us through Father Grigory, otherwise all would be lost.

So I did what Father Grigory advised me to do and invited Anya back into our family circle, waiting in vain for her apology, or at least for some sort of shamed acknowledgement of her sins, neither of which, to my fury, was ever forthcoming.

Instead, it was Anya who sulked and shot me unkind looks whenever she thought I wasn't looking at her. Indeed, she maintained such an air of affronted innocence that I began to question my original feelings on the matter. Was it all in my mind? Was I the heartless, suspicious woman my mother-in-law had cast me as being, and whom so many others believed me to be as well?

I did not think so then, and I do not think so now, and in the sad end, what did it matter? For, as Father Grigory had so tactlessly said, I had few friends, and despite my being sorely aggrieved with her and her iniquitous behavior, my greater grief was that I had missed her terribly.

So we resumed our old family life, and if the water was murkier underneath the placid surface of appearances, I chose not to peer into it too deeply. To achieve any sort of peace in life, it often requires that one should choose not to examine rigorously the underlying substance of things.

Chapter 6

I found, to my own surprise, that I rather enjoyed Irinia and Felix's wedding.

The young pair shone with such beauty and promise that I found it hard to prevent myself from crying out of a combination of sentimental affliction and regret, for hadn't it been but a few moments since Xenia and I had first become young mothers together, her Irinia being born only weeks before my Olga.

I ducked my head to conceal my foolish tears, noting that when I glanced across at Xenia she was crying too. Seeing this, I smiled at her and we exchanged a look of loving sorrow and pride, and for a moment I forgot the things that had separated us: her ghastly husband; her loud and ugly boys; and her endless loyalty to my despised mother-in-law.

I saw only the proud young mother she had been with her first baby.

Back then, we had been only a tiny bit older than the beautiful young woman standing today at the altar, just girls, newly married to the men we loved, and with all of our lives in front of us – lives that had appeared then to stretch out ahead of us like one long, glorious summer's day. How quickly all that had come and gone, and yet how could I regret the passing years when they had brought as much joy as sorrow?

They had, hadn't they?

I shook off my foolish question. Truly, these sorts of thoughts seemed to be coming at me with distressing regularity, as though a part of me were running away with itself. How ridiculous it was of me to question my time in Russia. Of course, my marriage and life here had been the glory of my existence. Why, I had only to look at my own four girlies and my so precious son. Baby was a page boy at this, his cousin's, wedding, so tall and handsome and well, his limp, the dread mark of his ordeal in Spala, almost totally extinguished so that no one who wasn't looking for it would ever notice it.

Then there was Nicky, looking every inch the Emperor that day as he escorted Irinia up the aisle. When he returned to my side, he winked at me and whispered roguishly that it "was good practice for me."

I poked at him playfully, but when I looked over at our big Olga standing in a line with her sisters behind Irinia, all clad in court gowns, I furtively crossed myself.

Olga, my first tiny one, was ready for marriage already – at least by the standards of royalty – as she was eighteen. However, unlike her pretty cousin Irinia, I could not be sure that when her great day came she would be wearing such a radiant expression.

I glanced once again at Xenia to find that she was still wiping her streaming eyes. Now she was becoming annoying. What did she have to cry about? Her daughter had been allowed to marry the man of her choice, had she not, although, in order to be allowed to do so, she had been obliged to sign over her own rights to the succession, a silly formality that meant nothing, for I had provided Russia with an heir, and if, God forbid, something should befall Baby, there were any number of male Romanovs in line for the throne before her, starting with Nicky's brother Michael, and then Nicky's uncles and their sons. So her daughter's meaningless gesture was just that, as were her tears over "losing my darling." It would be I who stood to lose my darling girls as they were picked off, one by one, to make politically expedient marriages. Xenia's daughter was not from the ruling family: she could marry a commoner and Xenia could see her every day if she felt like it. She would be able to hold her grandchildren and not just pore over them yearly in photographs. I had given birth to four beautiful angels, only always to be aware that I would inevitably lose them to dynastic unions.

Olga had been distant and cold toward me ever since that unfortunate luncheon in Livadia, and she viewed the approaching trip to Rumania to meet Prince Carol and his parents with both dread and anger.

"Mama, you always said that you and Papa married for love and that you wanted that for us. Well, what I want is to stay in Russia and to marry for love. Why are we going to meet this foolish prince? I won't have him, I won't, I won't, I won't. I'm Russian and I mean to stay in Russia. Why are you making me go?"

Naturally her anger was directed at me and not at her precious Papa, who, because he was a ruling Emperor, was the very reason for it all.

I tried to explain it all yet again.

"Darling, you know that your old Mama was nobody much, just a little princess from a little duchy, so it didn't matter at all whom I married, or even if I got married at all. You all know that story. Indeed, Mama would not have married anyone at all if it had not been for your papa. But you girlies are little grand duchesses and must marry members of ruling houses."

"You certainly can't say Papa wasn't from a ruling house, can you, Mama? You can't say that because he was the Tsarevich and he got to choose whom he married. What is a grand duchess compared with the heir to the throne? No, it's not right and it's not fair. You can't make me do it!"

We had spoiled them, Nicky and I.

Stiffly, I tried to explain to Olga that with her elevated birthright she owed her life in obedience to the crown and her heritage, and that those of us chosen by God to occupy elevated positions must at times serve His will uncomplainingly.

"Like you do, Mama?" Olga shot back with poisonous innocence.

I told Nicky that night what she had said to me, but to my annoyance he showed more concern for Olga's despair than he did in regard to her dreadful behavior toward me.

Scratching at his beard with his free left hand, his right hand holding a cigarette as always, he smiled sadly. "It is hard on them, I know. I remember so well how I felt when Papa and Mama were pressing me to marry that strange girl Mossy and then Princess Hélène, while I only wanted you, my own darling."

"And so this case has nothing to do with ours, Nicky," I underlined, refusing to be mollified, "as Olga has not loved only one other since she was a wee childy. And moreover, what in the world do you think she meant by implying that I haven't sacrificed everything to God's will."

"Sunny darling, of course she didn't mean that. She's merely young and upset. All of our children, all of Russia, and certainly your old hubby, know what you gave up, and continue to give up, for our family, for your adopted country, and for me in particular. Please, darling, do not upset yourself. We are all emotional from the wedding and a bit off-balance about our trip to Rumania."

I let him soothe me into his arms and into sleep, but the next morning I was still disturbed and in need of reassurance, so I stupidly discussed the matter with Anya over morning tea, who, after hearing what had passed between Olga and me, pursed her lips, sighed deeply, and said, "Ach, well, Alix, I now see that you are as cruel to Olga as to me, proclaiming that the only person in Russia worthy of marrying for love is you – and you aren't even a real Russian."

Anya's mind was such an odd one that at times her idiocy and her wanton lack of tact, as on this occasion, intrigued me more than it angered me; so, instead of slapping her on the arm, I languidly sipped at my tea and merely raised an eyebrow as if only vaguely interested in her cavalier airing of her rebellious streak.

"I am sorry, Anya," I said, "that you fail to acknowledge me as your rightful Empress, since I am, as you say, not truly Russian," I smiled to temper my words, "but tell me then who *are* you loyal to? You do know, I hope, that all Russian empresses hail from other countries. And after you have explained this to me, then maybe you can also tell me who else I have prevented from marrying for love, since apparently my own daughter is but one of countless others of my victims."

Unperturbed, Anya nodded as though impressed by her own wisdom, before saying in a consoling tone, "Oh, I don't suppose you're any less Russian than any of the other empresses. People just think that way because they never see you. It's why they call you '*Nem...*' "

She broke off, flushed, before noisily gulping at her tea.

I waited for her to continue, but she remained red, silent and perspiring.

I spaced out my words dangerously. "They call me *what*?"

She shook her head.

"I don't ... I don't ... I don't know what I was saying. I don't know what they call you."

She burst into noisy sobs.

I continued implacably. "Yes, you do, Anya. It is n-e-m, and then what? *Nem* what?"

Standing and waving her arms, her face puce and dripping with tears, crumbs flying from her mouth, Anya finally shrieked, " '*Nemka.*' They call you '*Nemka.*' Everyone does. I hear it everywhere. I'm sorry. I'm sorry, it means –"

I knew what it meant, and Anya was going to take quite some time spitting it out, so I interrupted her. "It means 'woman,' or more precisely 'a German woman,' with the emphasis on *German*. Kindly calm yourself." I said this quietly, for I did not feel either angry or agitated at this ugly foreign word to describe a foreign person. I did not feel anything at all.

However, my exhortation to her to calm down seemed only to upset Anya all the more, if that were possible. Sobbing and stumbling, she knocked over the tea table, caught her shoulder as she bumped into a wall, and then started fumbling desperately for the door handle.

I watched her unmoving and unmoved, and remained silent as she bumbled her way out of the room and down the corridors.

The palace was either particularly quiet that day or my hearing was preternaturally acute, but it seemed that I continued to hear her, and nothing else, for a long time, her sobbing and bumping, scrambling and crashing.

Was I all alone here?

I tried to reach for the bell, but my hand was stiff and clumsy, like Anya's for once, and I managed only to knock the bell onto the carpet where it made a muffled '*tink*,' before all immediately around me was a grand silence invaded only by Anya's now far-distant kerfufflings. Maybe it was better that I should be alone as I didn't really want Maria or her army of maids fussing about me. Maybe they would even be thinking that word that Anya had said everyone called me.

So, rising slowly as if I were very old and fragile, I made my way carefully around the overturned table and its mess of spilled food and tea, to the doorway of my bedroom, and once there, I lay down on my side and stared blankly out at the darkening sky.

It was barely past noon, but already here in this frozen land, night was encroaching again. Good! I wished for neither light nor comfort. I would lie here with no fire to warm me and no spectral servants to offer me their false allegiance. No, all I wanted was to sleep, and later, when I awoke, I knew that nothing would be changed except that I would be more capable of maintaining my habitually false face.

I needed no mirror to examine my real face now, but I was cruelly aware that, if I had been brave enough to look at it there and then, I would have seen a reflection on it of the wretched despair I felt for being so hated in this accursed country, that and the shadow of a growing fear spreading across it, for I was shivering with dread at that moment, knowing that something was coming for me out of the darkness, a terrible thing, not yet fully assembled but inexorably gathering together its forces. I could feel too that it was near, that it was maybe already in my quiet house, hiding in the darkness, waiting for me.

Yet I couldn't let people see that I was afraid, especially not my dearest little family who looked to me to be their sunshine, as Nicky called me. As a mama, I could bring them happiness or let my despair infect them, and despite what even my oldest girlie thought of me – and I knew what she saw: a selfish, pampered invalid – I did try always to show joy even in my darkest times. I knew that, even if Olga did not. So, I needed to be alone, because if I was seen in this state, I would never be able to hide my fear from them or keep from sharing it with them.

Nicky found me hours later in the unheated, dark room and was scandalized.

"Darling, my Sunny, my precious one, what in the world ...? Where are the servants? Why are you here?

60

We thought you had gone off somewhere with Anya. Darling, talk to me ..."

I was muddled and headachy from my nap and from the cold, and I didn't want to tell Nicky what Anya had said. Always when one is accused, even when innocent, one is shamed nonetheless by the accusation. I was no different in this regard than any other human being. So I did not let Nicky rage at Maria when he rang for her and she arrived flustered; I claimed I had a migraine and asked them send for Dr. Botkin, thus avoiding all need to speak.

The next day, when Nicky brought me an invitation for our girlies to attend a ball at Anichkov that their darling grandmamma wished to hold in their honor, I only smiled and commented on how kind it was of her to think of them.

Chapter 7

Naturally, Minnie's ball was hailed as the highlight of the season, although in truth it was the usual ridiculous Petersburg affair, with ten thousand beeswax candles and a matching number of roses that had been sent up from the Crimea during the bleakest month of winter.

I commented upon this to Nicky as our carriage arrived at Anichkov, for the boulevard outside was lined with the ominous-looking black scarecrows of the populace, huddled and shivering outside to stare at us with their hungry and, it seemed, resentful eyes. No one bowed and no one cheered; they just stood there, skeletal and cold and judging.

"Nicky," I said, "I think this whole silly affair is ill-judged, don't you, darling? The people do not seem to like it at all."

Nicky frowned at me and gestured toward the girls, all four of whom were listening avidly to our conversation.

Tatiana appeared ready to speak, and doubtless to agree with me as always, but at Nicky's look sat back in her seat staring at her hands.

"No, Sunny, it is not ill-judged. It is what the people expect from us, indeed what they want from us. For hundreds of years it has been one of their great pleasures to watch the nobles and members of the imperial family at play. It adds color and glamor to their lives."

"It looks to me, Papa, that they'd be more interested in having heat and food in their lives." Anastasia interjected saucily, prompting all of us, including Nicky, to burst into laughter.

I believe my unusual gaiety was much commented upon that evening, for oddly I did rather enjoy myself. It had been so very long since I had danced with Nicky and I was terribly proud to see how admired all four of our girlies were.

When, at last, I prepared to depart, having remained at the ball to the uncharacteristically late hour of midnight – due as much to my own inclination as to the pestering and begging of my two smaller ones – I kissed Nicky goodbye and managed to thank Minnie rather graciously, before herding Anastasia and Maria off to the carriage to take us to our train, where, on the ride home, I was nearly as giddy from the evening as those two little monkeys.

I had left behind my lady-in-waiting Sophie to act as an extra chaperone for Olga and Tati, no doubt somewhat to her displeasure, as those two talked their indulgent papa into staying on at the ball until four-thirty in the morning. The girls then slept nearly all day, but poor, dear Sophie was obliged to be up and about again in order to join Anya and me for tea, where she related that Nicky had told her on the train ride that he had morning meetings scheduled for nine a.m. himself. He did look terribly done in at luncheon, but I showed him no mercy, teasing him about being the beau of the ball and blaming our girlies for keeping such late hours.

I think back now on that winter at Tsarskoe Selo, the last time that we truly lived without fear and in happy expectation of our futures, and I am glad that the gift of future sight is only granted by God to the few. I pity them for it, and yet I still puzzle as to why Father Grigory sounded no warning to us then, when all that was to come could have been avoided. It doesn't matter now, I suppose – nothing can matter now – and, at any rate, on we merrily went, unknowing and preoccupied by a matter that seemed at the time to be of the greatest importance: I speak of our journey to Rumania to let young Prince Carol, my cousin Missy's son, and grandson of King Carol I, meet our reluctant Olga.

Nicky was already feeling exhausted and overcome by his haranguing ministers and the endless quarrels and decisions that they and the wretched Duma members were always trying to involve him in, so it was at his suggestion, and not mine, despite the endless criticism I heard of my "hatred for the capital," that we returned to Livadia at the beginning of April in that momentous year of 1914. We had Anya with us, and as the girls had requested, we brought their beloved lady-in-waiting Sophie Buxhoeveden along with us too. That created some dissatisfaction with Anya as she tended to be foolishly jealous of anyone who attracted the smallest bit of my affection, including, I think sadly, my children.

It is an odd thing that I had not noticed before that Anya and the girls disliked each other so much. I had received their funny little notes asking if Anya was still coming to tea on days that I had felt too unwell to see them, but until Olga had blurted out her comments about Anya at that luncheon, which seemed to be seconded by all my girlies except Tatiana, I hadn't known – or maybe I hadn't wanted to know – the extent of their animosity towards her. As for Baby, I think he and Anya were fond of each other ... or I hoped so. She always made a great fuss over him and he had never told me he did not like her.

Well, the whole truth of Anya is that things were no longer the same between us by then, hard as I tried to hold onto our companionship, and much as Father Grigory wished me to do so. Try as I might, I could not forget her ridiculous throwing of herself at Nicky the previous year, and nor could I continue to ignore her petulant reaction to my giving anyone else the least of my attention, my own children included.

Equally, she was no longer the same with me either: she was simply no longer amiable. Whereas she had once expressed agreement with my every statement, now she seemed determined to offer up a contrary opinion on everything I had to say. She laughed at odd times and she gave the impression of studying me with an unsettling interest when she thought I wasn't looking at her. Only when Nicky was about did she again become the affectionate, amusing figure that I had long loved. If, when I first met her, she had been the person I knew now, I would never have offered her my true-hearted friendship nor let her become virtually a member of our family. It was, I realized, too late to change things between us, as Anya had become a habit with me, if no longer a pleasure, and while I did not relish her constant presence, I could not see our being without her. So, on she stayed, a reminder of happier times maybe, I cannot truly say. As for dear Sophie, she remained mostly with the girls, thus avoiding Anya's ill-concealed ire.

In early June, we all traveled on board The Standart to visit Missy, her husband Crown Prince Ferdinand, and their son, Carol.

It was the strangest summer. Everybody across Europe was commenting on the weather, because, no matter where one was that year, hot blue days followed each other in relentless succession, and Nicky, who rather enjoyed heat, unlike me, made our captain drop anchor all across the sea so that he could indulge himself in his passion for swimming.

Baby and the girls begged to be able to join him, but I forbade this as I feared danger from the sea creatures lurking in the depths. I did, however, allow them all to run about the ship barefoot, something that no doubt would have scandalized my mother-in-law. In fact, as the heat continued, I often surreptitiously removed my own shoes, a pleasure that made me understand the children's delight in doing so. Unfortunately, Anya chose to imitate me, and the sight of her enormous, welty, flat feet slapping about the deck was most unappetizing.

Between the heat, my preoccupation with the coming visit, and my own problems, I did not keep a close enough eye upon my four daughters, and so it was only the night before our arrival in Rumania that I noticed over dinner what mad jackanapes our children had become, and by then it was far too late for me to do much more than gasp out in horror as they noisily tramped into dinner, resembling nothing so much as blackamoors! Somehow they had managed to expose all of their arms, and certainly their faces, to the sun's punishing rays, and they were each in varying shades of deep reddish-brown – so maybe they better resembled those fierce Red Indians than blackamoors.

"What have you done with yourselves?" I exclaimed.

They all fell about laughing at my shocked question, and Nicky, that naughty boy, joined them!

Tatiana, at least, had the grace to look away from me in shame, although, if she blushed, it was impossible to tell.

They looked awful, and Olga looked the worst of all, for her nose was so burnt it had swollen from sun poisoning and grown into a large red potato.

Maria and Anastasia were so excited at being such bad girls that they began running around the table making war whoops, which naturally caused Baby to join them! I grabbed him by his shoulder and pulled him against me before he could hurt himself, whereupon Anastasia, either deliberately or by accident, smashed into Anya's chair, making her spill the contents of her plate all over herself, her shrieks of outrage adding to the general cacophony.

Less gently than I had reached for Alexei, I snatched at Anastasia before she could make another circuit of the table, and pulled her in front of me.

"Stop this nonsense immediately!" I told her sternly.

She stilled in my hands and gazed at me with her merry half-animal eyes, and grinned.

"What, Mama?"

"Anastasia, why are you and your sisters so burnt?"
She laughed.

"So we would all look like savage animals and make stupid Prince Carol not want to marry any of us."

She finished this mutinous statement with another war whoop for emphasis, starting Sophie off giggling, to be followed by Olga and Maria, while Anya put her hands over her ears. Tatiana merely looked down and bit her lip.

It was the combination of Alexei and Nicky's own raucous amusement that made me release this, the most errant of my four very errant daughters.

"Nicky and Baby, there is nothing amusing about this at all!"

"You like it when I'm sunburnt, Mama," Baby said innocently. Nicky merely shook his head and wiped tears of laughter from his eyes.

I was shocked that Nicky could so easily laugh off Olga – all of them – behaving like this. I wanted this for my daughters, this safety, but what did I mean by that? So, unwilling to argue with Nicky in front of the children, I chose to address only Baby's comment.

Pulling his little face to mine, I kissed him and said, while eyeing the girls over his head, "Yes, my precious wee one, Mama does like it when her boy is sunburnt, because on a boy, or even on a big grown-up like Papa and the officers, it makes a man look well and healthy. But on girlies, you see, it makes them look like dirty peasants, as your sisters all know, and that is why it is different for them and very naughty." Then, dropping my pretense at speaking to Alexei, I addressed Olga severely. "Olga, you have ruined your complexion, and your nose now resembles Father Grigory's, who, although a saint, is also a peasant. I doubt very much that His Highness Prince Carol will find this new fashion of yours to be an attractive one. He may rather be concerned about your mental stability, as am I. Explain yourself, please ..."

Olga, who could be quite defiant when alone with me, was clearly embarrassed by my addressing her so frankly in front of everyone and shot Nicky a pleading look, hoping her dearest Papa would intercede on her behalf. Instead, Nicky took note of my severe shaking of my head, looked pitifully in my direction, and lit a cigarette, refusing the request in Olga's hopeful eyes, eyes that filled with tears as she started to speak.

She swallowed and looked down.

Anastasia, never missing an opportunity to be center-stage, smiled sweetly and said, "So what if he doesn't like her, Mama. She doesn't like him, or she won't when she meets him, at any rate. It's very mean of you to try and make her marry him. None of us want to be parted from each other. Why do you want her to go? I know you don't like any of us as much as you like Baby, and maybe Tati, because she spends all her time trying to please you, but –"

She was cut off by Tatiana resentfully reaching over and cuffing her over the ear, at which Anastasia gave a shout of distress and fell into merciful silence, doubtless plotting her revenge. Anya snorted with laughter.

Baby stared at me with huge eyes and asked me shakily, "You do truly like my sisters, don't you, Mama? And I don't want Olga to leave either," finishing by bursting into tears himself.

I began to comfort him, but not before I saw a gleam of triumph flash into my eldest daughter's eyes.

Chapter 8

As The Standart approached the landing stage at Constanza, I could see that Missy and her entire family were there awaiting us, a gesture that touched me deeply as, in my youth, I had not liked Missy much more than her completely objectionable sister Ducky, my former sister-in-law, now wife of Nicky's ghastly Cousin Cyril.

Missy had all of her pretty children grouped about her, which, while charming, was also rather awkward as rumor had reached Nicky and me that at least two of Missy's brood had not been fathered by her husband, Crown Prince Ferdinand, although we were quite sure of Prince Carol's heritage as he had been born in the first year of their marriage when Missy was only seventeen.

To add to this discomfort, I saw the strangest looking woman I had ever encountered standing near Missy. I whispered to Nicky, "Is that her, Carmen Sylva?"

Nicky nodded and stifled a grin, for we were close enough now to be overheard.

I stared at her, fascinated. Carmen Sylva was the most scandalous royal personage in Europe. She wasn't really named that, of course; she had started her life much like me, a princess from a minor royal house, and had in fact been my dearest Grandmamma's first choice for her son Bertie, the late Edward VII.

I shuddered at the very thought of what might have become of England if the girl born as Princess Elisabeth of Wied had indeed become the Queen of England. Why, poor Grandmamma must have died thanking God that such a fate had been averted, for some time after

Elisabeth had married the ruler of Rumania, King Carol I, and had officially become Queen Elizabeth, she took up writing under the pen name of Carmen Sylva, and although I had not read any of her books, it was well known that both her books and her poetry verged on the pornographic in the style of George Sands. Both Nicky and I had been a tad uncomfortable at the thought of the girls meeting this odd creature, but then again she was a reigning queen and so we had placed our concerns to one side.

Now, as we viewed her coming towards us with outstretched hands and a wide smile, I nearly fainted in shock.

"Nicky, her hair is down, and what in the name of heaven is she wearing?" I whispered frantically to him.

It was too late, though, as she was upon us, and Nicky's long training as an officer and an emperor served him well. He smiled and made a bow to her strange majesty, who looked more like a creature from mythology than a queen from a European ruling family. There she stood, her long white hair whipping about her, wearing what I think, but cannot be sure, was some sort of Greek costume.

I heard Anya gasp and all five of my ill-behaved children then giggled at my back as they beheld this apparition.

Naturally, Anastasia had to speak. Moving out from behind me, she curtsied to Her Majesty and asked with frank interest, "Are you a witch? You look like one. And can everybody here wear their nightclothes during the daytime? I know I'd like to, if that's all right."

At that, the odd thing threw her head back and laughed with obvious pleasure, and curtsying slightly to our naughty Nastinka, said, "Welcome, Your Royal Highness. I do so hope you are the Grand Duchess Olga, for I see my grandnephew, his Royal Highness Prince Carol, is going to be most enchanted with you."

Before I could blurt out either an embarrassed or an indignant response, Nicky smoothly stepped alongside Anastasia and, putting his hand on her head with what I noted was a little more than affectionate pressure, smiled and said, "Fortunately for your ruling house, and for Prince Carol himself, this one is our youngest girl, Anastasia. Allow me to present the real Grand Duchess Olga to you, Your Majesty."

Anastasia squirmed under his hand and managed to wriggle her way free, her dignity much ruffled. "Papa, you nearly squashed me," she announced indignantly, "and it's very rude to interrupt when people are talking, as you always tell me."

She was cut off by the laughter of both the Queen and Missy – more formally Crown Princess Marie – who slid around everyone to enfold me in a hug, exclaiming happily, "Alicky, it is so wonderful to see you!"

I sighed, resigned to the fact that there was no possible way to restore any dignity to our arrival, and somewhat half-heartedly returned Missy's embrace.

Missy, my beautiful young cousin, the sweet and not very bright younger sister of the appalling Ducky, was, I saw, even prettier now than she had been in our youth. What she saw as she pulled back from me and examined me closely, I wasn't quite sure, because her face clouded a little before she smiled and said with evident insincerity, "You are even more beautiful than when we were young, Alicky. How do you do it? And you the mother of all these beauties of your own!"

After that there was a quick flurry of introductions, during which I noticed a poorly hidden look of distaste cross Prince Carol's face on his first beholding Olga, his prospective bride.

Everything was very hurried. The visit had been planned in the maddest possible way to last only one day, and rather than try to make it a simple dignified day to allow the young people to become quietly acquainted with each other, the Rumanian Royal Family had decided, I believe, to try and murder me instead, as a list of inescapable activities had been planned that would have tried even the stoutest of creatures, let alone Baby and me.

First of all, we were all bundled into a series of waiting carriages for a state drive through town so that all could gawp at us. This was followed by a service in the cathedral, an event I might have enjoyed save for my exhaustion and inability to understand a word of the service. Following this, we were all taken to the city palace for a "small intimate family luncheon," while our suite, Anya included, was whisked off to a party of their own hosted by the Rumanian Prime Minister, Mr. Bratianu, where they all had a lovely time.

My own experience was not so pleasant. Nicky was faultless, as always, and quickly engaged King Carol I, Carmen Sylva's husband, in a lively discussion about the growing industrial and military might of Germany, a topic destined to bore all the ladies present. I, always lacking in small talk, was therefore left to feign an

73

interest I did not have in Rumanian social affairs with Carmen Sylva herself, discovering, to my horror, that in addition to all her other peculiarities, the woman was a raging socialist!

"I find the plight of your dear Russian peasants to be such a heartbreaking one, don't you, Your Majesty?" she enquired of me with effortless, if false, charm.

Startled from my private reverie of watching Prince Carol speaking to my daughters, I replied in confusion, "What? Our peasants? What plight?" adding pointedly, "What is your knowledge of Russia, Your Highness, let alone of the lives of our peasants?"

Of course, at that very moment, the orchestra that had been serenading our party at deafening volumes for some time with what sounded like the screeching of dying animals, chose to fall silent, so that my question boomed across the assembled dignitaries, causing even Nicky to break off his chatter and gaze at me in astonishment, only for Madame Sylva, as I thought of her, to continue smiling at me unperturbed.

"Oh, I have a great fondness for Russia and her people. You see, I visited your great country when I was a girl and it left a lasting impression upon me."

Nicky, seeing my color rise, quickly interjected.

"I am glad you enjoyed your travels in our land, Your Majesty."

Completely at her ease, despite her bizarre attire, Carmen Sylva decided to repeat to Nicky what she had just said to me.

Nicky smiled back graciously.

"As I have pointed out to many charming and well-intentioned observers of our country and its ways, there are deep and eternal feelings that pass between our peasants and ourselves. Day-to-day hardships are not what is most important to them."

"Nevertheless, Your Majesty," Carmen Sylva replied, "I must confess that I entertain some sympathy for the point of view of your social democrats, especially in view of the inaction and corruption of your Russian nobles. It seems to me that the peasants only want what is their due in nature, that all classes of people should have similar rights according to the law. I believe that the republican form of government, such as they have in England, France and America, is the only rational one. I cannot understand why the common people should be so foolish as to continue to tolerate our kind, can you?"

I thought Nicky was going to have an apoplectic fit right there, although the children, to my horror, and particularly Olga, seemed most interested in this mad speech, one that I could not help but see as against all nature, and positively mutinous coming from a queen, albeit a minor one.

I glanced at Missy for help, and she in turn looked across at her husband, Crown Prince Ferdinand, who cleared his throat and changed the subject by asking Nicky if he enjoyed Scottish smoked salmon.

"I had it quite recently," he said. "Nice little Georgie," he was apparently referring to King George V of England, "sent me some. Quite fine, I must say. It had a very different flavor from anything I had ever tasted before."

Nicky eagerly seized on this topic and a lively discussion ensued as to the respective merits of different fish and how they were prepared. It was obvious to me from her resolute stare that Carmen Sylva wished nothing more than to re-engage me in the topic Crown Prince Ferdinand had saved us from, however I foiled her from gabbling her anarchic ideas by bringing up with Missy my looming worry about the tea I had invited all of them to on board The Standart. This was, I knew, going to be quite grueling for me as I was already collapsing from exhaustion. I had not anticipated that Missy's odd family would choose to subject us to so many activities, and because of this I had not been able to slip back on board and check the arrangements for my tea.

So, wishing to evade the attentions of the Mad Red Queen to my right, I discussed my fears with Missy, who was most sympathetic and even offered to accompany me back to The Standart right away so that I could check on whether the officers had set up the deck chairs properly.

I thanked her and rose to my feet, neatly escaping Carmen Sylva's clutches entirely. Nicky, King Carol and Crown Prince Ferdinand seemed a bit startled by my sudden seizing of the moment, but immediately rose to their feet in their turn.

I held out my arm for Nicky to take, which he did, hastily adding, "Sunny dearest, I cannot return to The Standart with you as Their Majesties have invited Alexei and me to inspect their new ships."

I glanced at Baby, who had purple circles forming beneath his eyes, and was just preparing to say that he needed to return to The Standart with me for a rest, when Baby anticipated my decision with great tears filling his eyes. Fearing that I might provoke a scene that would be spoken about all across Europe, I simply nodded and excused myself from the luncheon with the bare minimum of fuss.

It was only as I approached my waiting carriage that I realized that three of my four daughters had also chosen to go and see the stupid ships instead of assisting me back at The Standart, and that only my sweet Tatiana had elected to help me.

"Don't worry, Mama darling," she assured me, "as soon as we are back at The Standart, please go and lie down. I'll see to the tea. I cannot imagine we'll have that many guests anyway, but no matter, you're not to worry about a thing."

I studied her affectionately. This kindest and, to my mind, most beautiful of our four girlies, what a queen she would make one day! At this, a cold shadow temporarily eclipsed the sun and I crossed myself superstitiously.

Tatiana, looked at me, worried.

"What is it, Mama? Is it your heart?"

I reached over and patted her hand.

"No, darling, just a goose walking over Mama's grave." My disavowal did not seem to allay Tati's fears, so I continued with, "Actually, your old Mama was just thinking what an accomplished wife and companion you would make for a lucky king one day, and I suppose not too long from now either."

Tati's face clouded over, and her huge gray eyes, eyes so like Baby's, so like mine, betrayed her distress.

"But I don't know if I want to get married, Mama." She searched my eyes for reassurance and hurried on. "I mean I do, but then Olga, well, she told me she thinks

77

that Prince Carol looks like a trout, and I don't want to marry a trout either."

"A trout?" I exclaimed, torn between horror and laughter. "Wherever did she come up with that silly comparison?"

Tati shook her head impatiently.

"Oh, it was Nastinka. When Papa and Prince Ferdinand started talking about fish, she asked Olga which fish she thought Prince Carol reminded her of."

I frowned in annoyance.

"Your sister has the manners and tongue of a shrike ... or for that matter of a social democrat."

Tati giggled.

"But truly, Mama, if all the princes in the world are as funny-looking as Carol, who would want to marry any of them? I mean, his ears are very odd, and he has no manners. Why, I don't think he addressed two words to Olga. He was too busy staring at Maria."

"What?"

"I said that he has no manners, and if they are all like him, or maybe even worse than him – if that's possible – then no one would want to marry them."

That was not the part of Tati's statement I was reacting to.

"Why did you say he was staring at Maria?" I demanded.

She shrugged impatiently at my ignoring of what she considered to be the greater issue and muttered sulkily, "Oh, everyone noticed it, Olga especially, I imagine."

I felt one of my dreadful headaches coming on, so I chose not to pursue this line of questioning. Instead, I closed my eyes to signal to Tatiana that I was in no state to discuss her or Olga's worries at that moment, and, upon arriving at The Standart, I proceeded immediately to my stateroom and rang for Maria to bring me my valerian drops. After all, Tati had offered to finish organizing the tea party and I saw no reason to prevent her from doing so; she and Olga were big girls now and needed to become more accustomed to taking my place on occasion. My long years of serving the Russian people as their Empress had weakened and aged me beyond my worst fears. There was surely no better time than on this minor sideshow of a trip for them to learn that the privileges that come with high birth are always paid for in full by the endless demands we are called upon to meet, demands neither Carmen Sylva nor her beloved social democrats, who only seemingly wanted to accord the common people their natural rights, would ever be able to manage, I reflected as I slipped into sleep.

My nice little tea party ended up as a mad scramble as our Rumanian hosts were so inconsiderate as to decide, without discussing the matter with us or warning us, to invite along every official in their country, it would appear, and their wives. There were simply hundreds of people and not nearly enough food or tea for them. I suppose, as I later commented to Nicky, they had simply come to stare at us, and of course Olga, who might have been their queen one day.

Anyway, it was a dreadful melee, and by the time they all melted away like ill-bred peasants at a country fair, I was unable to do much more than sit grasping the arms of my deck chair for fear of fainting dead away.

Unconscionably, considering the day we had already had, a further outing was expected of us immediately following my calamitous tea party, as King Carol had organized a review of his troops and we were all therefore obliged to drag ourselves back into open carriages and set out again to display ourselves. I was, of course, completely done in and merely shook my head at Nicky when he asked if I could please come. I also insisted, over his protests, that Baby remain on board ship with me. Anya and Sophie were sent along as chaperones for the girls, and I was told breathlessly later by Anya that it had proven in effect to be a parade of our joint royalty like prize livestock before anyone willing to stand along the route.

"The crowds! The dust! Oh Alix, you would have died of discomfort," she exclaimed. "I nearly did. Those Rumanian carriages were made to be pulled by donkeys, I think. The seats weren't even sprung and I was terribly jolted."

"Anya," I interjected, "could you tell me about how the girls were received by the crowds, Olga in particular?"

Anya, who hated interruptions, which is too funny for she was by far the worst offender in this regard, glared at me balefully before puffing out her lower lip and answering my question.

"Olga was seated in the carriage with Prince Carol, but I can't say that I saw much conversation pass between them. I did, however, overhear quite a few people in the street commenting disapprovingly on how dark Olga's complexion was. Such a shame! A lady's complexion is truly her greatest asset if she wants to attract a husband."

I waved away Anya's final remark with marked irritation, for the divorced woman before me was herself the proud bearer of a large, red, sweaty tomato of a face to go with her no doubt large, red, sweaty tomato of a body.

'Some people, and especially great fat vulgar lumps, possess no sense of self-awareness whatsoever!' I thought to myself.

This, the most distressing and exhausting of days, ended with a State dinner at the palace, during which King Carol and Nicky exchanged speeches. I was nearly unconscious by then, but I did feel that Nicky's clear elocution and handsome smiles were a great deal more impressive than King Carol's performance. The poor old man looked almost as ready to keel over in a dead faint as I did, and his speech was wandering and slurred. Not that I blamed him: any king married to such a madwoman as Carmen Sylva was bound to succumb to both exhaustion and the bottle in the end.

As for Carmen Sylva herself, she appeared at the banquet in what appeared to be another sheet, possibly her formal one. At any rate, she was a most unappealing sight in her odd drapery, and, to make matters more awkward, if that were possible, the silly thing had forgotten to wear one of her diamond orders, or possibly she had misplaced it somewhere. Therefore, to be polite, I was obliged to remove my own orders to put her at her ease, not that she gave any indication of appreciating my magnanimous gesture.

During the meal, Missy breathlessly explained to me that the setting for this dinner had been built expressly for "this great and glorious event," by which I assumed she was referring to the impending engagement of our children, so there we were forced to sit for countless hours in this outlandish room which resembled nothing so much as a Moroccan seraglio. Finally, King Carol had the good grace to lay his head down partially onto the table and partially into his dessert plate, and began to snore, at which point Nicky seized the moment to effect our blessed escape by leaping to his feet, only for our endeavor to be thwarted by the announcement of the start of an enormous and interminable fireworks display that we were invited to view from the balconies of the palace. By then I couldn't stand and nor could I bear the hideous din all around me, so I resorted to sitting weakly on a chair with my hands pressed over my ears, and virtually had to be carried out to our carriage afterwards by Nicky.

All of this – the parades, the awful tea party, the banquets, my near-certain return to ill health, and the whole extravagant mess that I am certain the Rumanians could ill afford – soon proved to be for nothing after all when Nicky came to sit beside our bed, where I remained prostrate, raised my hand to his lips, and proceeded to relate with a bemused expression his meeting with young Prince Carol who had joined him on board The Standart for breakfast earlier.

"Well, darling, that was a bit of a shock. It seems that the foolish boy is indeed interested in marrying into our family, it's just that he would like to do so with Maria instead of our poor Olga."

Aghast, I sat up.

"What, he actually said that?"

Nicky nodded, clearly torn between amusement and outrage.

"He did indeed. He said that he found her much more congenial."

I pounded at my bedcover.

"What did you say? I hope you gave him a piece of your mind."

"I was polite. There is no use in making enemies. I just said that Maria was still a schoolgirl, just a child, and that we were not considering marriage for her at this time."

"I should hope not," I puffed indignantly, but then, curious, I had to ask, "Did he accept that with good grace? Did he say anything about Olga at all? Oh, I knew her sunburn was going to make the worst possible impression on him. Oh, Nicky!"

He smiled at me and stroked my face.

"Well, the stupid boy actually did try to press his suit with regard to Maria by saying that his own mother had married at seventeen. He seems to be truly smitten by her. As for Olga, he said that she seemed much older and more serious than he had anticipated. Never mind, Sunny, you look all done in. I want you to rest now."

"No, Nicky. I must see Olga. The poor darling, she must be devastated."

This made Nicky laugh outright.

"Possibly, but at present she is roller skating around the deck, acting as though she were six again, and she hasn't stopped grinning since I told her that there would be no engagement. Of course, if you are truly up for a visit, I can send her in."

I thought about this for a moment. It was odd because, contrary to what I might have expected, I didn't feel relieved at the thought of my girl's release from a foreign marriage neither she nor I wanted for her. Instead I felt that same strange, cold sense of foreboding that had overcome me in the carriage with Tatiana the day before, and I heard a voice in my head saying, "Save one by marriage, save one." I had no idea what it meant, nor did it seem like my own voice. In fact, it sounded like it came from my own long-departed mama.

Nicky saw me grow pale and anxiously snuffed out his cigarette before grasping me by the shoulders and gently lying me back against the cushions.

"Sunny, what is it? You look like someone has just walked over your grave."

I placed my hand to my head and looked back at him, frightened.

"Nicky, I just heard my mama's voice. She said I must save one of the girls by marriage. Good God, do you think The Standart is going to sink again?"

Nicky lit a cigarette and patted my hand.

"You've just overtired yourself, Sunny. Nothing is going to happen to any of our girls. And your mama is in heaven along with both of our papas, helping to watch over all of us, as you know." He warmed to his theme. "I know how much Father Grigory means to you, darling, and I myself find him to be a very good fellow, but as a peasant he is hampered in this respect in so many ways that our poor dead parents are not. It would be very much better for us to look to them for our safety."

"Hampered in what ways, Nicky?" I asked, my voice deceptively soft.

He shrugged, but I saw that he had recognized my anger.

"I didn't mean anything, Sunny. I was simply trying to say that our dear peasants tend as a whole to be terribly superstitious, and as they aren't educated or in most cases able to travel to hear any contrasting opinions beyond their own thoughts, it just seems to me that, no matter how much one likes one of them, it wouldn't do to get caught up overmuch with their fears or their ideas of how things might be."

"Or could it be," I interrupted, "that they are more open to hearing clearly the voice of God as they are not forced to pass every minute in silly social nonsense, gossip, and dissipation, as we are. I can assure you, Nicky, that Father Grigory, to name but one peasant, does hear the voice of God, and he says that everyone in his village understands all too well what is to come."

"Alix, how do you know?"

His question caught me off guard. Confused, I asked him, "How do I know what?"

"How do you know that what he is telling you is the truth?" Nicky raked his free hand through his hair, agitated now. "Because, so help me God, and I wish he would, I can no longer tell who is telling me the truth about anything. One minister says this and another the opposite. King Carol tells me Germany is arming against Europe, while Willy assures me he is devoted to world peace. Georgie says I cannot believe a word Willy says.

And Mama says things, and you say things, and Father Grigory says things ... But, you see, no one says the same thing, and so how is one ever to know where the real truth lies. Must I go to live in Pokrovskoe myself? Is that where truth lies, Sunny?"

Nicky looked and sounded so lost that the very best I could manage was to stutter out, "Nicky, precious one, I ... I ... I did not know you thought like this ..." I fell quiet for a moment while his hand reached for mine. Then, as if God had indeed spoken to me, I knew the answer. "You can trust your wify. Father Grigory was sent to us by Our Savior. I will guide you. We will guide you. You need never fear lies again. It is all going to be fine, darling. Just trust in me, as I do in Father Grigory and God, and your reign will continue to be glorious, as will Baby's, after you and I are gone."

Nicky withdrew his hand from mine and slowly got to his feet, stooping to kiss my forehead with a sad little smile on his tired face. It was funny how I had not noticed in the midst of my own exhaustion how worn out Nicky was looking.

"I know that I could never have survived this long without you by my side, my precious Sunny," he said. "As to my glorious reign," he shrugged, "I can only hope that your truth is the right one. I am going to go up and visit with the officers. Then I will be back to eat with you down here. Would you still like me to send Olga in to you?"

I felt off-balance. Nicky did not seem reassured by my words at all and I no longer felt up to lecturing Olga.

I shook my head.

"No, thank you, darling. I think I shall just rest now. Oh, but you could send in Anya?"

This request aroused Nicky's curiosity.

"I thought you wanted to sleep. Do you find Anya restful again?"

I laughed and so did he, our good humor restored almost as always by Anya, even *in absentia*.

"I know, isn't it funny, Nicky? She is never quiet. Often she is past endurance, and yet ..."

"I know exactly what you mean, Sunny. At times she can be the sole person in the world who makes one's troubles go away or at least allows one to forget them."

He said this a bit too knowingly for my liking, but I didn't make any comment. A wise woman knows when to ignore such matters. I merely smiled steadfastly, waved as Nicky took his leave, and waited for Anya to come and join me so that we could gossip about my cousin Missy and Carmen Sylva.

Chapter 9

The next day dawned, hot, clear and blue, as it seemed every day of this summer had, and our journey back home promised to be a true pleasure cruise.

Indeed, I might have been able to recover from our grueling, if short, visit to Rumania, but life in the imperial family does not allow us to set aside one moment for ourselves. Private family life is a luxury we are considered to have no right to indulge ourselves in, and if we are at sea, it is ministerial wisdom that we should take the opportunity to drop into any and every reception, unveiling, or opening of a cow shed that happens to be taking place along our route.

I was thinking about this with great weariness when I opened my eyes to yet more blazing sunlight, wishing only that I could close them again and disappear back into sleep as we approached the port of Odessa, where we were to become entangled in yet another series of interminable, pointless receptions, to be followed by conscripted attendance at a service of Thanksgiving at the cathedral.

The latter did not displease me entirely, as I was always happy to find myself in a place of worship, but first I would have to endure a tedious ladies' reception, stuffed to the rafters with curious, cloying, overdressed and over-rouged women who would all stare at me as if I were some kind of exotic, and vaguely disappointing, novelty. As for the church service itself, I knew that, as Empress, I would yet again be denied the restful joy that should come with the opportunity of spending time alone in the presence of God, contemplating what He might be requiring of us, that every one of His other faithful servants could take for granted.

However, just as my sour thoughts were beginning to overwhelm me, there was a great bustle at the door and Anya entered our cabin huffing and puffing.

Intrigued, I sat up in bed.

"Good morning, Anya. Have I sent for you and then let it slip my mind again?"

Anya slapped at her amazingly clad thigh to signal that she had every intention of interrupting anything I might have to say next.

"It's after ten and I couldn't wait another moment to see you," she wheezed.

All ideas I might have had of returning to sleep, and all my morose sentiments arising from the rumination of the overwhelming nature of my imperial duties, vanished at the sight of her.

"Anya, what are you wearing?" I exclaimed, for she resembled nothing so much as a giant orange and red root vegetable, topped with a sweaty beetroot face. Had she absconded with a pair of somebody's ghastly, discarded orange velvet curtains and had them run up into a ...? I hesitated to describe it even to myself as a gown. What on earth had she been attempting?

Caught off-guard by my question, she preened for a moment.

"Do you like it?" she asked. Without allowing me to answer her, she plowed blithely on. "I have been writing to Mama for all this time, telling her that that I am the only woman at court who has been seen over and over again wearing the same dress day after day, and she sent me this. According to her, this is the color everyone is wearing in town and in Paris this summer. I think it does rather flatter my complexion, does it not?"

I tilted my head to one side as though considering the matter and fought the urge to laugh.

"Well, Anya, I would say that it certainly draws attention to it. But tell me, are you not hot wearing velvet in summer and in this heat?"

She raised her hand to wipe at her dripping face and I recoiled at the large damp patches under her arms, but she merely shook her head as if annoyed by my question, or possibly what she considered to be my interruption of her train of thought.

"No, I'm never affected by heat," she said. "I suppose you'll wear white to the reception, as always, but that's not why I came to see you, Alix. It's about what I saw this morning. It … it ... Oh, I can't even say."

Unbidden and seemingly overcome by her mysterious and apparently fraught experience, Anya sat down heavily on the end of my bed and continued to fan herself with her puffy hands.

"What did you see Anya?" I asked.

"Naked men, thousands of them!" she shrieked, before covering her face and bursting into noisy gasps that forced me to avert my gaze so as not to become transfixed by the lurid sight of her trembling hulk.

"Anya, if you could possibly bestir yourself from your shock long enough to ring for my tea, I would be most grateful … And by thousands of naked men, I am guessing you are referring to His Majesty and his officers taking their morning swim …"

Anya, clearly unwilling to let go of the drama of it all, shuddered and nodded, then mumbled, "They weren't wearing bathing costumes, Alix. They didn't have a stitch on. And after they had finished, they just climbed up the ladder, naked ... horrible ... and shook the water off their bodies like dogs ... His Majesty, too."

I reached over shakily to ring for my tea myself and then rolled over face down and howled with laughter.

"Anya, I hope you had the decency to avert your eyes. Oh never mind, I can't bear to hear another word."

I was so engulfed in irrepressible gales of laughter when Maria arrived with my much-wished-for morning tray that she nearly dropped it, fearing that I was suffering from some kind of fit of convulsions.

"Your Majesty?" she enquired solicitously.

I wiped my eyes.

"Oh, I am fine, Maria. Bring the tray closer. I am quite parched, although, after having to hear all about Anya's escapades this morning, I should probably have requested something stronger than tea."

Maria sniffed.

"I imagine she was telling Your Majesty about how she stood on deck staring at His Majesty and the sailors bathing for several minutes, and then wouldn't leave, so they were forced to climb up the ladder right in front of her in a highly vulnerable state. Everyone on board is talking about it, quite shocked, but not surprised. 'What can one expect?' they keep saying."

Maria sighed heavily and backed out of the cabin before Anya could respond. For my part, I clutched the tea tray protectively to prevent Anya from knocking it over in a moment of distraction, and decided not to call

Maria back to reprimand her for taking leave of me without my permission and before she had even served me, for fear that Anya would become yet more agitated should I do so.

Instead, I was just pouring myself a much-needed cup of tea when Nicky strode in, and, upon espying Anya, gave her a sharp look of reprimand.

"Nicky, darling, what a lovely surprise," I said. "Have you come to have breakfast with me? Oh, I am silly. You will have eaten ages ago. Anya was just leaving, but she did tell me the funniest story about catching you, my naughty one, bathing this morning."

"I wasn't leaving." Anya said stupidly, then cast a glance at Nicky that I couldn't puzzle out, but didn't like anyway.

"You *were* leaving, Anya," I insisted. "I shall see you in an hour or so when we leave for the reception. You might wish to profit from that time by changing into another costume. The gown you are wearing looks like it has been caught in a shower."

"It does not!" she protested. "But I'll leave if you want me to."

She stormed out, managing to set several of my icons tottering as she breezed past them, despite the spaciousness of our cabin.

I sighed and poured Nicky a cup of tea while he lit a cigarette.

"So, my boysy, you have had quite the exciting morning, I hear …"

Nicky shook his head in exasperation.

"I cannot decide whether Anya is half mad or lacking in most of her mental faculties, which I suppose could amount to much the same thing. Will she ever stop behaving like a child? Anastasia knows more about life than she does."

"I think Anastasia is smarter than nearly everyone, darling, so she is probably a poor comparison. Father Grigory says so, anyway – that Anya is a mere child and a simpleton. Her simple nature does, however, serve to teach me patience, a service I fear I am too often sorely in need of."

I smiled at Nicky, who stood up, leaned over me, and kissed my hair.

"Oh, I don't know, darling. Look at how terribly patient you are with poor hubby. But for now, I shall leave you to dress for the reception, dearest. You are not too tired, are you, Sunny? You know my mother is here."

"Yes, I know she has come all the way to Odessa to support us in our ordeal here, and we would not want her to have yet another opportunity to talk about how she was never too tired, or too pregnant, or too anything at all, to do her duty when she was the reigning Empress. According to her, not even death would have prevented her from fulfilling her obligations. So, yes, I do know Nicky and, yes, I am exhausted and my heart isn't feeling famous, but I shall be there nonetheless, so there is no need for you to fret."

Nicky's face fell.

So much for my attempts to be more patient, I said to myself as I bit my lip and managed a thin smile as I shooed him out. I then summoned my maids to begin the arduous process of dressing and grooming me for what I had correctly labeled an ordeal, the ordeal of watching

93

people pointlessly flattering me to my face and then gossiping about me the minute they had moved past me down the reception line. Still, this was where God had set me, and this was what he required of me, and on I must go, despite not having been blessed with Minnie's near-peasant-like physical robustness and appetite for endurance.

Three hours and an eternity later, I had to be helped back to my cabin by two stout sailors. The reception and the church service had been interminable, and I had been forced to stand the entire time. Neither Baby nor I were up to such Olympian feats, and although he did not collapse in church, as I nearly did, I could see that he was growing paler by the instant and whispered as much to Nicky. Nicky gave us a concerned, if vexed, glance and gestured for a Cossack to escort Alexei and me out, without his electing to join us. The girls looked at us, worried, but I indicated that they should remain behind as well.

Anya managed completely to ignore me as I shakily tottered out, trying desperately to keep to my feet. If I could have caught her attention, I would have beckoned her to accompany me, but, as it was, she remained behind, too, to attend the unveiling of a statue, followed by a dinner reception. I was absolutely furious that she was clearly determined that her place should be with my daughters and my husband, rather than with me, but what could I do about it as the entire congregation stared openly at poor Baby and me as we retreated, my mother-in-law's eyes flashing the coldest of all?

From Odessa we moved on to Kishinev for the unveiling of yet another monument to Nicky's long dead papa. It seemed to me that Minnie, who was always commissioning these silly statues, did so in order to justify her nearly constant traveling and the millions of rubles it cost to do so; that and to bedevil me by following us about on her favorite yacht, The Polar Star, to see how much I could endure before my health failed me completely.

Nicky, who naturally did not see Minnie's maneuvers the same way as I did, said that his mama, who "truly understood the Russian people" – implying, I felt, that I did not – "knew that these ceremonies bind the Russian people always to our glorious past and at the same time allow them to see and adore their reigning imperial family."

While it is true that, due to my health, I was not always present at these fine events, when I was there I didn't sense so much adoration as idle curiosity among the people who attended. The attitude toward us of the true, dear Russian peasants, however, was another matter. Although, again, I did not often see them myself, I was assured constantly by Father Grigory that they, to a man, were filled with a devotion towards us almost equal to their collective adoration of God. These were, I knew, the true Russians, and as I pointed out over and over again to Nicky, they were unchanged by time and did not read the filthy lies printed in Petersburg or Moscow papers. Nor did they listen on street corners to mad student agitators, or leave their fields for some foolish strike, as did the workers in the cities whose minds had been so hopelessly poisoned by their environments that they could no longer hear the voice of God at all.

In contrast, the true Russian peasants knew that their Tsar was Our Lord's earthly representative, there to care and watch over them as a loving father must.

I believe Nicky did agree with me on this – no, I know he did – but only when he was with me. For, later, he would come to me, his head filled with doubts again, after his mama had ranted on to him about the growing discontent in the country, the thought of which made him depressed. If I pointed out to him in my turn that this so-called misery existed only in the cities, I would calm him down again, only for him to meet with his silly, ineffectual ministers, or, worse, read the Duma's reports, and become agitated all over again, saying to me, "But the discontent in the cities is spreading out from there all across the country. My minsters remind me that the French Revolution did not begin in the fields of the countryside, Sunny, but in the verminous streets of Paris."

I hated Nicky's defeatism, and ended as always by reminding him that France was not Russia, and nor could it ever be, so the two cases were not to be compared. Whether or not I ever convinced him of this, I still do not know, and, considering everything, I cannot blame him for that, but then again, who would have ever imagined that anyone might look upon the history of the French Revolution with envy?

Chapter 10

Mercifully, given my exhaustion and the relentless heat, after Kishinev we were able to return to Tsarskoe Selo for a while. I would have much preferred to have spent the next few months in our cool marble seaside palace at Livadia, but we were expecting the arrival of a long-scheduled and highly-esteemed visitor, and so back to Tsarskoe Selo we went.

One great benefit that came from our return there was the opportunity to see Father Grigory before he departed Petersburg on his own summer travels to his home in Pokrovskoe. He came to tea the day before he left, simply brimming with high spirits, and I received him in our bedroom as it was not a famous day for either my heart or my poor weak legs.

He strode in, radiant with health, and although I knew he had just arrived from the city, I fancied that I could smell the scent of freshly-cut grass upon him, and commented upon this.

My remark was met with an eager nodding from my visitor. "Yes, it's quite a funny thing, Mama, and I have noted it myself. If I think a great deal about my village, I begin to smell like it." Before I could express surprise at this, he continued prosaically, "It's much less noticeable in the winter, of course, for who notices the smell of snow? But once, last spring, I was entertaining visitors, and one poor lady fainted because she said that I smelt very much of manure. My wife and son, I was later to learn, were spreading manure on our vegetable garden on that very day. I suppose," he sighed as I coughed to cover my amusement at this, "that one has to be grateful for every miracle Our Father sends us, but I'm glad, for your sake, Mama, that today is a reaping day in Pokrovskoe, or you might not wish to see poor Father Grigory. Is that not so?"

When I finally caught my breath, I replied honestly, "No, Father Grigory, I do not think there is a single thing that would stop me from being glad of your blessed company. I will miss you very much while you are away. Tell me, what are your plans for Pokrovskoe this summer? Will there be a pilgrimage for you?"

He shook his head and gazed out of the window beside me.

"No, I will be too busy in Pokrovskoe with visitors who wish me to pray with them and teach them about the purity of peasant life. And Praskovia and I are adding another room to our house, so that will create much busyness."

Funnily, I was never comfortable when Father Grigory spoke of his wife Praskovia, an older peasant woman he had married in his far-distant youth. I did not much mind his daughter Maria being mentioned, but the thought of Father Grigory having a wife at all I found somewhat disconcerting. I suppose this was because, to me, he was not just a wandering holy man, but my true and personal priest and confessor, and such people are not in general married.

My distaste for her made me feel guilty, so I tried to show some genuine interest in Father Grigory's family situation by asking, "Oh yes, and what will this extra room be for? Is it for Praskovia – a sewing room perhaps…?"

"Oh no, we peasants aren't much for sewing," Father Grigory assured me. "We have time to mend things, that is all. No, the room is for more guests. Well, it's really for Praskovia and our boy Benjamin. You see, Mama, because you and Papa love me so much and have believed in me, other people who know of your wisdom say to each other, 'That Grigory, he must be a man of God we should listen to,' so then they come to Pokrovskoe when I am there. But it's a small, poor village, and where are they to sleep? they ask."

"I suppose there are few rooming houses there," I agreed, whereupon Father Grigory threw back his shaggy head and roared with laughter. Then, without asking leave to so, he stroked my hand, his touch electrifying my skin.

I blushed, but if he noticed this, he did not say so or remove his hand, instead carrying on in a delighted tone, "We call our hovels rooming houses, Mama, but we room in them ourselves. If I said to a neighbor, 'Hey, Ivan, we should build hotels and a restaurant here,' he would say to me, 'Yes, Grigory, but what is a restaurant?' and I would say, 'It is a grand place where they bring you much food if you ask for it,' and he would say, 'That must be heaven itself, for here in our village even the cockroaches won't come, for they are natural boyars, those cockroaches, and know that not one speck of food that falls on the floor goes unfought for here. But tell me more of these hotels you speak of ...' And I would say, 'Ivan, they are grand places with beds that you can sleep in all alone, and steam heat, and windows.' "

"… And he would say, 'Oh, not windows too, with real glass inside?' I exclaimed, wishing to be caught up in the fun, my headache and exhaustion having magically dissolved in Father Grigory's joyful presence.

Father Grigory laughed again and shook his head. "No, Mama, I would never tell him there are glass windows in these hotels, for he would think I had gone off my head. Also, I would have to try to explain what glass was, and that is a tale too tricky even for a *starets*."

"So then what does Ivan say in response?" I asked, hoping to prolong the merriment.

Father Grigory tilted his head. "He says, 'Well, Grigory, we must build one of these grand places and all move into it!"

I clapped my hands in delight, but took care not to dislodge his hand away my arm.

"Yes, Father Gregory, that is a grand idea, so why do you not build one, or why does Ivan not build one, or lots of Ivans? Why live in hovels?"

Father Grigory shook away my hand and stood up, turning his back on me as he gazed out of the window.

"I know it's funny, Mama, and that we peasants are very funny to you. We think we are funny, too, sometimes. But come, let us discuss the beauty of the day, for I have many things to attend to before I leave in the morning. The day is like sadness, isn't it? One moment all is dark, and then, ah, there is the sun rising again, and all sadness is over with."

"No, I don't want to talk about the weather," I sulked, my headache returning. "You are displeased with me. Why did you try to change the subject? Surely it is not a bad idea for your fellow peasants to try to improve their lot. You did, and it seems to me that, rather than bemoan one's fate, one should try to do better."

He turned back to me and, sighing, sat himself down on the edge of my bed.

"Beautiful Mama, Mother of the Russian people, it is not for them to do better, but for those who keep them in such misery to do better for them."

Coldly, I replied. "That is the job of our *zemstvos* and the Duma. His Majesty and I are ever vigilant in our concern for our peasants, as they should know."

He nodded, a strange smile crossing his face.

"Yes, they know that, but when the dark and the cold come, and come they do, as it seems forever, and the hunger arrives, and the children cry until they are too weak to cry anymore, only weak enough to die, and we stack their bodies outside with our few pieces of wood, waiting until spring comes when we can bury them or join them in death, it is sometimes hard to remember that our betters are concerned for us." I began to speak, but he shook his head for silence and continued. "You mention the *zemstvos* ... No one helps them, though they are good people and of the Russian land. A young teacher in our village starved to death waiting to be paid. The *zemstvo* leaders wrote and begged for her money, and no one heard them, or if they did, we did not hear of it. You then speak of the Duma. You and Papa hate the Duma, but when your people cry for help, you say it is for the Duma to help them. The Duma, in its turn, says it is for you and Papa and the ministers to help the people, but, back in the villages, live tens of millions of us who only know one truth ..."

Subdued now, I asked quietly, "And that truth is, Father Grigory?"

"That no one hears or sees us, or ever will. God does not hear our prayers, for he is too far away, and so is the Tsar."

"What?" I demanded indignantly.

He rose up again, stretching himself and smiling at me.

"Nothing, Mama. It is just a thing we peasants say. But we are a foolish lot." He took my hand and kissed it, making the sign of the cross over me. "I will go now, and I will pray for you, and wish you a happy summer, for you and Papa."

"And you will pray for Alexei too, won't you, Father?"

Father Grigory seemed strangely wearied now after his earlier exuberance, and, moving stiffly all of a sudden, he nodded. "I always pray for little Alexei, and I always will, for as long as I am able."

Concerned, I asked. "What do you mean? Why would you not always be able to pray for him?"

He looked away and gestured toward the window.

"Who can know what each new day will bring? There are many who wish poor Father Grigory harm."

"No, I won't hear of this. Has not His Majesty ordered our ministers to make your safety their first priority? Are there not always police around you to protect you?"

Father Grigory waved his hands.

"Yes, those good fellows never leave my side. They are down by my car now. They are on the staircase at my apartment. They are under the tables I sit at in restaurants. But there will not be any in Pokrovskoe, though, because there is no room and I am a happy fellow about that."

"Is that why you and Praskovia are building a new room?" I asked, returning to our original conversation. "Because, if so, His Majesty and I will send some builders to help you. I do not like you being anywhere without protection."

Shaking his head, he said more cheerfully, "No, Mama. Peace! My village is for me and for my family, and for whatever friends or pilgrims choose to come to see me. That is what the room is for. There can be no policemen following poor Grigory about or the peasants will say, 'Look, there goes that bighead Grigory with his policemen. He is not one of us.' For you see, Mama, bringing the police to my village will be as welcome as when Papa's tax collectors come with their whips."

"Yes, but you must remain safe. I will be sick with worry."

"And if you order that your police travel with me, Mama, I will have no place to go. They hate me here in the capital because I am a peasant, and –"

"No, they only hate you because we love you, Father Grigory," I interjected plaintively.

He threw back his shaggy head and roared with laughter.

I smiled uneasily, glad to have made him smile again but uncertain as to what I had said that was so funny.

Father Grigory cleared up my confusion between snorts of mirth.

"Forgive me, Mama, you are very funny, and maybe what you say is true. But I think it doesn't matter so much why one is hated. The fact is that I am hated in Petersburg, whereas in the village I am still one of them. But, if I am followed about by a group of policemen, I will not be one of them any longer, and then I will have to always be alone wherever I go. I will not belong anywhere, you see?"

Appalled by his insensitivity, I could only nod stiffly and say coldly, "Since I am hated by all classes of society, I think I understand quite well your predicament, so I wish you a good journey, Father Grigory. I hope that you will find time to write to us between entertaining all your friends."

He looked at me curiously but said no more, only giving me one of his awkward sideways bows before leaving.

I let him go with a frost still remaining between us.

Chapter 11

That summer proved to be a mad one that would not allow me the time to dwell on the ill feelings between Father Grigory and me. Indeed, the next day our honored guest, the King of Saxony, arrived.

He was a kindly gentleman and a widower, so I hardly minded his intrusion in our lives, as His Majesty was much given to following Nicky about the grounds to enjoy long walks in the stifling heat. This left me free to take to my bed and attempt to recover the strength I had dissipated during our endless traveling and entertaining, and therefore constituted a saving grace as I was still not well, although, truth to say, I was scarcely any better when, immediately following His Majesty's departure, we were obliged to entertain the Commander of the British Fleet, Admiral Beatty, and his fat English wife for luncheon.

The event was long and tedious, as was to be expected, but enlivened by Anya's embarrassing attempts at imitating a British accent, which had us all in gales of laughter, save Mrs. Beatty, who was most visibly offended.

Later that night, I commented in bed to Nicky that I could not remember a single previous summer during which we had had so many visits forced upon us, whether as hosts or guests.

"Does it not seem to you, Nicky darling, that everyone is just sailing about for the sake of it? I am beginning to consider yachts something of a curse. With all this withering sunshine we are experiencing across the whole of Europe, everyone is escaping to sea on board the stupid things, keen to sail them anywhere that will supply them with a cool breeze."

Nicky chuckled, maneuvered my head a few inches away from him as he sat up to light a cigarette, and then answered with a surprisingly serious tone in his voice.

"I do not know that the phenomenon is quite that innocent, Sunny. I do hope so, but you know, it is a funny thing … Do you remember a few years ago when Willy and I met at sea and he so admired The Standart?"

"Yes, and he made that tasteless joke about how he would gladly accept it as a gift. I remember that quite well. And you made a very clever joke back."

"I made a joke of it, yes, but it is not what I would do now. If he were to ask me for The Standart, I would give it to him."

I sat bolt upright, jostling Nicky so that his cigarette fell into the bedclothes, and then had to wait impatiently for him to find it and smother it out before we all went up in flames. Inevitably, he then elected to light another one.

When he was finally settled, I unleashed my ire.

"You would do *what*? Have you run mad, Nicky. Why in the name of heaven would we gift that buffoon with anything, let alone our yacht?"

Nicky raised his hand.

"For the sake of peace, darling. We would do it to ensure the peace."

I shook my head.

"What in the world are you talking about, Nicky? We have peace."

"Yes, but I have been advised to expect it to end at any moment, Sunny."

My anger died, to be replaced, as is so often the case, with a shock of cold fear so that I slid down into my blankets, although the room was unbearably stuffy, and whispered in a voice so small I didn't recognize it as coming from me, "Why do you say that, Nicky?"

Nicky stroked my shoulder absent-mindedly without looking at me.

"I don't know, Sunny, and maybe old hubby is just being silly, but it is odd all the same. All summer, wherever we have been, and whomever I have spoken to, it keeps coming up that we are only a spark away from war, that Germany is ready for war and may even be eager to have one, that we cannot avoid a war now. Even good old Admiral Beatty thinks so, and you know the English, Sunny, they are never alarmed by anything. Just today Admiral Beatty told me that Georgie and his Parliament have been discussing funding in case a mobilization is needed, and I am very much afraid that Willy does want a war, that maybe everyone does."

"But war ends everything, Nicky. Why would anyone want that? Do not forget our troubles with Japan and the truly terrible time for us that followed on so quickly after that."

Nicky shrugged agitatedly and inched away from me.

"No, of course I have not forgotten any of that, but that was nearly ten years ago and we've made great strides since in building up our munitions and in developing our railway infrastructure."

Speaking slowly, I turned on him.

"Why, you want war as badly as Willy, don't you, Nicky? As badly as any other stupid boy who wants war. Why, Nicky? Is it the glory of it all? What do you think that war will bring us, Nicky? What do you think it will bring Russia?"

"Darling, we are leaving early for Peterhof tomorrow. You can always rest there. It is so much cooler by the sea. I do not think there is any point in discussing this further. Doubtless nothing will happen, and, at any rate, war is not the province of the fairer sex. So let us go to sleep, shall we, and forget all about it."

With that, he sunk down into our bed clothes and cuddled against me while I lay there stiffly.

"Nicky, war should not be the province of anyone, whoever they may be," I said resentfully. "Any fool, however stupid, should know that wars are always a mistake."

Nicky merely chuckled and kissed the back of my head.

"Yes, dearest, I am sure you are right. Goodnight, my Sunny."

Shortly after our arrival at Peterhof, to soothe my fractured nerves and also because there was nothing he enjoyed more, Nicky proposed that we cruise among the Finnish Fjords simply for our family's pleasure.

Nicky was under such terrible and constant pressure at all times that he never truly had a moment to enjoy his own wee ones and his beloved exercising unless we were at Livadia or out on our little floating home. Whether we were all at our happiest in Livadia, at our dear, white seaside palace, or on board our beloved Standart, it is hard to say, but for us, finding ourselves aboard The Standart signaled blessed release from the torments of Petersburg. Our family was a simple one and we really never wanted anything beyond being with each other and having just a tiny bit of time to be alone together.

Nevertheless, it was while we were resting on our floating refuge this time, ironically enough, that we received the worst possible news.

Nicky rushed to me while I lay on my chaise in the shade, his face bleached of color, and a crumpled telegram in his hand.

"Sunny, dearest," he said with a catch in his voice, "prepare yourself. It is Father Grigory. He is –"

"Dead? He's dead?" I screamed, clutching at my heart. "He's dead and now we will all die, but Baby first, for without him what will become of us?"

I found that I was wailing as Nicky dropped to his knees beside me.

"No, no, darling. I am so clumsy and stupid. He is not dead, but he has been badly injured."

My heart stopped for a moment and then caught again. He was not dead after all, it seemed.

I clutched at Nicky.

"Give me the telegram. Now! No, wait, just tell me what it says, my eyes are poor today. Oh my head, my heart! Nicky, I am so distressed."

"Shhh, dearest, my Sunny. Here, I will tell you. It is from his daughter Maria. What seems to have happened is that yesterday some madwoman attacked poor Father Grigory with a knife outside his house. He managed to get away before she could strike at him again, and that alone shows how strong he is. She only managed to wound him once, in his stomach."

"Nicky, we must send Dr. Botkin. No, never mind that, we must send someone better, a specialist. Instruct Kokovstov to do so immediately. He can make himself useful for once."

"Darling, he is our Prime Minister. I am not certain that it would be fitting to ask him personally."

"Tell him!" I screeched.

Nicky flinched and nodded.

I continued speaking through my sobs.

"Oh, and tell him to that I want Father Grigory brought to town. I will nurse him myself."

My barrage of urgent demands was interrupted by a series of bloodcurdling screams, but Nicky did not even turn his head in the direction of the noise. Rather, he met my eyes and shrugged.

"That, I imagine, is Anya on becoming acquainted with the news. We will want Botkin to sedate her or we will all be driven mad by that hideous sound. But, Sunny," he raised his voice to be heard over Anya's hysterics, "I need you to remain very calm"

"Calm?" I exclaimed. "Have you already run mad? How can I remain calm when he might die and then all of us will die?"

Nicky grabbed my hands to stifle their frantic fluttering.

"He most probably will not die. He is strong, and I will send our best doctors, and they will advise us if he can be moved to town straightaway or not."

I had a brilliant idea.

"Nicky," I said, "we could go to him. Order the captain to set sail for the nearest port to Pokrovskoe. Or, wait, Pokrovskoe might be on a river. We can go up the river on The Standart! Yes, yes, that is what it would be best to do. We shall go to him, and Anya and I can nurse him, and, if he can be moved, we will bring him aboard and take him back ourselves. The Standart can act as a hospital ship, but much more comfortable for him. Oh Nicky, tell the captain right now." Nicky did not move. Instead he continued to smoke and stared nervously at me. "What, Nicky? Do something!"

However, rather than rushing off to follow my directions, he sat down heavily in an adjacent deck chair and looked around to make sure we were alone while Anya's screeches continued from a distance.

Becoming more frightened, I leaned towards him.

"So he is already dead and you could not bring yourself to tell me, is that it?"

"Calm yourself, Sunny," he said. "Be very calm."

But I was not about to calm down yet.

"You lied to me," I flailed, "because you were afraid I would be driven out of my wits like Anya. Oh God, no! What will become of us, Nicky?"

"Alix, darling, it is not that. I did not lie to you. Father Grigory is alive. It is that, well, you see ..."

I waited for him to complete his sentence, but he could not bring himself to do so, merely continuing to smoke and avoiding my eyes.

I tried to stand up but my legs gave out, and if Nicky had not leaped up and caught me to him, I would have fallen to the deck. He held me against his chest. I could feel his heart thumping against mine. He kissed my temple.

"Sunny, please, don't you see, it is just …"

He tried again to finish what he was saying and failed as I crumpled against his shoulder.

"Can't you say it, Nicky? Why are you always so afraid to say what you think, even to me?"

He straightened and helped me back to my chaise.

"You are right as always, darling. I am often afraid to speak the truth, for everyone, wify included, tends to receive it very badly. And you will not like what I have to say this time either. Nonetheless, I shall tell you."

I have to say this: Nicky's bizarre pronouncement did indeed have the effect of calming me down, not that he necessarily was intending to do so. I was now feeling much more annoyance than fear and was able to pull myself together sufficiently to bring myself to say quietly and steadily, "Tell me, then."

He brightened at my change of mood.

"Sunny, everyone in Russia, and the rest of the world too, is watching us to see how we react to this event. Father Grigory's attack made the London papers, for pity's sake! And here at home there is not a newspaper in Petersburg or Moscow that will write about another thing until this news has been milked to the last drop. Don't you see that if we go to him, or if we bring him to us …"

He stopped again and just stood there, a vacant expression on his face, a cigarette burning at his jaundiced fingertips.

I sighed, turned my head, and waved my hand at the sounds of the caterwauling emanating from Anya.

112

"Yes, of course I see, Nicky. Silly of me to forget that only I, Empress of all the Russias, am not allowed to have friends or to care if the man whose daily prayers keep our son alive is hurt. Thank you for reminding me. No, please don't say anything more. Go and fetch Botkin to attend to Anya before she deafens us all, and I shall write to Maria myself. Do not concern yourself that anyone, you included, will ever see my torment." Nicky made a half-hearted gesture toward me, but I shook my head, my lips pressed against the unsayable things I wanted to tell him. "No, go please. I wish to be alone now."

Remarkably, despite my white face and shaking limbs, he did just that and with a barely concealed look of relief.

After that, I did what I could for Father Grigory in secret, although finding myself much hampered by my location. I telegraphed his daughter Maria, I communicated with a surgeon I sent to him, and I read the daily dispatches in private. What I did not do was to speak to anyone save Anya regarding his progress or of my misery and fear.

Our summer pleasure cruise through the Finnish Skerries thus continued unabated, and if Nicky shared my terror, he was a past master at concealing it, for he bathed each morning in the sea and instructed our captain daily to find an estate with a dock available to pull into. From there, he and a small party – often including the girls and, disconcertingly, Anya – would happily troop off to try to find someone who had a tennis court, and, if successful, would play happily before being invited to stay for tea by the awed and delighted householders.

Anya's grief and worry about Father Grigory abated peremptorily moments after she was told that Nicky did not wish to hear any further shaming displays of this kind. What an agreeable creature Anya always was for Nicky. Also, the reports from Pokrovskoe were encouraging. God, it seemed, had heard my prayers in this matter, if not in others, and I was beginning to feel hopeful and rested again, when, a few days after receiving news of the assassination attempt on Father Grigory, on yet another of those seemingly endless blue and golden days of that accursed summer, came a fresh horror, the news of the successful assassination attempt, this time of Archduke Franz Ferdinand, heir to the throne of Austro-Hungary, and of his wife, shot by some madman during their visit to Sarajevo in Bosnia to investigate the unrest there.

Naturally, this horrible crime greatly shocked Nicky and me, as it did every right-thinking person. Royal blood, anointed blood, had been spilled, and this is always a peculiarly grievous sin in the sight of God, so Nicky declared that the whole court should wear mourning attire, which was a great imposition given the heat, but we donned it all the same. In addition to this, Nicky and I also called for special prayers for the souls of Franz Ferdinand and Sophie to be said throughout the land, and we both wrote personal letters of condolence to poor aging Emperor Franz Joseph, who now had no heir left to take over the running of his empire.

In private, however, Nicky, despite his genuine shock, had mitigating thoughts on the matter.

114

"It is hard to know what that poor old man truly thinks of the situation. He never liked his nephew Franz Ferdinand much, and he only made him his heir after a great deal of thought and considerable delay. Then there is the fact that Franz Ferdinand's marriage to his poor wife was only a morganatic one and their children are not in line to inherit the throne, so who knows what Franz Joseph plans to do now. I suppose, given his age – he is nearly a hundred, I believe – the Austro-Hungarian Empire risks being shared out between Germany and Turkey, with Willy in overall control of the situation. That will please him as much as it displeases us."

"Willy?" I exclaimed indignantly. "What does he have to do with it?"

Nicky chuckled at what he, as a man, obviously considered to be my womanly ignorance in these great matters.

"Well, darling, over time Germany has eaten up great pieces of the former Austrian Empire, much as Anya and the children eat up your tea cakes." He looked at me to see if I was amused by his silly analogy, but I merely nodded for him to go on with his explanation, straight-faced.

Lighting his cigarette from the end of the one still burning, he shrugged and continued.

"So, Prussia continues to grow as the greatest power in what was once the vast Holy Roman Empire, which has shrunk down over the years to become merely Austria and Hungary. Willy is now ever more its great protector, savior, and I suppose master, much as I am the protector of the vulnerable Slav peoples of the diminishing Turkish Empire and the Balkans, except that, unlike Willy's, mine is a sacred trust."

Amused by his sweet pomposity and presumption of my ignorance on a subject every educated and well-read German knew about, I playfully took his cigarette and inhaled from it, then threw my head back dramatically as I blew out the smoke. Anya had recently shown me this trick, one that she was convinced made her look like an American film star, although, unlike her, I had learnt to do it without either coughing or dropping the cigarette on myself with the attendant risk of setting myself alight.

Nicky's eyes sparkled with admiration at my maneuver, adding that special glow that only I could induce in them.

"A sacred trust, Boysy, that sounds grand," I said.

"No, but truly, Sunny, it is a sacred duty. We tsars are Slavs in our souls and they are true Russians in their lives and in their ways of life, only to be imprisoned and demeaned by foreigners, the kind of treatment they can never be expected to accept. For those of us chosen to rule here, it has always been understood that we must protect them to our fullest capability, and that one day…"

It was Nicky's turn to falter.

"One day …?" I prompted.

Nicky laughed gently, but I could tell that he was utterly serious as he answered me.

"One day, darling, I would like to be the tsar who returns all this land to Russia, including Constantinople, as has been promised to us, thus uniting the Greek Church with our own sacred Orthodoxy, all under the care and protection of a Russia gloriously restored, a completely Slav-Orthodox country that would end all divisions and stop this deuced looking outward at Europe that my ancestor Peter brought us to." Nicky's eyes were truly shining now. "All of it," he continued, "every bit of Russia's discontent, has come from Tsar Peter trying to make us part of a wider world, a wider world that has adopted democracy, and industrialization, and other such evils, and that has in turn led to nothing but discontent among our people. No one sees this as I do, that only the Tsar and Orthodoxy brings contentment to our people, and that we must therefore return to it. Then and only then, when I am called before God and my ancestors, well then, Sunny, I can face them proudly in the knowledge that I have left a strong country for my son. This is the sole purpose of the Autocracy. Only this leads to happiness for all. And I want to lead us back to it." His voice broke. "And maybe then I shall not be remembered only as 'Nicholas the Bloody.' " He raised his hand as I bleated a protest. "Oh, I know it is what they call me, and have since that so-called Bloody Sunday, but maybe they will call me 'Nicholas the Savior' if only I am given a chance to restore Russia to itself in all the good old ways."

"Nicky, dearest, I do not think that conquest will lead to your being called 'Nicholas the Savior' by history. How many people would have to die to accomplish your ...?" I threw out my hands. "I don't want to call them crazed dreams, but you have to admit that they are somewhat feverish ones."

I gave him a final smile that he did not return.

"Do you remember, Sunny," he said, "that I once referred to the people having fevered dreams?"

Bored now, and wishing to send a telegram to Maria about Father Grigory, I answered somewhat dismissively, "No, Nicky, I am afraid I don't."

"It is nearly word-for-word what I said to the *zemstvos* just before we were crowned. I said that their wish to have a voice in my government was nothing but a senseless dream, and now you say it back to me all these years later. It feels like a portent, Sunny."

I stared at him in surprise. His face was gray and drenched in sweat. I stood up and led him to a chair where I waved for a servant. When one came, I sent him to fetch Dr. Botkin, who also became alarmed upon seeing Nicky, and who, despite Nicky's voluble protests, insisted on dosing him with up with veronal and escorting him back to his study to rest.

This entire, strange incident got me wondering whether Nicky was not perhaps becoming too wrapped up in his superstitions and an overwhelming sense of his destiny, and consequently gave me a profound longing for reassurance from my dear friend who was at that moment lying wounded a great distance away from me, leaving me alone on that great blue sea with its pitiless sun.

Chapter 12

In later days I would look back on that particular conversation with Nicky and wonder if I should not have seen the end coming. There again, no one ever does see that, do they, at least not until after it is all too late. All I knew then was that Nicky seemed unusually tense as a result of the dual attacks on Father Grigory and Archduke Franz Ferdinand, a tension that I shared and considered to be an appropriate response at the time.

In contrast, I met the next piece of dispiriting news concerning the imminent arrival of yet another visitor, this time of the French President, M. Poincaré, with no especial interest and much lassitude. I knew that the assassination of the Archduke had led to an inevitable fuss arising between Austria and Serbia – because it had been a Serbian who had assassinated the Archduke and his wife in Bosnia – and that poor old Emperor Franz Joseph was loudly demanding some sort of justice and apology, as was to be expected, but by then I was wearied by the whole business and somewhat dismissive when Nicky told me that he and Willy were intervening in the dispute to try to effect a settlement between the warring parties.

Or possibly it was Anya who told me this, since she tended to hang onto every trivial word Nicky addressed to our officers at luncheon. Anya, unlike me, was not otherwise preoccupied with obligations to a husband, children and country, and so had more time to devote to such matters.

In point of fact, I was most preoccupied at that time with our plans to travel to Livadia for the end of summer and the entirety of the autumn, and I had decided to invite Father Grigory to stay with us at the palace to recuperate. He had never stayed there before, Nicky having always seemed cool to my wish that he should do so, therefore, up until now, he had been forced to stay at a local inn while we were in residence there. I knew Nicky would not raise any arguments against my proposal this year as we had come so near to losing our dear friend, although I was prepared to point out, should he prove recalcitrant to my wishes, that there was no one to gossip about his presence amid the safety and peace of Livadia

Nicky and I both hated to return to Petersburg, even to Peterhof, a moment before we had to, so we continued sailing aimlessly about the dear Finnish Skerries for some time, with Nicky, Anya and the children bathing and picking mushrooms. It was lovely, truly lovely, and there wasn't a cloud to be seen on the horizon, and I mean that in every sense, as we finally sailed back home to meet our honored French guest, who arrived on July 19th, a fortnight after the death of Franz Ferdinand.

We all greeted him at the landing stage, and he utterly delighted the children by having his sailors offload an enormous pile of astounding gifts for them. Olga and Tatiana received gold toilette sets that had them nearly swooning with pleasure, and Baby was given an entire new army of toy soldiers and a cunning miniature car that I think even Nicky envied. Unfortunately, Maria and Anastasia were both given enormous and beautiful dolls they were hard put to smile about, Anastasia making a point of dragging hers face-down all the way back to the palace, and Maria, always the more tender-hearted, managing at least not to display her disappointment at her gift, although I had to whisper to her a reminder to thank kind President Poincaré for his thoughtfulness.

After his arrival, the French President lunched privately with Nicky and me, and I found him to be a most charming man and one of those rare Frenchmen who spoke perfect English. Then, later that night, we attended a grand ball that Minnie had arranged in his honor at the main palace. As always, my poor heart was unable to carry me through to the end of the evening, and so I departed early, together with the wildly complaining Maria and Anastasia, leaving my big pair to act as the official hostesses, alongside Nicky and his impossible mama.

I despised the court and intensely disliked being stared at, and so we never stayed in the main palace at Peterhof – Peter the Great's acclaimed masterpiece – preferring to have our accommodation in the cottage there. So, in common with the grand Catherine Palace at Tsarskoe Selo and the Winter Palace in town, its vast rooms remained empty and shrouded as I felt no family life could be cozy in such cold settings.

As you might expect – and I certainly expected – my preference for small, sweet homes was ceaselessly criticized by my mother-in-law, and in consequence by all of Nicky's family, every member of the nobility, and by every member of lesser society too. They all called me "the old woman who lived in the shoe," merely because I wished to recreate the happy family life I had known during my childhood in Germany. What did they care for our family, for closeness, for affection? The sad conclusion I had long ago come to was that they did not care about any of that kind of thing at all, only for balls and pageantry and display, bejeweled pastimes that attract only empty-hearted and equally empty-headed fools. Was it any wonder that the ordinary people grumbled about their lot?

I had just concluded, and not for the first time, that such glitter and artifice were the foolish province of the frivolous and the indolent, and I was just giving a final glance across the ballroom to make sure that the girls remained under the protective wing of their papa as I took my leave, when I was suddenly overwhelmed by the sheer grandeur and majesty and, well, enormity, of all that was taking place before my eyes. I was so taken aback that I audibly gasped at this unexpected realization of the glory of our collective Russian history, where nothing had changed since the days of Peter the Great, who had either wrested Russia from a dark and ignorant past into an age of progress, or who, alternatively, had destroyed what was best in her, as Nicky so often argued. In simple truth, this all-powerful ruler had conjured something magical out of what had once been a swamp, whichever way one looked at it, and I found myself the unwitting and enchanted victim of a convulsive surge of pride and awe at the sight of the tens of thousands of white wax candles, and the hundreds of banked, white roses, and the twinkling of the jewels born by the ladies as they danced with their dashing officers, sweeping gracefully together back and forth across the glistening marble and gold floors.

It was an entrancing scene, and one which I could not help but feel enhanced all of our lives by its mere existence.

Then the moment was gone as I watched Sandro and Xenia waltz by me, offering up demeaningly small bows in my direction, mixed with very wide smiles, as a sharp reminder to me that Sandro despised me, and that Xenia, my once dear little sister-in-law and friend, had come to view me with considerably less affection and admiration than she had once held towards me in a far-distant past. Nevertheless, here in the glimmering, scented ballroom I smiled and nodded back, and it seemed to be less an occasion for hypocrisy on all our parts than a grace note.

Silly Sandro, I thought. He never ceased to rail against the intolerable misfortune of having been born a grand duke, and he regularly dined out on his tales of privileged tribulation and his plangent denunciations of the mad rituals, of the horrible, never-ending extravagance, and of the meaninglessness of his peripatetic life, while he and Xenia and their six sons made royal progress between Petersburg and Paris, and between the Crimea and the South of France, with his devotees and hers in tow, accompanied by an entourage of dozens of friends and followers. Yet what, he would ask languidly, is this all about when there is such great suffering in Russia?

I wondered why no one during one of these tawdry recitations of his ever suggested that he just give it all away and retire to Siberia to free himself of the burden of the Romanov legacy. Poor Sandro, he couldn't have survived a moment without all this panoply, yet I, who cared nothing for earthly glory, had managed in that one dazzling moment of insight to understand the need for it at last. This was what the ordinary people wanted us to be, the way they demanded that we should live, whether they admitted it, or even understood it about themselves, or not.

Those with the misfortune of not being born noble – and this, I am certain, has been true since the days of Adam and Eve – want something to look up to and worship. Adam and Eve and their children had God mostly to themselves for many years, but then there were more and more people, and I suppose it was impossible just to ponder His glory in an increasingly ordinary world. So He began to make semi-divine humans down here, and earthly kings and queens were created to give the rest of the people a taste of the glory of heaven and keep them from falling into sin. After all, it is written in the Bible, 'in my father's house there are many mansions,' which is, I suppose, a reassuring thing for humble people to hear, but if they have never seen a mansion, let alone a palace, how can they be expected to obey the Church in order to accede to a mansion in the afterlife?

Why, all one had to do to see this truth was to look to France and our nice visitor, their president. The French people had unwisely railed against God's natural order and murdered those set above them, and this despite the French royal family's unusual generosity towards their people. I had read that the reigning family used to allow all sorts of peasants and sundry others into their presence to watch them eat their meals. I shuddered at the very thought of this, of course, for in my case it would have meant allowing them into our bedchamber, but that was hardly the point, which was that the poor king and queen were beyond kindness itself to their people. Now the bloodstained French had their Republic, but they still wanted to retain all the glory and pageantry of the *Ancien Régime*, and the new Republic duly gave it to them.

In contrast, our own Russian people were more than contented with their imperial family, eccentric and selfish as some of us could be. In us they truly had it all. Courtesy of the bottomless extravagance of my mother-in-law and her adherents, they had all the pomp and theatrics they could wish for; and in Nicky and me, they had a true, hardworking, and loving family to act as a supreme example to our nation. So, for the first time in twenty years, I had finally realized that a happy populace required all that we offered between us, and this enabled me to smile lovingly at Nicky as I departed, and even to give a somewhat grateful nod to my mother-in-law in recognition of her contribution towards the whole endeavor.

The next day, Nicky, Baby, all the girls – and, it seemed, every member of the court and the ministers who were at Peterhof – accompanied the delightful President Poincaré to the officers' training camp at Krasnoe Selo so that he could see with his own eyes the flower of our Russian Army. Nicky said later that the President "seemed reassured" by what he saw.

"Reassured, Nicky?" I asked. "Why would he need to be reassured? What do you mean?"

Nicky shrugged off my question with some mumbled nonsense about all allies needing reassurance, which in no way reassured me, I must say, but during this visit I had little time to rest or poke about, as I had agreed to attend a performance of 'A Life for The Tsar' at a small local theater, although I was subsequently obliged to leave early because I had developed a terrible headache. I was told later by the ever-helpful Anya that my departure caused much whispering and murmuring, "and that it was ever so."

As always, I tried to shrug off the ill-feelings that such unkindness towards me created, but they stung me nonetheless, particularly after I had made such an effort to be there in the first place. So, on the President's last evening with us, hosted upon his ship The France to return our hospitality, I steeled myself against a terrific onset of pain in my heart, my head and my swollen legs, and resolved to stay the course, no matter what.

I managed it, too, although after dinner, during the excruciating clanging and clashing of cymbals emanating from his band of honor, I did shriek out briefly from the pain and place my hands over my ears, whereupon the kindly President gestured it into silence and hurried to my side in deep concern, accompanied by a very worried Olga.

"Mama ...?"

"Your Majesty ...?"

I smiled at them weakly.

"It was just that the music was a bit loud," I explained.

"Mama, let me take you back home," Olga suggested. "I'll send for the tender."

I shook my head.

"No, Olga darling, I would like to stay on a bit and speak with President Poincaré."

I inclined my head towards the President with a faint smile and he duly sat himself down beside me as Olga stood there expectantly.

The French President gave her a reassuring nod.

"I shall watch out for the well-being of Her Majesty, Your Highness. Please go and enjoy the rest of the evening, as all those who are young and beautiful should."

Olga looked at me and I nodded in agreement, waving her away.

Alone with this kindly man, yet one whose very presence augured things that I knew to fear, I was direct, a trait that I believe is not always esteemed among the French, or amongst politicians in general.

"President Poincaré, have you come here to ensure that Russia will support France if there is war? Do you believe a war is coming?"

"Please, Your Majesty, do not trouble yourself with such matters this evening. Your lovely daughter would never forgive me and it is such a beautiful night. Let us speak of more pleasant things."

"No, I would prefer that you speak frankly with me. I am in my origins a German after all."

The President smiled thinly.

"Ah yes, the plain speaking of the German people, or as I believe they say in America, 'the plain shooting.' Is that not what they say?"

I was confused. "I do not understand."

"Perhaps I am being elliptical, as one would expect from a Frenchman." He laughed. "Well then, let me try to speak like a German, much as my lifelong training and upbringing are against it, or maybe as an Alsatian … To speak candidly, I believe that war is now inevitable, largely because Germany is speaking out plainly about its desire for a war, any war. And if a country as powerful and industrialized as Germany has become is determined to start a fight, we are in no position to refuse to respond wholeheartedly. We learnt that lesson forty years ago when Germany seized Paris. Germany is much stronger now, but it is to be hoped that France will not be standing alone this time. Is that what you wished to hear?"

I clutched at my heart and fainted out of my chair. I didn't see President Poincaré ever again, so I had no occasion to answer him.

Chapter 13

Later I would always say that the declaration of war came as a great shock to me, and this much is true: I was indeed shocked, horrified, and stricken numb with the sort of fear that makes one taste iron in one's mouth. I had only felt this truly terrified once before, on the forever dark and infamous day when the doctors in their arrogance and conceit removed all hope from me of saving Alexei.

Often one knows something without knowing it, until the terrible fear is confirmed. Then at that moment it does not matter an iota that one might have suspected, or truly known, what was coming. All that foreknowledge falls away when the announcement is made and one is confronted by the inevitable consequences of the event, as if one is considering the enormity of the situation for the first time. For, in truth, whether one is Empress or peasant, none of us truly believes that we are going to die. No young girl catching her reflection in a mirror, or in a pond, believes that one day her fresh young visage will resemble that of a wrinkled old crone. We all know that our destiny is death and, for most, old age, but none of us believe it as a solid fact. How could we ever rise in the morning if we believed that what we knew to be true would inexorably come true?

Everyone recollects differently the moment they heard that war had been declared. For me it was sudden. Nicky had come to me a few days before and said almost idly, "It seems old Franz Joseph is going to cause a bit of trouble after all. He is asking the King of Serbia for a rather impossible set of reparations in revenge for his countryman and subject having murdered his unlamented nephew and his wife." He ran his hand through his hair and continued. "I cannot imagine that they will agree to his demands, but don't worry, darling, Willy and I have this well in hand."

"Willy," I protested, "never has anything in hand, ever. What can you mean, Nicky?"

Nicky shot me a distracted look, lit a cigarette, and then turned his back on me to stare out at the placid sea from our private deck.

"He's not a bad fellow really, Sunny, and like me he desires peace. We have been corresponding with each other quite often by telegram."

"Telegrams about what, Nicky? What business is any of this of his? For that matter, what business is it of ours? If that old creaking gate Emperor Franz Joseph chooses to bully silly little Serbia because that man shot his nephew, why should we care? Father Grigory always says the Balkans are not worth thinking about and that all their people are crazy."

"That is all well and good, darling, but the opinion of an ignorant peasant from Pokrovskoe that I, as Emperor of all the Russias – all the Russias – should turn my back on my sacred duty to act as protector of the Slavic peoples is barely worthy of serious consideration."

"How dare you speak of Father Grigory that way!" I shouted.

Nicky turned towards me and held his hand up angrily.

"Stop it, Sunny, please … Just stop. Here is how things are, and how they have always been, and how,

God willing, they will always remain. The Emperor of Russia has a sacred obligation to protect the Slav peoples. Germany is obliged to protect Austria. In consequence, it would seem rather obvious, given the old Emperor's mad adventuring, that Willy and I should do all in our power to try to plead the case for reason to prevail. Willy is pleading his case with Austria and I am in contact with the Serbian Government, encouraging it to respond calmly to Austria's demands, no matter how insulting they are. In this way we hope to steer this crisis into calm waters and away from war. Still, my ministers are advising me to mobilize my armies lest Germany do the same."

Somewhat cowed by Nicky's newly-acquired demeanor of strength and resolution, I asked quite humbly, "Oh, and will they do that, do you think?"

Nicky shook his head.

"In all sincerity, I do not know. Willy says he does not want war, and I know I don't. His telegrams are kind and considered, and I feel he is being truthful. It is just…"

He paused.

"Just …?" I asked.

"Well, it is the ministers, you see, and Nikolasha as well – all the generals, in fact. They say that we must mobilize, no matter how the talks between Willy and me are progressing. But if I give in to them, will not Willy, or Austria – which is the same thing – judge our mobilization to be an act of aggression on behalf of Russia and therefore an act of bad faith on my part too?"

I rose shakily to my feet. Clearly my husband needed me, much as I needed Father Grigory, more than ever

131

before, but Father Grigory was far away from me, lying wounded in his bed, so I had to help Nicky all on my own.

Carefully keeping the distaste I felt from my voice, I laid my hand on his back and said gently, "I think Austria and Willy will very much see mobilization as an act of aggression, darling. And as for your ministers, I should tell them to wait to see what really happens in relation to Franz Joseph's demands on Serbia. Maybe the Serbian Government will accede to his demands."

"My generals will not agree to that, Alix."

My voice turned steely.

"Your generals are foolish, pumped-up peacocks, silly men who have grown old under your years of peace, darling, and now they yearn to recapture a glory that they never had in the first place. And Grand Duke Nicholas, your cousin, your darling Nikolasha, is the stupidest and most prideful of the lot. You would do better to listen to anyone other than him. And his wife is a poisonous creature too. This is probably all her doing. You know she is my enemy, and Father Grigory's."

I knew immediately that I should not have made that last remark. Up until then I had Nicky convinced of my argument and his eyes had been alight with renewed hope and strength, but at the mention of Father Grigory he pulled away from my hand and resumed smoking and staring out at some horizon only he could see.

His response served only to anger me more, for I hated his resistance to Our Friend. How could Nicky continue to resist the wisdom of the only man, a gifted man of God, who had been able to save our son, whose holy advice could save us even now, were he but here?

Instead, all I had, all we had, was me, and I had lost my temper yet again.

"How dare you, Nicky!" I repeated.

Nicky turned to face me and his look of puzzlement seemed genuine, which only enraged me more.

"How dare I what, Sunny? What in the world are you talking about now?"

I stamped my foot. "Father Grigory!" I shouted, and a terrible pain shot up my sore leg, forcing me to stumble. Nicky caught me before I fell and guided me gently back to my chaise. I waited until he had finished arranging me comfortably there before saying more softly, "Nicky, don't you see, none of these decisions can be made before consulting with him? If you turn your face from Father Grigory, you turn your face from God, and how can anything come right from that? And Nikolasha and his awful wife, darling, they hate me and Father Grigory. And if you love me, how can you listen to those who wish to bring about my destruction?"

"Sunny ..." He paused. "My wify ... One day I hope you will finally understand that, because of who we are, we cannot always let our personal feelings dictate our thoughts and actions."

"Oh, Nicky," I said beginning to shake in earnest, "when will *you* finally understand that our feelings are exactly the things, the sole things, we should listen to in order to dictate our actions?"

Chapter 14

Austria declared war on Serbia a few days after the latter had completely capitulated on all of Austria's demands, proving that old Emperor Franz Joseph did not wish to die quietly in his bed, as Nicky had hoped, but attain one last round of glory on this earth, if war is glory. In response, we mobilized our armies on Austria's border to show our great sympathy for the poor Serbian peoples. Willy and Nicky's telegrams continued to flow between them, but they no longer declared eternal devotion to each other or evinced a resolute commitment to peace.

No, on Willy's part now it was all, "You mustn't mobilize or I will consider it an act of war," accompanied by mendacious, self-serving statements such as, "Only you can avoid this mad conflict, Nicky."

Nicky, as always torn apart by indecision, and desperate to please the last and strongest voice he had heard, first cancelled his partial mobilization, and then, after Nikolasha and the other generals pounded their fists at him, reinstated it.

None of this mattered. On July 19th, according to the Russian calendar, or as the rest of the world remembers it, on August 1st, Germany declared war on Russia.

Nothing better illustrates the sad hypocrisy and confusion of those days than a letter that Nicky wrote in reply to one he had received the day before from King George of England. Sweet Georgie, who had believed that there would be a favorable outcome from the Willy-Nicky correspondence, had innocently written that he and England felt assured that, between these two great emperors who controlled such vast terrains, this silly conflict between the Balkans and Austria could be resolved amicably, saving all from the destruction of war.

Nicky sobbed as he read to me the answer he had given to Georgie.

My Dearest Georgie,

I would gladly have accepted your proposals for saving peace had not the German Ambassador this afternoon presented a note to my government declaring war.

Ever since presentation of the ultimatum at Belgrade, Russia has devoted all her efforts to finding some pacific solution of the question raised by Austria's action. The object of that action was to crush Serbia and make her a vassal of Austria. The effect of this would have been to upset the balance of power in the Balkans, which is of such a vital interest to my empire as well as to those powers who desire maintenance of balance of power in all of Europe.

Every proposal, including those of your government, was rejected by Germany and Austria. It was only when the favorable moment for bringing pressure to bear on Austria had passed that Germany showed any disposition to mediate. Even then Germany did not put forward any precise proposal. Austria's declaration of war forced me to order a partial mobilization, though in view of the threatening situation my military advisers strongly advised a general mobilization owing to the quickness with which Germany can mobilize in comparison with Russia.

I was eventually compelled to take this course in consequence of complete mobilization on the Austrian border due to the bombardment of Belgrade and the concentration of Austrian troops in Galicia as well as my knowledge of "secret" military plans being made in Germany. That I was justified in doing so has been proven by Germany's declaration of war upon us, which was quite unexpected by me as I had given most categorical assurances to the Emperor William that my troops would not move so long as mediation negotiations continued.

In this solemn hour I wish to assure you once more that I have done all in my power to avert war. Now that it has been forced upon me, I trust your country will not fail to support France and Russia in

*fighting to maintain the balance of power
in Europe.*

God Bless and Protect You.

Nicky

"I dictated it straight to Sir George," Nicky said proudly, referring to the pompous English Ambassador, Sir George Buchanan.

"Oh yes, and what did he say about it?" I asked with no curiosity at all, for I had fallen into a stupor of depression since Nicky's unexpected announcement at luncheon the day before that we were at war. Personally, I found the lengthy telegram to Georgie to be self-serving and undignified in its pleading tone, but following my initial breakdown at the news of war, I could not yet muster my usual energy to fight back.

Nicky, who was a man so changed that I could not recognize him, puffed out his chest, pulled on his cigarette and said proudly, "Oh he was deuced impressed, I can tell you. In fact he said that he did not see any other path ahead for England but to declare war upon Germany immediately."

"Yes, otherwise his country will miss out on this collective madness."

I rose to my feet and started for my room.

Nicky goggled at me.

"Alix, Sunny, what are you saying? I did not want this. Were you not listening when I was reading my telegram to you?"

I stopped and turned to him.

"No, I was not listening fully, not with my complete attention. I get distracted by the sound of a distant drumbeat drawing closer every moment. We will no doubt know what it means when it is all too late, Nicky."

He was so very altered already by his barely-concealed righteous enthusiasm for this madness that his only response to me was to remind me tersely that we would all be leaving for town within the hour for our state visit to Petersburg, where Nicky would formally sign his own declaration for a war that had already begun.

Unsteadily, I tottered to the elevator, and, upon reaching my rooms, rang for Maria, and then sat like a stuffed doll while she and the maids dressed me and did my hair, not even flinching when one of the stupid creatures stabbed me with a hatpin.

What did it matter? For well over a day now my poor head had been so riddled with hot pain that my own reflection caused only a distant interest in me. Except that it was more pale than usual, with slightly reddened eyes, I looked much the same. How could this be? I wondered. Should my head not have grown to the size of great balloon to match the agony I felt going on inside it? Should not my face reflect my inner turmoil and the roiling fear I was experiencing?

After Nicky had read to me his telegram, I received another one from Pokrovskoe that night. Somehow my dear Father Grigory, so far away and still so weak, had learned of Nicky's mobilization and of his monstrous new resolve. How this could be, I did not know; maybe God had whispered it in his ear as he lay on his bed of pain. The telegram came addressed to Nicky, but as always in these new days, Nicky was closeted in his study with bombastic generals and forthright ministers, and the object of his new affection, a telephone. Up until the last few days, Nicky had determinedly disdained this device as being overly intrusive, but now he had ordered, as a matter of urgent necessity, two new handsets just for his study alone, I suppose so that he would never miss out on a single piece of ill-judged advice from anyone. As a result of this, and of the fact that the telegram was marked as urgent, Count Fredericks brought it to me.

"Your Majesty, I regret to disturb you at this hour, but I wanted to be assured that His Majesty would receive this telegram tonight before he retires to bed as it is marked 'urgent and personal' and I hesitate to leave it with any member of the staff."

"Just give me the telegram, Count Fredericks, and go to bed," I said dismissively.

Every sentence Count Fredericks ever uttered was accompanied these days by a lengthy bout of hand wringing, which made our every interaction tedious in the extreme. Over the years he had deteriorated into becoming a senile old fusspot and no longer the amusing old, fuddy-duddy creature I had once found him. Only two days previously he had subjected me to a particularly sustained and tedious discourse on the state of our linen cupboards, and on the laxness of our maids, that had nearly provoked me into sending him staggering out of my presence propelled by the force of my boot up his behind.

"Why is it," I wondered to Anya afterwards, "that as people age, their ability to speak in concise sentences just seems to vanish completely? Have you noticed how those of advanced years invariably use a thousand words to describe a situation that could be explained in ten?"

Anya nodded enthusiastically and then told me an endless story about how her 'old' mother (a woman of exactly my age) could no longer manage any sort of simple explanation but just "went on and on, until I could faint from boredom."

Listening to this, I had also wished to faint from boredom and was much irritated by my own stupidity in having addressed this topic to Anya, of all people.

Having been handed the telegram by Count Fredericks, I nearly laid it down on Nicky's side of the bed, as he received many hundreds of telegrams I had no interest in knowing the contents of. However, something prompted me to examine this one.

I tore the telegram open and the first few words erased any guilt I might have felt about doing so. He was speaking to me, telling me the words that I knew could save us if they were only heeded, or would predict our future if they were not.

LET NOT PAPA PLAN FOR WAR STOP FOR WITH WAR WILL COME THE DESTRUCTION OF RUSSIA AND YOURSELVES STOP YOU WILL LOSE TO THE LAST MAN STOP

GRIGORY EFFIMOVICH RASPUTIN

After that, sleep was impossible and I decided to wait up for Nicky, who did not come to bed until well after midnight,

140

I handed him the telegram in silence and with shaking hands. He read it and before my streaming eyes tore it into shreds, letting the individual pieces fall to the floor. When I screamed out my protest at this, he shook his head vigorously and stared at me through exhausted, angry eyes before turning away from me and departing for his dressing room. Aware that the ever-present servants would be watching me and that they would gleefully pass on my every misstep, exaggerating any apparent distress on my part until it was reliably reported as uncontrolled hysteria, I decided not to follow him and merely lay back on my pillows to will myself to endure my never-ending headache and my ever-flowing tears.

Chapter 15

From this distance, I cannot truly remember my wedding day at the Winter Palace, save for two things: That my head ached so badly that I had trouble keeping my feet; and that the sheer amount of people crowded around me had helped me to do so.

Even as a wee childy, I had always been terribly nervous around people I did not know, and for me, unless I was conversing with my immediate family, more than four people in any room seemed to me to be a crowd. I therefore truly feared and, yes, disliked those who kept pushing and shoving their way to the front of the crowd at our wedding, their hungry stares burning up my skin.

Ella reminded me later that it was only natural for people to be curious about me, to want to see me, to wonder at me. After all, was I not their future Empress?

No, no, no, I replied. On that day I was only a bride, a girl in love, but that was not whom they had wanted then. They had not wanted an individual but a symbol, a symbol they could form a judgment about, even then, even on that day!

Naturally, like all young girls in love, I had thought less about what role I should play in our marriage and more about the man I was going to marry. That was wrong, it seems. In my time, whatever a woman's walk of life, she was thought ill of if she married only for love. Princess or peasant, she was expected to marry first of all in the interests of her family. If she were poor, then she must seek to marry a man who had 'prospects' – a trade or a small farm – and woe betide her if she had no dowry to offer, and it was the same in royal circles, if not worse.

On my wedding day, what the Russian nobility knew about me was that I was a very sorry sort of princess, selected from a grand-duchy of no consequence, one with no wealth and only limited influence. I brought with me to my new country no great lands and no great hereditary power with which to exert pressure on the world stage. That I was extraordinarily pretty for a princess was acknowledged well enough, but what did that matter beyond that it made me pleasant to stare at? That I loved my prince terribly, and that he loved me in return, mattered even less. I was not there for Nicky's happiness, let alone my own; I was there for their pleasure and they did not feel particularly delighted by me at all.

Not only was I poor, but I was also too tall and graceless. When I nodded at them in greeting, my head had a tendency to jerk. Overall, they considered me charmless, but maybe some hoped I would improve with time. "She couldn't get any worse, could she?" they whispered. They would wait and see, and be on the lookout for any signs of improvement in my general behavior and appearance, but they had no great expectations in that regard; they would not be holding their breath.

Now, on the day of Nicky's declaration of war, I was back in front of the same staring crowd, mobbing the staircases and the hallways, filling even that enormous palace, and this time they cleared a narrow path for us, and bowed, and scraped, and wiped away tears of pride and adoration from their sweating faces as they gazed at Nicky and at our children … and maybe even at me. However, for me their looks would always be of distaste, and their smiles would always be smirks, as I bowed my aching head towards them. After all this time on the throne, I knew I was still being judged to be the greatest of disappointments to them.

Today we had come amongst them to declare publicly a great war, to bestow our blessings upon them, and to ask, in return, for their blessings on that war. Undoubtedly they would grant them to us with much enthusiasm now and equally certainly return them with bitter hatred towards me later if their vainglorious dreams of a quick and easy triumph were not met.

It would have to have been all my fault in some way, would it not? I must have pushed and nagged Nicky into declaring this war, just as I had inveigled him into marrying me – and look how that had turned out. I was selfish and wrong to my bones, and if the outcome of this war failed to heap ever greater wealth and power on our nation, it would be because it was conceived by me in selfishness and criminal error.

I began to cry again as I passed through them, and glancing behind me at my children, I conceded that our long ago choice to marry for love had indeed been self-serving and wrong, and that because of our selfish choice, our own children were insisting on placing their own happiness ahead of any sense of duty they owed to our country. They would forge their own paths, and duty be damned!

My smart, bookish Olga had rejected Prince Carol because she was intent on marrying for love and staying in Russia, and that decision might have cost us a much-needed ally in this war. My beautiful Tatiana was a princess worthy of any ruler, any place on the world stage, but I had spoiled it all for her, holding her so close, so sheltered, that she said she might never marry at all in order to remain by my side out of love and duty towards me, almost like a pet, "like Anya, Mama." Already she was stiff and shy, and I could see the crowds eying her and recognizing that she was like me and therefore of no use to Russia at all. My big Maria, a girl who already drew the eye of every man who saw her, did not aspire to being a queen or a ruler; rather her dream was to marry a soldier and to produce twenty babies. Anastasia, my comedian, was more dutiful: she did not want to marry a soldier; she wanted to be one.

Then there was Alexei, my Baby, the crowning glory of my marriage, and the son I had at last given to Russia. He had knocked his ankle a few days before and had suffered nights of agony, so that today he could not walk and was being carried in the arms of a Cossack. Total shock and disapproval at this were on display on every face, and this too was my doing. I was *pech vogel,* a bird of ill omen, and what I touched, what I initiated, always turned to ashes.

I finally understood all this the way the Russian people had realized it all along, and as we processed to the balcony to greet the crowds – a million people it was later said – to give our special blessings on them and on our war, I asked myself why they were cheering. Did they not know what a catastrophe this new adventure would prove to be, as I did?

Nicky's speech in the Salle de Nicholas, the largest hall in the largest palace on earth, was so ridiculous and moving that I wondered if he had not written it all by himself, encompassing as it did all of his love for Russia and all of his foolish belief that this war was right and just for his adored country. He went on at some length in front of the worshipful crowd inside the Salle about how this war would arouse the national spirit lying dormant in the soul of his people, and he finished with tear-filled eyes by promising never to "even whisper of peace as long as one enemy remains on Russian soil."

Then we progressed onto a balcony under which millions of people from Petersburg, who had hated us the week before, knelt as one in adoration of us and of Baby in order to sing 'God Save the Tsar.' If ever there was a greater collective moment of delusion in Russia than this, I have yet to identify it.

There were so many things I knew by now I would never see again after this supposed moment of triumph and jubilation; some that I had already anticipated and others not.

I knew, for instance, that I would never board our dear Standart again. Right before war was declared, we had been planning our customary annual cruise through the Finnish Skerries as we made our leisurely way to Livadia and our dreamy white palace that awaited us there. Indeed, our bags had already been sent on ahead and had to be recovered from there on the declaration of war.

As I declared to Nicky, little to his amusement, "I feel it is all up with us. We shall not see The Standart again for some time. And, of course, we cannot return to

Livadia until this stupid war is over. It would be scandalous for us to do so when we will be sending off so many men to fight for us."

Nicky shrugged irritably.

"I suppose a cruise is out of the question right now, but I do think we could plan to visit Livadia for Christmas. It is such a terribly cold and depressing time here, and I imagine we will all need a break from the war, if it is not already over by then. I suppose you are right, though, Sunny about using The Standart this time. It would look bad. However, we could certainly travel to Livadia on Mama's old Polar Star, if she has no need of it herself at the time."

I did not trouble myself to argue with him over this, nor to point out to him the likelihood of our having to sail right on by under the noses of millions of armed enemy soldiers, but within a day Nicky himself began to realize that this war might not be the gentlemanly game of high jinx and flowering patriotism he had envisioned from the start.

This onset of reason was provoked, somewhat funnily, by my mother-in-law. That year, Minnie had been off on her usual summer travels, this time visiting her widowed sister, the Dowager Queen of England, Alexandra, and they had had such a lovely time together, doubtless reminiscing about the old days, that Minnie had decided to stay on in England for an additional month. This decision resulted in her being caught even more unawares than I had been on the declaration of war. Naturally, Minnie insisted upon returning home immediately, intending to do so in tow with Sandro and Xenia and their enormous family, all of whom had been hedonistically pursuing their customary summer idyll in the South of France.

I do not know why they all assumed it would be possible for them to travel all across Europe on Minnie's private train as war flared up around them, especially as the planned route would take them straight across the heart of Germany, our newly-minted principal enemy, but they could hardly have expected it to have been a joyous family outing, their royal progress approved by the ever-affectionate Willy and cheered on by rapturous crowds.

Not, I must admit, that I bothered to think about their predicament too much as I was already far too busy opening hospitals, and I suppose, if I must admit this also, I was more than relieved not to have to deal with my ever-contentious mother-in-law while attending meetings with the Red Cross, of which Minnie was President. Preparing hospitals and setting up field stations was critical to the war effort, and the efficiency of these operations would be little enhanced by being presided over by two empresses who were also at war with each other.

This and the urgency of the situation dictated that matters could not be placed on hold until Minnie's eventual return, so I was faced with no alternative other than to take it all over and do nothing but hold silly balls to raise money in this time of terrible crisis, one I had not wanted but that was upon us all the same. It was, fortuitously, my first chance to be the sort of empress I had long wished to be, and where my German organizational skills and work ethic could serve our dear soldiers and their families well.

Given this, I suppose that I had good reason to laugh secretly to myself after Nicky had burst indignantly into my boudoir waving a telegram, his face purple with rage.

"Look, just look what those German swine have done to Mama!"

For a terrible moment I thought maybe that they had ... well, it didn't bear thinking about, which didn't stop me from doing so.

Therefore, curious but not greatly alarmed, I asked him mildly, "What have they done, darling?"

"They have held Mama's train. The scum won't let her pass through. She and Xenia and her family are all trapped there in the sidings, trapped like rats ... a Russian Empress ... it's unthinkable."

He then sat down heavily, buried his face in his hands, and burst into sobs.

Anya, who was with me as always, joined him, wailing in sympathy.

"Oh no, the poor dear Empress. What will you do, Your Majesty?"

Since I well knew that Anya had long ago picked up on Minnie's distaste of her, and fully returned it, I was not a little impressed at her display of manufactured and hysterical grief. Conversely, Nicky was visibly relieved to find someone close to hand who truly understood the gravity of the situation.

"I have sent a strongly worded telegram to Willy, you can be assured of that! Imagine the Dowager-Empress of Russia, the sister of the reigning Emperor, and a grand duke and all their children trapped in a train car like rats, like sardines, at the mercy of God knows what sort of abusive elements."

149

"Has Willy answered your telegram?" I asked impassively, while Anya wailed out her own greatest fear by asking, "How will they eat?"

Nicky, whom I am certain was all too well aware that I was feeling less anger than gratitude towards Willy at that moment, chose to ignore me and to answer Anya, by which I understood that Willy had not replied to Nicky's indignant demand for safe passage for Minnie and her family.

"Oh that is so kind of you to ask, Anya," Nicky said, shooting me a look, "but I imagine the kitchen and supply cars were well stocked in France before they set off and got caught up in Willy's little trap."

Anya was sufficient reassured by this to allow herself to resume munching contemplatively on her cake.

I allowed myself a moment to imagine our being trapped on our train with Anya – a thought that made me shudder – before saying, "I suppose he will let them pass through sooner or later. He is just making a silly show of things. Will Sandro be joining our armies when he does return, Nicky?"

"What?"

"Will Sandro be taking up some command within our army when he returns?" I elucidated patiently. Then, when both he and Anya stared at me as if I had run mad, I added, "The army! Because we are now at war!"

"I am all too aware that we are at war, Alix," Nicky snapped back. "What in the deuce has got into you today?"

I shrugged.

Nicky continued sullenly, watched avidly by Anya.

"I am proposing, as it happens, that Sandro be placed in charge of Russia's first air operations."

I laughed bitterly. "Oh well, that *is* a relief. Maybe he can improve his little flying containers to the point where we can use them for food deliveries."

Nicky sighed heavily and Anya exclaimed worriedly, "There are food shortages?"

I shook my head, irritated, tired and wishing they would both leave me now.

"No, Anya, no one is out of cakes … yet, but I have a letter here from Father Grigory that has raised some concerns and I –"

Nicky cut me off.

"Forgive me, darling, forgive me, Anya, but I must leave you two together now. I must go to inspect the officers leaving for the front."

Then, with a cold kiss on my forehead, he was gone.

Anya, however, was impatient to hear what Father Grigory had to say, and although she could have been of no help to me whatsoever at that moment, I did want to tell somebody what he had said, and, as usual, Anya was all I had.

"Father Grigory," I proceeded to tell her, "has pointed out that if all the men are taken from the fields, there will be no one to collect up this year's harvest, and if all the trains are taking all the men, there will be no space left in them to bring the wheat and the food into the cities anyway. He says that if the war is not won by Christmas, the people will begin to starve, and that if it continues through the planting season, there will be no harvest later in the year, with the result that there will surely soon be as many dead from hunger as from bullets."

Anya looked at me with gratifying horror, her eyes filled with tears.

"Will you tell His Majesty this so that he can see it doesn't happen?"

I smiled sadly at her, warmed, as always, by her innocence.

"I will try to do so, but you saw how he left us at the mere mention of Father Grigory's name. He is particularly angry at him now."

"Why?"

"You know why, Anya. I told you what was in his telegram, the one Nicky tore to shreds. Nicky was incandescent with rage. He said it wasn't Our Friend's place to say such things, and, indeed, that it could be considered treasonous for him to have done so." I gave a little laugh to denote amusement I didn't feel. "In fact, I think he would have exiled him to Siberia if he hadn't already been there recovering from that attack."

"He's coming back, though," Anya assured me.

I nodded. "Yes, of course he is coming back, as soon as he is well."

Anya shuffled agitatedly.

"No, I mean he's coming back now. He sent me a telegram and I had a call from his daughter, Maria. She's already in the city, preparing his apartment for his arrival and finding him a nurse, too, I think. He may already be here, I'm not certain."

I was brought alive by this news, so much so that I feared to let Anya catch my expression, not that it mattered. It was just ...

I smiled, straightened, and said briskly. "Well, he will have a pleasant surprise when he comes to see us, then, won't he, Anya?"

"We could put on a special tea for him," Anya suggested enthusiastically, for, to Anya's mind, what could possibly be of greater import?

I shook my head.

"No, Anya, it is wartime and we are going to open up a great many new hospitals and get trains of our own started … supply trains and hospital trains for the wounded."

"How could there be any wounded yet?" Anya protested. "The war has only just started."

I goggled at her. God in heaven, she was stupid, comically so I chose to think, and decided to laugh.

"No, Anya, but there will be and soon. My papa was a soldier and the very first thing that happens in a war is bloodshed. When it happens, and it will, we shall be ready."

I nodded emphatically to make my point and she smiled tentatively in return.

"Oh yes, that's a very good plan, but still, shouldn't we plan a special tea to welcome Father Grigory home?"

Chapter 16

Everything is different in war, and our long time marriage became different, and so did I.

I was no longer tired; I was no longer sick; my heart, long damaged, began to beat as regularly as any other; and my weakened legs, although still troublesome to me, seemed to strengthen each day as my headaches vanished in a trice.

I asked Father Grigory about these small miracles and he shared with me a vision he had had.

"I saw Jesus last night, Mama, and his hands were bleeding. He raised them up and the blood fell from them upon the ground where a white rose began to grow. It grew so fast, and then it bloomed, and I awoke and I saw you, Mama. You! You are the white rose. He has fed you with his holy blood so that you can heal the bloody ground that this war will create."

I was naturally comforted by this explanation of Our Creator's grace, but troubled by the knowledge that Father Grigory had not so long ago said this war would bring down ourselves and Russia.

I asked him what he saw now and he twisted his hands and looked away. For a brief, terrible moment he reminded me of Nicky, or, more kindly, of Baby when he was caught out of bed and I knew a lie was coming. But then Father Grigory was incapable of lying, even if he wished to. He spoke for God. Only Satan and his minions lied. Oh how stupid I was to have these doubts, how vain and wrong!

It pains me to remember this now, that I once believed that only those who wished me evil ever lied. What ruler has ever been told the truth, and when they were, how well did they take it? But that wasn't a thing I knew, or at least let myself know, not then, not when it would have mattered.

Poor, wise, martyred Father Grigory, he knew this about both Nicky and me, and although lying came hard to him, he tried, from that day forward until nearly his last, to tell us what he knew we wanted to hear. This was not for his own advancement or power – as so many said then and later – no, he lied because he knew that if he told us what he actually saw and what he knew was coming, we would banish him – not just Nicky but I too. So, instead, he told us what he could and softened the rest. However, now that I consider what he did, I'm not sure that he really lied to us at all; it was much more that we didn't listen to him very well.

Anyway, what he said that particular day was this: "Mama, I have told this to Papa and he did not like it. I do not think he likes me either now, but I did tell him this already."

"Tell it to me now, then, dear friend and redeemer. Tell me, then I will know."

"I will say this again, but never after this. There is a menacing cloud over Russia, and with it lots of sorrow and grief. It is dark and there is no lightening to be seen. There is a sea of tears as immeasurable as blood. What can I say to you? There are no words. The horror of it is beyond words. If these madmen who have brought this to us should conquer Germany, then what will come of Russia? Truly, will there have been any greater suffering since the beginning of time? Is she not to be drowned in blood? Terrible will be the destruction, a destruction without end, a terrible grief to come and to remain."

"What? No, no, no. You did not tell him that! You did not see that! No, take it back!"

He rose to his feet, wearily shrugged into his old bear coat, and then, grimacing from the pain of his healing stomach, he knelt before me.

I stared at him, my eyes streaming, my hand shaking over my trembling mouth.

He waited until I was quiet, bowing his head, his face twisting in discomfort.

"Will you bless me, Mama?"

I raised my hand intending to do so, but then pulled it back.

"Father Grigory, these visions ..."

He sighed and raised his tired eyes to mine.

"Yes, Mama, I do not ask for them, and I did not ask you to ask me about them. Please, the blessing. I need to go home now and sleep."

"Yes, of course, Father, forgive me for delaying you with my concerns, which are only those of Russia. Here..."

I blessed him hurriedly and he arose, groaning. I could almost see the wheels turning behind his eyes. I was angry at him and he knew this. He knew, too, that I had asked him to tell me. He always knew everything, but that did not stop his from being kindness itself, so he smiled down at me.

"Tell me what else worries you, Mama, besides the fate of all of Russia."

"My son is the fate and the future of all of Russia, Father," I answered him sternly. His expression did not change and my voice hardened in fear as I asked, "Will he remain well?"

He shrugged infuriatingly.

"I have told you, Mama, that as long as I am with you, no harm will come to him."

"Yes, but what if you do not happen to be with us?"

I made a sweeping gesture that knocked over a small table, and the ensuing sound of breaking china shattered my nerves yet further. I was as clumsy as Anya.

Father Grigory actually laughed at that moment, and it was then that I saw him, as I knew Nicky did, as merely a peasant, a mad and maddening peasant.

"If I will not be here, Mama, none of us will," he said.

"I do not care about you, or the war, or anything," I screeched, "I do not care about anything except my son. Tell me about my son!"

Without asking my permission to take his leave, he headed for the door and replied over his shoulder, as if none of this mattered much to him one way or the other, "Oh, Alyushka will be fine. If he lives to be seventeen, he will live to be an old man. If not, the blood will drown him as it will drown all of Russia. But for now, Mama, I am still here."

This whole experience, as well as Nicky's far too short answers to the daily letters I had begun to write to him, left me feeling deeply frustrated, for, as my health returned, so did my earlier self, the long ago little German *hausfrau* who loved to snoop around and see

157

everything that was going on, and then fix things. At this same time, my burgeoning plans for the Red Cross had been derailed by Minnie's return from her dreadful capture at the hands of that "barbarous beast, Willy," because, immediately on her arrival she took up her position at the head of the organization and began doing "what was truly needed," which was naturally to raise money by holding yet more balls and receptions.

I, on the other hand, being the daughter of a soldier, knew what was truly best to be done, and left Minnie and her noble ladies to their own devices without a murmur. What were really needed were hospitals and hospital trains, and I planned to have a chain of them running all the way between Petersburg and Odessa in the extreme south. I therefore approached Ella, and our relationship, so long strained by her allegiance to Minnie and her narrow-minded views, as well as by the gossip brought about by my association with Father Grigory, was finally renewed as we began a daily correspondence between us, accompanied at times by telegrams and telephone calls when either of us became too excited to wait for a return letter.

For Ella, like me, was at her best in times when she could help those in trouble, and while I had, it is true, long wondered at her strange decision to become a Sister of Mercy, and even questioned her commitment to it, I was filled with pride at her dedication to the alleviation of suffering now. For yes, already, even at the onset, there was suffering and her home town of Moscow was the first to feel it.

Moscow, unlike Petersburg, was situated near the vast farming lands of Russia, and it was from these small peasant farms and enclosed villages that the men were taken off to war.

In a letter to me that I tried not to view as an attack on Nicky, Ella wrote this:

> *It is hard, Alicky, to see them, they come now daily and in greater and greater numbers, old men and women, and young women and little children. Some of the young women have babies in them, but all of their stomachs are empty.*

> *The poor live very close to starvation at the best of times in Russia, and now without their young men to hunt and fish for them they have already begun to slip into severe hunger. God knows what will become of all of them by harvest time, and who will bring it in.*

I knew she was telling the truth, so I did not bother to ask Nicky about it. Besides, I was far too busy.

As I said to Nicky one day, "I am sorry, darling, but I am late for a meeting. We will speak again after dinner tonight, shall we?"

"A meeting?" he asked curiously. "What about, Sunny?"

I smiled at him, already on my way.

"Oh, I am quite busy nowadays, dearest. I am setting up so many hospitals and medical trains. Why, our big Catherine Palace is almost ready to receive the wounded." Then, not meaning to be unkind – or at least I

159

do not think I was – I remarked with affected nonchalance, "I fear we will be getting many wounded for me to help soon. Goodbye, darling. I will see you later."

I did not really have a meeting to attend that day as such, but I did have a project in mind, one I wanted to surprise him with. I had in fact signed up, alongside Anya, Olga and Tatiana, to take lessons in nursing from the only female surgeon that I had ever heard of. It was Ella who had told me all about the brilliant Dr. Gedroiz, poor Dr. Gedroiz, who had clearly been so overwhelmed by the honor of my first receiving her and then informing her that she should train us, that she had refused me utterly.

"Your Majesty, this would be too great an honor for me to bear, and I do not know who would care for my patients while I was engaged in this. We are so short-handed."

I responded to her appropriately self-effacing protestations by clapping my hands together briskly.

"You are too kind and modest, Doctor, which is as it should be. All the same, I trust you to instruct us, and we would like to start tomorrow, directly after luncheon. So, shall we have you attend to us here in the Red Room at one-thirty?"

Given no further choice but to be abashed, the kind doctor then curtsied so deeply that she almost hid her face and reddened, no doubt from the great honor of it all.

It is odd, considering how every pair of hands would prove so necessary to the war effort, that my plan to become a full nursing sister was met with almost universal disapproval and derision, starting with Minnie, as one might have expected, who was the first to begin the wave of gossip that would soon spread to every drawing room in Russia, and then, I fear, to humbler dwellings.

Nothing I could do, or ever did as Empress, could ever be adjudged to be the right thing. Here we were at war, with thousands of young Russian men being horribly wounded every hour at the hands of the German and Austrian forces, and instead of putting on my finest gowns and sitting uselessly about in this or that drawing room, I had chosen to clad myself in the raiment of a humble nursing Sister of Christ, with a red cross rather than a diamond pendant on my chest, and instead of receiving praise, what I heard were comments like these:

"Oh, how clever! She's found a way to avoid being our Empress and having to meet anyone, even while we are at war."

"She doesn't care enough about the soldiers even to see off the trains. The Emperor, God bless and keep him, has seen off nearly every one of them leaving for the front."

"It's a miracle, isn't it, how she can suddenly rise from her bed like a Phoenix and scurry off to the hospital. I suppose we should all be grateful for that, and for Rasputin!"

"Anya", I began, after wiping away my angry tears on hearing the first few ugly things she had rushed back from town to report to me, "the last thing you said, does that not show that some people are pleased with my taking up nursing and finally that they understand about Father Grigory?"

She shook her head so wildly that spittle and crumbs flew about.

"Oh no," she began, helpfully trying to correct this false impression of mine, "it doesn't mean that at all, Alix. You see, they said it in a very mocking sort manner, like this ..." She accordingly scrunched up her face and stuck out her cream-coated lower lip to illustrate a typical expression.

I sighed; it was ever thus.

Pulling my shoulders back, I smiled sadly.

"Well it does not matter. We will not let it matter, shall we?"

"What doesn't matter?"

"We have our first instruction today with Dr. Gedroiz. And, oh well, I wanted to wait to surprise you and the girls later, but I truly cannot wait." I picked up the bell and rang for my dear old Maria. When she arrived, I told her to go and fetch Olga and Tatiana, and to tell the seamstress to bring in the surprise.

Her eyes twinkled, more with pleasure at my pleasure, I think, than at the surprise gifts I was about to bestow, for Maria, like Dr. Botkin, was terribly concerned that my new burst of health would subside, leaving me in a worse case than before.

While I appreciated her concern, if not Dr. Botkin's, who some days reminded me more of a silly old clucking hen than a physician, I was determined upon my course, so I narrowed my eyes at her now lest she spoil my fun by making yet another worried remark.

My fun and Anya's ... as Anya was nearly bouncing upon her chair, making it creak ominously, she was so excited. I had to smile at her, annoying and clinging and tactless as she was, but also childlike and loving, and the latter for me always outweighed the former.

My girls, who were always excited by any summons to my boudoir, rushed in, flushed and smiling, followed by the seamstress closely on their heels, staggering under the weight of her load.

I gestured at her to drop all of it onto the chair and said mischievously to my curious ones, "Would you like to unwrap them now or should we wait until later?"

Their responses were characteristic of each of them. Tatiana smiled and asked me which I preferred. Olga shrugged as if it did not much matter to her either way, her standard response that she knew was sure to annoy me. Whereas Anya, she immediately jumped off her chair, knocking it into the tea table and spilling everything everywhere, to Maria's obvious horror and Olga's eye rolling. She then made her way over to the brown paper-wrapped pile and greedily tore into it, asking over her shoulder, "Is it a present for everyone to share or do we get our own?" Before I could answer, she said, clearly disappointed, "Oh," and moved away without even picking up one of the specially designed nurses uniforms I'd had made.

Tatiana, seeing my face fall, moved over to them, and reaching for the first one, held it up gaily and said, "Oh

163

Mama, they're beautiful! Olga, I think this one must be for you. I'm far too thin for it."

Olga, to my relief, joined in with Tatiana's giggles, for, by sheer good luck, the one Tati had picked up was obviously several sizes larger than the rest and therefore clearly destined for the buxom, and now pouting, Anya, who complained, "Why do we have to do this? I don't even know if I want to be a nurse, I don't much like sick people, and I'm certain I'll faint if I see even a drop of blood."

Now it was my turn to roll my eyes and even Maria giggled, although Anya did not. Olga, who was often openly disdainful of Anya, remained quiet.

Despite these small setbacks, I suggested that we all surprise Nicky by appearing at luncheon in our new garbs, and this idea appeared to delight everyone.

Nicky was indeed gratifyingly shocked and delighted by our appearance, to the point that he insisted upon addressing each of us at luncheon with our new titles of "Sister," calling me adorably, "Sister darling," which caused much mirth except from Anya who remained stubbornly displeased, her mood not helped much by Anastasia's observation that she had never seen such a fat nurse before and that she thought that the very sight of Anya would cheer up the men and make them laugh.

"You've certainly made me laugh," she said.

At that, Anya sniffed and looked pointedly at Olga, "Well, I may not be as thin as some, but I'm not a lot fatter than others," she said, clearly meaning Anastasia, who stuck out her tongue back at her and then looked away. "And at least I'm not a silly schoolgirl hiding in

164

the nursery, but a grown up lady who is ready and willing to help our dear wounded."

To this, Maria said, "Mama, I want to help the wounded too. Oh please let me be a nurse along with all of you. I'm sure Anastasia would like to be one, too. We really don't need any more lessons."

"No," said Anastasia, "I'm going off to the front with Papa when he goes. When are you going, Papa?"

A wail of protest from Baby followed Anastasia's pronouncement.

"I'm the heir. I'll be the one going to the front with Papa when he goes, stupid girls."

He followed this up by bursting into tears, which made everyone at the table cease from arguing and gather around him to offer him words of comfort, for if Baby became upset in any way, there was always the chance of his rupturing a blood vessel in his nose. Colds could cause this as well, so we all had to be very careful at all times and guard him against any upset or uncontrolled sneezing.

Nicky, who always hated to see our sunshine in distress, took this as an opportunity to slip away from the table, and by the time we had managed to restore Alexei's good spirits with various promises, it was well past one-thirty, and Anya, Tatiana, Olga and I had to face a thoroughly exasperated Dr. Gedroiz for our first nursing lesson.

Chapter 17

"This war is bad," I told myself in between changing blood-soaked bandages and holding the hands of the dying while prayers were whispered, and it was worse when I had to hold the hands of men while they were having their shattered and gangrenous limbs removed.

"Be brave, God is with you," I would say, "and I am with you, too."

They were indeed brave, often not screaming as the saw was applied to them, and not crying when the end came. I, however, was becoming less brave by the minute because it never ended. The wounded kept coming, and soon the entire, gigantic Catherine Palace was filled with men so damaged by this very modern warfare that they could scarcely be considered to be men at all.

Despite the horrors, the moment we began to visit the wards, we all studied our hardest for Dr. Gedroiz, and within a short time the four of us had graduated from nursing assistants to full Sisters of Mercy, although, a mere two months in, only Tatiana and I remained working on the wards.

It came as no surprise that Anya proved to be a complete disaster as a nurse. I was of course disappointed that this should be the case, but that is a different thing. It seemed to me that if she had ever put any effort into anything at all during her training, it was into annoying poor Dr. Gedroiz more than anything else, while Dr. Gedroiz herself let it slip in many small ways that she would have much preferred to have been working on her own wards than teaching us. I am certain one of the main reasons for this was Anya and her complete inability to grasp the simplest of concepts in nursing. Between her endless questions and her constant clumsiness around the instruments we were practicing on, I was in a state of near collapse from embarrassment at her clueless antics.

Fortunately, both my girls did me great credit and somehow we all muddled through. Indeed, within the first week, Dr. Gedroiz complimented both my own and Tatiana's "cool nerves," and moved us over to work in the operating amphitheater, where we even assisted with surgeries, including holding steady a limb while it was being cut off, and in some cases carrying it away for incineration. These were terrible things to have to experience, worse than terrible things in truth, but they were soon to get even worse when the morphia ran out, as did so many other supplies, and then the men had to be operated on while fully awake.

"Matushka, Matushka, hold my hand that I might be strong," they would whimper piteously to me, and I can still hear their pitiful sobs as the surgeon determinedly cut into them, and shall continue to do so until my dying day.

My Tatiana was a dream of kindness and efficiency as well, and thankfully she was not so easily recognized in her simple uniform and wimple as I was.

And then there were Anya and Olga ...

Anya, naturally, managed to alienate every other nursing sister with her high-handed manner and her frequent absences, presumably at the refreshment cabinet. Nor did her ghastly screams and sobs endear her to any of the doctors, and least of all to Dr. Gedroiz, who in short order asked my permission to banish her permanently to the bandage sorting cupboard, a request to which I readily, if guiltily, acceded, although I found the case of my oldest girl Olga very much more disturbing.

Olga had always been a fine student and had only recently finished her schooling. She was also truly assiduous in her attentions to Dr. Gedroiz, and once allocated to the wards, she proved a quietly attentive presence to the sisters, and both kind and efficient in tending to the needs of the wounded. However, she soon developed a tendency suddenly to grow pale and for her hands to shake so badly that the other nurses were obliged to take over from her in distributing the medicines.

It was therefore quickly apparent that she would never be asked to assist in operations, and that fact seemed at first to cause her to be less nervous, but then she began crying all the time, and saying that her head hurt, and that her legs were cramping, whereupon Dr. Botkin diagnosed her with a mild case of rheumatic fever and put her to bed for a fortnight.

The proposed fortnight stretched into months, and although I hesitate to give voice to any dark suspicions about my own childy, I couldn't help noticing that Olga's health seemed to rally whenever there was an event she wished to attend, and then collapse again at the prospect of her resuming her nursing duties.

When one considers the life of duty that Nicky and I had modeled for her during her entire life, her sudden descent into hypochondria and weakness of will was, I will admit, a great disappointment to me. I am sure that this was the case for Nicky as well, although instead of speaking to her sharply about it to encourage her to develop a more resolute disposition, he chose rather to mollycoddle her with long, soothing visits when he was home, which he was less and less.

Two new things had become apparent to me, or as I said to Anya one evening as I collapsed onto my chaise, too tired even to allow my clucking Maria to help me out of my bloodstained nursing garb, "Do you know, Anya, I think Nicky is enjoying this war."

She gawped at me and shook her head.

"Oh no, he hates the war. He is so concerned about how things are and all the suffering."

"Anya, when exactly did Nicky say that to you?"

Anya yawned and rubbed her back, as if exhausted from an entire day of hiding among the linens at the hospital, in order to evade the issue I was raising with her about her habit of conducting private conversations with my husband, her Emperor, behind my back.

Not, apparently, that my tone had any apparent impact on her as she glanced at me with a small smile and sighed as though I were boring her.

"Oh, he writes to me about his worries and the things he is thinking of."

This admission would have made me incandescent with rage had I not been so exhausted from my long day at the hospital caring for the sick and dying, the sick and dying created by this rotten war. Instead, I merely felt sad for myself and for my husband. For no matter how long my day had been, I wrote nightly to Nicky before retiring to bed. Sometimes my thoughts outpaced my

169

hand, and at other times I would collapse into sleep before I could finish, but in those cases I would squeeze out precious minutes of free time at dawn to continue my correspondence so that my letter could be posted to him, and so that, no matter what, he would hear from me each day.

By now, Nicky was nearly always either at the front or traveling around Russia making inspections. What he was inspecting, I could hardly imagine, although his ever-cheerful letters would go on happily about such matters as his investigating a captured German artillery gun, or mention how many new babies he saw the Cossack women holding up for his approval as he passed.

"New subjects for us! It gladdens my heart!" he declared on this occasion.

Sometimes he wrote about the rousing walks he took at Headquarters alongside that ghastly old Grand Duke Nicholas Nicholaievich. "His nerves are steady and he sees what must be done," he would say.

I refrained from commenting in my return letters that if the Grand Duke's nerves were steady, no one else's were.

By that first winter, the war had turned against us and we seemed to be losing every battle, due in part to the frightful lack of bullets and shells available to our troops. Nicky and I had a conversation about this one day when he was at home.

"My God, Sunny, their field machinery sends out a hundred bullets a minute. My generals tell me that the men have never seen or even imagined such a thing and are demoralized, those who are not cut into pieces immediately, that is. They still have muskets, most of them, and so few bullets!"

"What do you mean, Nicky?" I asked.

He couldn't look at me.

"We weren't ready for a war on this scale, you see, darling. We didn't have enough munitions factories – the ones that make the weapons, the ones that make bullets – and so the officers have had to tell the men not to use more than six bullets a day, whereas the German army has as many bullets and shells as it needs."

"Germany was prepared for war and has lots of armaments … Yes, I see."

He looked at me and reached for my hand, grasping it hard.

"The railroads are failing us too. We are missing hundreds of miles of track that are needed to supply us at the front, Sunny. Supplies, men, they all have to travel on foot as there are not so many horses, and those that there are have to be used to pull the carts. And now that the winter is here …"

"Yes, it will be much worse then, won't it?"

It was ruinous. Due to the lack of munitions available to our armies and to the ability of the Germans to move their troops quickly across the whole front on their railroads, our men were being killed at a rate of sixty Russians to one German. Our young officers had even taken to going off into the forests after battles and shooting themselves in the head, this gruesome activity having begun after Grand Duke Nicholas and Nicky had signed a joint order that officers must not place themselves in the front line of fire.

Now I watched Anya, fat, funny, lazy Anya, and asked her quietly, "What do you write about to His Majesty?"

Without bothering to stifle yet another yawn, she replied, "Oh, I tell him about quarrels between the nurses and how badly upset Mama's cook is about the butter shortages in town, and then I tell him how I see the men looking so lovingly at his portrait there in the hospital – those sorts of things. Not very interesting, I suppose, to a man at the front, but then, you know, Alix, I like to help the wounded officers at the hospital to write letters home to their mamas or their sweethearts, and I read to them the letters they receive too, and none of the letters they get from home are ever about sad or worrying things, so I try to do the same in my letters to the Emperor."

"Yes, quite. I see."

I stared into the flames for so long that eventually I heard Anya beginning to snore. I rose wearily and rang for Maria. I thought of rousing Anya and then decided to let her sleep where she sat, the fat, smug creature. It was so nice for her and so nice for Nicky that they could correspond about such happy matters. My letters, I had to admit, would have made for much more difficult reading, and maybe he wished that they wouldn't come at all, speaking as I did about all that worried me and all I saw of the young blasted men I had to nurse. Still, I always tried so hard to reassure him of my deep and endless love for him, for I missed him terribly, although sometimes I was no longer certain why.

I had not felt much more than anger for him after he had begun this war, or after Willy had – I could not seem truly to understand which of one of them it was who had started it. Or, no, was it all that sad old Emperor of Austria's fault?

I leaned back on my suddenly shaky legs in my elevator, and pressed my hands to my eyes with a moan. No wonder he liked Anya's letters, and maybe Anya herself, more than me. I was behaving like a mother towards him, although not his mother. Oh no, she was all gaiety and interesting stories of her travels around Russia for the Red Cross. Even Ella, who I also knew wrote to him, was probably more cheering than I was.

I staggered out of my little cage and down the corridor to my rooms, where I collapsed into Maria's waiting arms in sobs.

She brought elderflower wine and rubbed my aching head with her gentle callused fingers, but she didn't say anything soothing or ask me why I cried. Maria was of the people and she didn't need to.

Chapter 18

By the winter, Dr. Botkin was becoming concerned about my health again. I had fainted twice during operations and my headaches were returning to overwhelm me. He pleaded for complete bed rest, but I couldn't, not during the war, so instead I planned an informal tour of inspection to visit some of the outlying hospitals I had funded. My trip would end in the faraway small town of Grovno, where I would meet up with Nicky.

Naturally, I took Anya with me and included Tatiana as well because she was looking nearly as pale as me and I wanted her to have a rest and a treat. I had not planned on Olga joining us, given her ill health, but to my intense irritation she had gone behind my back and written to Nicky herself, asking him to intercede so that she could see "her dearest, darling Papa."

This latter decision created a great storm with the younger children, as was to be expected, and Nicky, who was away somewhere – I had lost track of exactly where – was not there to have to deal with any of it, of course. Anastasia protested vigorously that Olga had done nothing to deserve this treat as she was no longer nursing, and didn't "go to school or do anything much at all that I can see." Maria said tearfully that she could barely sleep for missing Papa and that she did not understand why she had to continue with her lessons anyway since she "muddled them all, and, Mama, all I want to do is to get married and have twenty babies. I want to marry a soldier and you're going where there are

174

soldiers, and when I do get married, he won't care much whether I know the capital of Moldavia or not!"

In vain did I point out, over and over, that this was not a pleasure trip and that there would be no spare time for seeing things. Besides, I would only meet up with Nicky at the very end.

Baby became so hysterical that he banged his elbow in rage and screamed for hours afterwards until at last Father Grigory was found and brought to the palace at dawn to pray over him, and the pain vanished once again.

Because I needed the rest, and because I would be on and off trains for nearly a month, and trains risked injuring Baby with their bumping and swaying, I steered a firm course on this matter, and so, as I made my departure, I received not a single kiss goodbye from my three little ones, although they did all send loving greetings to their adored papa who had created this mess in the first place.

First our little troop traveled to the towns around Tsarskoe, but soon we forged other paths to faraway Pskov, Vilna, Kovno, and finally Grodno, where Nicky joined us.

I hadn't seen Nicky for so long that he seemed all new to me again, and it seemed he returned my feelings, with the result that for a few days on the train we were as young lovers.

Possibly the intense cloud of emotion that hung over Russia at this time also contributed to our renewed mutual affection, because it had become all too apparent even then that there would be no quick resolution to the war, and no Christmas homecomings and celebrations. Instead, the first winter of the war came with its iron grip of cold and a new round of suffering. Daily, our train was forced into sidings to allow the dozens of overcrowded troop trains headed for the front – or the slower ones heading south with all the wounded – to pass us. After a few days I could no longer bear to look out of the windows of my compartment at the huddled women and children, who often remained standing along the tracks long after the trains taking away those they loved and depended upon the most were out of sight.

Early one dark afternoon when we had been sitting in a siding for what seemed like hours, I summoned Count Fredericks, who was traveling with us, to my presence.

"Count Fredericks, why are all of these people still standing out there? It is freezing out there and, moreover, they are making me uncomfortable staring at our train. Why don't they go home?"

He shook his head sadly.

"They don't seem to want to, Your Majesty. I have sent some of the guards out to speak to them, but they say there is nothing at home for them anymore."

"But it is so cold and they look hungry. It is ridiculous for them to loiter about there. They have little children with them too," for, as a mother, I was growing angry at their lack of care for their small ones.

Count Fredericks bowed and said rather slyly, I felt, "It seems that they have no winter fuel or food, so it is possible that one place is much the same as the next to them. And I think they are hoping to catch a glimpse of Your Majesties as well."

I drew myself up to my full height.

"Certainly not, Count Fredericks. His Majesty and I have made no such plans and will not be chivied into this. Tell the engineers clearing the tracks to get on with it and to get us away from here as quickly as possible."

"Yes, Your Majesty."

"Immediately please, Count Fredericks."

Count Fredericks bowed and backed away, and soon our train was departing along the tracks across the snowy wastes, leaving those terrible ghostly-looking people behind us.

Much later, lying warm in Nicky's arms, I asked him about the people lining the sides of the tracks and he shrugged against me.

"It is sad, I agree, Sunny, but war is difficult, and at such times one must put one's patriotism and love of country ahead of one's immediate comforts. Such sullen displays do little credit to the brave soldiers they have sent off to do their duty for Russia."

"Darling, I could not agree more. I mean, look at us out here adrift on this frozen wasteland, being shunted from one miserable hospital to the next, but Count Fredericks said they were hungry and it reminded me of what Father Grigory has spoken about, and I have to wonder if there is anything more we can do to help."

"Sunny, my angel, please don't upset yourself, unless you wish to join me in deprecating this latest piece of self-pitying nonsense from Misha. I mention it as we are speaking of those who whine about any sacrifice for their country, even members of my own family."

I sat up with real interest, completely diverted from my dark thoughts over those frozen-faced women we had left behind us.

Misha, Nicky's utterly charming, utterly spoiled by his mama, younger brother, had for years been indulging in the sort of behavior that made all of us a laughingstock in society. First, he had openly courted a fellow officer's wife, one Madam Natalia Wülfert; then he had been named as a correspondent in her divorce; then he had fathered a son out of wedlock with that same shameless hussy; and as if all that weren't enough, and to drive everyone mad, he had used the cover of Baby's near death at Spala to secretly marry her after giving Nicky his solemn promise that he would never, ever, do so. The entire sordid affair had nearly killed Nicky and my mother-in-law from the shame of it all.

I cannot pretend to have been too concerned for the health and well-being of my mother-in-law, but this was truly appalling behavior, and very unfair on Nicky and myself – and indeed on the standing of the family as a whole – so I obviously could not countenance such a personage as Mrs. Wülfert ever being received by us. The marriage was morganatic, which meant that any issue could neither stand in line for the throne nor hold any titles, although it seemed that Mrs. Wulfert – or Countess Brassova as she had now styled herself since the wedding, this being the name of one of Misha's estates – was not intending to have any more children in any case, so she and Misha would have to content themselves with poor little George, their bastard child.

"What does the letter say, Nicky? Can I read it?" I asked because I did genuinely wish to think of lighter matters, and no matter how keenly Misha felt for his own suffering, it would, I knew, pale into comparison against the very real suffering I was seeing all around me and thinking far too much about.

So, when Nicky handed me the letter with a shrug, I began to read it eagerly at first, and then more slowly, and by the time I had finished reading it, I felt wretched. If that is what Misha intended by writing it, I could only conclude that he had been successful.

Dear Nicky

As I am leaving for the war, from which I may not return, I want to ask you one request, in which I hope you will not refuse me and which depends entirely upon you.

It is very hard for me to go away, leaving my small family in such an ambiguous position. I wish only for the son I love so dearly to be accepted by society, as my son and not as the son of an unknown father, as he is presently listed on his birth certificate. It hurts me when I think about it, which I do constantly and I am possessed by this worry at a time when my soul is full of longing and readiness to serve and if so willed by God to die for our beloved country.

Remove me from the burden of fear that if something were to happen to me, my son

179

would grow up with the stigma of illegitimacy.

Where other people are concerned the question of legitimizing children born before marriage is easily decided by the court, but in the case of my son the court is powerless! You alone can do this, it is your right. I beg you now to use your prerogative and give the order for my son Georgy, born to Natalia before our marriage, to be recognized as our legitimate son. Please Nicky, spare him in this way from the difficult position I have outlined in the future. At the moment he is too little to be aware of the situation but in the future he will feel it very much.

And after all, he is not to blame! Take pity on him and on me as a father, as a brother. This is perhaps my last personal request. To expedite the matter, I enclose the certificate of the birth and baptism of my small Georgy.

I embrace you warmly, dear Nicky, your very loving

Misha

I set the letter back onto the covers with shaking hands and swallowed. "Oh!" was all I could manage to say.

"Yes," was all Nicky replied.

"Why didn't you say that it was such a sad and terrible letter? Why did you let me think it would be amusing?"

Nicky shrugged and failed to meet my eyes. I thought for a moment and then felt a flush of embarrassment and anger creeping up my neck.

"Oh, I see, you wanted me to read it for myself. You thought that if I did so, I would say, 'Oh, we must help him!' while you thought that if you just asked me, I would say no. Or if you went ahead and did what you are clearly intending to do anyway, which, as Misha points out is well within your power, that I would make things unpleasant for you when I found out." I began to choke on my angry sobs. "You think I am a coldhearted monster like your mother."

"Alix!"

"Well, she is. She has never even bothered to meet the little boy, her own grandson, and she would say no to this, I know she would! But I wouldn't, Nicky, I wouldn't say no. Grant what your brother asks for his child and stop trying to make me look like the monster of the piece. My God, if you saw what I see every day at the hospital, if you heard their cries, if you only stopped for a moment and thought this might really be the last letter you will ever receive from Misha, and then asked yourself why this is, you would know who the monster of this piece is." I should have stopped there. The expression on his now dead-white face should have stopped me, but I was too lost in my own pain by then, and instead sobbed out lamely, "You would know who the monster is."

He nearly fell out of bed in his hurry to move away from me, grabbing at his robe and cursing as he found it to be inside-out. I, on the other hand, was calm now. All of my anger and tension had drained away when I had stepped over the abyss.

"Where are you going, Nicky?"

"To my study. I have just remembered that I need to go over some letters with old Fredericks."

I did not bother to point out that it was well after midnight and that poor old Count Fredericks would have long been asleep. I simply turned over and pulled the covers up over my newly chilled body.

Nicky had left me without saying good night, and when I awoke in the still, black winter morning he had not returned. Maybe he had slept on a couch in the dining car for all I knew. What I did know was that we had lost a very valuable part of our marriage, our habit of always standing together. It is true that we had not always been in agreement on every matter, and may even have annoyed each other in tiny ways, but our constant familial closeness had created soft places so that we did not rub up against each other in a jarring manner. Now that was gone and we were as strangers with a well-remembered past that somehow would not feel real to either of us. I wondered how we would ever again become that family we had been before the war, and be able to love each other and not simply endure each other, and probably poorly at that.

182

Fortunately, there was little time to dwell upon Nicky and my situation because the war demanded all of my attention and that very day after our fight I was taken out of my own problems by a visit to the small hospital in Grodno. It seemed that one of the young wounded soldiers had learned that Nicky and I were nearby and had said he would wait to die until he could meet me. *Me not Nicky*. He wanted me.

I was both thrilled and moved, and gave orders for the train to return there at full speed, and once we reached Grodno, I hurriedly put on my nurse's uniform and went to see the soldier.

He was a handsome young officer, but as white as the sheet he lay on.

I took his hand.

"Thank you for coming to me, Your Majesty," he whispered.

"Thank you for waiting for me," I whispered back.

But he was already dead.

On unsteady legs, I made my way back to the carriage, which duly became stuck in the heavy snow, so it was over an hour before I could collapse back into my train compartment.

I heard laughter coming from the salon and recognized it as coming from Anya and Nicky. I minded that I did not mind it at all.

Chapter 19

Nicky traveled on to Dvinsk to make inspections there, and Anya, the girls and I started back for Tsarskoe Selo, mostly in silence, a silence that was broken at our first stop when the mail was brought to our train.

Nicky, it seemed, had written to me immediately upon gaining his own train and the freedom to write, and I had done the same, and in our letters we poured out all the love and concern and kindness we had for each other that we could not seem quite to manage in person. So I sat there in innocent happiness, reading his sweet words, not even noticing that Anya had also been in receipt of a letter of her own until she made a silly show of herself by giggling loudly, kicking up her feet as though she had sat on a pin, and finishing off this bizarre display by clutching the letter to her ample bosom with a gusty sigh.

Olga, who had fallen back into her torpor right after Nicky had left, stared at her incuriously and resumed her vigil of staring out of the window at the frozen landscape.

Tatiana, who was looking particularly beautiful having rested herself on this trip, smiled at her and asked, "Anya, have you a secret sweetheart?"

Anya turned magenta with pleasure and giggled madly.

"Oh no, it is someone I may never call my own."

Tatiana, who had a very well-developed moral sense, answered severely, "Then you shouldn't receive letters of that sort. Besides, Anya, why do you say that? Surely you are no longer married ..."

"It is not I, Tati, who make it so. Not all are free to love."

At that, Anya burst into some ostentatious lamentations and started kissing the letter.

I had been trying to avoid being drawn into this nonsense as I was puzzling over another letter I had received, this one from Ella. It was such a strange letter that I could not quite make out what she meant by it. It contained a request for me to visit her hospitals in Moscow and my own, but it had an unsettling undertone. It seemed to represent a sort of warning, if I had not misunderstood her last line of, "But, Alicky, expect little in the way of adoration, for Moscow has begun to turn."

'Turn what?' I thought irritably as I read this.

I would have much preferred to discuss my letter than whatever stupidity Anya had obviously involved herself in with some wounded officer she had encountered. 'He must have been badly wounded in the head if he was writing to Anya,' I told myself, but my complacency was shattered a moment later when Olga suddenly roused herself and impatiently grabbed the *billet doux* from a startled and shrieking Anya.

She briefly examined it, and then, before I could chastise her for her rudeness, she said slowly, "This is from Papa."

"What?" gasped Tatiana and I in unison.

"We are friends, and friends may write to each other," Anya protested sullenly, all traces of girlish delight wiped from her face, but neither did she look ashamed.

I was beyond appalled.

Olga handed me the letter and wordlessly left the salon car.

Tatiana stared at me, concerned.

"Mama?"

I shook my head, but only slightly as I feared any great movement might shatter me to pieces. I was the Empress of snow and ice in that moment, which was entirely fitting given our location, I suppose.

"Tati darling, perhaps you should retire to your sleeping car."

"But I'm not tired, Mama. It's not even three yet."

"Then maybe you would like to go and see to your sister," I managed to say between gritted teeth, piqued by her obtuseness.

Tati glanced between Anya and me, finding a remarkably unperturbed Anya, I might add, and her forehead wrinkled in consternation as she worked on puzzling things out in her mind. For the first time since her birth, she resembled Nicky more than me.

Anya sighed.

"Dear Tati, you should leave us for a bit. Your poor mama is very upset with me and wants to say unpleasant things to me that I am sure she would not wish you to hear."

"Tatiana, please ..." I added.

"But, Mama, I don't want you and Anya to quarrel." She was close to tears. Why did we all spend half our lives in tears, even Nicky?

"Tatiana, if you do not go now, you and I shall soon be quarreling too," I said in a tone of voice my children seldom heard.

Sobbing audibly now, and casting me a reproachful look, Tatiana finally left me alone with Anya, but by then my head was pounding away to the point where the salon car swam before my eyes, shades of my favorite mauve blending together with the early dark from the windows until all was a graying blur. Only Anya with her tomato-colored dress and large red face retained her spots of color.

I gripped my chair, not wanting to appear weak in front of her, but she knew me so well; we had been together so long.

"You're getting one of your headaches, aren't you, Alix? You should go and lie down. And you should say you are sorry to poor Tati, too." I gaped at her. She gazed back at me calmly. "And why are you looking at me like that? You have my letter in your hand. Why don't you just read it instead of making such a fuss about nothing?"

"I ... Anya, you cannot say things like that to me!"

It was I, the wronged party, who was now finding myself thrown off-balance, and I could not read the letter because I could not stop the words from swimming and swirling around my vision. Instead, I dropped it as if it was burning my fingers and we both watched it flutter to the floor,

Anya half-rose.

"May I have my letter back, please," she said.

I gestured my assent. Nodding might have killed me.

Anya rose up and bustled over to where the letter lay, all fat and healthy and complacent – everything I wasn't.

There was so much I could have said, but only this came out, to my horror and doubtless to her pity.

"Does Nicky love you, Anya?"

Having regained her precious missive, Anya sat back in her chair and studied the remains of her tea with distaste. Then, without asking my permission, she rang the bell. There would only be moments now until our privacy would be interrupted and I sensed that there would not be any other opportunity to discuss this matter with Anya. Anya was, I suddenly understood, a past mistress of evasion. The question that remained for me was whether she was also my husband's mistress.

"Does he love me?" she repeated back to me slowly.

"Yes."

"I believe, Alix –"

"Please address me by my title."

Anya tilted her head and smiled.

"I believe, *Your Majesty*, that *His Majesty* the Emperor loves all his subjects, as I'm certain do you."

"You said ... did you not say that you dared not call him your own? And you acted ..."

"How did I act, Your Majesty, as a subject delighted by the slightest acknowledgment of my existence by my Emperor? Haven't I witnessed hundreds of his subjects bowing down to kiss his shadow ... and yours too?"

There was an inflection in her voice that implied that my being the object of the bowing was something of an afterthought for all involved.

"But you said ..."

I started the sentence and then forgot what she had exactly said and what I had wanted to say about it. I was also finding that my tongue had grown abnormally large for my mouth and that my face was numbing up. "You

188

said ..." I repeated and those hated tears began to flow again.

"I said ...?" Anya prompted me, sweet as poison.

I could hear footsteps approaching in the corridor. It was always the case when my headaches came that all sounds were magnified a hundred fold. I needed Dr. Botkin. I needed medicine. I needed sleep.

I heard a soft knock and cried out, "Wait!" at the same moment that Anya imperiously invited the person to enter.

There was a confused shuffling.

I only had a few seconds left, I knew. My pain was dreadful, but my pressing need to address this issue with Anya overrode any such considerations and I loudly blurted out at a volume whereby the waiting servants could undoubtedly discern every word, "You said you dared not call him your own. How could you? *How could you?* He is mine!"

It all came out in a wail, or maybe a scream, and the train seemed to shake more as it swayed along the rails and I clawed for purchase at my seat.

Anya went over to the door and opened it.

"Set those things down on the table," she said quietly, "then go and fetch Dr. Botkin immediately. Her Majesty is very ill."

I tried to protest, but they obeyed Anya.

She came over to me and laid her hand on my shoulder. I flinched.

"Poor Alix, always so ill and confused, and yes, I daresay I did say it, and I meant it. How could I call him mine, Alix, for here you are and we are both so devoted to you?"

189

Then there were hands helping me up. Was she helping me? I don't know. I couldn't stand. I couldn't think.

Soon after that I found myself in bed amid the coolness of my sheets, being fed a draught by Dr. Botkin, who was clucking over me.

"Overtired ... strained, as I feared ... all too much for her."

I wanted to protest, to tell him why I was so upset, but I was too sick and far too ashamed. Later, I would fix this, stop it all, but now I had to sleep. The black winter outside was within me, mad, sick Alicky, poor Alicky! That was what my family had said when I was sick as a little girl, and doubtless it was what Nicky and Anya said when they were alone together, she being so healthy and young, so calm and frightening. Yes, I knew they whispered and smiled, and intoned, "Poor, sick Sunny ..."

And then at last I did not have to think at all.

Chapter 20

The next morning I was feeling much better, although still quite weak, until Maria informed me sourly that Anya had abandoned our party during a fueling stop, pleading that she had just remembered she had some appointments that she couldn't break in Petersburg, and promising that she would see us again at Tsarskoe Selo.

I received my first telegram about it from Father Grigory soon thereafter. Anya it seemed had been busy.

"Mama, poor Anyushka is very troubled by your anger. We must all live in love if Russia is to achieve peace, but then who teaches about love better than you?"

I crumpled up this nonsense with some irritation, reflecting that Nicky was sometimes right about Our Friend after all.

Nicky ... I had to see him, to confront him, to ask him ...

I needed denials and protestations of undying love, but there was no way to see him as he was on a train barreling towards Pskov and mine was on its way to Petersburg. Trains that pass in the night ... And if I did order my train turned about, what would the girls think, what would be the inevitable gossip, and what would I do if he only blushed and refused to meet my eyes?

I would die at his feet, I supposed, but there was so much suffering in Russia beyond my own that I knew this would be a great sin.

That thought angered me too. A great sin indeed! How could he have let things reach this sorry state?

What was it about Anya that could have made him feel...?

But no, of course this was not Nicky's doing. This all came from the fevered imagination of my poor, fat, besotted Anya. After all, she was constantly indulging herself in hysterical fancies. She couldn't help herself really, and hadn't I almost encouraged her to do so as a source of amusement? In truth, I had been half mad myself to even think there might be something there between Nicky and Anya.

This thought made me feel a lot better, but I still needed to let Nicky know that I didn't like this situation, whether he was at fault or not, and whether he knew of her stupidity or not.

The letter ... Yes, I would read that ridiculous letter, the one that started it all, and then I would write to him something light and amusing but with a subtle admonishment embedded in it to remind him that poor, unstable Anya might misunderstand the things he said to her in kindness. Yes, that was the best way to handle everything.

So, forgetting that Anya had in fact taken back her letter from Nicky just before I had collapsed in the salon, I summoned Maria and told her that I must have dropped a letter I had received from one of the nursing sisters at one of the hospitals I had visited recently, and that I very much needed her to find it as it contained a request for much-needed supplies I had agreed to order.

"I am certain that I left it on my chair in the lounge, or maybe under it. If it isn't there, you must ask the maids what they did with it while they were cleaning."

Maria dutifully went off to seek it out, but returned after a full half-hour with a troubled look.

"Your Majesty, it wasn't in the lounge, not anywhere, and I summoned all the maids and questioned them most carefully, and I am convinced of their honesty in the matter. The letter that has been misplaced is nowhere to be found. Could one of their imperial highnesses have picked it up by mistake?"

I knew she was right, and that troubled me, as I wished only that the girls would forget what they had witnessed the previous day. Moreover, while I was completely certain that Nicky had only filled this ill-judged missive with platitudes relating to his activities – for he never varied from doing this in our letters – reading their father's letters to another adult was not right. Equally, while I had built up an iron-clad certainty that he had communicated nothing amiss to Anya, I preferred not to have to defend anything he had said that might be misconstrued by my sweet girlies, so I still had to have that letter.

Olga was sullen and said she had left the salon before I had lost "stupid Anya's stupid letter," so how could she be expected to know about it?

Tati burst into tears all over again, which renewed my headache and made me wish I had not asked her about it.

"Is Papa in love with Anya, Mama? Oh what will you do?"

Wearily, I explained to her that she was being ridiculous as she knew Papa loved only me. To suggest otherwise was to be as silly as Anya.

"So why does it matter about the letter?" she asked reasonably, her tears drying.

Inwardly groaning, I decided to handle her question simply … and lie.

"Because it does not matter at all. I was being silly and now I want to give Anya her letter back unread. I would never read another person's correspondence, Tatiana, and neither should any of you girls. It is a most unpleasant habit."

Tatiana raised her eyebrows.

"Well, since I've never done it, and I don't think any of my sisters have ever done it either, it could hardly be called a habit, could it, Mama? Besides, it's quite simple to see what has happened here. Obviously Anya retrieved her letter from where you'd been sitting before she left for town."

This was so clearly the truth of the situation that I gasped in a sudden shock of recognition before I could stop myself when I remembered that Anya had indeed retrieved the letter from the floor before I had been led back to my bed.

"Mama?" Tatiana was immediately at my side, her face twisted in concern.

I lied again.

"Oh sorry, darling. Mama's heart had a little spasm and it took me by surprise. I suppose I had better follow silly old Dr. Botkin's orders and stay in bed and rest up until we reach Tsarskoe Selo." Seeing her beautiful eyes fill with tears once more, I stroked her sweet face. "No, dearest, Mama will be fine. I just need to have a little nap now. Don't worry your sweet little self. Go and find your grouchy old elder sister and see if you can cheer her up a bit."

That made her smile ruefully.

"All right, I will, Mama, if you promise to rest now."

I nodded dutifully and waited until she was gone to begin my own tears, the terror having started up inside me again. Oh how I wanted Nicky with me!

After I had mastered myself again, I calmly wrote to Nicky all about this fraught episode.

How dare she call you "my own"? Only I may do so! She must never, never, do so! You must tell her!

Oh Nicky, oh my boysy, this has come near to killing me. Is that the fate you wish to visit on wify, that poor wify should be driven near to death with anguish?

Oh tell me it is not so! Tell me she is mad and you are all agog at receiving this letter! And tell me quickly, my own, my darling, my naughty one. I pray that you write back to me by return, for until then I only wish to die. I think I may be dying, and, if so, I shall find it in my heart to forgive you both.

Your Sunny

His reply did indeed come by return and proved to be as puzzling as the rest of this affair.

My own beloved Sunny, my darling, my dearest little girly and wify, I have just finished luncheon, and read through your sweet dear letter with moist eyes.

I paused in my reading to wonder what sweet dear letter he could possibly be alluding to.

It was so difficult to leave you on your train and to go upon mine. I managed to keep myself in hand but oh what a struggle!

Lovy mine, I miss you horribly, much more than my tongue can tell you. Isn't it a funny thing, my Sunny, that after all these many happy years together, I am still shy to show and say how I feel, that you are my only joy. I am not clever with words as all remind me, but here I can be more free so I shall try to write often, as, to my great surprise, I find I can write while the train is moving!!

My hanging bar is very useful!! I hung upside down on it and climbed it a lot before eating. It is really good for one in the train and shakes the blood and the whole system up!

Lovy mine, it is such joy and comfort to see you well and doing so much work for the wounded. As Father Grigory told you, it is God's mercy that at such a time for Russia you should be able to do and stand such a lot! Believe me, my sweetest love, my eternal darling, do not fear, but be more sure of yourself and me when you are alone with troubled thoughts. Then everything will go smoothly.

God bless you, my very own wify little girly.

I kiss you.

Nicky

His letter was calming, for it was very like Nicky, so very boyish in its way that Baby could almost have written it, and as loving as any longstanding wife could ever wish for. But was there a sort of warning in it?

"Do not fear," he had said.

No, I shook myself off, Nicky was not warning me, he had no reason to, nor to apologize. Nothing had occurred, nothing ever would. Anya was a very stupid woman who had become inflated with a false sense of her own importance and of her attraction to others, which was derived, ironically, solely from her constant inclusion in the affairs of our family. Nicky was right. Father Grigory was right, although not in the way he thought, for I had every reason to be shocked and horrified at Anya's behavior, whatever foolish words my husband might have said or written to provoke all this.

Anya had absolutely no right to think of Nicky that way; she had no right at all.

She was a child, a large, annoying not-all-that-bright child; my child in a way. No, that wasn't right either; she was my friend – and not a very good one – but she was the only one I had. I had to laugh if only a tad bitterly at that: She was my only friend!

It had been clever then of Nicky, and of Father Grigory, to have refrained from explaining all this too directly to me, and for Nicky rather to say that my worries were groundless, and for Father Grigory to say that Anya was sad at my silly lack of understanding of her. Yes, I would have to forgive her and try to forget what had happened, or I would be alone without a friend or companion in this world.

I was glad indeed that there was no one alive who would be brave enough to say that to me, besides myself.

Chapter 21

I did not allow myself time to brood on my own pains and worries, for that terrible first year of the war, 1914, commanded all of my time and most of my attention. Thus I only permitted myself a fortnight at home with my three small ones before once again wearily mounting my train, this time for Moscow, together with Anya, Olga and Tatiana, just as I had for the trip to Grodno, but for different reasons.

I took Anya with me because Father Grigory had asked it of me, and because she was long a habit of mine, I suppose, and it felt wrong not to. Naturally, Anya being Anya, she showed not the slightest gratitude for my accepting her back at my side but acted instead like a wounded victim.

Olga was there because I wanted to keep an eye on her, and because I feared leaving her lying about sulkily in Tsarskoe Selo. She and Anya spent most of the trip sniping unkindly at each other, while I turned a blind eye to their petty feuds.

In Tatiana's case, I needed her sweet companionship and thought it would be unkind to leave her behind to endure the endless and bloody grind of nursing, a poor reward for her endless patience and uncomplaining compassion.

Inevitably, the little ones bemoaned their fate, "trapped at boring, stupid Tsarskoe Selo with nothing to do." I had not expected to win on that score, and it seemed that, as the first year of the war drew to a bitter close, the Russian army could not win on any score. No matter what strategies that idiot Nikolasha or his generals adopted, Father Grigory's predicted sea of blood was surely determined to drown them all. By now, Russian men were being cut down at a rate of between thirty and one thousand times that of Germany's.

This whole dreadful war, this open slaughter, was becoming a mistake so great that no one could deny it, and yet no one could see how to escape it either without a massive loss of face for those who had begun it.

Nowhere were we bleeding as fast or as hard as in Russia, and the reasons for this, which I had made it my business to find out, were shocking ones. We had one munitions factory for every fifty that the Germans had, and even if there had been more, the state of our railways presented themselves as an almost insurmountable hindrance to success in their own right.

Half our railway lines had gaps of hundreds and hundreds of miles in them, meaning that even if we managed to build several more munitions factories to supply guns, bullets and shells to the front, they could not reach there by train because they had to be packed onto horseback for the considerable distances where there was no track, and even that depended on the availability of horses to carry them.

As for the horses – those that the starving men hadn't slaughtered and eaten – they were required to transport not only munitions but also food, clothing and other supplies across those same hundreds of miles of trackless wilderness. Meanwhile, wherever the troops were engaged in battle, our men, who were severely lacking in both food and footwear in the depths of winter (and, oh, when wasn't it winter in Russia?), were told that they would be shot if they used up more than six of their precious bullets a day, if they had any bullets at all, that is.

Most of our soldiers were therefore required to wait until the men in front of them, or beside them, had been cut down by the Germans – who had lots of guns, bullets and shells at their disposal – and then either pick up their dead comrades' guns or simply hold up their bodies to shield themselves until they themselves died or the assault was called off.

That we did not surrender, and that we did not lose the war outright during that first winter was a testament to the sheer stubborn pride of my husband and to the grotesque reality that we had so many more men available to be killed than the Germans did.

No one would give me the exact numbers (maybe no one had them), but I know that we lost over a million men that first year. These were men who were loved, men who were needed, men who would never return home to the land their ancestors had cultivated for generations. Therefore, even that first year, the people began to starve, and the lines of refugees – women and small children, the old and the infirm – began their sad, slow migration from the only places they had ever known towards the cities. They went there in search of food and in search of news of their loved ones, because hope is always the last thing to be killed in a human being. They vainly hoped that maybe, despite the months without a word, they would find the names of their husbands, children or parents on the lists of wounded posted at street corners or on buildings, if only they could get there and find some kind person to read them out to them.

I think they knew I could see all of this in their faces when I steeled myself to look out of my train windows at them. I did not manage to do so very often, for at every station, along every piece of track, they knew the royal train was passing and they would stare silently at it, no longer bowing.

Maybe they were already too bowed by grief to do so, I don't know, and maybe it wasn't a question of resentment, or even of hatred, that I saw on their faces when I did open my shades and look out. Maybe they didn't even see me at all. What could we even do for them? This was why I almost always refused Count Fredericks' requests to "let the people see you."

"Let them gawp at me, you mean, Fredericks. I think not. This is not a theater and I am not an actress. Tell them no."

"But, Your Majsety …"

"I said no. Please do not ask me again."

Then, bowing, he would take his leave of me and the train would pull away, while I would work to silence the nagging voice inside of me, the one that sounded suspiciously like that of my mother-in-law.

"The people do not want another nurse, Alix," she would admonish me, "they want their Empress. They want you to come and bless them, to show yourself, to remind them that there is something greater in life than their present day misery and fear. You must for once rise above your limitations and become a Romanov!"

But she was wrong. It was in fact the nurse who was more needed, and whether there was a war on or not, I could not be her kind of empress, not now after all this time. I could not bear the scorching intensity of a thousand pairs of eyes on me, whether peasant or peer, and no one should have asked it of me. I was doing the best I could, and oddly, in my uniform, I did not mind people's eyes looking at me, for they merely wanted a nurse and what help and relief she could bring, not the mystical Empress who would always disappoint them when they found out that she was all too human.

I did what I could, and I did help. My hospitals saved lives or helped bring about good deaths, and when Ella, who had been silent for months, busy as she was with her own hospitals, asked me to come to Moscow to see them, I eagerly agreed. I was doing what I could and that was something.

Chapter 22

Moscow during the winter of 1914 struck me as being a frozen hell on earth, but then I had never liked Moscow, although I disliked it for vaguer reasons than Petersburg, which I loathed. It was the old capital and much more Russian than Petersburg, and it was the cradle of Orthodoxy, of course. Unlike Petersburg, it was not a false city built on mud and water to stoke one man's vanity by recreating the grandeur and elegance of Europe in Russia. Nor was it filled with lazy, self-important, judging nobles.

No, it is as Russian a city as London is an English city and Paris is a French city. Moreover, I retained happy memories of my girlhood trips here, and to nearby Ilinskoe, to visit Sergei and Ella. We had been crowned here too.

Yet I never liked it.

Nicky did, he even claimed to love it, and he often made wistful comments about making Moscow Russia's capital city again. When we spoke of it, he and I both agreed fervently that Petersburg wasn't one atom Russian, and that Moscow was even now a glimpse of the true, ancient Russia and its ways.

That may also have been why I had disliked it on sight and had made certain that our trips here were few and far between, coming here only for ceremonies from which there was no escape. Funnily, Nicky never pressed me to come here more often either, even when we were young and newly-married and still the firmest of friends with Sergei and Ella. We went straight to

Illinskoe for our visits, never stopping off in Moscow. Nor did Nicky's mother ever come here except for ceremonies. No Romanov that I knew ever did.

Of course, I never said I did not like it. That would have been held against me for sure, certain proof – as if more proof were needed – that I was a foreigner and, like Petersburg, not one atom Russian.

No, Nicky, and all his family, and the Petersburg nobility, all simply adored the "true Russia of Moscow," but they never went near the place. It was much like their love of the peasants, "the true Russians," greatly idealized until one had actually to see, meet or deal with one of them. It was the expression of a sentiment that was of sentimental value only.

This was not true in my case, though. I did indeed love and respect our peasants, and knew that they felt the same way about me. It was just Moscow I did not like. Moscow was so strange; it looked, spoke and smelt different, eerily different.

I had traveled to Italy with Grandmamma when I was a young girl, and Italy had not seemed strange or otherworldly at all, but Moscow did. It was not just that the language was different – it had been different in Italy too, and, of course, in Petersburg – nor that it was warmer than in Germany or England – it had been sweltering in Italy, especially for Grandmamma and me who always preferred to be cool. No, it was that everything in Moscow was both familiar and unfamiliar all at the same time, bizarre in its way, but not bizarre enough to require me to learn its ways from the beginning. It was like crossing over into the world of Mr. Lewis Carroll's wonderful novel 'Alice in

Wonderland,' infused with the feeling that one had entered a realm where some aspects of one's surroundings resembled buildings, furnishings and artefacts from one's past, while fully aware that one was nowhere one had ever been before or had ever dreamed of being. It was like a world where a fork suddenly turns into a table cloth and a chair into a lion.

It was due to this disquieting otherworldliness and those unsettling sensations it immediately evoked in me, that I did not like to be there at all and avoided it if I could.

Here is another thing – so did all the other Romanovs. Say what they liked, toast the special status of Muscovites as "real Russians," as they so often did, but where were they to be found when not in Petersburg or on their estates? Paris or London, not Moscow. Their great Moscow mansions and nearby country estates remained empty year after year, with only spiders dancing in their ballrooms. They felt the disturbing strangeness of Moscow too. In Russia, Petersburg and the Crimea were the places that made them feel part of the civilized world, whereas Moscow reminded them that Russia is a vast wilderness set out on a limb of Western history, with its Slav roots, and its struggles for independence as vassals to the Mongol Khans, and its endless wars as much to the south as to the west.

Now here I was again, and without Nicky, espying my estranged and beautiful sister Ella waiting for me on the platform. I closed my eyes and thought about how long ago, and yet how recently, it had been since the young Emperor, Nicky, and his pretty bride, Alix, and their newborn baby, Olga, had arrived at this station on a hot sunny afternoon, to be met by an imperious but loving Sergei and my beautiful, bejeweled and complacent sister, then a grand duchess, and now a nun – a kind of nun. I wasn't quite sure what she was really; I never had.

That complex, magnificent and sometimes overwhelming couple, Sergei and Ella, had dominated my young girlhood, and they had loved Moscow, but there again they had been virtual Emperor and Empress here.

"Where is everybody?" Anya asked petulantly, her question interrupting my thoughts.

I turned to look at her in confusion. I hadn't even heard her approach, so lost had I been in another time, a time before Sergei's violent death, before Ella's descent into sainthood, before the wars, and before the onset of middle age. None of my four younger ones had even existed then. So much had gone.

Now here I was in my train with Anya, and she was asking me a question.

"What?" I replied automatically to give myself a moment to recover myself.

"I said, 'Where is everyone?' Look, the station is empty!"

I shook my head and stared out. She was right: There was Ella shivering in her robes, another nun standing beside her, and the stationmaster, but not one other person.

I laughed a little to throw Anya off the fact that I was puzzled to the point of shock and even dismay, and then Count Fredericks joined us, saving me from having to speak right away.

He bowed.

"Well, Your Majesty, here we are. All the arrangements have been made for your apartments in the Kremlin."

"Count Fredericks, Mrs. Vyroubova and I were just wondering where all the people are. Are we far ahead of schedule?"

Count Fredericks appeared flustered by the inference that he had managed our visit with less than clockwork precision.

"Not at all, Your Majesty."

He pulled out his pocket watch, a gift from Nicky that he proudly displayed at every opportunity, and examined it carefully, before nodding to himself in satisfaction and announcing pompously, "Ten o clock exactly, and look," he gestured out of the window at Ella, "there is Her Imperial Highness the Grand Duchess who has arrived to meet you. If you were expecting something more in the way of fanfare, I would remind you that this is a private visit."

"It is hardly a private visit, Fredericks," I protested indignantly. "I am here to inspect my hospitals. Has General Djounkovsky, the Governor, been notified of the time of my arrival?" He nodded but not emphatically enough to convince me that he was communicating the truth as I stared at him icily and his gaze dropped. "Well, did you, Fredericks?"

"I did, through the Office of Court Protocol ..."

"I see. Well, please investigate urgently whether they followed your orders, for it would appear not. In the meantime, I shall greet my sister." Turning to Anya, who had been listening avidly, I smiled to hide my discomfort and said brightly, "It seems that through the gracious intervention of Divine providence I am to be spared the usual round of gawping and gasping onlookers that would have greatly delayed our progress. Please go and tell the girls to come and greet their aunt."

"They're already out there, Alix."

I looked out again and so they were. Olga was being held loosely against Ella's side and Tatiana was standing politely opposite Ella's companion who was curtsying to her while Sophie and Maria were curtsying to Ella.

"Oh yes, I see."

I moved to the steps, and taking the arm of a Cossack in attendance, I descended to the platform, preparing to hug and be hugged by my sister.

I had missed Ella, or maybe, as always, I had missed the idea of Ella and the sisterly closeness that we had achieved so rarely over recent times. At any rate, I was quite glad to see her.

She moved quickly towards me and I held out my arms while she dropped to my feet in a deep curtsy.

I blushed and the girls giggled nervously.

"Ella, for Heaven's sake, get up. It is me. Let me see you."

She stood up and I clasped her to me before she could do anything else to embarrass me in front of the mere smattering of onlookers. She was so stiff in my arms and there was no warmth in her answering embrace, so I stepped back and tilted my chin.

"Quite the chilly welcome to Moscow, Ella. Can you explain it?"

She raised an elegant eyebrow and glanced around as if just noticing the deserted platform. Her wimple moved gracefully with the icy wind. She was still so beautiful and looked years younger now than me. I noted this with the usual feeling of discomfort she had always aroused in me. It made me impatient, angry, and frustrated at us both.

I raised my own eyebrows.

"Does your habit perhaps impair your vision, Ella?" I demanded.

My remark was greeted by a chorus of gasps from my daughters and the nun who was accompanying Ella, and a poorly stifled derisive laugh from Anya betraying how much she disliked her.

Ella chose to return my attack by addressing her response to Anya.

"Mrs. Vyroubova, do you no longer curtsy in Petersburg to members of the imperial family? Is this a new fashion we have yet to become acquainted with?"

Anya stared at her open-mouthed, her breath pluming into great clouds in the icy air.

"But you're a nun, aren't you? I don't generally curtsy to nuns. No one does, not in town, not anywhere."

Ella stiffened, looking every bit the Empress I was supposed to be.

"I remain a member of the imperial family, Mrs. Vyroubova, something I believe that, despite your situation, you are not. I am a grand duchess after all."

"Her Highness the Grand Duchess Elizaveta," Count Fredericks intoned thoughtfully.

Ella gave him a small smile and returned her gaze to Anya who continued to stand there stubbornly.

I might have interceded on her behalf, for Ella's current status was indeed confusing, but the memory of her recent behavior lingered on in my mind.

It was all ended by Olga, who snapped, "For God's sake, curtsy to my Aunt Ella, Anya, so we can get into our cars before we all freeze to death out here."

Anya started to crumple gracelessly in front of Ella, managed to slip as she did so, and slid forward, almost knocking Ella over onto the icy platform floor, at which point the girls and I convulsed into laughter as Count Fredericks emitted shocked groans and hastened to help her to her feet.

From there we proceeded carefully to the awaiting cars where Count Fredericks covered us with furs to fend off the bitter cold.

I nodded for the driver to go ahead, and as we began to move off, Olga and Tati, who were turned completely around on their knees in order to see out of the back window, narrated for me what was happening.

"Oh Mama, poor Anya," squealed Tati. "Aunt Ella is looking ever so fierce. I wouldn't want to be in a car with her."

"Anya is a complete menace, Mama," Olga countered. "One day she's going to kill us all."

I should have reprimanded her, but Ella's reception of me had been so icy and the subsequent events so comical that I merely pursed my lips and tried to look severe.

Tatiana was scandalized, naturally.

"Olga, shame on you! Mama, can you believe what she said?"

Tatiana, angel that she was, could be very tiresome at times, but of course always correct, which I adored her for.

"Yes, that was terribly disrespectful and wrong of you to say such things, Olga. I will expect you to make a full confession about it to Father Yanishev when he attends us for prayers this evening."

Olga settled herself back into her seat and gave me a sullen nod as she drove her elbow into Tatiana's side,

Tatiana yelped. "Mama!"

I sighed.

"Girls, do be quiet. I swear you are both acting as though you were in the nursery, and making Mama wonder whether she should have brought you here at all. Please remember that we are here to see the poor wounded of Moscow."

"Mama, Olga hit me and I didn't do anything wrong."

I ignored her and looked out onto the streets.

"I don't see a single soul out there," I said. "It is so odd."

There really wasn't a single person to be seen on the streets all the way to the Kremlin. Where was everybody? Once a million residents had stood a thousand deep to catch a glimpse of our carriages as they passed.

"Count Fredericks, where are the people and will the Governor be awaiting us at the Kremlin?"

He looked at me worriedly and shrugged.

"I truly do not know, Your Majesty. As I said on the train, everything was arranged. I ... I... am sorry, Your

Majesty, I shall make inquiries as to what has happened as soon as we are at the Kremlin."

I nodded coldly at him.

"See that you do, Count Fredericks. I await your explanation."

My anger had at least made the girls quieten down and the four of us spent the remainder of the journey avoiding each other's eyes.

Several minutes later we drew up outside the towering red walls and decorous towers of the Kremlin, the ancient seat of Tsarist power and a reminder of how sovereigns who had not always enjoyed the love of their people had been forced to live.

While modern tsars had called it affectionately "the village of palaces," it was in fact a walled fortress, where, during more turbulent times, tsars had lived their entire lives behind its walls, behind the same walls that had been penetrated by anarchists in order to assassinate Ella's late husband, Sergei.

It was of the heartbreaking and devastating loss of Sergei that I was thinking as we alighted from our car, with Ella's pulling up within seconds behind us. My poor sister! I smiled at the set of her face as she exited, the red and pouting Anya on her heels. Ella was still scowling furiously as she stalked towards me, the girls trying to muster a smile as I met her halfway.

"Ellie, you look as exhausted as I feel. Let us hurry inside and hope we can encounter someone to conjure up a cup of tea for us."

Ella nodded and produced a warm smile for the girls who rushed her, each grabbing one of her hands.

Tati shrank back. "Aunt Ella, you're frozen stiff." she exclaimed. "

Ella turned on me. "Alix, whatever do you mean?"

I shrugged, not wishing to get into any further discussion of the marked absence of living souls until we had reached our, preferably warmer, apartments.

"We shall talk in a minute, Ellie," I said. "In the meantime, I really should go to rest for a bit. Fredericks, please see that Mrs. Vyroubova is settled comfortably, and contact the Governor to acquaint yourself with his whereabouts. And send Maria to me also. Oh, and please escort Their Highnesses to their rooms and make arrangements for tea for all of us. I shall have mine in my rooms with Baroness Buxhoeveden after I have had a chance to rest. And then, Ella, I wish to inspect the two largest of my hospitals before dinner."

With that, I continued up the staircase and made my way to Nicky and my private apartments in this building full of ghosts.

If Ella and I had been as close as we once were, I would have asked her to spend time with me to help me change and lie down for a bit, and we would have talked about Mama and how she had always seen and heard ghostly things too. But we were no longer close and I was happy enough to see sweet Sophie and my Maria enter the beautiful rooms that had been decorated so long ago – or was it yesterday? – for Nicky and my coronation celebrations. Ella had decorated them for us, all in shades of her favorite pale blue, and I found them cold, but pretty, I suppose.

She had also picked out all the fabrics and furniture in the apartments we had meant permanently to occupy in the Winter Palace in Petersburg, but as here, she had wasted her time, and the rooms had remained empty and haunted by shades of a much younger and more hopeful Nicky and me.

The other ghosts here were not so benign. I know that Ivan the Terrible's ghost was said to haunt the Gatchina Palace in Petersburg, but this place was full of the ghosts of unhappy tsars and their tsaritsas too. I could even hear their cries as I entered our apartments. They were saying my name. 'Why now?' I asked myself. This had never happened before. Indeed, they were so loud that I clasped my hands over my ears.

"Your Majesty?" sweet Sophie inquired, concerned.

"Do you hear them, Sophie?"

"*Them*, Your Majesty?" She smiled uncertainly and then more widely. "Oh, I do," she said. "It's the tea trolley coming. Well, thank goodness, I could do with a cup of tea, and I imagine you could as well, Your Majesty."

I studied her plain, kind face for any sign of deception but could find none. So these voices were only meant for me, then, as a kind of warning or perhaps a lament.

Mercifully, there was no time to dwell on the strange forces hovering around me as I had to change into my nurse's uniform and visit the hospitals, accompanied by Ella and her companion, although not by Anya or the girls who had elected to stay in the apartments and rest.

As we were not alone in the car, and were very busy seeing patients and speaking to doctors and nurses regarding supplies and care, there was no time to talk of uncomfortable matters until that evening when I asked Ella to sit with me before dressing for dinner. It was not that I particularly wished to hear what Ella had to say to me, but there were many issues that had built up against us in Moscow over time, at least in Ella's mind, and she had been visibly dying to spit them out to me all day. Now was the time to do what my mother-in-law had expected of me for so long and to shoulder my burden as Empress, for if it wasn't Ella and her circle who were to blame for the streets being so empty for my arrival, then at least she would know who was.

This matter had to be dealt with. We were at war and I was fighting alongside my husband and my son for the sake of Russia, and therefore I must overcome my natural disinclination to address unpleasantness and discover how we could regain the respect and trust of the citizenry of Moscow.

"Ellie," I began, "we need to speak ..."

Ella nearly leapt at me from her chair.

"I have been praying, Alix, oh so hard, you cannot know how hard, that you would finally be ready to talk. People keep saying to me, 'You must tell her, tell them,' but how could I when you seemed to act as though I wasn't even your own sister anymore? You never invite me to Tsarskoe Selo. I hardly ever get to see the children, my own nieces and my nephew. You even prefer the company of that treacherous creature Madam Vyroubova to me."

She burst into sobs and put her hands over her face, rocking backwards and forwards in her distress.

I was stunned. Ella had never been emotional and I did not know whether to find this scene endearing, with my iron-willed sister finally opening herself up to her frail, womanly, less controlled side, or to slap her back to her senses. Truth be told, I was leaning towards the latter option, for, in the jumble of accusations she had just bombarded me with, there had been much to anger me.

'Where to start?' I asked myself, and then out of force of habit decided to defend Anya.

"Ella," I laughed lightly, "I realize you are not fond of Anya, but to call her a treacherous creature seems a bit much."

Ella's hands dropped and she leaned forward, forcing me to ease myself back in my seat to avoid our clashing our heads. Her eyes, while reddened, were no longer tear-filled.

"Oh does it, Alix? Can you really say that while that woman spends so much of her time with that crazed monster, either as his creature or he hers, I can never really tell? Not that it matters."

I stood up quickly and backed as far away from her as I could, my sudden movement stopping her in full flow.

She started up again, but this time in an uncertain voice, as though she had finally remembered who I was now rather than who I had been in the Darmstadt nursery of our childhood.

"Alix …?"

"*Monster*, Ella? I assume you are referring to Father Grigory. You claim to be the holiest of women, do you not, Sister Ella, but apparently you are not so holy as to constrain yourself from encouraging the lowest, the filthiest gossip being spread around about Father

Grigory. I see now who has poisoned Moscow against me! Do you not understand, Ella, that what you say and do here poisons people against Nicky, and that when you attack me, you attack the throne? So who then is a treacherous creature, dearest sister?"

Ella, agitated, rose to her feet in her turn and began to pace back and forth across the room. I suddenly wished that I had a cigarette to offer her, and the thought of it made me chuckle. Ella glared at me, appalled, but not, I was sorry to see, cowed by my accusation. No, my sister was intent on having her say. Fine then, let her get it over and done with.

I seated myself again and said with a studied calmness, "Ella, you look half mad. Maybe you are. Maybe that would explain, if not excuse, your actions here. But please have your say. Sit down, though. You make me nervous with your pacing."

"I may speak freely?" Ella asked, surprised and tenuous, which was good. That was how I wanted her to be towards me.

"You may. Sit," I said waving her towards her chair.

I reached for the teapot.

"Shall I pour? Would you like a cup of tea, Ella?" Ella sat down and murmured something so quietly that I could not catch it. "What was that, Ella?"

Ella looked at me, her eyes dim. There was fear there too now. I did not know whether I was gratified by that or not.

She waved her hand.

"Oh nothing, really … your saying that about pouring the tea so reminded me of Mama. What would she think of us … of this? Do you ever think of Mama, Alix?"

I shrugged. Of course I thought of Mama, all the time – just a few hours earlier, in fact – but it didn't matter. I did not want to take a trip down memory lane at this precise moment; I wanted Ella to finish what was obviously a rehearsed speech and then leave me in peace.

"No, not so much anymore. Please, Ella, you are all a-twitter and obviously bursting to say more about Father Grigory. Tell me, I'm curious, is your dislike of him the same old one or have you found something new about him to outrage you?"

Ella stared back at me, no longer agitated or seemingly angry either, and reached for my hand, but I shuddered and pulled it away. With a great sigh, she settled back in her chair and reached for her teacup, not that she drank from it, preferring instead to stare down into it as if looking for all the answers to her questions among the tea leaves.

"The church considers all necromancy a sin, you know, Ella," I said snidely.

She looked at me confused.

"What?" she asked, startled.

I gestured towards her tea cup.

"You looked as though you were trying to read your tea leaves."

She smiled faintly.

"I think I would if I could." She looked up and met my eyes squarely. "Oh Alicky, please try not to be so angry at me all the time, angry at everyone. Those two creatures you nurture and protect keep your head filled with nonsense."

At this continued insulting of Anya and Father Grigory, I clenched my fists, driving my nails into my palms to try and refrain from throwing my tea into her face. I could imagine it hitting her. Splash! Throwing tea in people's faces was becoming a recurring fantasy of mine.

"Ella, give me one fact about Father Grigory that should make me distrust him. Not your megrims, not gossip – a fact."

She straightened.

"All right, Alix, I will. Is it not a fact, for example, that you have dismissed your long-time nursery maid, Miss Tutcheva, a fine young woman from an ancient and respected Moscow family, a young woman who has cared for and loved your girls with all tenderness and devotion since the days of their births? Is that not a fact?"

I inclined my head and smiled faintly.

"If you say so, Ella. It is certainly a fact that she has been in our employment, yes."

"But she is so no longer. Why is that, Alix?"

"You would have to ask her, I am afraid, Ella."

"I have."

"Then I am at a loss, Ella. Are you planning on hiring her for a position in your little nunnery? I am not sure she is suited for such a role, but there again I wouldn't really know."

I yawned elaborately, stretched myself, and then sipped from my tea as if bored by it all, which was far from the truth as my heart had begun to pound so madly that I wondered whether Ella could see it thumping through my shirtwaist.

"You dismissed her for talking, didn't you, Alix? You dismissed her because she told that idiot busybody of yours, Madam Vyroubova, that she had seen that false priest Father Grigory in your girls' chambers at night when they were in their nightgowns. Is that not true? Is it not true that she spoke of this in great distress and shock to Madam Vyroubova, who then waddled off to you shrieking that Miss Tutcheva was a tale bearer against your dear friend Father Grigory?"

That was it. I had heard quite enough of these scurrilous and nonsensical lies. I could not bear any more of this twiddle-twaddle.

I stood up and pointed at the door.

"I want you to leave now, Ella. I would prefer that you not attend this evening's dinner, but I suppose if I tell you not to, you will spread yet more filthy gossip about our family. If I find that you have ever repeated this story to anyone ever again, I will have the Archimandrite close your little vanity project of a nunnery and demand that Nicky exile you from Russia. I will tolerate your loose tongue no more." I then raised a finger in warning, for she too had risen to her feet and looked desperate to continue the conversation. "Not one word, do you understand?"

She hesitated, nodded and then curtsied deeply to me before turning swiftly towards the door.

My voice halted her.

"Ella, you do not turn your back on me. I am your Empress."

Ella spun around, her habit flying about her, and began to back out as I had demanded. However, before she reached the door, she managed to add, "God help me. I wish I could forget all of it."

I was utterly shaken by this confrontation and had to lie down clutching my chest for some time.

Oddly, I wanted Anya – Anya knew what lies these all were – but I couldn't summon the energy to call for her. All I could think of were the ballrooms and drawing rooms where they were all sitting around, here and in Petersburg, talking about us, about me, about Father Grigory, in delighted, scandalized whispers, and nothing of what they said was at all true, none of it. Yes, Father Grigory entered the children's chambers one night to pray with my girls after attending to Baby's sore arm; yes, they had been in their nightdresses; but it had all been innocent and pure, like him. They had all been praying together.

I hadn't wanted to dismiss Tutcheva but there was no choice because she ran to Anya, and when Anya scolded her, she went to see Minnie to warn her about "a risk to the Grand Duchesses."

When Minnie fed the story back to Nicky, feigning grandmotherly concern and embellishing the whole adventure with an extra layer of venom all her own, Nicky became angry with me and cautioned me that if Father Grigory were ever found in the girls' rooms again at night, he would be permanently banned from Tsarskoe Selo.

The worst of it was that the nasty-minded thing so terribly distressed the girls by telling them why she was being dismissed – or at least why she was claiming to have been dismissed, not for gossiping and spreading malicious rumors, but for trying to protect them – that since that time, which was over a year ago now, neither Olga nor Anastasia had ever seemed to want to see Father Grigory again, and there had not been a single thing I could do to correct the situation.

As Empress, I had the power to dismiss evil-sayers from my presence, but not to split their tongues, as the old tsaritsas who haunted this very palace had once done; nor could I fail to appear downstairs for dinner that night rather than tolerate Ella's presence before me, because to do so would have been to add more fuel to the fire lit all around me, and I was certainly not going to leave the field to my accursed sister, my accursed sister the nun, of all things.

Moreover, not one person alive would have agreed with my assessment of her if they had watched her at dinner that night. The proverbial butter would indeed not have melted in her mouth, nor would ice have done so. Ella was serene beauty incarnate.

That night, we were to dine with a selection of generals and the sullen-looking Governor Djounkovsky – who had been appointed by Nicky as Governor of Moscow, but whom I had never met – and we were certainly not off to an auspicious start.

General Racine, a kindly old man whom I had encountered many years ago during Nicky and my visit to Moscow during the Tercentenary, was the one who presented Governor Djounkovsky to me, whereupon the Governor kissed my hand, bowed, and murmured that it was truly an honor to meet me. I remarked back that it was evidently one he had been able to put off for the most part of the day, as he had not been at the station to await our arrival. We each ignored the other's words; there was a lot of that during that dinner.

I wasn't speaking to Ella, and neither Ella nor Anya were speaking to each other, and Count Fredericks seemed so sunk into his own private gloom that not even my girls, who adored him, could raise much more than a smile out of him and some platitudinous comments to the effect that, "Yes, Your Imperial Highnesses, my rooms are quite warm enough, thank you. It is so kind of you to ask."

I sighed audibly. I was already miserable from this trip and at home I never attended dinners when it was just our own dear family, let alone subjected myself to state functions. This was Nicky's job. He could speak to anyone at any time and on every topic.

Desperate for someone to break the silence, I looked over at Anya, but she was too busy staring mutinously at Ella to notice me.

Just then, nice General Racine relieved the silence by addressing the Governor.

"Tell me, Governor Djounkovsky, why have there been no receptions or official welcomes in honor of Her Majesty and Their Imperial Highnesses yet?"

Everyone's head jerked toward the Governor as Anya nodded her frantic agreement to the question.

"Yes, it's been horrible," she said. "It's like we aren't even here. The streets are so empty. Has everyone in Moscow gone on a trip somewhere?" She giggled at her awkward jest and I closed my eyes, fearing what was coming, but I will say this: between General Racine and

224

Anya, the stultifying lack of conversation at the table did indeed come to an abrupt end.

Governor Djounkovsky looked coldly at General Racine, ignored Anya completely, and said in a carefully considered, matter-of-fact tone, "I was given to understand that this was to be a private visit by Her Majesty and that she was intending to travel *incognito* as a nursing sister. So, I assumed that it would not be welcomed if I were to organize official greeting committees for Her Majesty or put on elaborate receptions for her, especially at this time."

"Yes," Ella agreed, "the war has removed from us the flower of our youth and visited many privations on all of us, sparing no one, so it would not have been right at all, would it, Governor Djounkovsky? Do we not all agree?"

Ella's voice was oddly shrill and I stared at her curiously and all at once understood what had happened. Then, before I could stop myself, I blurted out, "Ella, it was you who told Governor Djounkovsky that I was not to be met at the station and that no one in Moscow was to be told I was coming, is that not right? What could you have been thinking of?"

As soon as I had said it, I realized my mistake because I now knew that the orders had probably come from Count Fredericks, but it was far too late by then, for Anya instantly exclaimed, "I knew it!" and Olga turned on her to hiss, "Be quiet, you! It is none of your business, you numbskull!" to which Anya started screeching wild protestations of outrage.

Tatiana tried to calm things down.

"Mama, I'm sure Aunt Ella only wished to save you from having to see more people than necessary." She

225

turned on Olga. "Olga, you should apologize to Anya at once. Mama, make her apologize!"

Ella smiled serenely as she addressed both Tatiana and me.

"You are right, dearest Tatiana. I did want to spare your mother all of that. I know how very much your nursing means to you, Alix. Heavens, I of all people understand what it is like to have a calling. I have to confess," she added with girlish self-effacement, "that I was thinking more of your comfort, Alix, than of protocol. If I made a mistake in doing so, please forgive me. I assure you, I was thinking only of you."

Anya gawped at her and said, "But you made me curtsy to you!"

I groaned, but everyone was so busy talking across each other that Anya's peevish complaint failed to register except with Olga, who said *sotto voce*, "And a good thing too. You should curtsy to me as well."

It was a suggestion that did not please Tatiana.

"Olga, you're an idiot! Anya is family. Mama, what has got into her?"

Nor did it please Anya, who in response slapped her hand so hard and carelessly onto the table that she accidentally hit her soup spoon, thereby catapulting it and its contents full in the direction of poor Count Fredericks, who was seated next to her, and splashing him quite badly, an unforeseen assault that drew from him a sharp intake of breath and an understandable nervousness on his part as to how, why and when Anya was likely to strike at him next.

General Racine stared at us aghast.

"This is appalling," he declared, and I agreed with him but I did not have time to speak before the up-until-now subdued Governor of Moscow smiled thinly about him and said, "I am beginning to feel more assured by the second of my decision not to put on a public banquet for Her Majesty. The situation in Moscow is terrible enough without our having to be subjected to the level of additional devastation I am seeing at this table ... Although it does give me the idea that if only we could arm our soldiers with soup instead of failing to supply them with bullets, we might finally win the war."

At this, Count Fredericks and General Racine gasped simultaneously, and Count Fredericks bristled with indignation sufficient to exclaim, "Your Honor, you forget yourself!" but I knew he secretly agreed with the Governor, which added a sting to my already distressed state.

Count Fredericks had once been so devoted to Nicky and me that he had referred to us lovingly as *"mes enfants."* Now he loved only Nicky and addressed me resolutely as "Your Majesty," evidently blaming me for Nicky's failings and for drawing our dear Father Grigory into our lives, which, as he saw it, tarnished irrevocably the reputation of the imperial family.

Maybe he also secretly believed the worst of the rumors about me: that I loved Germany more than Russia; that I was a German spy; and that I had earned the title of *"Nemka"* that people gave me behind my back. Nevertheless, he always defended me in public and I was pathetically grateful for that at this moment.

Governor Djounovsky inclined his head towards Count Fredericks but made no apology, and General

Racine looked as though he was considering defending me but instead shook his head, averted his eyes, and began to fiddle with his napkin.

Count Fredericks looked sharply at Ella, Anya, Olga and Tatiana, who were still arguing, and suggested that we adjourn, while Governor Djounovsky and several of the generals noted our collective behavior with severe expressions on their faces. There would no doubt be some terse and amusing recitations of events escaping from their lips at society evenings over the next few days. I could imagine them only too well.

'Such an unfortunate thing! The poor Empress, so long an invalid, and, of course, as we all know, terribly nervous in company, had such a hard time trying to keep her unruly brood under control. What a disgraceful scene! I am most grateful that you were not there to see it. It was quite the spectacle!'

This would naturally be followed by shocked and delighted gasps, and a battery of questions inquiring as to the nature of the spectacular scene under discussion, the answers to which would leave the baffled but titillated audience shaking their heads and sighing their inconsolable grief to the well-worn theme of, 'Of course she's always been mad, hasn't she? The poor Emperor! The poor Dowager-Empress! Now there is a woman who knows how to manage things properly. Never puts a foot wrong!"

Finally, my dearest Tatiana saw that I was struggling to deal with the situation and decided to take matters into her own hands.

"Ladies," she said, "It is time to leave the gentleman to their port. Let us all withdraw next door, shall we?"

228

She offered me her arm, smiled at the men, and scowled at Anya and Olga. "Gentlemen, thank you for your company and for a most entertaining evening."

She then gripped my arm firmly and, as though merely out of affection, wrapped her other hand around my waist. It was so adroitly done that I doubt anyone realized that she was holding me up as we left the room.

However, as soon as we reached the privacy of the hallway, Olga shoved at her sister, causing her to let go of me, and I collapsed to the floor, moaning. At that, Anya started her caterwauling again, forcing Ella to put her hand over her mouth to quieten her down. I saw that Anya was just about to retaliate by biting or kicking her, but it was then that Olga finally remembered that she was a grand duchess and should behave like one, and glared Anya into quiescence.

Ella, freed from having to deal with Anya, knelt down beside me and put her hand to my face. I flinched but she did not withdraw it as she adjusted my aching head to lay it on her lap.

I closed my eyes and heard Tati and Olga whispering urgently among themselves, doubtless trying to decide how to move me from in front of the door before someone opened it and a new scandal was let loose.

I was past caring and might have lain there partially insensate all night if Anya hadn't at that moment tripped over something in her fury and keeled over right on top of me, expelling all the air from my lungs.

"Oh my God!" I exclaimed as Ella and the girls tried to haul her lumpen body off me. Then I began to laugh.

"Darlings, will you please help Mama up too and get me to my rooms before Anya kills me?" I said, reaching out both arms to them.

I patted Anya's arm and smiled at her with genuine affection. My poor, clumsy Anya, the constant thorn in my side and the one person guaranteed to help me forget my troubles.

It was an awkward but kindly, or maybe just exhausted, little group of women who steered me gently to my bedchamber, undressed me, and elected to braid my hair themselves without troubling the maids. Then all four of them kissed me goodnight and I fell asleep.

Chapter 23

We left Moscow as inconspicuously as we had entered it. No one was on the platform to see us off, any more than they had been there to greet us, or so Anya informed me later. I had been put on strict bed rest by Dr. Botkin and had not raised the shades on the train and had no intention of doing so either.

Our route would not take us directly home, but rather via some of the larger towns between Moscow and Petersburg, such as Tula and Orel, so that I could inspect hospitals there, except that I had informed the girls and Anya that they would have to be my eyes and ears, and represent the family, because the nursing was taking too great a toll on my constitution, and I would consequently be obliged to retire from it.

Yet that all changed in the way that the sun appearing from behind clouds can turn a miserable day into a bright and happy one, when Tatiana rushed into my bedroom behind Maria, who had brought my morning tea, declaring, "Oh Mama, it's so wonderful! There are thousands and thousands of people outside! Just look!"

I sat up.

"Darling, what are you talking about? Maria, what is she saying?

Maria grinned.

"Her Imperial Highness may be exaggerating slightly, but there is quite the crowd of fine-looking people waiting for you out there, stretching as far as the eye can see. Would you like me to open the shades?"

I nodded and then checked myself.

"No, I …well … How close to the train are they?"

"They are everywhere, Mama, can't you hear them?" Tatiana said excitedly.

She was right and I didn't know how I had missed all the singing and shouts of welcome.

I put my feet over the edge of my bed and swayed a little, both Tatiana and Maria rushing to help me.

"Your Majesty, you must not try to get up," Maria exclaimed. "I'll go and fetch Dr. Botkin for you."

I shook my head at her and smiled reassuringly at Tatiana.

"You can go and fetch him if you like, Maria, but not until you have helped me dress. Please bring out my nurse's uniform. Tati can do my hair."

Maria stepped back and folded her arms.

"Dr. Botkin will want you to stay in bed, Your Majesty. I heard him say so."

I drew myself up straighter. Much as I loved my old Maria, and much as I treated her at times almost as a friend, it was not her position to advise me and even less to presume to give me orders.

"Maria, bring my uniform to me and do so quietly," I said sharply. "You are giving me a headache and I will not have another word from you. Please just do as you are told."

Maria's chin was shaking. I nearly said something to soothe her, but now was a time for discipline not sympathy. I said as much to Tatiana shortly afterwards when she stared at me in the mirror as I sat at my dressing table while she arranged my hair.

"Darling, I know that you love Maria, we all do, but she must show me the deference I am due."

"But Mama, you've never even let the servants call any of us by our titles, just our ordinary names."

"Tatiana, please do not argue with me or question your papa's and my decisions. An ungrateful child is sharper than a serpent's tooth."

After that I refused to look at her in the mirror. She too must learn.

I reflected that this trip had been rather good for me after all. Clearly discipline and respect for my authority had been slipping. Both Russia and our small circle of family and servants needed an autocrat, particularly in these dark days, to give them direction and surety, and I could be that for them if I stood firm.

I straightened my shoulders and looked into the glass, ignoring Tatiana's reflection behind mine. The years had been unkind to my poor body, leaving me an aching, nearly crippled, mess, but my face was still beautiful, and my hair, the hair my daughter had just brushed and braided to put under my nurse's veil, was still the long, lustrous, red-gold mass that had made Nicky gasp in admiration of me the first time he had seen it unbound.

To Nicky's family, I was a disappointment, but to the people I was not. They just needed to see more of me and then they would be mine. Minnie and I were at last in agreement on something. How delighted she would be. I vowed to make more appearances until the war was won. What had occurred in Moscow must not happen again.

Feeling ill, but resolved, I rose to my feet and asked Tatiana to hand me my sable cape.

In a calm voice, one that I hoped would convey a balance of forgiveness and firmness, I said, "You wear yours too, darling. We are going to see the little hospital here, but we want the people waiting outside to see us looking at least a little regal, do we not? Oh, and tell Olga to wear hers as well." I saw a hesitation cross Tatiana's face. "What is it, Tatiana?"

"Nothing, Mama, I wasn't going to argue with you. It's just that I know Olga will not be wearing her cape."

I sighed.

"And why would that be?"

Tatiana furrowed her forehead, managing to remind me of Anya in that moment with an expression that galled me.

"Because she didn't get up this morning, and when I asked her when she *was* going to get up, she told me she wasn't going to get up at all, and that's why she won't be wearing her cape today."

I took my cape and allowed Tatiana to help me fasten it.

"Fine, I shall speak to her about it when we return. Go and finish getting ready, and find Anya too and plan on us departing in a few moments."

Amazingly, given the horrendous few days we had just undergone, our afternoon in Tula was a sheer pleasure: The crowds were most satisfactory; they all shouted out "God save the Tsar" in gratifyingly loud voices; and every wounded soldier at the small hospital we visited cried and asked for my blessing, so that when the three of us returned to the train that evening, I was quite amazed at how buoyed I had been by the success of the day.

I said as much to Anya.

"You know how I have always simply dreaded crowds, and yet suddenly I am finding them so delightful. I didn't feel a bit shy today either. I suppose I am changing my ways in my old age."

"You're not old at all," she replied earnestly, "and you're still so pretty. I heard everyone saying it as we rode by. Well, of course, you're old compared to me, but most people are," she finished contemplatively, rather ruining the compliment.

"Yes, Anya, thank you, but I am interested in what you think about my newfound lack of shyness. Is it because I am a nurse, do you think?"

"I don't know," she said. "Maybe you just got tired of being in bed." It was a remark she found so pleasingly ironic that she could not resist explaining it to me. "You see, bed is where most people go to rest so that they will feel less tired."

"Yes, Anya, I see, and as usual you have got it all tangled up. I am not tired of being tired, as you so ridiculously state. My chronic poor health is something I have long prayed over. It has nothing to do with my being in bed."

Anya yawned without covering her mouth.

"Anya!"

Anya waved her hand in the air idly.

"Well, you did ask, and now you're talking about being ill again, and that's mostly what we've always talked about and it's not very interesting. But here is a thing to think of: Did you see the way that general was looking at me when we were at the hospital today?" She was referring, to a young, wounded officer, who was probably at best a captain and not a general, but who had indeed gaped at her.

"Anya, that poor young man was clearly frightened of you. Who knows what can happen when you are around, especially when you choose to perch on their cots so presumptively? I do not regard it as very appropriate behavior."

"All four of your daughters do it too," Anya fought back. "Olga even fell in love with a young officer once, and another officer gave Tatiana that little dog she has, the very ugly one."

"Stop it, Anya! Little Ortino was simply a gift to Tatiana in gratitude for her kindness, and I will not have you gossiping about my daughters while they are still innocent children."

"Olga is twenty and you wanted her to marry Prince Carol. Tatiana and Maria should have already come out by now. All the girls at court do so when they are sixteen, and most are expected to be married by Tatiana's age. Your own niece Irinia is expecting her first baby and even she is younger than Olga."

"By a month!" I snapped.

I could feel a red rage against Anya building up inside my head. Did she ever do anything other than plague me nowadays? My daughters were still only young girls at heart. I had kept them pure and innocent, and away from dangerous influences at court, and they were all the happier for it.

Imagine having brought up poor Irinia, who was indeed expecting her first child by that extraordinary young man Yusupov, who, as Anya so frequently reminded me, was nothing but a sodomite – well, not always a sodomite, apparently. Why, that poor child Irinia must spend her nights begging God to reverse it all and send her safely back home to her mama and papa, although they too were the very portrait of unhappiness themselves. No, my girls were safe and happy, terribly happy, as happy as it was possible to be during wartime.

I must have spoken some of this out loud, for Anya said curiously, "as happy as you can be in wartime?" Her eyes looked kind now and she was my friend again.

"I was only thinking – well saying, I suppose – that I had always planned ... we ... Nicky and I had always planned to let Olga and Tati come out together, this last summer, actually, but then the war came along."

Anya reached over and patted my hand.

"It's all right, Alix. Yes, the war has changed many things. Everything is different now." Her face brightened. "And it doesn't matter, anyway. I'm quite happy being a spinster myself and there's no reason your daughters won't be either."

"You are not a spinster, Anya, but a divorcee. If you were a spinster, you would still be living at home with your parents and not allowed to go about freely in society as you do."

Anya tilted her head and then smiled disarmingly.

"You know, that's quite true. Perhaps the girls should marry and shed their husbands as quickly as possible, and then they can be as happy as I am."

I stared at her for a moment to try to discern her real meaning behind this extraordinary idea. When I realized she was being quite disarmingly sincere, I relaxed and doubled over with laughter, and like the child she truly was, she joined me, just happy to have amused me with her quaint ideas.

My fine mood held throughout the next few days, helped on by the people in the small town of Orel who were so tumultuous in their greetings that poor Anya was separated from me and knocked headfirst down a flight of stairs outside a church where I was presented with a particularly beautiful icon, although I feared that this was no random accident, but rather carried out by Olga whom I had ordered to accompany us.

I was becoming worried about my big girl and it was a sobering realization to me that I had missed so many signs that her disposition was changing, and not for the better. Now that I considered it, the last time I had seen her happy and laughing had been during our cruise on The Standart to meet Prince Carol. Or no, had it been in Livadia? I couldn't remember and that made me feel ashamed of myself, comforting myself with the thought that if anyone should have noticed what was going on with Olga it should have been Nicky because they were so close. All our girlies loved their papa, of course, although Tatiana and Baby loved me more, but for the other three girls, Nicky was the sun around which they spun.

It was an odd thing to think that I did not truly know three of my children.

Olga had once been my sole baby, and then, later, one half of a darling set of perfect little girls. However, by that time I had already begun to despair of not having produced a son. Tatiana had been such an astoundingly beautiful and sweet-natured baby, never crying but

238

lighting up in a very special way whenever I was near her – everyone agreed that she was a miniature version of me – yet I had been so ill with her birth, and she had weighed nearly ten pounds, and that pregnancy had been the first one that had reduced me to having to make use of a wheeling chair.

All of this had maybe contributed to my not spending enough time with Olga, but when I had seen her, she had been an enchanting little girl and seemed more than delighted with her baby sister and the opportunity to follow Nicky around on her spindly little-girl legs. There had been no time for us to play and read alone together, for I had no son and had to become pregnant again as quickly as I could, whatever my state of health.

Then Maria had come and I had barely been able to look at her for the first several months of her innocent life. Oh, I had nursed her myself, as I had the other two, but she was a disappointment, a third girl, the baby who would prove to the entire country, let alone to Nicky's family, that I was incapable of having boys. Three girls – my God! And Maria was an enormous baby at nearly thirteen pounds, and I never regained my health after having her, and Olga was by then already completely Nicky's creature and slipping ever further away from me as my life darkened into continuous ill-health.

The emotional distance that developed between Olga and me felt natural enough too, for Tati, small as she was, had already begun to show her sensitivity towards me and would come to see me with funny little wilted bouquets of flowers or crooked pictures she had drawn. Olga would do no such thing. She would come to visit her new baby sister with Nicky holding her hand, and stare at me from beside him, her kisses dutiful.

By the time of my fourth pregnancy, I was so ill that I could barely raise my head to be sick, and that state of affairs was to last until delivery. I couldn't see any of my girls, but I still tried to be their mama. I wrote little notes to them, and while Tati and Maria were too young to read them, they responded with joy when their nurses told them what I had said. For her part, Olga, who had learned to read early, never even attempted to answer my notes, not until later when Mama had to tell her to behave and sit up nicely, based on reports I had received from her tutors and nurses. Only then did she take the time to respond to them and only so that she should argue with me.

We developed a long, silly correspondence one summer when she was nine over her habit of knocking down her little sister Maria, something, which I might add, that never occurred with her even younger sister, Anastasia.

Oh, Nastinka – she had come out of my womb on a long, hot day of interminable labor, enormous like her sisters, though funnily not the disappointment that the previous two had been. For, before her, there had been poor Msgr. Philippe's promise of a son that had resulted in my humiliating false pregnancy. After that, any actual pregnancy was a relief, and, unlike the previous ones, this time I just prayed for the delivery of a baby to prove I still could make one. I think Nicky felt the same, for, in contrast to his reaction to Maria's birth, he did not vanish into the park for hours, "walking," when Nastinka arrived. She was, and I suppose remains, the child we share, each of us equally enamored of her courage and her wit. Maybe because, from birth, Anastasia has shown a complete lack of need of approval from either of us, we both delight in her and adore her almost in defiance of her distracted nature. Olga had no need of me to tell her not to bully this little one; Anastasia was born with teeth.

Olga was ten years old when my sunshine was born. After that, it was as though I was a mother to only one child. This wasn't true, of course, but Baby's importance and his terrible illness made it true in ways that I think all four girls felt. Well, maybe only three of them were so affected, because the lack of my time and attention never seemed to touch Anastasia's limitless enthusiasm for life. This was not true of the others, but what could I do?

Now they were all grown, or nearly so, and I did not know two of my daughters at all. Olga was now a strange, depressed soul who, I could admit to myself privately, looked ten years older than she was and acted twice that. She seemed to have none of me in her at all, save her desire to lie in bed, but unlike me, she remained untouched by illness. She brightened around Nicky, but Nicky was no longer much with us, and so she spent the majority of her time deep in an impenetrable fog, rousing herself only to make fatalistic predictions about the future course of the war that made Father Grigory's visions seem positively euphoric by comparison.

To make her presence all the harder to bear in my eyes, she had somewhere along the way developed an unreasoning hatred of poor Anya, or maybe it was just a jealous reaction to her for all the time Anya had spent with me that she had missed. Not that she seemed to enjoy my company, far from it. For, unlike Tatiana, I sensed she found me unduly burdensome.

I resolved to raise all this with Nicky when we met up again in early December, in the run up to Christmas. This was going to be a wonderful, exclusively family, celebration in the midst of a war, and had taken no small amount of arranging on my part to bring about.

The plan was that Nicky would join my train at Voronezh, wherever that was, then together we would visit some other small and out-of-the-way places as we made our way back towards much-dreaded Moscow, where – joy of joys! – Baby, Maria and Anastasia would be meeting us. Then we would have our whole family together again for the first time in so long.

After that, all the children, along with Anya, would return to Tsarskoe Selo to prepare for Christmas, and Nicky would return to Headquarters, with the hope that he would manage to free himself up for a few days in order to join us for my favorite holiday.

So I decided right then that the first quiet moment Nicky and I could find to be alone, I would broach the subject of Olga. Clearly it was time for her to be married, and sooner rather than later, as already her girlish bloom had faded and she was full set to become a sour spinster. That this transformation had happened right under my nose was terrible, and that I hadn't forced the issue of marriage with Prince Carol, that was ill-considered in retrospect too, although Prince Carol had not exactly shown much interest in asking for her hand on their meeting in Rumania either. No, it had been our little Maria he had wanted, a child of sixteen.

I moaned into my hands. We had been far too indulgent with Olga, letting ourselves be persuaded by her talk of wishing to stay in Russia, a noble idea, possibly, if there were a single suitable candidate for the hand of the Tsar's oldest daughter anywhere in Russia, but there wasn't. No, it was past time that she marry, and if that meant losing her to a distant country, so be it. Nicky would have to be brought around to the idea, but I was sure that could be accomplished without too much difficulty. It was a shame, however, that we were at war with the country that traditionally had furnished us with the most fertile opportunities for matches of this kind. Germany was so full of suitable princes and grand dukes. Grandmamma, who, like me, had a great many daughters, had always looked to Germany for suitable husbands.

My own dearest papa, he had been her choice for Mama because her German husband, Prince Albert, had made her so happy, but now Germany was our arch-enemy and I could not even mention the name of my own adored brother Ernie lest everyone cry "traitor!" Even after the war, I doubted that Nicky would agree to a German alliance for any of our girls, so I would probably have to look to England.

Therefore, after I had returned to Tsarskoe Selo, I would write to May and see what she and Georgie could come up with. She would surely be anxious to help me find an English husband for Olga, war or no war, and no one could fault me for looking in that direction. After all, England was our other great ally. Then we could go for long visits to England to visit Olga at Windsor or Balmoral in the spring when the lilacs were drenched with that soft rain. Oh England!

I pushed up my shade and stared out at the relentless blackness, broken only by snow flurries, and, placing my hand against the glass, I felt the implacable cold of a Russian winter meet my palm and I shivered. Winter again and it had only just begun. Endless winter! One day, how grateful Olga would be to her Mama for sending her away from all of this.

Despite the freezing temperatures and the long delays due to heavy snow, and having our imperial train shunted to one side on a frequent basis to allow troop trains to pass, our journey was quite moving in the spiritual sense, too, as all through this loneliest part of our vast empire I was daily gratified by shows of adoration from the true Russian peoples.

In one funny little town, one so small I am not even sure it had a name, there were no cars and all the horses had been sent to the front, so I was dragged to the hospital in an antique coach by a group of peasants. They had somehow even found branches to decorate it. In Kharkov, hundreds of students met our group, waving portraits of me, of Baby, and of Nicky. By the time we reached an old monastery in Bielgorod, one I insisted on visiting for I had been told by Father Grigory that it was a sacred place to pray, I was physically spent and yet spiritually filled with a sense of peace and joy. It was all as Father Grigory had predicted: the real Russians adored us; it was only amid the filth of the cities that they had become deceived and disloyal.

When we arrived at the monastery in Bielgorod, it was dark, and then there was a sudden flare of lights as the monks ran out to greet us bearing torches. The whole feel of the welcome was profoundly medieval, and as they bowed in the snow around my carriage, I felt I had become a Tsaritsa of old. Then, once inside the monastery, it was my turn to fall to my knees. I prayed for peace; I prayed that all wars would end now and forever; I prayed for Nicky to grow in wisdom and in strength, and for my precious only son to be a great Tsar for his people when the time came. I felt that God was listening. I felt a power come into my body through the icy stones I knelt upon. I drew deeply of the frigid air and felt the Holy Spirit enter me.

Rising without assistance, I looked at my daughters and Anya, and smiled serenely at them.

"All will be well now," I said. "God has told me so."

Chapter 24

All my storms in a teacup with Anya vanished at the fresh beginning of 1915 when she was nearly killed in a horrible railway accident. Poor Anya, it was a dreadful thing, and yet through her suffering came two miracles.

It was an ordinary day, the second of the New Year. Anya had taken tea with Tatiana, Sophie and me, Sophie's presence no doubt provoking Anya into making her hasty and ill-judged decision to surprise her parents in town that evening with a visit. Sophie Buxhoeveden and I had become good friends, as had another young lady named Lili Dehn, and I had unusually asked them to stay on with me as Ladies-in-Waiting. Naturally this caused Anya to start up her typical nonsense of pouting and whispering in my ear that they were not really my friends, and so on, nonsense I had been obliged to listen to all too often in the past, and so this New Year I decided override her objections and include Sophie and Lili more often in my company.

So, off Anya went on her haughty excursion, but it was barely an hour later when Count Fredericks announced in hushed, but not particularly stricken, tones that there had been a terrible crash involving Anya's train. Somehow the track signals had failed, and two trains, one of them carrying Anya, had slammed into each other head-on and at full speed. A great loss of life was feared and a young Cossack had just reported from the scene that Anya had been pulled out of the wreckage and was clinging on to life by a thread.

246

Horror-stricken, I ordered her to be taken immediately to our own hospital at the Catherine Palace, and then, after summoning my girls to join me, rushed to her side.

Once at the hospital, I met with our own Doctor Gedroiz, the brilliant woman who had trained us all in our nursing duties. Dr. Gedroiz, a woman of few words at the best of times, merely shook her head resignedly.

"I am sorry, Your Majesty, I fear she may die. There is nothing I can do for her, and as you can see …" She threw out her hands to indicate the chaos around us.

Indeed, our beautiful ballroom, which had been turned into an operating theater and a cot arena, now resembled a scene of suffering of Biblical proportions, with bloodied people leaning up against walls or rolling on the floor in agony. The sounds of their suffering echoed terribly against the high ceilings. Then there were the blue, abandoned bodies of the dead.

My little girls, even Anastasia, recoiled in horror at this sight and leaned against me. Olga, who surely should have been used to such a scene, swayed on her feet as though about to faint. Only my Tatiana rose to face the nightmare we were confronting. Shrugging off her sables, she stood tall and, though dressed for home in a silk skirt and blouse, addressed Dr. Gedroiz calmly.

"Please, Doctor, tell me where I can best be of use."

Dr. Gedroiz raised an approving eyebrow and looked at me. I nodded my permission. Then, taking Tati by the arm, she said, "This way, Your Imperial Highness," and they vanished amid a sea of bodies.

Olga scowled and swayed again.

"I feel unwell, Mama. I want to go back home. Anya is going to die, Dr. Gedroiz said so, and I don't want to see that. And the little pair are distraught."

Maria had indeed burst into noisy sobs, but Anastasia, while maybe wanting to cry, refused to do so.

"Hush, Maria," Anastasia said commandingly. "Mama is very upset, so be quiet! If Anya is going to die, so she is, but Mama will want to say goodbye to her. Olga, rather than standing around waiting to faint, shouldn't you go and find someone to tell us where Anya is."

"Anastasia, really!" I said in reproof, for I too was beginning to feel faint.

Anastasia puffed out her lips.

"Well really, Mama … what …? It is better that Olga be given something to do." Then, addressing Olga, she added, "You were a nurse here before you took to your bed and starting acting like Mama."

Both Olga and I braced ourselves to react to this most insulting of remarks, but before we could do so, Maria shrieked out, "Papa! Papa's here! Look!"

I did and it was true. There was Nicky, and even amid confusion on this scale people were parting for him. Even better, following closely on his heels was Father Grigory.

Nicky reached my side and drew me to his chest.

"Dearest, you must be so worried. Volkov informed me just an hour ago, and, as you can see, I sent for Our Friend."

"Father Grigory!" I exclaimed in relief, pulling back from Nicky to gaze at him. "You came! But how did you know?"

"I felt your fear and heard your prayers," Father Grigory replied solemnly.

"I sent a car for him as soon as Volkov told me about Anya," Nicky said flatly, whereupon they traded annoyed glances, but Anastasia was pulling at Nicky.

"Papa, I don't know how we'll ever find her in this scrabble."

Nicky smiled down at her.

"We'll just follow Volkov, Nastinka. He knows."

Nicky's valet bowed at this compliment and gestured for us to follow him, which we did, while trying to avoid stepping on the wounded who moaned ever the more loudly at the sight of Nicky with piteous cries of "Little Father, Little Father, hold my hand. Give me your blessing." Nicky did not interrupt his stride as he crossed that vast room, but Father Grigory paused time after time by the side of the afflicted to make the sign of the cross over their poor heads, his lips moving in constant prayer as he did so.

At last we came to a small, curtained alcove, and Volkov, somewhat conceited for having found her, threw open the curtains, bowed and gestured to a pile of broken, bloody flesh that I was supposed to believe was my dearest Anya.

I gasped and stepped back against Nicky, and the girls did likewise. None of us wanted to approach the poor thing until Father Grigory stepped around us in order to address her.

"Anya, open your eyes!" he commanded. "Open your eyes, Anya!"

There were beads of sweat standing out on his forehead and his face was almost as white as the exsanguinated head of poor Anya. Then the miraculous occurred. Despite both her eyes being terribly blackened and swollen, she lifted her lids.

"Nicky," she said and moaned.

I was instantly furious, even in the face of her lamentable state. How could she call him by his Christian name in front of all of us, and so intimately?

The sound of Father Grigory's labored breath drew my attention back to him, and Nicky's too. Father Grigory's visage was bleached, his eyes as colorless as if they were silver coins, and he was swaying rapidly back and forth.

Maria, always helpful and strong as an ox, made an exclamation of distress and put her arm around his waist to anchor him, and Nicky winced.

Father Grigory didn't even notice what Maria was doing, and after what seemed like an age, he stopped, glared at Anya, and proclaimed, "You will live, but forever be a cripple."

And then, without a word, he turned and left us all.

Later that night, we returned Tsarskoe Selo after we had all made soothing noises around Anya, and I had persuaded Dr. Gedroiz to finally allow Anya a bit of morphine, something she was stubbornly reluctant to do for a dying patient, but willing to do, after some persuasion, for someone who might live. I wasn't even angry at her, because it was true that the hospital was very low on morphia and that all the doctors were now only allowing its use for surgeries involving amputations. I hated to pull rank on the good doctor, but immediately after Father Grigory had awoken Anya, she had begun to scream, and none of us could bear to leave her until she was sedated.

In fact Nicky and I were nearing nervous collapse ourselves by the time we arrived home, so much so that we allowed Dr. Botkin to dose us both with cocaine to calm us, and then, still unable to settle, we wandered down to Nicky's study and I joined him in a brandy, much to his delight and surprise.

The fire was banked low and his curtains were open to the blowing snow and blackness. I shivered. Nicky raised his head from his glass, and gesturing with his cigarette, said, "I saw it. I did see it. But what did I see?"

I looked at him, puzzled, and then I realized what he meant and became angry all over again. He had seen trouble afflicting Baby so many times, but why just now with Anya?

No, I didn't want to argue with him. I was grateful to him for having called Father Grigory.

I smiled softly at him.

"You saw a miracle. I have always told you that God works through him. That God favors him."

Nicky rubbed his face.

"I know that, darling. I know that is what you truly believe."

"But what, Nicky ...? You have seen him save Baby how many times ...?"

He turned in his chair and looked out of the window.

"I have never known what I saw there, Sunny, you know that. The doctors tell me one thing and you tell me another."

"Doctors try to fool you. What do they know? They cannot help him, so they hate the man who can. But, Nicky, you know … you know he is a man of God."

Nicky swiveled around, his face red.

"I do not know anything, Alix!" He pounded his fist on his desk, something I had long wished him to do with his ministers but had never seen. I recoiled. He ignored me and in an anguished tone said, "All of my life I have believed that God has placed me here."

I nodded; it was obvious. I told him as much.

"Well, of course He did. All rulers are chosen by God. What does that have to do with Father Grigory?"

"Alix darling, don't you see?"

"Don't I see what, Nicky? You are overtired. Maybe we should discuss this another time."

"No, it must be said, Alix. I must make you understand."

My exhaustion suddenly caught up with me. I wanted to go to bed and I did not want to listen to another of his excruciating speeches on how God had chosen Him for martyrdom.

I knew what was coming but I stayed. What else could I do? I was his wife.

Sighing, I indicated that he should continue.

"If God chose me to be Tsar, and He must have for how else could I be Tsar …? Do you see what I mean?" I covered a yawn and nodded. He nodded too in satisfaction that I was managing to follow his argument. "… Then it should be me, Sunny, to whom God speaks, to whom He gives visions, to whom He dispenses the power to heal others. It is what the people need and want from their Tsar. And so I ask myself, Alicky, why him, why an ignorant peasant who can help no one, when I am in a position to do so much?"

I could not bear to hear any more, and I stood up and moved towards him.

"Nicky darling, don't you see? God loves the humble. The lowest amongst us shall be first. But it is you, you and all rulers, whom He favors, and you, my boysy, above all, for He not only chose you to rule over Russia and its peoples, He sent you one of His humble holy men to guide you. Has anyone ever been more favored in this than you, my darling?"

His eyes had become glassy, but his stare was still piercing.

"Can it be so, Sunny?"

I stroked his face.

"It is so, my darling. All that has ever stood between you and God's perfect grace, which will bring your reign to true glory, is your failure to understand that He sent Father Grigory to you, to us, to guide you."

Nicky's eyes filled with tears.

"I am so foolish, my darling. How disappointed you must have been in me all these years, for you are right. Our boy, our sunshine, he lives because of this and because of your faith in this man of God. I have been so filled with pride and doubt that I couldn't see what was laid our clearly before me, but I do now. I saw Father Grigory raise Anya from the dead. Only a messenger of Christ could do that. I understand everything now and everything will be different from this day."

Chapter 25

The spring and summer campaigns of the war began in earnest, but despite Nicky's newfound and quite touching faith in Father Grigory, God did not smile down upon Russia during that brutal season. In May, the villainous Germans and their cowardly Austrian counterparts launched a great offensive against us on our Western Front.

The Battle of Galicia the previous August had been a great triumph for us and had nearly destroyed the Austrian army and shown mad Cousin Willy that Russia was not the half-slain beast he saw us as. Our brave soldiers had also continued to fight throughout the winter, the fierce, wretched Russian winter, the one that had humbled Napoleon and that he had called "General Winter." This outstanding and selfless courage and fortitude had enabled us to further rout the Austrians in the Carpathian Mountains and to submit them to yet another crushing defeat. However, now that Germany realized that Russia was the powerful enemy we were, and that we had at last gained her respect, she was even more determined to destroy us.

Nicky explained it all to me after he had broken down in sobs at the recent loss of our once dearly won Galicia and our seemingly endless series of retreats.

"They think ... Willy thinks," he gulped, coughed, smoked and cried, "that they will break us this year and force us into a separate peace. Force me, force me, Alix, to betray our allies and leave the war. And after I said , after I promised our people, that this would never happen. Not one German on Russian soil!"

He could not go on.

I patted his hand but felt distaste for him, although I was careful not to let it show.

"Yes, you promised that you would never sue for peace as long as one enemy soldier remained on Russian soil and that you would never betray our great allies," not that I was as enamored of our allies as Nicky was.

During many long fireside chats over the previous winter, I had discussed this whole situation with Father Grigory, for owing to exhaustion and the effort and time it took to care for Anya, I had all but given up nursing.

Father Grigory pointed out that so far Russia had sacrificed the lives of over a million men to the war, while the French had suffered "cataclysmic" losses of only twenty thousand men. True, the English were suffering terribly, but compared with us, even their casualties were miniscule.

"You see, Mama, they do not think we are much. They do not count our empty villages or the piles of our dead. They do not care that we starve, and freeze and die. To them, we are nothing, of no more consequence than sandbags set out to soak up German fire."

I feebly tried to defend the position of our allies.

"Well, I don't know that they feel that way about us. You see, Father Grigory, we lose so many men owing to a lack of munitions. Nicky says that our allies are most trustworthy and estimable."

"He is too kind, Mama. Our allies have many factories and they should send us more munitions and other supplies so that we can do our work better for them and die less easily for ourselves."

I did not particularly mind Father Grigory criticizing France, a country I despised, despite its constantly being acclaimed as "our dear friends," for one of my most valued possessions was the great Vigée Le Brun painting of Marie Antoinette, the queen whom that ungrateful nation had first brutally imprisoned and then foully murdered. Such unjust treatment, I felt, was indicative of the presence of an ingrained moral turpitude and therefore a stain forever on its character. Moreover, was it not more than faintly ridiculous that the proud autocracy of Russia should find itself yoked alongside the perfidious and unapologetic Republic of France.

However, I did not appreciate Father Grigory casting his aspersions on England; besides, he was incorrect to do so.

"Father Grigory, the bravery and loyalty of England cannot be questioned. It has pushed its factories to their very limit on our behalf. I had a letter from May just yesterday about it, and of course Georgie is in constant communication with Nicky on the matter, and if its munitions are not getting through to us it is because those iniquitous Germans have blockaded them. Poor England is suffering at least as much as we are, and I will not have you say otherwise."

Father Grigory raised his hands and bowed his head.

"Peace, Mama, forgive me. What do I know of foreign places, a peasant from the Siberian countryside?"

"Oh, I didn't mean that. Please, Father Grigory, enough of these discussions. It is better that you discuss these things with Nicky. You are meeting with him after this, are you not?"

Father Grigory smiled happily, baring his yellowed teeth in forgiveness.

"I am. Papa and I are now the greatest of friends. He likes me to pray with him and then sometimes we talk. Today I think we will talk about Nikolasha." His face darkened as he said that name.

I had very much wanted to talk about my latest troubles with Anya, who was becoming daily more awful, but my old hatred of the Black Sisters, Grand Duke Nicholas's dreadful wife Stana and her equally ghastly sister Mitsia, reared its head and caught my interest.

"Oh, what about Grand Duke Nicholas?" I asked, and by using the title gave a gentle reminder to Father Grigory that even here, and alone with me, he should show respect towards a member of our family.

"Yes, him. He will be sorry, Nikolasha will," Father Grigory said, ignoring my covert instruction.

I tried not to smile as at that moment he resembled Baby when had been told he had to go to bed. Instead, I nodded as though I were taking him seriously.

"I see. What has His Imperial Highness Grand Duke Nicholas done now?"

"I wrote a very nice letter to him and gave him much excellent advice. Then I told him I would go to Headquarters to bless him so that he might do better for Russia."

I looked down to hide my amusement. I could only imagine the pompous Nikolasha's wrath.

Father Grigory continued. "He sent me this!" He thrust a crumpled telegram at me and I looked at it curiously.

Yes, do come to Headquarters so that I can shoot you. Stop.

I gasped and fell back in horror.

"He dares do that?"

Father Grigory nodded emphatically.

"Yes, and I shall tell Papa myself and show him this telegram. When he sees it, he will not be pleased."

"No, Father Grigory ... I mean, yes, of course, show him the telegram, but do not speak out too openly against the Grand Duke. Nicky loves him and trusts him, and now is not the time to move against him. I will sense when it is and I will speak to him about it then."

"Oh, it is the time, Mama, if your son matters to you at all. It is the time to rise to my defense."

"My son? Why do you bring up Baby?"

Father Grigory closed his eyes.

"I am in danger. I dream it and I feel it. Nikolasha," he opened his eyes to see if I would correct the name again, but I remained silent and he closed them and continued, "seeks my destruction, for he knows that if I am killed or sent away, the heir will soon die, and then he will become Tsar, he or some puppet of his choice. He has no love for Papa and even less for you, Mama."

I shuddered.

"Please, Father Grigory, do not ever speak of Baby's death." I crossed myself. "I cannot bear to hear such a thing, and besides, you told me last week that he was much better and that the doctors think so too. I believe that hideous disease is vanquished now."

"It is not, Mama. I pray – Oh how I pray! Sometimes I do not eat or sleep for days as I am locked in my room asking God for this one thing. That alone is the reason that your son has seemed so well. It is true that I have received a vision that if my prayers can keep him alive until his seventeenth birthday, he will be free of the bleeding disease forever, but there are many years to go yet and many ways for me to fall."

"No, no, no, nothing will happen to you. I stand firm even if he does not." I broke off, feeling it wrong of me to discuss Nicky's weaknesses in relation to Father Grigory, though of course he knew all about them. He knew everything. I resumed more calmly. "But you must in turn give me your solemn vow that my son will live to be Tsar."

He raised a long, dirty finger in caution before saying, "As I have promised, as long as I live to guard him with prayer and healing until his seventeenth birthday, then yes, he will be Tsar. But you know, Mama, Papa does not believe that this will ever come to pass."

I stared at him, confused.

"Of course he does. How ridiculous! Nicky and I discuss so many things about the future and about Baby's future. How, with his strong will, he will be a great, but possibly fearsome tsar. Why, Nicky used to joke that he would one day be called 'Tsar Alexei the Terrible.' "

I laughed gently. Father Grigory did not.

"It will, I think, have been long ago, Mama, since he made that joke."

I frowned and then thought about it.

"Well yes, not since Spala, that is true, but only because Baby has become so much calmer and less prone to outbursts of temper since then."

He was shaking his head vigorously.

"That is not why. Even if I did not have God to show me things, I would know, as you should have known, Mama, for I see that Alexei Nicholaevich does not know many things. He does not go to the classroom with his tutors, as his sisters do. He does not do his lessons."

"He does! Monsignor Gilliard teaches him French, and Mr. Gibbes teaches him English, and Master Petrol instructs him in Russian."

"But he does not know any of these things, does he, Mama?" He asked this quietly, his hands spread wide, and before I could answer him, he said devastatingly, "I have asked Alexei when I visit, what does he learn of Russia, of government? He laughs and shows me his soldiers. He will be twelve soon. I ask him whether his papa tells him about Russia, and he looks at me, Mama, as though I were as mad as some others think me to be. Do you find it not strange that Papa does not oversee his progress, does not discuss with the heir to all the Russias his education, his plans for the future?"

"I ... but you see, Nicky, he –"

Father Grigory reached out and grasped both my flailing hands, and, as always, bestowed on me the tranquility that only his touch could bring me.

"Mama, I know. I know that Papa does not involve himself with such matters, in the same way that his papa did not involve himself with him, because he does not believe it matters."

"Why would he not believe that?" I whispered.

I knew why, of course, but I wanted Father Grigory to tell me.

"He does not believe that Aloyishka will live to be a man, a husband, a father, a tsar. That is why he does not care about what he knows or does not know."

"It is not true," I protested. "I can explain this so easily, and you will see how wrong you are. You see, the war, it occupies all Nicky's time, that and his ministers who are rotten to the core." I choked, cleared my throat and started again. "He would very much like to supervise Baby's education, but there is no time, and of course Baby himself, he is still so very young and he does not enjoy learning yet. As you know, when he becomes upset, he risks hurting himself, or if he has a tantrum, his nose might bleed, and so I do not force him to do what he does not like. There is still so much time yet. Why, Nicky is not yet fifty."

"He believes the doctors, Mama, and not me and not you."

"He has never said, never shown by one instance any of that."

He smiled sadly and shook his head.

"Ah, Mama, I know Papa is weak, and that he will do and say whatever you wish him to. All of Russia knows."

"You go too far!"

Father Grigory carried on, unperturbed. "He loves you. He knows, as do I, your strength and your wisdom, but what a man says, what he does ... well, up here," he tapped the side of his head, "this is where it matters. Maybe not to others, but here a man is free. Even you, beautiful Mama, cannot own his thoughts."

I glanced at the small clock over the mantel. I knew that Father Grigory was supposed to see Nicky at five p.m., and was dismayed to see it was not yet a quarter-to. I wanted him to go.

His eyes followed mine and he laughed and rose.

"I will go now, Mama. I see you are angry with poor old Grigory." He shrugged. "I am not trained in the ways of the thousand people who live here in velvet lies and silence, and who know to bow and scrape when you are angry, and smile and sit down at tables to say nothing true." He waited to see if I would respond as I usually did, with a smile, with thanks for his peasant honesty, but I wished him to leave me to what he had just referred to as velvet silence.

Seeing that I was no longer in the mood for any more of his wisdom, he departed, as he always did, without a word and without permission, and I heard him make his customary thanks to my silent Abyssinians as I pressed my lips together in annoyance. Father Grigory either adored the Abyssinians or despised them, and neither they nor I could be sure of which it was, for he liked to poke them and say things such as, "My good fellows, how are the doors today? Is the wood behaving?" and then laugh uproariously at his joke and their silence.

He reminded me of the small boys I had seen outside Buckingham Palace when I had visited Grandmamma, who made faces at the sentries there to try and get them to react. Sometimes I found Father Grigory's teasing of the Abyssinians amusing, but today was not one of those days. Today I could hear the voices of my mother-in-law and her court in my ears.

'She lets that filthy peasant into their most intimate family life. Nicky sees more of him, and worse, hears more of him, than he does his own family and ministers. She is mad, mad.'

Could any of it be true? Was he a man of God or just a whim of mine? Yet, without him, would not my son be dead?

Spala, I could never forget Spala. Father Grigory had saved him, and since then he had soothed him a hundred times more. And, of course, I had seen the miracle of Anya, Anya who lived, and complained, and bedeviled me with her whining and her moaning, true, but I suppose that if she had died, she would have left me bereft.

However, Anya was not why I clung to, and sometimes, like today, endured the man the world called Rasputin. That was because of Alexei, my sunshine, my agoo wee one, my Baby, the precious boy who was so much more than just my adored son, the one who would one day be my savior in Russia. Nicky's reign was, I now understood, something of a disaster. It was as though he, and because of him I too, had been cursed. He had forced me to marry him immediately after the death of his father, when I had not wanted to. I had wanted to leave that smelly corpse behind, not ride all over Russia in a funeral train and marry in the dead cold of winter in the middle of their mourning season. Weakly he had clung to me, for that is something I learned from him and see now in Anya – the tyranny of the weak.

Oh how he clung to me, just as she did, too, now. It seemed that he could not live, could not reign, could not breathe if he could not be near me. I had capitulated, and look what happened! Instead of a beautiful summer wedding, which could so easily have been delayed until after his coronation, I was instead a funeral bride, feared by a superstitious populace and hated by his mother and her coterie for being so insensitive as to take Nicky away from her in the midst of her grief. Maybe the disaster at Khodynka Field during the coronation would have happened anyway, but I would not have been blamed for it later on. So, instead of being a triumphant summer bride, I had become a funeral wife, stuck living with Nicky's horrible mother. I became the newly-crowned Empress of Khodynka, and the people's superstitions had hardened to hatred, for their worst fears had been realized. I was indeed a curse on the Russian land – I, not Nicky.

After that, I produced four girls for which I was also blamed, while he busily mismanaged every decision he undertook as Tsar. First he plunged Russia into a stupid war with a nearly non-existent country because of some mad expansionist dream of his, one sixth of the world not being enough for him, apparently. This then created a revolution that made him huff and puff and cower until he signed away three hundred years of autocratic rights and created a Duma that he claimed was the bane of his existence, so he cleverly ignored its existence, which in turn stoked the revolutionary fervor yet further.

The people he did choose to listen to were a group of militant lunatics who called themselves "The Black Hand." They proposed that anytime someone complained too loudly in Russia about anything, the situation could be solved by a pogrom on the Jewish people, and so, with Nicky's enthusiastic support, they burned and raped and murdered thousands of his own subjects, much as had happened when he had, as always, ignored his ministers to let his troops shoot scores of innocent civilians on the day the world knows as 'Bloody Sunday.'

And during all of this, who was hated, who was blamed? Why, me of course, although I knew nothing of what was happening, not any of it, until after it had already happened, because I was busy trying to do the one thing that Nicky and Russia said they wanted me to do, to produce a son. Apparently, by giving Russia four beautiful, healthy little girls, which kept me pregnant and ever sicker with each pregnancy, I was still managing to cause each and every disaster to hit Russia. "You would at least think she could manage to produce a son to cheer us all up in this new disastrous reign," they told each other.

And then, during Nicky's ill-considered war with the "yellow monkeys," as he termed them, I did finally produce a son, thereby providing Russia with an heir. After that you would think all would have been well: that useless German woman that I was considered to be had done something right for a change.

Maybe even Nicky thought so, because he triumphantly named every soldier in his army to be Alexei's godfather, but he lost that war anyway, and we plunged into a revolution anyway, and as a result of that and Nicky's perennial weakness, he robbed our son of a perfect and ancient autocracy, and saddled him with an argumentative and divided Duma.

All these things that had damaged Russia and the crown had been his doing, but I held fast to my Baby, and I kept him alive when it was discovered that he had inherited my family's bleeding disease. And I prayed, oh how I prayed, for God's assistance, for I had nothing from Nicky but hand-wringing, tears and the occasional sullen look, which was his sly way of showing me that he knew Alexei's illness was my fault. He also made sure to let his Mama know what he thought too, and, through her, his condemnation of me spread to the rest of his family and to the whole court. In this way, despite all he had done and all he had failed to do, he was the victim, the lamb, and I was the one ultimately to blame. How marvelous for him!

It was always said that I dominated him, and those who said it were right to say it because I now felt increasingly desperate about leaving anything in his hands, but my domination of him was limited to the sphere of our domestic lives.

When I found Father Grigory, or rather when God sent him to me to save Baby, I used everything in my power to keep him by my side for Baby's sake, only for his sake. Or maybe that wasn't wholly true, for Baby's sake was also my sake, and I admit that I have always known that. Maybe I have always known that Nicky did not believe our son was going to live either, that he did not believe me or Father Grigory. This was maybe why he declined to appoint a special governor to educate Baby as Nicky had been educated as a boy, and why he neglected to oversee his education or to care that Alexei

266

sometimes behaved badly, for yes, I knew that too. He was wrong about this, as he was always wrong. I saw far and Father Grigory could see all in the future and in the past, and understood the present as well.

When Nicky had fallen into this current dreadful war, Father Grigory had tried to tell him it would be the end of Russia and of his monarchy, but he had also secretly shared with me that what it would really bring about was a new Russia, one governed by my son, which, given Baby's tender years and present ill-health, meant Russia would have to be governed by me.

"You are the true Empress, Mama," he had said, "another Catherine the Great. You will never flinch and you are what Russia needs."

He was right and it should not be considered to have been a treasonous thought. I did love Nicky, but he always faltered and failed, and Baby must rule one day. I would help him, and he in turn would help me to finally achieve the love and respect and gratitude of these strange childlike people whose hated and despised Empress I was. Baby loved only me and he would never allow me to be treated and spoken about as I was, as Nicky had allowed me to be.

I rose, yawned and smiled tiredly at my reflection. Thinking of Baby made me long to see him. It was just coming up to five and I knew that he would be in his little rooms, playing with his soldiers and planning out great battles. Father Grigory was mistaken in this one thing: when the time came, Baby would know how to rule just fine.

Chapter 26

And still there was no ammunition or guns for the Russian armies. I blamed Nicky's glorious and fearless uncle, Grand Duke Nicholas, for this state of affairs, but it appeared that I was wrong to do so.

"It is not him, Sunny, it is that useless War Minister Sukhomlinov who has been sitting there twiddling his thumbs instead of organizing adequate supplies for our armies. I have so many telegrams from him assuring me that he had everything well in hand. Well, does this look well in hand? God help us!"

He pounded his fist against the bed clothes as I remained silent.

Sukhomlinov was a name I was familiar with, not simply because he was our Minister of War but because Father Grigory had mentioned him affectionately on a number of occasions, calling him "a grand fellow" and a good friend to himself and Russia.

Nicky looked at me, knowing this and wondering, but as I remained quiet he drew a deep breath, lit a cigarette and continued.

"I am appointing a new man, General Polivanov. He seems resolute and will sort things out, but sometimes I wonder if what is lost can ever be regained."

He trailed off and tears appeared in his eyes. I could not bear that and snapped out, "Nicky, please do try to pull yourself together."

He pulled back his shoulders and lit another cigarette from the one he was holding, saw that he had two going at once, and irritably stubbed one out in the ashtray. I coughed and waved my hands around as the smoke was choking me. Nicky looked at me guiltily and opened the window, letting in the cold night air. Such was summer in Russia.

"Forgive me, Sunny, it is just that I had believed, truly believed," he thumped at his heart for emphasis, "in here, that we would have ended the war by now, and instead, well you see. I was told that since we had Galicia and Poland, Austria would capitulate, Willy would open peace negotiations, and Russia would be victorious. But now, thanks to that arch-villain Sukhomlinov, our army is still without bullets and Willy has sent troops to help out the Austrians, and we simply cannot shoot back. So it is retreat after retreat. The men have no bullets, and no boots, and no food. The trains do not help either."

"Yes, I know they are inadequate, that there are not enough of them and there is not enough track, and what there is is old and outdated. I know all about the trains from my own travels to visit my hospitals. But Nicky, you must have known the state of our trains before we went to war. Why have no preparations been made?"

He looked at me, genuinely puzzled.

"Well of course I knew. My ministers bleated on and on about it. That idiot Witte even wrote to me promising doom and gloom. But what could I do, Sunny? There wasn't time to fix everything and then the war came."

"So why did we go to war, then, Nicky?"

"Be careful, Sunny. There is no call to sound defeatist. Defeatism is the enemy of patriotism. And we were winning the war, despite these problems. It is just that now –"

269

"… we are not," I finished for him.

"That is not what I was going to say. It is true that we are in retreat, which is difficult for morale, but in time I am certain this supply issue will be corrected, and then we shall launch a counter-offensive. But it is all blasted difficult because we will only be fighting to recapture what we have lost, and that is hard for the average soldier to understand as being any sort of real victory. And these poor Polish refugees are causing so many problems for the army as well."

"What refugees, Nicky, are we talking about this time? Why are there refugees and where are they coming from?"

"Why, from every village, town and piece of land that our army has to retreat through. Where do you think? If Warsaw falls, the numbers will grow to a million, I fear."

"If Warsaw falls …? But Nicky, I still do not understand. Why are there refugees? Are they fleeing the Germans?"

Nicky looked away and started fiddling with his lighter. "Maybe."

"Nicky?"

"All right, Sunny, please stop badgering me. I came to you seeking sympathy not recriminations."

"Why are the refugees causing problems for our armies?"

"Because all their homes are burnt. Because all their stores and warehouses and fields are burnt too. Because they are starving and they do not know what else to do, so they are following our armies, hoping they will feed them, or if not that at least they might tell them which

270

direction the cities are in, because they think there will be food and shelter there. Maybe work too. Maybe word of their lost ones, I don't know. It is an awful mess, Sunny."

"So is it that our armies, our soldiers, are doing all the burning of the villages, Nicky? I thought the Polish people were on our side, were our people."

"We are doing it to keep it from the Germans, Alix. How can you not understand that?"

I laughed bitterly.

"I have no idea. I must be simple-minded. I suppose all those displaced and starving people completely understand what you are doing. It's just me who doesn't."

Nicky stood up and tightened his robe, readying himself to go off and sleep in his dressing room. I was glad of that.

"Of course they don't understand, don't be ridiculous! But you of all people should. Read this. You will enjoy it, I think. It is from Moscow. Your damned sister sent it to me. She would make a fine social revolutionary, I have no doubt of it."

Dearest Nicky, I write to you today with a heavy heart. This holy city, my dear home and the place where I have lived the only meaningful years of my life, marriage to my beloved Sergei, and then learning through prayer to abjure all the concerns of material life, yes this place! Ancient city of tsars, has become changed and unrecognizable since the war. The retreat

271

has angered so many, and with a lack of available food because the farms are all fallow, because the men are all gone, Muscovites have begun to be hungry.

Two days ago a group of one hundred seamstresses arrived at my small convent to receive their sewing work for my hospital committee. But Nicky I had to turn them all away! You see there was no material to give them to sew for our poor soldiers and refugees, there was nothing available! Nicky, they would not leave, they began to shout and scream accusations at me, me who lives to serve them. They said "The German Grand Duchess has given our work to a German sewing firm."

Then more and more people arrived until my convent was completely surrounded by a mob, I feared I would be seized and killed. I was only saved by the arrival, not a quick one I might add, of the military governor and his troops. I am all right thanks to the grace of Our Lord and Savior, but the city is not quiet, the rage of the people grows apace with their hunger, and I think we must all now fear the morrow.

Nicky, please look deep into your heart and pray. Ask God if this great burden he has put on you as a ruler cannot be shared with the Duma. At this time in our history when we face such a great foe as Germany from outside, can we stand if we are torn from inside too? Our Lord in his humbleness had disciples, can you not have them as well?

I remain your humble and loving sister in Christ,

Ella.

I crumpled up the letter and tossed it on the floor. Nicky raised an eyebrow. I shook my head.

"Ella has obviously run mad," I said, "comparing the ghastly Duma to the Disciples of Christ. Really, what will she come up with next?"

Nicky nodded, and seeing I was angry now at Ella and not at him, he moved back from the door and perched once again on the bed.

"I agree, and of course I am not listening to her."

"Good."

I nodded firmly and for a moment we were in perfect accord, but then his eyes shadowed again. I sighed inwardly, preparing myself for more grim news. He was truly the most terrible company tonight.

I did not wish to encourage much more of this, so I stifled a yawn and changed the subject.

"Have you seen Anya today, Nicky?"

273

He glanced at me, puzzled, and then at the clock. It was nearly ten.

"Oh, well, no, darling. I have been a bit busy …"

"Of course you have, dearest, but you know she sets such store by your visits, and if you don't go to see her, she whines and cavils about it, and it makes life much more difficult for me, as you can imagine. And the girls are not much help. Olga detests her, Tati is lovely with her but is mostly at the hospital, and the little pair are busy with school and visiting their officers. I dare not take Baby with me when I go to see her, obviously."

"Why? Is Alexei unwell?" Nicky interjected sharply.

I smiled, gratified by his return to what was important and to have distracted him from his endless self-pity.

I leaned forward and kissed him as a reward.

"No, he's fine. Perfect. I really think he has turned the corner on this disease, and Father Grigory assures me that everything will be fine as long as we have him by us."

"Then why don't you take him to see Anya?" Nicky insisted, already sounding bored.

"Because her house is so crowded with small tables and a really ludicrous amount of chairs that I worry he will bruise himself."

Nicky's shoulders relaxed and he chuckled.

"I have always wondered about all of those chairs. Why do you think she has so many?"

I grinned at him in complicity.

"It is too funny, darling. A year or so ago, a few officers dropped in for tea to thank her for her kindness to them at the hospital, and she didn't have enough chairs. So a young captain joined her on her settee and she bleated and wailed afterwards that she could feel his thigh pressing against hers all the time he was sitting there. Of course, I am sure it was simply that Anya is so fat that there was not enough room for the two of them, but right after that she ordered a dozen chairs, and now the place is a veritable obstacle course."

Nicky roared with laughter and I smiled, happy to have lightened his mood, for wasn't it a wife's duty to soothe and distract her husband away from his cares and woes.

Nicky wiped his eyes and shook his head ruefully.

"Poor old Anya. It is too cruel of us to make fun of her, and especially now that she is a cripple."

I shrugged.

"Oh, she is all right, or will be in time. I think she is making the most of it all for the attention she gets. It is not as though she has anything lasting wrong with her, such as a failing heart."

I sighed and Nicky reached over and stroked my arm.

"Of course not, my darling. I did not mean to imply otherwise."

I grabbed his hand and raised it to my lips. He sighed in pleasure and moved closer.

"I know you didn't, boysy. It is just that I think it best if we bear in mind at all times in our dealings with her that treating her as an invalid can only lead her down the road of self-pity to self-indulgence, where she may begin to feel that she is more injured than she really is. Both her broken legs are healing now, although I was told she will need surgery on one of them to insert a metal rod into it, like the one she has in her back and her neck. It is marvelous how far medical science has come, isn't it,

275

darling? Although, when you consider how little they can do for Baby, I suppose I shouldn't say so. Thank God we have our dear friend Father Grigory."

Nicky stiffened under my hand.

"Yes, we are most fortunate. You know, though he can say some very curious things at times, darling."

"Oh yes? Such as?"

"Well, this afternoon he told me that all my ministers lied to me and kept me from my people."

I nodded.

"Yes, that is true."

Nicky stared at me curiously.

"You realize, darling, that if I wandered about the towns and countryside like Father Grigory – and it was his suggestion that I should, by the way – I would soon be killed. Also we discussed this most worrying strike in Kostroma on which he had most vexing opinions."

"Oh?"

"Yes, it is really quite a worrisome one. Women, this time. Moscow is also having a great many strikes. It is all highly treasonous, of course, in the middle of a war when our soldiers are sacrificing so much for us and for their families at home. Imagine asking for greater wages at such a time! They cry out about how much things are costing, but are they on the front lines dying and bleeding for their country? I think not. And in Kostroma, these hopeless women at the linen factory pay no mind at all to the general suffering as long as they get paid more for their work which risks their lives not at all."

"I suppose it is difficult for women in particular to die and bleed on the front lines," I commented sarcastically. Why couldn't Nicky go ten minutes without saying something stupid?

Nicky shook his head, annoyed, and lit a cigarette. Come to think of it, why couldn't he go ten minutes without another cigarette? Nonetheless, I wished I had kept quiet.

"Thank you, Sunny. Yes, well, obviously ... But at any rate, these ridiculous women went off on strike at the linen factory and, naturally, they were immediately ordered back to work, and the silly creatures refused. The Governor came and spoke to them himself, Alix. It was quite moving, his speech. I was sent a copy of it. He told them that all factories were now supplying the needs of the Fatherland during a time of war, and that to strike at this moment was both to break the law and to aid our enemy."

I imagined the poor women with children to feed whose men had been taken away from them by the war.

"What did they do?" I asked.

"Appallingly, they ignored this good man and took their silly grievances to the streets with lots of marching about and waving of banners, so that the soldiers had to be called in."

"Naturally," I said dryly.

Nicky ignored me and continued.

"Yes, the soldiers were called in, and when they tried to stop these harridans marching about and shouting and causing trouble, they threw stones at them!"

I was now fascinated.

"Good heavens, Nicky. What happened then?"

"The Governor ordered the soldiers to fire into the strikers."

"No, Nicky, not like Bloody Sunday?"

"That is what Father Grigory said too."

"Oh God, Nicky, the foreign papers will have a field day with this."

"And damn them to hell if they do! They had better not – they are our allies, Alix. But it is worse than that. Please let me tell it all to you."

I waved one hand and pressed the other one over my heart. It really was like Bloody Sunday all over again.

"You see, the soldiers deliberately fired over their heads. They were not willing to shoot at the women. They only meant to scare them. And at that, instead of being grateful, the women started shouting, 'Don't worry, they don't even have anything to shoot us with. They're out of bullets."

"Oh Nicky, stop, I cannot bear it!"

Inexorably, as though lancing his own wounds, Nicky went on, each word hitting me like the stones the women had thrown.

"But they did have bullets and the women were wrong. And the soldiers showed them how wrong they were!"

I was feeling numb.

"There were deaths?"

"Several of the women were killed, and some children too. They had brought their own children with them and got them killed! A terrible sin! But what else could the soldiers have done? Here, darling, read this. It is some scurrilous propaganda that these women – or so-called women, for they are really nothing more than filthy anarchists in skirts – have been putting about."

Nicky reached into his pocket and handed me a piece of paper. It was titled 'Proclamation of Kostroma Women Workers to Soldiers,' and read:

> *Soldiers! We are turning to you for help. Defend us. Our fathers, sons, and husbands were taken away and sent to the war, but healthy well fed soldiers are shooting at us defenseless, weaponless women. They say to us, work peacefully but we are hungry and cannot work. We made requests but they didn't listen, we made demands and they began shooting. They say there is no bread. Well where is it? Can the Russian land bear fruit only for the Germans?*

Shaking, I dropped the piece of paper onto the floor beside Ella's letter to Nicky that I had discarded earlier.

"What did Father Grigory say to you?"

Nicky looked at me, his own face white, his outrage having passed.

"He said that we are on the brink of revolution and that I must save us by taking charge of the army, by leading it, and that if we do not achieve a quick victory, it will all be too late."

Chapter 27

"So you see, Mama, the only way to save us all is for Papa to go and fight for Russia."

It was August and very hot at Tsarskoe Selo, and Father Grigory, Anya and I were having a light luncheon at her little house the day after Warsaw fell.

I was at Anya's that day because, due to the camarilla who controlled the endless stream of gossip, or better to say propaganda against me, neither Nicky nor I felt it was safe to meet Father Grigory openly at the palace. There, our every move was watched and reported upon by guards who often seemed more like jailers or spies to our eyes. We hated the gossip but could not stop it, and so we now met our dearest friend and savior like criminals sneaking off to some basement to avoid detection. Nicky humorously compared us to the filthy Bolsheviks who were known to move from place to place for their meetings to avoid detection by the police.

"At least, Sunny, we cannot be sent off to Siberia for our activities, but still ..." Turning serious, he cautioned, "We should avoid giving anyone anything more to speak about. He is so hated by so many people, you see, darling."

"Because we love him," I added angrily.

He agreed, and I was forced to agree with him and to see Father Grigory at Anya's in secret to try to stop people saying that we were lovers and that I had let a dirty *moujik* compromise the Tsar's daughters, to name but two of their grossly unfounded accusations. I had always hoped that Nicky would exert his authority and defend me, but he didn't or couldn't, and now I agreed that we needed to be careful as the mood of patriotic fervor that had existed a year earlier had long gone and our enemies were turning on us again. Russia was losing the war, our armies were in retreat, and what may be forgiven in victory becomes ever more resented in defeat – the lives sacrificed, the mutilations, the missing men, the scarcity of food, and the unaffordable prices. Sooner or later people were inevitably going to be asking themselves and others what the point of all this was, and that moment had already arrived.

Of course, as always, I was the one being blamed for Nicky's choices. On the one hand they said I had dragged them into this bloodbath with Germany against the will of the country, and yet, coming at me from the opposite direction, they accused me of being a German spy working behind the scenes to negotiate a separate peace. It would have been nice if they could have made up their minds as to where my guilt lay.

I did not say any of this aloud to either Anya or Father Grigory, nor did I tell him that Nicky and I couldn't really see him at the palace, although he knew the score well enough as it had all happened before five years earlier. Instead, I just made a point of being at Anya's each day for tea. She whined so terribly if I did not visit her a great deal anyway, and sometimes in the evenings she would call us at the palace and then both Nicky and I would know he was there and we would go over. The whole subterfuge was simply degrading.

Anya found Father Grigory's proposal that Nicky should take over command of the armies from Grand Duke Nicholas very exciting, which meant that she was speaking all over us and repeatedly interrupting everyone, as she always did when she was excited.

"And he wishes to kidnap Alix and have you killed, Father Grigory, so that he can be Tsar!" she exclaimed.

Father Grigory nodded as though this was not news to him, but I started in my chair so that my tea cup rattled.

"What, Anya? What do you mean? Where did you hear that and what do you mean by it?"

"So many people come to see me, and they write to me too. I'm sure Grand Duke Nicholas' wife, Stana, put the idea in his head. You know she has always hated you and plotted against you, Alix, and I'm certain she sees herself as the next Empress!"

Ridiculous as Anya's claims might have seemed, I believed her instantly, for it was true that Stana was terribly ambitious. But to plot to kidnap me? This was treason and I said as much.

Father Grigory shook his shaggy head.

"There will be no proof of it, Mama, of that you can be sure. She is a cunning woman. No, what will occur is that, one day soon, the army led by Nikolasha will march on Tsarskoe Selo and demand that Papa make him Tsar. Then they will take you away to a nunnery and hunt me down like an animal. I have seen it all in my dreams."

"Please don't call the Grand Duke 'Nikolasha,' Father Grigory," I pleaded, giving myself time to take in what was being said. "Nicky would not like it at all if he heard you. But do you believe it is true?"

Father Grigory nodded emphatically.

"It will come soon, Mama. It is coming. Only Papa taking up the reins of the armies from the Grand Duke,

282

as it seems I must call him, can stop him." He scowled. "The Tsar will save us all, for we can only continue to lose under such a man as the Grand Duke. Papa will bring us victory and Russia will be strong again. He must do this!"

"Nicky will bring us to victory?" I said, making sure that I understood him properly. "You are certain that this is what God has told you?"

He crossed himself, and Anya and I automatically bowed our heads.

Then Anya said breathily, "He'll be magnificent at the head of the troops. Oh, can't you just see him astride his horse?"

For a moment, but not for long enough I later realized, I wondered if I wasn't just an old, sickly woman, exhausted from too many cares and too much suffering, and Anya wasn't just a young, hysterical simpleton given to misunderstanding everything she heard and yet repeating it anyway, and Father Grigory wasn't just a strange, dusky, dirty peasant who believed God spoke to him but who was really just a madman. What nonsense were we concocting here?

But no, if Father Grigory was just a deluded, crazy peasant, how could anyone explain how he had healed Baby so that he would survive until he reached seventeen years old and could become Tsar. No, he was truly a man of God and I would kill my own precious child if I believed otherwise. This being the case, I must surely help him to make Nicky see his divine duty, although this was indeed a fearful thing. Nicky had never been lucky or brave or competent, and everything he touched turned to ashes, and yet ...

I lifted my head and met Father Grigory's eyes, then fell to my knees before him.

"Bless me, Father, and promise me Nicky will achieve victory."

Father Grigory closed his eyes, made the sign of the cross over my head, and intoned in a voice that sounded too deep to be his, "Papa will lead us to victory. It may not come as soon as we all hope, but we will triumph over our enemies and drive them from the Russian land. If Papa hears me and I remain by your side, this shall come to pass. It has all been foretold to me by God Himself."

Nicky, as it turned out, required little convincing, and by that evening he was thoroughly enthusiastic about his new mission. He, as Tsar, would save Russia! The Tsar and his people, the true Russians, would fight together to secure victory. However, while all four of us were agreed on this, the rest of the world was not, although Nicky held firm. This was what he had long wished for. This was what his great ancestors expected of him. It was the job of the Tsar to lead his armies to victory or to sacrifice himself accordingly!

Not that he would have a word said against Nikolasha.

"He would never raise a hand against you, Sunny. His loyalty to me is undoubted. He is a great general. Our losses, our retreats are not his fault. I believe firmly that this is all the result of problems with supplies of munitions and equipment. If I am head of the army, I will be kept informed of the state of munitions and supplies and the railways, as well as knowing every movement of the army and all of its needs. The ministers and the army will work together to win the war."

His statement filled me with pride in his resolve, but also left me with nagging doubts. How would it be that, after twenty years of misunderstandings and distrust with his ministers during peace time, Nicky could make everything run smoothly from now on amid the tumult of war? Yet Father Grigory had promised that victory would be ours and it was surely time for an old, arrogant and vain fool like Grand Duke Nicholas to be replaced by someone with fresh ideas, so Nicky must stiffen his spine and do what needed to be done.

Those days before Nicky left for the front were fraught with activity and discussions as the ministers and other naysayers lined up outside his door to wring their hands and predict doom and disaster if Nicky were to go ahead with his plan to take over the armies, pointing out that morale in the cities was getting worse, that there were still severe shortages of supplies for the front, and that there were increasing difficulties getting food into the cities that would lead to yet more trouble soon enough. Did Nicky really want to become personally responsible for all these things? Shouldn't the Tsar distance himself from such matters? And if these things were a problem now, what would happen when the winter came, and the railway tracks and roads were impassable, and the aging equipment fell apart with the cold. Worse, coal was becoming short. There were now over a million refugees from the war living under bridges in Moscow and Petersburg who constituted an impossible strain on available food supplies and a disheartening sight for all to see. If Nicky were far away at the front with the armies, there was a risk that civilian discontent would mushroom out of control and then who knew what might come?

Nicky conducted himself marvelously during this time, asserting with great majesty that, "these were mere opinions and not facts, and I, gentlemen, deal only in facts."

"Here, then, Sire, is a fact," suggested old fat, pompous Rodzianko, the President of the ever-troublesome Duma. "Grand Duke Nicholas is most beloved of the army and of the entire country. The recent and terrible losses we have sustained are not laid at his feet. Should you remove him from his post now that we are in retreat, it shows that you blame him alone, and should the losses continue, you will be held doubly accountable – for the dismissal of the Grand Duke and for the new defeats."

Nicky looked away, rose to his feet, and turned to face his long windows, commenting that the weather outside was most pleasant, while Rodzianko and Guchkov exchanged despairing looks as they took their leave. Visitors had long been instructed that when Nicky stood up and looked out of his windows, this was a signal for them to depart without any further ado. What they did not know was that I was secretly listening to them from the balcony above.

Funny thing really: when I had designed Nicky's study, I had been quite in love with the Gothic style, one that dear departed Grandpapa Albert had incorporated into the building of Osborne House for Grandmamma, and in Gothic rooms there are always balconies so that minstrels can play from them. So, naturally, I had a balcony built into Nicky's study. With the mere addition of a dark green velvet curtain, which was not noticeable from below because the walls were also dark, I could listen unobserved to everything that was happening. So there I sat on a chaise I had ordered moved there, and I was firmly resolved to stay there so that I could hear what was truly being said rather than having to rely on Nicky's unreliable versions of proceedings.

Today I had been there to hear Rodzianko's petulant arguments so that I could step in forcefully the minute he left.

"He will put me away," I stormed. "He will take Baby from me. I will save Nikolasha the trouble. I cannot bear to live like this. Bring me a knife, Nicky, and I will kill myself now, this moment, rather than watch you allow him to kill me slowly. It is what you want, what everybody wants, that I should be gone. I will give them what they want!"

It took Nicky hours to calm me down, even after I had been strongly dosed by that clucking old hen Dr. Botkin. Yet my tears were righteous ones and the groundwork I laid proved fertile, because the next morning I was told by Tatiana, who had replaced me on my chaise in the balcony as I was still incommoded, that when the ministers had returned, all Nicky had said was, "My decision is final, gentlemen. I leave for Stavka tomorrow. Should any immediate decisions be needed in my absence, speak with the Tsarina as she will be acting as my regent."

Chapter 28

I had not expected Nicky to put me in charge of the country while he was away, and at first I was a completely overwhelmed by his trust and by the responsibility, but I quickly came to realize that he had at last, for whatever reason, finally understood that I alone, with Father Grigory and God's help, could save Russia for him and Alexei.

I had always felt that it was wrong that I should be deprived of having a say in the affairs of state, for I was the granddaughter of the greatest queen who had ever lived, one who had commanded a full quarter of the world during her reign, and even here in Russia the only ruler other than Tsar Peter to be termed "the Great" had been a woman. All these things were true and yet during my time they wanted to confine me to acting as a consort who entertained the nobility and produced sons. A bad tsar, Tsar Paul I, the ungrateful son of Catherine, had made it law that no woman could be a ruler in Russia, but that had been over a hundred years ago, and times had to change. My own son, who was far from ungrateful towards me, might even see fit to reinstate the possibility of women becoming reigning empresses in the future. After all, women are often so much more courageous and wiser than men.

In this mood, I sent for Count Fredericks and told him to let the ministers know that henceforth they were to make their reports to me and that I would begin to see them once weekly. After giving that order I felt so well that I was able to dress in my nurse's uniform and go off to visit my hospital at the big palace.

I had recently begun to allow Maria and Anastasia to go and visit the hospital as well as soon as their lessons were over. They were obviously far too young for nursing, but they would play chink-a-checkers with the soldiers, help some to compose letters home, and perform sundry other small tasks for them. They both enjoyed such excursions a great deal and adorably referred to the men as "our soldiers." However, on this occasion it was Olga whom I asked to accompany me there to give her the opportunity of an outing and a chance to see her sister Tatiana bravely going about her nursing duties, but she claimed she had a headache and closed her eyes as though our brief conversation had been too much for her.

All of the children, with the exception of Tati, had taken Nicky's departure for Stavka very hard, but Olga had taken it worst of all, for she had always been in very thick with her father and was accustomed to eating breakfast with him every morning when he was home. For the little girls, their time with Nicky was between luncheon and their afternoon lessons, when he would take them, and Baby if he was well enough, for long hikes with his collies, so this was the time they missed him the most.

At the beginning of the war Nicky had been gone a great deal, visiting Headquarters and traveling to inspect various regiments, but this past summer, when all had fallen against us, he had remained at Tsarskoe Selo, so the children now had to learn all over again to do without him.

Naturally, I missed him keenly as well, but I wrote to him at least once daily, and then, of course, between governing the country, nursing and motherhood, I was falling into bed and asleep nearly before my head hit the pillow, and up like a rooster at the crack of dawn, raring to go again, the next day.

Nicky decided to salvage Grand Duke Nicholas's pride by sending him out to the Caucuses to command the army operating against the Turks. I did not much care for so implacable an enemy of mine to have a command at all, but at least this one kept him busy far away from Petersburg or Moscow, and for now that would have to be good enough. Later, when I had things managed properly, I would have Nicky strip him from the army altogether.

The ministers were a great trial to me and I began to have some sympathy for what my husband had been forced to endure all these long years.

"Come, gentlemen," I would chide them, "bring me answers not more problems," but seemingly they were not designed to do so and at this time the Duma was beginning to agitate badly as well.

The patriotism of members of the Duma had vanished as quickly as it had come, and now they wanted to control the government entirely by wresting it away from Nicky and me in this our darkest time of war. If I had had my way, they would all have been sent to the front, while Father Grigory recommended that I shut the Duma down and call for new elections, which would render them powerless for at least a year, but only Nicky could command this to be done and I did not like to ask him to appear to rescue me so early on in my regency.

The Duma wanted to be able to choose "a leader who had the people's confidence." What was that but an absolute blow against the Autocracy? Then there were the *Zemstvos*, the small, so-called local governors in villages across Russia. They were clamoring to be given a say in food distribution and for an end to the taxation of crops as there were no men available to bring in the harvest.

These lofty peasants, whom Nicky had told the truth to at the beginning of our reign when he called their aspirations to be heard in government nothing but "senseless dreams," were now nurturing a renewed hope of greater power built on the losses of our armies and the growing discontent across the country, but I wouldn't have it. Nicky's weakness and his sweet nature had allowed a certain deterioration in the respect the people had for the crown, but I would regain it. I did not say any of this to him, of course, at least not then. I wrote to him of homely things, our children and our dogs instead.

I also sent him valuable items to keep him safe: A bell that dear Msgr. Philippe had once given me that would ring of its own accord if liars were nearby; a stuffed fish on a branch that Father Grigory had blessed; a broken comb that had belonged to Father Grigory, who assured me that if Nicky were ever confused, he should use the comb and clarity would return to him. All this I did, although I did miss my bell, for I too was surrounded by liars, but as Father Grigory reminded me, I had the innate ability to see things and people so clearly that Nicky was much more in need of such an object than I was.

As I viewed things now, my first and most important duty was to make a show of stability. This was particularly important given the states of mind of Nicky's timorous ministers and the mutinous members of the Duma. Both these parties wished for Nicky to dismiss Goremykin, our present Prime Minister. It was true that he was very old and constantly begging to be allowed to retire, and indeed that he had been retired several times, but in the end we kept coming back to this dear old fellow, for he was truly devoted to Nicky and me, and was always kind towards Father Grigory, who assured me that any lapses he had in memory or ability were more than made up for in a loyalty that was scarce on the ground nowadays.

The whispering campaign against me had reached so far that I had begun to notice a change even at my hospitals. Those first wounded men who had begged for me to come to their sides and hold their hands in order for them to be more brave during their surgeries were, of course, long departed, either to heaven or back to the front. This newest crop of torn, bleeding men did not ask for me, rather they would turn their heads away and I even heard some mutter, *"Nemka"* as I passed amongst them. Not that I blamed these poor soldiers as I knew all this to be the handiwork of my enemy Grand Duke Nicholas, who had obviously poisoned the minds of our soldiers before being sent away, and I knew that in time this misguided anger would leave them, but it did wound me.

The exhausting days passed quickly with all I had to do, and I scored a small victory when Nicky bowed to my wishes and agreed to retain poor Goremykin and even to order the closure of the Duma, but what he asked for in return was a higher price than I had ever dreamed of paying, for he demanded that Baby join him at Headquarters.

All his reasons were good on the surface. He told me, near tears, how his own papa had never included him in any sort of responsibility and it had made him shy and uncertain of himself, and unprepared to be Tsar when the time came. This was true and we had all suffered for it, but my little boy ... I had never been separated from him and what if there were an accident ...?

"... and what if there isn't?" Father Grigory asked. "Aloyushka has been well for nearly a year now, Mama," he said, spreading his hands and smiling up at Anya's ceiling, having arrived within the hour after my urgent summons. "I will always be with him in prayer, and maybe I shall visit Headquarters to bless the troops too. Then I can be of help if an accident does befall him. Has Papa said anything about bringing me to Headquarters?"

I blushed and looked away. I had asked Nicky, but he had said that between the allied generals and the soldiers, he feared what sort of reaction such a visit might bring.

So, moving the conversation back to Alexei, I asked anxiously, "But you have told me that if he lives to seventeen, he will be Tsar."

"Yes, exactly." He clapped his hands together in delight. "If he lives to manhood, he will live a long life and reign over his people, and as long as I am alive and am able to help, the child will see that birthday. Since I am here," he comically patted at his own chest, "so too will he be. And so then, you see, Mama, if there is a small bump on a train or whatever might befall a happy boy, I shall attend to it. You must let him go and not worry about him."

"Yes, of course, Father Grigory, and I am not sure I could stop him going now anyway, for Nicky has already told Baby about it and he is so excited. But you are sure that he will be safe?"

He shrugged. "As safe as God's love can make him, which is all any of us can hope for or expect." I started to speak, but he continued softly, "God, it seems, does not hear the prayers of the peasant as often as that of the boyar."

I did not like him saying things like that, so I quickly changed the subject to ask him what he thought of Polivanov, our new Minister for War.

"He is not a good man, Mama. I went to see him and he called me a woman's name and ordered me out of his office."

"*A woman's name,* Father Grigory? What name did he call you?" Anya asked suddenly, having sat silently listening to our conversation without interrupting or wriggling for an unusually extended period of time.

"He called me 'Charlotte.' Much has been said about poor Father Grigory, but no one has yet called me a woman. He is a bad man and must go if Russia is to find God's favor and win the war against our enemies."

At this, he and Anya piously crossed themselves and I left moments later, anxious to see Nicky who was briefly back from the front, to share the joke with him.

"Oh, he probably called him a charlatan. Poor old Grishka!" chuckled Nicky, wiping tears of laughter from his eyes.

I laughed just as hard as he did and then became more serious in my tone.

"But really, Nicky, Polavonov is such a fool and he will have to go, will he not?"

Nicky stared at me, shocked.

"No, certainly not, never ... or at least not until we have victory. He's marvelous, darling, and our supplies have improved nearly miraculously."

"He is Our Friend's enemy, Nicky, and so can only bring us trouble. His post is far too important to be held by someone as dangerous to us and our armies as he is."

"Sunny, that is simply untrue. You know that Father Grigory has strange fancies. In fact, I would much rather that we not discuss military and government matters with him." Before I could protest angrily at this, he lit a cigarette and went on. "I know I laughed at what Polivanov said, darling, but not everything that is said is amusing. There are so many rumors about Father Grigory consorting with German spies, and what is said of him sticks to us, you see. I cannot punish all Father Grigory's enemies as I did poor Bishop Hermogen –"

At this, I gasped out, "He spoke out against Our Friend!"

"... And I banished him to the frozen wastes of Tobolsk for it, as you asked that I should ... as you demanded that I should ... and don't you see that it all makes a liar out of me, Sunny?"

Through gritted teeth, I managed, "How so?"

Nicky stood up agitatedly, accidentally knocking his ashtray to the floor, and for a moment I regretted this scene. We had been laughing happily together and now he would be leaving for the front in the morning and taking Baby away with him. How could I send him off with this memory? Oh, but he was so wrong, so tragically, stubbornly, blindly wrong.

"I tell them, I tell my ministers, I tell my generals – for do not think they do not speak of him either, Sunny – I tell my mama in letters, that anything to do with Father Grigory is a private family matter not to be discussed by others, that they are not to mention him and not to interfere in our family life. But they are right, aren't they? Through you, he interferes in every aspect of public life, and I cannot say no to my wife, and everybody knows it, and sometimes they laugh at me, Sunny, but mostly they are simply angry at us, Sunny, and disgusted."

"I want Polivanov removed, Nicky!" I insisted.

He looked at me aghast.

"After everything I have just said to you, that is your reaction, to move forward even harder with Grishka's recommendations, or your own, for I am beginning to find the line between those two points ever more of a blur, Alix?"

I merely inclined my head.

"I shall search carefully for a new minister, Nicky, and write to you when I have identified the right man. You should get some sleep now. The train leaves at six tomorrow morning and I assure you that Baby will give you no peace on the trip as you have so excited him about going."

"My God, Sunny, would you really have me replace our very competent minister because you are angry at me for taking Alexei to Headquarters? Is that what this is about?"

I shook my head and smiled sadly at him.

"Nicky, you sound as deranged as people say that I am. Don't be ridiculous! I simply understand, as you do not, that God has placed you where you sit, and that He has sent us Father Grigory, whose prayers for you arise day and night and are heard by God. This makes you the one true ruler in this mad world of war and shame, and if we forsake him, if we allow those who do not believe in him to retain their places, then we shall lose ours. I know this as you do not yet, despite the overwhelming evidence, therefore I trust solely to my own decisions. It will all be for the best, as you shall see."

Nicky left the next morning without saying goodbye and took my sunshine with him. By that evening, of course, I had received a loving letter from him and sent one in return. Nicky and I were always filled with passion when apart, I cannot say why.

I took his letter and went to Baby's room, and knelt by his empty bed and recited the same prayer I said nightly with him, a child's prayer.

Now I lay me down to sleep,
I pray the Lord my soul to keep.
If I should die before I wake,
I pray the Lord my soul to take.

Then I kissed his empty pillow and went off to my own lonely bed and hoped I was right.

It is the best any of us can ask.

Chapter 29

I replaced Polivanov with a minister named Shuvayev, whom Father Grigory had recommended. Everyone seemed to hate him, including Nicky, but I saw that he remained, and then, at Christmastime, Nicky brought Baby back to me on a stretcher, nearly bloodless, nearly dead.

Nicky had been careless and let Baby do as he pleased – run around barefoot, play all day, and not rest enough – so my agoo wee one caught a cold, then began to sneeze, then to bleed, and by the time he arrived at Tsarskoe Selo, he was moments from death. Thank the Lord that Father Grigory was by my side when Baby arrived home to fall to his knees at his stretcher. Then, as if it were but a simple thing, the blood stopped flowing and my dearest treasure lived to see his Christmas tree a few days later.

The following year, 1916, was a long and terrible year for me, for Nicky, and for the armies fighting Germany. We could not win our battles against the Germans, but nor could we seem to retreat or die fast enough to lose against them either. Fear of some separate peace that we might make with Germany ran through all our allies, but Nicky held firm that we would never surrender or make a separate peace with Germany because he deeply loved our allies, and Russia.

This love prevailed despite the fact that the French and English papers wrote about our repressive government and while they tried to court America into joining the war, which America refused to do as they did not wish to ally themselves with "a brutal autocratic regime." I often thought during that dreadful year that we needed to live up a bit more to what we were accused of, and wondered, with dark humor, what the international papers would print if they knew the truth, for we were not so much brutal as paralyzed, and that didn't seem very autocratic at all.

To my great sorrow, I found I was having to agree with Nicky that our dear old Prime Minister Goremykin might have to retire again after all. The poor old thing could barely keep to his feet, and his letters to Nicky begging to be allowed to go home and die in peace were piteous in the extreme.

It was then that Father Grigory introduced me to his good friend Boris Stürmer and said that a vision had come to him assuring us of victory should he be our next Prime Minister. There was nothing for it really. We needed a loyal and decisive man, and God, through the auspices of Father Grigory, had brought us one. I engineered a meeting between him and Nicky during one of Nicky's visits home and it was done.

The outcry from the Duma, which had been reinstated by Nicky, was fierce and he was loudly denounced as a German spy, amongst other ignominious things. Then even my own choice for Interior Minister, Kvhostov, resigned, saying he could not work with such a creature as Stürmer, so in a fury I talked Nicky into appointing Stürmer as Minister of the Interior as well as Prime Minister.

This was when the Duma passed from covert treachery to open treason.

A radical deputy named Milyukov, whose family stretched back centuries, stood up in front of all the other Duma members and the hundreds of idiot strikers who, having nothing better to do than to spend their days at the Tauride Palace listening to rabble-rousing, gave them all their money's worth. For that was the day that Milyukov coined the phrase "ministerial leapfrog," referring to the unavoidable changes in key positions of the Government that Nicky and I had made in this terrible time of war. He then pounded the bench he was sitting on and screamed out, "Is this stupidity or is it treason?"

His words were repeated throughout Russia within hours. Even horrid Minnie, skulking in Kiev where she had retired after demanding that Nicky choose between her and Father Grigory, heard them and bestirred herself to catch an express train to Nicky at Headquarters and demanded that he replace Stürmer. I was at the time frantically telegraphing Nicky, demanding that he have this filthy dissenter Milyukov either hanged or sent to the front, and pointing out that Milyukov himself had said it best when he had said, "Is it stupidity or is it treason?" while the one deserved hanging and the other made him worthy of becoming cannon fodder, but Nicky was too busy with all his other visitors to respond to me.

At this point, the traitorous foreign ambassadors, the English Sir George Buchanan and the slimy Frenchman Maurice Paléologue, added their unsolicited advice and met with Nicky to tell him that, in their informed opinions, the internal situation in Russia was so bad, so dangerous, that unless he allowed the Duma more power, more voice in appointing ministers, we were looking at a possible revolution to rival that of 1905. They also advised him, although I did not know that they had done so until too late, that he should move the troops living in the barracks in Petrograd and Moscow to the front.

It seems there were some one hundred and sixty thousand of them living in reserve in those two cities, daily exposed to propaganda of the worst sort, and there had been rumors that they were fraternizing with the strikers, of which there were many thousands more, all of Petrograd and Moscow seemingly having gone on strike to protest heaven knows what.

Then Nicky went behind my back and asked for Stürmer's resignation while I was on my own train heading for Headquarters to join Nicky's other importuners.

Minnie left when she heard I was on my way, and so, there alone with Nicky, I spent four days making him listen to me until he backed away from his cowardly plan.

That trip was rather eye-opening for me as it was my first visit to Headquarters without the children. The children and I had gone there periodically and it had been rather a treat for them. For Tatiana, it was a chance to rest from her nursing duties; for Olga, it was a chance to see Nicky; and for Maria and Anastasia it was a welcome change of pace from the classroom. As Anastasia put it, it got them "out of boring, horrible old Tsarskoe Selo, where nothing ever happens or ever will." For Baby it was a chance to put on his uniform and proudly show me and his sisters his place in this greatest of all adventures.

So, when I had come before, the girls and I had stayed on the train, and Baby had slept with Nicky at the Commander's House as usual. Because of this, I really only saw Nicky at dinner, and there we were joined by General Alexeev, who was the general in charge of all the armies under Nicky.

I suppose I assumed Nicky took meetings all day when we were not there and ordered troops about – or well, who knows what men in charge of armies do? – but whatever that was, I had assumed he did it busily. What I didn't anticipate, when I visited him alone, was the opportunity of having four uninterrupted days alone with him to discuss why we needed to keep a united front and maintain things as they were. I thought I would only get pockets of his time.

After all, when he came home to Tsarskoe Selo, he always looked so exhausted that oftentimes he was too unwell to see officials. It was a shock then to find out that his entire time was taken up by an enormous domino game in his study and by his swinging upside down on the hanging bar in his train. These activities were broken up by long walks and drives in the afternoon. So, the truth was that he was basically hiding up at Headquarters without a single pull on his time. He actually had the nerve to stare resentfully around me and glance at his watch to ensure that I was aware I was keeping him from these pleasant pursuits, going so far as to tell me, "When Mama came to see me, I still took my daily drive. She accompanied me on them."

And from the moment I arrived, he obviously could not wait for me to go, but he was stubborn and remained firm that Stürmer was "causing discontent in every area. I cannot keep him, Sunny, and that is final."

"If we show weakness now, Nicky, it is all up with us. I insist that you silence that idiot Milyukov with a noose. And then there is a lawyer in the Duma named Kerensky who lives for nothing more than to cause us daily trouble, and he is firing up the masses against Father Grigory. Make him be quiet at the end of the hangman's knot as well. Don't you remember 'Stolypin's necktie'? Sometimes such things are necessary."

"You bring up Peter Arkadyevich Stolypin to me, Sunny, the man you hated, the man you worked against, the man many say you and Father Grigory ordered assassinated? It is a rumor I do not believe, but I know you were glad when he was killed. This is the man you resurrect to argue your case?"

His voice had risen with every word and he was trembling with rage. I could only look at him curiously. He was so animated.

Before I could respond, he opened his desk and pulled out a pile of greasy, cheap newspapers and thrust them at me. Without thinking, I took them up, looked at them, and wished I hadn't. They comprised pictures of hand-drawn caricatures, filthy, unmentionable depictions of Father Grigory and me. I did not bother to read the captions underneath, nor did I cry or scream. Instead I balled them up and threw them at his head.

He flinched.

"So, Nicky, this is what you spend your time reading?" Before he could answer, I shook my head. "No, don't bother. I write to you, I am sure Stürmer keeps in excellent contact with you, Father Grigory sends you telegrams you do not bother to answer, but this is what you read? God help us! No wonder we are in such a state of crisis in Russia."

"Alix, do you believe these cruel things you are saying to me? Do you think I do not read and listen to everyone who addresses me? But I am crushed by this. Whichever way I turn, it falls against me. And then to see my own wife daily maligned in the papers and for me to be called a cuckold by the common man on top of everything else ... They talk of you and Rasputin," he nearly spat on saying Father Grigory's name, "in the army, all the way out here."

He finished by placing his face between his hands.

I moved from his desk, where I had been sitting, in what I suppose could have been mistaken for a threatening manner, and stood idly by before flicking my finger at his elaborate domino set-up. The dominoes made such a clatter as they fell that I was momentarily sorry I had done it, but the way he jumped up and ran over to his fallen toys caused a savage delight in me.

"You see, Nicky, it all falls down if you are not keeping a close watch on it. I do watch. I have trousers on under my skirts and eyes in the back of my head to see it all."

Thereby, I won a pathetic victory, for he was not armed for war, with me or with anyone else.

Shortly after that Father Grigory brought me assurances that, despite all appearances, Russia would win the war, but he said that he too was concerned about the internal situation.

"An empty stomach makes for an angry head, Mama," he said.

I wrote that down and sent it to Nicky at Headquarters, along with the name of the truly admirable man whom Father Grigory had recently introduced me to, Mr. Protopopov. Father Grigory had brought this small, well-dressed man to meet me at the palace, and at first I had been quite hesitant as he was a member of the Duma, which I despised, but Father Grigory had been so persistent and finally, as always, had been so right.

When Mr. Protopopov appeared before me, he did not bow, but instead fell to his knees, fixed his gaze on something beyond my shoulder, and frantically crossed himself.

"Your Majesty, I see Christ behind you," he said.

How could I see him other than as a man of true vision after that?

I told Nicky all of this, but he was still sulking about his spilled dominoes and only said, "Oh yes?"

This infuriated me anew and I let him know, in no uncertain terms, that I had arranged for Mr. Protopopov to go to Headquarters in two days' time.

His reaction was … well, nothing. At times like this I tried to convince myself he was born to be Tsar because he was opaque and unknowable; at other times I secretly agreed with those who said that he was merely empty inside.

In either case, their meeting went well and Mr. Protopopov was duly appointed Minister of the Interior. The Duma, who the day before had loved this kind man, now hated him with a ferocity only matched by their hatred of Stürmer, and me.

Chapter 30

There was not so much time left with him. I wish I had known. If I had, I would have never let a day pass without hearing his dear voice, without listening to his sacred words, but I was not blessed, or cursed – depending on how one sees it – with the ability to see into the future.

Nicky stayed away almost constantly; and, at intervals, and if he was well enough, I gave into Baby's begging and let him go join his papa at Headquarters, although not once the cold weather came. He resented me terribly for this, but I was not going to give nature another chance to make him sneeze if I could help it.

Meanwhile Nicky and I resumed writing the sorts of daily letters to each other that would have done young lovers proud, and it is true that, when we were separated, we were mad for each other, and I think this caused us more pain when, during either his brief visits home or during mine to Headquarters, we could barely find two words to say to each other unless we were arguing.

Sometimes at night ... well, there we found each other again, the old Nicky and the old Alicky, lovers, friends, and all was as it was, but it would vanish into awkwardness with the dawn.

In that November, Nicky fired Stürmer, my friend and confidant, as Prime Minister without telling me, and I telegrammed him frantically that I could not remain standing if he insisted on knocking the props I leaned upon out from under me.

He only answered that "any other course was impossible."

I bestirred myself to find out what I had done to bring what I could only view as my husband's treachery down upon me, and the results nearly broke my mind. They certainly broke my heart.

It was Anya who obtained a copy of Kerensky's speech denouncing Stürmer as a cowardly German traitor who was guided solely by self-interest and that "contemptible Grishka Rasputin." Poor Stürmer was then forced to walk out of the assembly amid boos and hisses, and then Xenia's disloyal and disgusting husband, Sandro, who fancied himself a man of the people for all that he ate off gold plate, wrote a series of telegrams to Nicky, signed by himself and his stupid brother George, another raving socialist grand duke, demanding that Stürmer be fired.

So, instead of Nicky hanging Kerensky and sending Sandro and George where they could do no further harm, he bowed his head and hurled that fine man Stürmer into the abyss, leaving him broken, and Father Grigory and me apoplectic.

Or rather *I* was apoplectic; Father Grigory was, I think, rather more frightened, and sent Nicky a letter at the end of that month from Pokrovskoe, where he had gone to pray for Nicky to become wiser and not to turn away from God. Nicky forwarded it to me by post, commenting only that, "Poor Father Grigory seems depressed and we should consider sending him to Livadia for a rest, maybe until after the end of the war."

Has ever one man been so blind?

Here is what Father Grigory had written, a last, desperate *cri de coeur* to his emperor:

I feel that I shall leave this life before January 1st.

I wish to make known to the Russian people to Papa, to the Russian Mother and to the children, what they must understand.

If I am killed by the common assassins, and especially by my brothers, the Russian peasants, you, Tsar of Russia, will have nothing to fear for your children, they will reign for hundreds of years. But if I am murdered by boyars, nobles, and if they shed my blood, their hands will remain soiled with my blood for twenty-five years and they will leave Russia.

Brothers will kill brothers, and they will kill each other and hate each other, and for twenty-five years there will be no peace in the country. The Tsar of the land of Russia, if you hear the sound of the bell which will tell you that Grigory has been killed, you must know this.

If it was your relations who have wrought my death, then none of your children will remain alive for more than two years. And

*if they do, they will beg for death as they
will see the defeat of Russia.*

*See the Antichrist coming, plague, poverty,
destroyed churches and desecrated
sanctuaries where everyone is dead. The
Russian Tsar, you will be killed by the
Russian people and the people will be
cursed and will serve as the devil's
weapon killing each other everywhere.*

*Three times for twenty-five years, they will
destroy the Russian people and the
Orthodox faith and the Russian land will
die. I shall be killed. I am no longer among
the living. Pray, pray, be strong and think
of your blessed family.*

"Why this is very good, isn't it, and it's typed, too,"
said Anya with great vacuity when I sat sobbing and
shaking after allowing her to read it.

"What?"

"Oh, I know, it's just horrible, but you see here, it's
typed. He must have had Maria do it up for him. She's at
the Smolny Institute, you know."

"Anya, did you see? I mean, did you read what he
said?"

"Do you think we will ever sail on The Standart
again?" she asked, confusing me. But before I could
even attempt an answer to this, she continued wistfully,
"Do you remember how we always played cat and

mouse, and I always won, and how the officers would get so excited when I fell upon them?"

I stared at her and then realized that what she really was was terrified, and my old protective instincts swept over me. Anya was a big baby. So, instead of forcing her to speak of Father Grigory's prophecy, I smiled sadly and nodded.

"Yes, Anya, you were a great sport!"

She nodded back eagerly and leaned forward, adjusting her crutches, for as in all things, Father Grigory was right: the accident had left her a cripple.

I understood all too well her desire to look back to our sunlit happy days on The Standart, and the game she was referring to had created so many hours of hilarity. We would sit in chairs on the deck. Well, I would be on my chaise, of course. And then two people would be blindfolded, and one would be the cat and the other the mouse, and the cat would try to catch the mouse, while both ran about wildly, shrieking and knocking into people, the officers adoring it as much as the children.

Usually Anya was the cat, and she tended to end up prone on some poor officer, or in some cases Nicky, having knocked them from their chair. Naturally, we could not allow Baby to play, so he would sit excitedly out of range on my lap and be allowed to give out the small prizes we awarded to the winners.

Thinking back on it, I could almost smell the water, hear the laughter, and feel the sun. But no, that was in the past, and maybe again in the future, although not if we lost Father Grigory, for I instantly believed every doom-laden word of his letter. I found I could forgive

311

Anya for not wanting to think or speak of it, but Nicky, no, that I could not understand.

Our new Prime Minister was Alexander Trepov, a man I knew virtually nothing about. It was just his turn, I suppose, as our old friend Goremykin had begged and begged us not to reappoint him. "Your Majesties, it would be wrong. Let me be the first to tell you that I am not capable of the great office you ask me to fill. At my age and given my health, I would no longer be of use to you in peace time, let alone in such a critical time in our country's history. Please, I beg you, do not ask this of me." Then he tried to bow, and the poor old thing fell flat with a piteous groan, and Nicky had to help him up to a chair until he could shakily stand again. I could barely look at him.

I could also barely look at Nicky, but, in truth, what other choice did we have, or what better choice did *I* have after Nicky took Stürmer away. The hideous truth was that, at that moment in Russia, there was no one I could trust in the Duma or in our own ministry except for that poor old man … well, he and my dear Protopopov … all the rest, every single one of them, wanted to see Father Grigory and me either dead or sent off to the madhouse.

I did suggest to Nicky that we appoint Protopopov as Prime Minister as well as Minister of the Interior, but even I had to agree that the consequences of that might be dangerous. Poor Protopopov was so very hated because of his friendship with Father Grigory and because I approved of him.

So a nonentity called Trepov it was.

Because of all this nonsense, food distribution had slipped even further back, and in addition to this, coal wasn't coming through either, and so half the factories were shuttered and that poured more angry and discontented people onto the streets.

Nicky at first tended to blame poor Protopopov, as did everyone else, for our worsening state, that fat idiot Rodzianko even going so far as to tell Nicky that Protopopov suffered from syphilis and that it had made him deranged.

As I pointed out to Nicky, "It's funny that Rodzianko never noticed either of these things while Protopopov was his deputy at the Duma. But the moment he begins to serve us, oh what a failed, demented creature he is!"

Nicky had agreed.

"It is true, darling. Any friend of ours is an enemy to all. Despite that, I am not certain that he is competent, and neither his former position under Rodzianko, who is an idiot, or even his friendship with Father Grigory, leads me to be certain of his abilities."

Before I could protest at this, Nicky shook his head.

"No, you know it is true, darling. Our Friend can have very strange ideas about people."

"God probably does sound rather strange to any of us when he speaks," I replied.

Oh, I did believe in him though, or at least I believed completely that without him our boy would die. And Alexei, with his beauty and strong will, was the answer for Russia. Unlike Nicky, I could see a time beyond our present situation.

I will admit that, if you considered only the situation as it was, it was grim due to a combination of anarchist propaganda, the strikes of people in Petrograd and Moscow, the state of our rolling iron that was in such poor case that half of it lay helpless and stranded in snows along unrepaired tracks, and the hardship of getting crops in with only old men and little boys left to harvest them and get produce to towns, while the rest of the wheat and corn rotted in the fields.

This made the people angry and they wrote letters to their kin at the front, telling them all about it, which led to many desertions. If a little family had been forced from their burned village and had taken to the road as refugees, as millions now had, their fathers, and husbands, and children inevitably felt the need to desert from the army and come to look for them. Desertions were running in the tens of thousands, and when the deserting soldiers arrived in the towns, they mingled with the strikers and read, or had read to them, the pamphlets passed around by disgruntled agitators who were now organized into so-called Soviets.

Many factories that were not on strike were still closed owing to a lack of fuel and supplies, and those who were laid off joined the teeming multitudes. Bread lines were growing longer and longer, and while I knew all of this was temporary, they obviously did not.

In all this, Father Grigory's was a soothing voice, reminding me, "Russia has always had her troubles and God has always saved her from them."

It seemed that no one else in Russia could remember that the country had faced all this before, and panic ran unchecked in every class and on every street corner in the country.

Father Grigory constantly urged Nicky and me to be brave and to ignore the chaos, and in my case I did, for, as always, I saw the glorious reign of my son shining out before me as Father Grigory had prophesied, although our situation still made my damaged heart nearly burst out of my chest with the never-ending worry of it all.

But Nicky and I were once again divided. He was so crushed by our losses in battle and the parlous state of a nearly unarmed and starving army that he could barely bring himself to address the internal strife at all, and in truth did not do so. As long as he was at Headquarters, he could somehow manage to ignore every report he received, and I think Father Grigory's letter was to him simply one more unpleasant thing that was best not thought of, while I knew it was the only thing worth thinking of, because, if Father Grigory was killed, so would we be too, and then what did anything matter?

I gave strict orders to Goremykin to increase our police protection, and I asked Father Grigory not to leave Petersburg – now renamed 'Petrograd' to make it sound more Russian – and I prayed for Father Grigory's well-being with the sort of fervor I had only previously used with regard to Baby, but then wasn't it all the same thing in the end?

As it turned out, I shouldn't even have bothered, for when Father Grigory's death came, it came from our family, as he had said it would, because he always knew everything.

Chapter 31

Dmitri, our nephew – the boy we had practically raised as our own – and Felix – the husband of Nicky's adored niece, Irinia – helped by two accomplices from the monstrous Duma, slaughtered Father Grigory like a pig in the basement of one of Felix's palaces. Then they threw his sacred body into a hole in the ice of the frozen Neva as though he was of no account at all.

He was found because one of his boots, an item that immediately became a sacred relic to me, was found on the ice, and his lifeless body was dragged out with his hand still making the sign of the cross even as he was being welcomed into the eternity of heaven.

After this, I had no more hope for the future. All must be as it would be. And Nicky was of no comfort to me at all.

I had cabled him as soon as I was told that Father Grigory had not come home from an appointment with Felix the previous night, and by the time Nicky had arrived home from Headquarters, it was all up: they had found his body and I had ordered the immediate arrest of Dmitri and Felix, and of Shulgin from the Duma. Yet none of my orders had been carried out as I was informed that "only His Majesty can order the arrest of his relatives."

As for Shulgin, I was told that the police would not touch him for fear for their own lives, so popular was he.

I had Father Grigory's body brought to us and we buried him at a little church Anya had constructed in the park at Tsarskoe Selo. The only attendants at this sad

317

ceremony were Nicky and I, the children and Anya. Father Grigory's wife and children were unable to attend as travel from the village of Pokrovskoe was not possible during the winter. Besides, they had been very ungrateful over my desire to bury him near us. His daughter, Maria, wrote to us and asked if it was not possible for his body to be stored until arrangements could be made to "bring Father home," but I needed him near me and had Count Fredericks reply that this was not possible.

It was mercilessly cold, and by early afternoon it was already growing dark. My legs were not working and my health was in shreds. Anya was crippled and Olga was ill, and so they rode with me in the sledge to the church.

Our confessor, Father Yanishev, presided over the rites, but he did so with little emotion. What he did display was nervousness as though wishing to be anywhere but near my dearest fallen one.

I did what I could for the comfort of those of us who remained. I ordered necklaces for each of the children and Anya, as well as for Nicky and me, miniatures of Father Grigory, his hands raised to heaven, which had been his posture when he had been dragged up onto the ice from the Neva, and I exhorted them to wear them at all times, but under their collars, as my lost friend was as hated dead as he had been in life.

In fact, even as I was placing a note across his chest, begging for his prayers for those of us left behind on this sad earth, celebrations for Dmitri, Felix and the other filthy swine who had killed him were taking place all over Russia.

"He is dead!" strangers would cry out to each other in joyful greeting, and exchange smiles and hugs. "We are free from Grishka and his evil reign!" This they said at the death of my only help and solace, and I understood that the assassins had in the eyes of people of all classes struck at me through the slaughter of Father Grigory.

Nicky did not immediately return to Headquarters, saying he wished to rest at home for Christmas and the New Year, even though I had no intention of celebrating Christmas that year, so grief-stricken was I over our recent tragedy. Nor could I grant him any kind of peace until he had finally signed arrest warrants for Felix and Dmitri. In the end, all he did was send Dmitri to Persia and Felix to his estates. Even this punishment, if one could call it that, proved too much for Nicky's family, and they wrote to him *en masse,* demanding that these young murderers be freed. They did not go so far as to demand medals for them, but even that was implied.

However, for all of Nicky's compromises between family and justice, not to mention the rule of law, no one ended up being pleased at all. I could barely look at him, and his mother, sisters, uncles and cousins were enraged by his decisions. Not that this mattered to Nicky, maybe nothing did any longer. Nor did he join me for New Year's Day when Protopopov and I summoned the spirit of Father Grigory. And, as the coldest January in a decade froze Russia further in its tracks, he neither returned to Headquarters nor met with his ministers.

Driven by idle curiosity one day, I had Maria push me very quietly in my wheeling chair to the balcony overlooking his study and there I found him seated by a great map that was spread out on a table, moving small flags about it, his face sunken and sallow.

It was the first time I had truly noticed how badly he had aged over just these last few weeks at home, and my heart turned over with pity, and then hardened again, for he was hiding somewhere deep down inside himself, buried in self-pity and obstinacy, living at a depth where no one could reach him or make him hear, and I was exhausted from trying to do so.

I therefore signaled Maria with a raised finger to my lips to push me back to my boudoir as silently as I had come.

Chapter 32

It was quiet for me at Tsarskoe Selo during the month of January 1917. Yes, ministers came, but no longer to see me. After all, the Tsar was in residence, so they went to him agitated, sometimes panicky, and they all left the same way, stoop-shouldered and gray of face.

"What do they want of you, Nicky?" I asked without real interest one night when he had chosen to eat with me off trays in our bedroom.

I was by that time so sick with heart pain, leg pains, and facial neuralgia that I had not been able even to dress myself and go to my boudoir for a week.

It was not just I who felt lethargic, either – the whole palace had sunk into such deep gloom since the slaughter of our savior, Father Gregory, that on the very few occasions in which I had seen any of the children, they had appeared greenish with fear.

Yet Tati still went faithfully to her nursing duties each day, and Maria and Anastasia, when not at their studies, were off visiting wounded officers and playing card games with them. In truth, I suppose, it was just my oldest and Baby who were the most changed by his death and by what it had wrought in Nicky and me.

Olga, who had always breakfasted alone with Nicky whenever he was home from the front, no longer bothered to do so, and examining him over my untouched plate, I could see why. His eyes were so sunken and pouched with black rings that he looked quite gruesome, and his hands shook so badly that could barely hold a cigarette, let alone a fork, not that he really ate anymore.

He was as choked by defeat as I was by loss, and by fear, I think. He was afraid generally by then, but of what specifically he did not say, and now in answering me, he merely mumbled into his tobacco-stained beard.

"The ministers want so many things, Sunny. Who can begin to hear all of it? And the armies too ..."

He trailed off.

"What do the armies want?"

I tried to speak gently to him, but he heard the boredom and impatience in my voice, and smiled faintly at me, shaking his head.

"I think from your expression, Sunny, I should rather ask you what you want."

He put a hand over his eyes and rubbed them heavily.

What did I want from this sad, broken man? I wanted him to end the war. I wanted him to have saved the poor Rumanians who had entered the war at our urging and were immediately slaughtered by the Germans. My cousin Missy was now Queen of Rumania, and her desperate letters for help had torn out my heart. I wanted him not to have begun the war in the first place, when any fool could now see that we had never had a chance of winning it.

I didn't say any of this. Instead I answered almost idly, "I wish you had not gone to war with Japan. Do you remember any of the things Count Witte warned you against at the time? That there were no railways to move around supplies and that there would be a terrible anger in the country if we lost. And we did lose and there was so much anger, but not like now of course." I waved my hand about. "Then the people were not starving, now they are, and now their anger seems to be much more frightening. Do you ever think about 1904 and all that happened afterwards, Nicky?" Before he could answer, I laughed sadly. "Count Witte gave you much the same advice at the start of this war, too."

Nicky dropped his hands and sat up straight. It was the first time I had seen him do that in weeks. I steeled myself for his anger, while knowing at the same time I preferred even that to his defeated stare.

"Count Witte, my father's beloved minister ... I never liked him, you know. He never liked me either. I was rather pleased when he died. He was spending all his time arguing for a peace with Germany."

"Father Grigory liked him very much. They met before he died and Father Grigory said that he was a wise man and one with whom one could converse quite plainly."

Even as I said this I knew I was stoking Nicky's fire, but I did not care much about that. Nicky's fire needed stoking.

Baby's disappointed little face hung in my thoughts.

"Is Papa going back to the war soon? Will he take me again? Why doesn't he talk to me or come to see me. Why is everybody so sad, Mama?'

Nicky's voice brought me back to the present.

"Witte would have hanged Rasputin by now, Alix, if he had still been my Prime Minister. Would you have liked him so much then? Why did you choose to fling his name into my face while I am drowning? Why did you bring him up now?"

I shrugged, wishing he would go, and my head was aching so badly that, without answering Nicky, I picked up my bell and rang for Maria.

"Alix, what are you doing?" he asked.

"My head, Nicky. The pain is becoming unbearable. I need Botkin."

"But we were talking."

"No, we weren't, not really. There seems so little to say and I am tired. You look terrible as well. We'll continue later."

I closed my eyes, Maria entered the room, and I heard Nicky ask her to fetch Botkin. I waited for the sounds of his footsteps which would signal he was leaving, but they didn't come. Then I heard Dr. Botkin's soft tap, followed by his voice.

"Your Majesty, is there anything I can do for you?" He fell silent, obviously surprised by the sight of Nicky sitting in the shadows of the room. "Your Majesty, forgive me. I did not see you there at first. I have been sent for."

"It is fine, Botkin. Her Majesty has need of you, don't you, darling?"

I heard, if Botkin did not, the distaste in Nicky's voice as I opened my eyes and moaned weakly, gesturing to my head.

"Ah, so the head is bad again tonight? Let me give you a shot to help you with the pain."

At his sympathetic tone and the promise of relief, I opened my eyes and let tears of self-pity spill down my cheeks, but, to my dismay, Nicky remained where he was, standing a few steps from our bed and watching dispassionately as Botkin gently swabbed my arm and injected me with the blessed relief of morphia.

Dr. Botkin was puzzled by his behavior as well, feeling obliged to say, "She should sleep now, Your Majesty," but Nicky still had no intention of leaving me.

Instead he said, "Thank you for your help, Botkin. You may go. I will stay with Her Majesty until she falls asleep."

Dr. Botkin bowed and backed away while the Abyssinians held the door open for him. Then he was gone and we were alone together again. However, as the drugs had entered my system by now, I was feeling calm and the pain in my head was receding, but I did not understand why he was still lingering behind in order to watch me. So often in the past he had been filled with sympathy and concern at such moments, but this was not the case now. Rather, he was eyeing me as if examining an insect under a microscope.

I could not take it any longer. I wanted him to go and leave me in peace, to leave me to sleep, which was the only peace I got these days.

"Nicky, what is it? Do you want something or do you want to tell me something? I must sleep. My head is hurting so much."

I clutched at the sides of my face and grimaced pitifully.

He merely nodded and then said nonsensically, "I received a letter from Sandro."

I gaped at him.

"And this is important enough for you to keep me awake when I am in agony?"

I could feel the hysteria building up inside me again.

"He has asked that he be allowed to visit us."

The sweet morphia tide was taking me and my thoughts were fragmenting. Sandro … I did not like Sandro … this was a house in mourning …why would he want to come here?

I did not care. I yearned for the tender release of sleep.

I held up my numbing hand and waved it in the air. "Yes, fine, I don't care. Do what you like."

"Good," he said, and he was gone.

It wasn't until the next morning that I wondered if I had dreamt the whole odd thing, so I sent for Count Fredericks.

"Your Majesty?"

"Yes, Fredericks, I was wondering, do you know if there are any plans to receive Alexander Mikhailovich shortly?"

I saw Count Fredericks wince at my use of Sandro's common name without the addition of his title. I occasionally liked to poke at him to let him know that I knew he no longer liked me.

He nodded stiffly.

"On His Majesty's orders we have been told to expect him for luncheon today, Your Majesty."

"*Today?* Oh no, that cannot be. Why, I was only informed about his desire to visit us last night. Is he not in the Crimea? How will he get here?"

"I believe His Highness has been visiting his younger brother and staying in the capital, Your Majesty. Would there be anything else?"

His studied civility grated on me, but I needed to stop this, so I merely said, "No, nothing else, except that you will please inform His Majesty that I wish to see him immediately."

He had already reached the door. He bowed.

"I will send someone out to look for him, Your Majesty, but he is out walking his dogs in the park and I believe the Grand Duke is with him. Shall I ask that they attend upon you?"

As he spoke he made an elaborate rigmarole of inspecting the gold pocket watch he carried and then at my bed.

I sighed.

"What time is it, Count Fredericks?"

"Just past eleven, Your Majesty. Will you be joining His Majesty and the Grand Duke for luncheon? If so, I shall make the necessary arrangements."

"No, of course I shan't. I am not well. And I do not want you to send for His Majesty after all. Merely give him word at luncheon that I am indisposed and will not be able to see the Grand Duke today. Please offer my regrets."

As soon as he had left I nervously rang for Maria, and when she arrived I gave out a quick spate of orders.

"Maria, send for the maids. I will need my hair put up. Also, I want the sheets changed immediately. Oh and the Alençon lace trimming, please. I will take a bath too and then put on a fresh nightdress and wrap, also with the Alençon lace. And do have the room aired. It is unbearably stuffy in here. And tea ... no coffee, immediately, please, Maria. We must get a move on!"

A few moments later I was in my bath, reflecting irritably on the nature of servants and how, if one issued more than one simple, slowly spoken order at a time, they fell apart completely. I would be fortunate to find even one task completed when I returned to my room.

My heart was pounding so ferociously I could see it through the wet linen gown I wore to bathe in. It would serve Nicky right if I died at this instant, for I feared Sandro's visit. He had not been to Tsarskoe Selo in years and our relationship had been reduced to a ghostly mockery of what had once been affection.

Sandro had signed the letter asking Nicky to pardon Felix and Dmitri, and I knew he was glad that Father Grigory was dead. I knew also that he hated me, as did everyone else in Nicky's family. I would never agree to see him. The simple knowledge that he was so close was enough to set me on edge. Why would Nicky have agreed to see him, now of all times? What could Sandro possibly have to say to him that would be of any help to us?

Chapter 33

Nicky had obviously made up his mind to force this meeting on me, no matter what my feelings were on the matter or the pitiable condition that I was in, because, within minutes of me sliding back into bed, I heard them both, and my children, enter my mauve boudoir next door. Nicky was clearly intending to make this as awkward for me as possible.

Worse, from their voices I could tell that they had all been having a jolly time without me. How dear of them to insist on joining me anyway, whether I wished them to do so or not, indeed when they knew full well that I did not wish to be included in their frivolities.

I made fists of my hands and prayed for the calmness and courage I would need to face all this, for face it I clearly was going to have to do. Still, I was curious: whatever Sandro wished to say to me, Nicky must already know about, and, knowing about it, he evidently was insisting that I hear it directly from Sandro's lips rather than relaying it to me later when he knew I would get angry with him all over again. That was why I was being ambushed in this brazenly underhand manner.

I heard Baby laughing adorably at something Sandro had said to him. It had been so long since any laughter had been heard here that for a moment I almost loved Sandro again, charming Uncle Sandro, the handsomest of all Nicky's tall and handsome cousins, the once-adored husband of Xenia, and the playmate of Nicky and me in our younger years.

Then, as if it had been ordained by God Himself, I heard Father Grigory's voice in my head, whispering at me from all the icons in the room at once, and a breeze ruffled my hair and coursed through my sleeves, although the windows themselves were sealed against the icy air outside.

"Mama, face him. Face the father of my killer."

I shuddered and made the sign of the cross. Sandro was not Felix's father, but his father-in-law. What did he mean?

"He knew what they were planning to do. He approved my murder. Face him, Mama!"

Yes, Father Grigory was with me, as I knew he always was. Then, a moment later, Nicky entered the bedroom with a hangdog expression and said, "Darling Sunny, how are you feeling today?"

I shook off his inquiry and held up my chin proudly.

"You had better bring in Sandro, had you not, Nicky? Let us start this nonsense the sooner to get it over with."

"Dearest, Sandro merely wants to see you and to speak of a few things that are on his mind."

Then, before I could repeat my order to let him in, there he was, tall, handsome Sandro, the aviation hero, slipping gracefully around Nicky to arrive at my side and kiss the hand I reluctantly held out for him. Such breeding these Romanovs had!

Nicky followed him and perched on the side of the bed, his hand reaching out to stroke my leg through the bedcovers. I shuddered and pulled away from him, which brought me ever closer to Sandro, who settled into the chair beside me.

Rejected, Nicky shrugged, lit a cigarette, and stared at the floor as Sandro prepared himself to launch into what was so clearly going to be an unconscionable harangue.

Before beginning, however, he addressed Nicky.

"Nicky, in my letters, as you know, I asked to speak to Alix alone ..."

"You wrote to Nicky, not me, about seeing *me*, Sandro?" I queried icily.

He looked taken aback and again addressed Nicky.

"You read my last letter and approved my coming, but I wrote to Alix. I don't understand."

Nicky refused to look at either of us.

"Why would you not give me Sandro's letter?" I asked him, "and why would you arrange for Sandro to be here so precipitously today?"

Nicky turned towards Sandro. "Alix was far too upset to answer letters. She was in deep mourning. She hasn't been well." Then he turned towards me. "Sunny, I thought we should hear Sandro out, but of course Sandro cannot see you alone in your current state of dress.

"Nicky!" both Sandro and I exclaimed simultaneously and we exchanged a look of complicity in our mutual affront. We both knew I was about to be verbally assaulted but I wasn't expecting to be physically raped by him.

Nicky shrugged and mumbled, "Well, at any rate, here we are. Let us get on with it."

He then lit another cigarette and resumed his contemplation of the rug.

Sandro then did a strange thing – he pointed at the icons behind me, the ones I had just heard Father

Grigory speak from, and said, "Alix, I would like to talk to you as if I were your Father confessor, as if I were one whom you might listen to."

I was so taken aback by this that I could only reply, "And if that fairytale were true, which is unimaginable given your private life, Sandro, what would you say to me, oh worldliest of priests?"

He gave me his charming laugh.

"Oh, Alix, I thought you of all people believed that the more a man sins, the closer he is to God."

"Don't you dare compare yourself to him," I roared at him.

Sandro held up his hands.

"Let there be peace between us, Alix. I didn't come here to argue with you but to advise you, and maybe to save Russia, so in that way maybe I am like a priest."

I sighed and glanced at Nicky, but he kept his concentration firmly on his feet, wreathed as he was in billows of smoke.

"All right, Father Sandro, tell me your holy thoughts …" I encouraged him with an edge to my voice.

"I thank you, Alix. I will. I believe or hope that you are aware that, at this moment, every class of Russian is against your husband's policies, which they see as being your policies. Revolutionary propaganda, once read only by the fringe elements of society, is now being taken seriously by tens of thousands in Petersburg, Moscow and the Urals. It has leaked into the armies and is taken for truth by all."

I bridled at this foul calumny.

"Sandro, nothing you say is true. The nation is still completely loyal to Nicky." I pointed at Nicky, but he

332

did not even look up, and that made me blush. Sandro looked at me with a level of sympathy that shamed me. I went on heatedly. I did not even hate him – I just wanted him to see the truth, the real truth. "You cannot understand, Sandro. It is only the treacherous Duma and those drunken cowards who make up Petersburg society who are our enemies."

"Alix, you are partially right," he conceded, which surprised me, but then he went on, "because there is nothing more dangerous than a half-truth." He looked me straight in the eye. "The nation is loyal to its Tsar, but it is likewise indignant over the influence that has been exercised over him by that man Rasputin. Nobody knows better than I your love and devotion for Nicky, and yet I must confess that your interference in the affairs of state is causing harm both to Nicky's prestige and to the popular conception of a sovereign."

"No, Sandro, none of this is true," I said.

"But it is true," he countered, slamming his fist into his palm so that Nicky flinched, but he did not try to stop Sandro's punishing words.

"Everything I'm saying to you is true, Alix. My God, please listen to me! I have been your faithful friend for twenty-four years. I am still your faithful friend. And as a friend, I am pointing out to you that all classes of the population are opposed to your policies. You have a beautiful family. Why can't you confine yourself to them? Please, Alix, leave the cares of state to your husband."

I looked at Nicky, who did not react at all, just continued smoking.

Seeing that Nicky had no intention of intervening between us, Sandro felt emboldened to continue his treasonous rant.

"Alix, I have always been opposed to any form of parliamentary rule in Russia. I'm a Romanov." He smiled and eyed me hopefully to see if I would return his smile. I didn't. "But now, Alix, now at this ever so dangerous time in our history, I believe that the only way to let out the steam from what is happening all around us is to grant to the Duma a form of government acceptable to it. That would lift the weight of responsibility off Nicky's shoulders, because otherwise they will kill him." We both looked to Nicky for his thoughts on this, but he just shrugged and turned away. Sandro continued in a pleading tone. "Please, Alix, do not let your thirst to avenge your priest dominate your thoughts. A radical change of policies at this moment would remove the heat from the nation's wrath. Do not let that wrath grow and grow until it explodes over all of us."

I laughed in his face.

"All this talk of yours is ridiculous, Sandro. Nicky is an autocrat. How could he share his divine right of tsarism with a parliament?"

Sandro regarded me earnestly.

"You are very much mistaken, Alix. Your husband ceased to be an autocrat on October 17, 1905. That was the moment to address the issue of his divine right to rule. It is too late now. Perhaps in two months there will be nothing left of this country of ours to remind us that we ever had autocrats sitting here in the first place."

"You sound like the revolutionary filth you warn me against, Sandro. You are just as stupid and gullible as they are."

The loudness of my denunciation of him took Sandro aback, but that did not stop him biting back at me with a reddened face that indicated that he was barely keeping control of himself.

"Remember, Alix, I remained silent for thirty months! For thirty months I never said as much as a word to you about the disgraceful goings-on in our government, or rather *your* government! I realize that you are willing to perish and that your husband feels the same way, but what about us? Must we all suffer for your blind folly? No, Alix, you have no right to drag us, your family, down a precipice with you! You are so incredibly selfish and such a fool!"

I fell back against my pillows and stared at him in horror, waiting in vain for Nicky to speak out and silence him. When he didn't, I drew on my every reserve to reply to him with thunder in my voice.

"I refuse to continue this dispute," I said. "This is ridiculous! Utter nonsense! Someday, when you have regained control of yourself and returned to your senses, you will admit that I have known better than you all along."

At that, he stood up without a word, clicked his heels smartly, and headed for the doors with crisp steps as the Abyssinians obligingly opened them for him.

I suppose half the palace had heard us, and in the dead silence of our room I listened to his footsteps clacking along the hallway.

I was never to see him again. I did not know that then, but if I had I would have been glad of it.

I fell back against my pillows again and stared blankly at Nicky.

"He is quite mad, isn't he?" I said. "Poor Xenia!"

Nicky only shrugged again and then said in a voice I had never heard him use before, a gravelly, deadened voice, "I don't think he is mad, Sunny. Have you ever heard a prophecy that was made in 1905?"

"Nicky, I am not in the mood for this. I am exhausted."

"Marvelous writer," he continued, "although at the time I nearly had him exiled to Siberia. A man by the name of Merezhkovsky. Look, I keep what he said right here and I read it often. It is good too, I think. I want to read it to you now, Alix."

"No, Nicky, I have heard enough today. I feel half-mad from all this as it is."

I raised my hand as though to push away any more words being thrust at me.

"No, no, I shall read it now," Nicky insisted, "and then you can sleep, if you can sleep. I find sleep so elusive these days." I lay back and closed my eyes, trying to ignore him, wishing the spirit of Father Grigory would return and thinking reluctantly about his prophecy that God would have helped us all if he had still been alive.

Nicky began to read.

" 'In the House of the Romanovs, as in house of the Atrides ...' That is from 'The Iliad,' you know. The Atrides were a royal family whose patriarch committed such atrocities that God cursed his descendants ever after. I see where this fellow found a parallel." I shrugged, feigning a lack of interest I did not feel and hiding the sense of horror I was feeling so keenly. "Yes, it is quite interesting and apt, I think," he continued, "so he wrote, 'In the house of the Atrides, a mysterious curse descends from generation to generation. Murders and adultery, blood and mud. The filthy act of a tragedy played in a brothel. Peter kills his son; Alexander the First kills his father; Catherine kills her husband. And beside these great and famous victims, there are the countless mean, unknown and unhappy abortions.' " I flinched at the language and Nicky smiled sadly at me. "Yes, the words are strong, painful to read."

"Painful to hear, too. Please, Nicky ..."

"No!" he shouted at me suddenly. "No, it won't just be me who has to hear and read and think of every awful thing all the time. What Sandro said is true. I am crushed by my responsibilities and it is you, Alix, who force me never to stop, never, ever, no peace, never! You are always making me hear your voice, your opinions, forcing me to listen to what you want to say, Alix, and what Grishka wanted me to hear when he lived, which was the same thing, wasn't it?"

His rage was greater than I had ever seen it. This was as bad, or worse even, than having to listen to Sandro. I was surrounded by madmen and hysterics.

"All right, Nicky, finish your little story, and then I think you had better take your leave of me so that I can rest. My heart is number three and I do not think that killing me like this will put an end to either your or Russia's problems, much as your family might believe otherwise."

337

"Sunny, I do not want you dead. I do not want you away from me. I still love you. Everything I do is for you."

"Not now, Nicky. Please, if you do love me, as you say, let us not speak of it now. Read me your prophecy, if you insist."

His face hardened, and he cleared his throat.

" 'The block, the rope, the poison, these are the true emblems of Russian autocracy. God's unction is on the brows of the tsars and has become the brand and curse of Cain.' That is all there is, Alix."

"Oh what a shame, Nicky! I could have listened to him all day! In fact, if you could have read it out to me until dinnertime, we could have finished up the evening drinking hemlock together in perfect amity."

Nicky's head jerked up in surprise at my sarcasm.

I shrugged, irritated beyond measure by now.

"Well, your little reading did mention poison. I was just trying to stick to the spirit of the thing. Now, if we have indulged our maudlin natures sufficiently for one afternoon, could you please send Dr. Botkin to me?"

"For your neuralgia, Alix? Or is it for your legs?" Nicky was actually snarling at me. "No, probably not. It is a Monday after all, so, according to the schedule, I imagine it must be your heart today. Ah yes, you did tell me it was three. Tell me, darling, was it Sandro or my reading that got it up there? Either way, I shall summon Dr. Botkin at once."

Everything went still in my head, except then I heard it, the faint ringing of a bell. I gasped.

"Nicky, can you hear it? It is Msgr. Philippe's bell …"

338

"Alix, that ridiculous thing is still at headquarters. You just heard one of the maids ringing for a footman to take away the dishes from next door. Good God!" Nicky then picked up the small bell on the bedside table and rang for Maria, who arrived within a few seconds. "Good afternoon, Maria," he said equably. "If you would be so kind as to fetch Dr. Botkin, it seems Her Majesty has taken one of her regular turns for the worse and needs help right away."

Maria betrayed no emotion at his request, curtsied, and left the room hurriedly. I couldn't say I blamed her.

"Nicky, the reason I wanted to see Dr. Botkin was to ask him if either Olga or Baby were showing any signs of the measles. If you will recall, it was your idea that they should share a room last week, and your idea as well that Baby could have those young cadets come to see him, one of whom was coughing terribly and has now gone down with the measles, I am told."

Nicky looked at me confused, clearly having forgotten, in his resentment of me, last week's small domestic dramas when Olga had succumbed to an ear infection and poor Baby had hurt his ankle and suffered from it greatly. He had been confined to his bed, growing increasingly bored and miserable.

Whereupon Nicky had emerged from his fog of depression long enough to take note of all this, and had decided that both Olga and Baby would be cheered by sharing a sick room together. So, Olga, who did not like this idea one bit, had been moved into Baby's playroom to complain vociferously that she was being forced to act as a nursemaid to Baby while ill herself, and Baby had complained that Olga "was an old stick." Nicky then ordered that some young cadets be brought to the palace to play gently with Baby and keep him occupied. He did not bother asking me about this, and I only found out about it when Anya was visiting me and mentioned seeing them as she had passed the playroom on her way to me.

Surprised, I had sent for Derevenko, Baby's sailor-nurse, who told me that he had not liked this arrangement as one of the boys was coughing badly, and in any case they had been far too boisterous for Baby in his condition.

I then consulted with Dr. Botkin, who advised moving Olga away from Baby in case of infection, so I had her put on the couch in the Red Room to convalesce, only to learn that silly Anya had visited her two days in a row to keep her company, a situation I found ironic as neither of them could stand each other. Then, the previous day, Tatiana came to me in distress to report that Anya's nurse had sent her an urgent note stating that Anya was showing signs of measles.

Frantic with fear for Baby, I had sent for Dr. Botkin and asked him to phone the cadets' sergeant and ask if there was an outbreak amongst the young boys there, and, "That, Nicky, is why I must see Botkin immediately," I finished angrily.

"Oh, I see. Measles, well it is too bad, but something best got over with. Perhaps they all should be allowed to catch it."

Dr. Botkin appeared.

"Your Majesties?"

Nicky stood up and clapped him across the shoulder, smiling.

I was puzzled. This news about the measles, which I considered to be quite calamitous, seemed to have quite cheered Nicky up.

"Her Majesty tells me," he said, "that we may have an outbreak of the measles in the palace. Is that so, Botkin? Have you heard any news of the cadets?"

Botkin bowed.

"I have, Your Majesty, and it seems that our worst fears are confirmed. They do indeed have the measles. Also, I have examined Madame Vyroubova and she has them too."

I groaned, regretting, not for the first time, my decision to have Anya move into the palace in the wake of Father Grigory's murder for fear that she would be the next to be struck down by assassins. Thinking, therefore, only of her safety, I had moved her into an unused suite and she had been a constant plague and nuisance to me ever since. Previously, Anya, who had always demanded as much of my time and company as possible, had at least been obliged to go home to sleep, and she was not an early riser. Now she liked to drop in on me at every moment, no matter the time. The sound of her crutches creaking down the hallway towards my door had begun to make me cringe.

Now she had the measles!

I sighed loudly as though I was the one stricken by them and Dr. Botkin nodded wisely.

"Yes, I fear she will be a difficult patient. Of course, it depends on the severity of the case. The effects of the measles can differ considerably."

Nicky decided he had heard enough of the good doctor's opinions and now wished to insert his own.

"What I think, Yevgeny Sergeyevitch, is that it would be better to let all the children catch it at once, then it will be behind them, and doubtless afterwards you will advise a change of scene for them so that the palace can be cleansed properly. Livadia would be the healthiest choice, do you not think?"

Poor Dr. Botkin looked all at sea, blushing, scratching his head, and glancing at me for support, but I turned away from him to study an icon.

"Your Majesty, yes, of course Livadia has an excellent climate for such a convalescence. It would be an inspired choice for them. But the disease of measles itself can present many dangers, and, as I was saying, its effects differ from person to person. The Tsarevich, for example, risks bleeding because the measles are often accompanied by terrible bouts of coughing."

I stopped him, having heard enough.

"Nicky, your idea is possibly too fraught with risk, so I think we should begin by moving the three girls who have not been fully exposed to the measles –"

Nicky was shaking his head almost as vigorously as Dr. Botkin was nodding in agreement, and rudely interrupted me by saying decisively, "No, my mind is quite made up on this already. We shall allow the measles to take their natural course. You, Botkin, will oversee their care and, if necessary, bring in all the other physicians you need should any complications develop, which I feel sure they will not, and afterwards we shall all decamp to Livadia so that they can all recuperate in the sun."

He sighed with pleasure at the very idea of it and all a pale Botkin could do was to bow to this reckless edict.

Chapter 34

Two days after Nicky's decision, both Olga and Baby were complaining of headaches and had developed very bad coughs. Dr. Botkin, wanting to please Nicky, I suppose, murmured that as far as he could tell, it wasn't the measles at all, simply a late winter ague.

Because Nicky had said no to any sort of quarantine, their sisters were still allowed to visit my two sick ones in Baby's playroom where they languished, and why not? It wasn't measles anyway, according to the ever-fearful Dr. Botkin, who, I was beginning to see, was more a measured mouthpiece than any sort of real doctor.

Dr. Botkin at least continued to acknowledge that Anya, who was far away in her new suite in the west wing, did have measles, and she was truly the most miserable of patients, driving her poor nurse to distraction and whining for my company.

Despite my continuing heart and neuralgia pain, I was therefore forced out of bed and into my old nursing dress to rush between the playroom of my sick children and Anya's room, and barely had a moment to catch my breath. I had asked that Dr. Federov be brought to the palace from town, and he was attending to all three of my invalids, and it wasn't until Maria had chased me away from Anya's bedside, insisting that I stop for some tea and food, that I heard that several panicked ministers had been to the palace that morning for an audience with Nicky, and that Michael, Nicky's brother, was even now closeted with him in his study.

I summoned Count Fredericks immediately.

"I have been informed that Michael is here. Is that true?" I asked.

Fredericks inclined his ancient head.

"Yes, Your Majesty. I believe his Imperial Highness is with His Majesty as we speak. Would there be anything else?"

I wanted to stretch out my hands and ask him why Michael was here as he knew everything that took place in our family, but I merely informed him that would be all, and, standing hurriedly, I looked into my cheval glass and pinched my cheeks for color.

I looked a ghastly shade of white, with pouches under my eyes and streaks of gray in my hair which had not been washed for lack of time. Michael would think that I looked old and ill, he would tell this to his mother, and people would … Oh, never mind, what did it matter anymore?

I left my boudoir on shaky legs and rode the elevator down to Nicky's study, motioning the Abyssinians to open the doors for me.

Nicky was alone, sitting at his desk, smoking. He looked up at me without interest.

"Hello, darling. How are the children and Anya?"

"Oh, they are as they are. Nicky, Maria told me that Michael was here and Fredericks just confirmed it too. Has he gone to visit the children?"

Nicky shook his head and smiled lightly.

"I wouldn't think so. I believe he is on his way back to town to consult with his dear friends in the Duma." He nodded as if to himself. "Yes, I am quite sure that is where my brother has gone. He wanted me to go with him, you know."

I sat down in the chair in front of him, my legs too weak to last a moment longer, finding it hard to breathe.

Nicky looked so awful. His skin was yellow and drawn tight across his bones, and he seemed to have lost more weight since I had last seen him that very morning, so I couldn't look at him when I asked, "Why did he want you to go to the Duma, dearest?"

Nicky fiddled with a small frame on his desk.

"He wants me to establish a constitutional monarchy. There are so many troubles and he said much of what Sandro did, but even Sandro did not suggest I become a constitutional monarch. No, it took my brother, the son of a Tsar, to bring this to me. He also said that he has heard that the armies are on the verge of mutiny. Well, why not?" He gave a mirthless laugh. "All of Petersburg is, after all."

I could barely get out my question through my suddenly frozen lips, whispering, "What did you say to him, Nicky?"

"Oh, I told him that I would have to die and be reborn again to be able to do such a thing. What would Papa have said, I wonder?"

Reassured, I said fervently, "Of course you could never break your coronation oath, and we cannot toss away Baby's inheritance just like that. As for the scuffles in town, it is just a hooligan element, Nicky, young boys and girls running about shouting for bread. I am concerned about what Michael said regarding the armies, though. He sounds hysterical but I wonder if there may be something to what he says."

345

Nicky stood up abruptly.

"I am going to leave for Stavka in the morning, Sunny. I cannot think here in this poisoned air. I have ordered the Duma to be closed down until the end of the war. They only seem to make things worse. I do not know if anything that Michael tells me is true. He seems half-mad to me, but I must show myself to my armies."

He glanced at me over his shoulder, framing the snow against the windows behind him.

"Sunny, what is wrong?"

My hand was at my throat and I must have looked as shocked as I felt.

"Nicky, you cannot go now. The children are sick and you have to stay and make the ministers and the police calm down. You were utterly right to close down the Duma but you cannot go anywhere at all right now."

"Look here," he said, "you are already downstairs and I have invited Dr. Federov to join us for lunch. The girls will be so happy to see you. It will be just us and dear old Fredericks, not even his wife, I think. He told me the poor woman was quite ill. So do come in with me, darling. Don't worry about your gown. I have always thought you looked so wonderfully simple in your nurse's dress, so much like Tati, and hardly a day older. It reminds me of that little gray dress you wore at Darmstadt when we were first engaged."

He smiled sweetly at me and held out his arm. I heard a distant bell. 'Oh God, I thought, it's Msgr. Philippe's bell of warning, I can hear it all the way here.'

Nicky heard it too, I could tell, for he nodded firmly, "Ah, there is the luncheon bell. Are you coming, darling?"

Numbly I took his arm and allowed him to lead me away, all the while thinking, 'He's quite mad now. Quite hopelessly mad.'

Chapter 35

That luncheon was to be our last as a reigning imperial family, although I did not know that at the time. What I was aware of was that I felt terribly alarmed, and wondered if Nicky should be sent away for a cure, but I did not see beyond that, for that day, as far as I could see, we were as secure as the family had ever been during three hundred years of Romanov rule.

Those three hundred years had never been untroubled. There had been wars, and uprisings, and assassinations all along the way. Russia comprised one-sixth of the earth's surface and was sparsely populated by a people who could seldom agree on anything at any given time, and what had always ended a period of uncertainty was that a tsar made a bold and forceful move born of unflinching courage.

On the other hand, Nicky's grandfather had faced a time of great troubles too when the *moujiks* finally rose up against serfdom and burned their way across the land, and so he had granted them their freedom and a right to own the land they had cultivated for centuries. How could that have been anything but right and wise? But the Russian people, a people so strange and unknowable that after over twenty years in their midst they still remained objects of confusion to me, did not like this concession and perceived his generosity as that thing that was most dreaded in a tsar, weakness, and so they raged on and clamored for even more, and then they murdered him.

In 1905, my own poor little hubby had been given two choices as the country boiled around us: a limited constitution or a military dictatorship. He caved in and gave the people what they thought they wanted, and then, like frenzied sharks in the water, they smelled the blood of a tsar who was frightened by them and a revolution broke out. Stolypin, my enemy, reacted to this by hanging and shooting thousands of people, and restored peace.

From all of this recent history I concluded one thing: it was weakness and hesitation that brought tsars down and decisive action that won the day.

Yet here sat Nicky, pale with fear despite being the head of the vast Russian armies, listening to anyone with the right of admittance and quaking before them as they all but ordered him to sign a full constitution, this when he could simply order them to be hanged or imprisoned for daring to voice opposition to him. Yet, with Nicky, anyone could voice anything and he would do nothing but smoke, and stare, and agree with them, and then reverse his opinion when they had gone so that nothing ever happened in the end.

Nicky's voice brought me back to the present. He was telling Tatiana about his plans to leave for Stavka.

After glancing at me, Tatiana looked disturbed.

"Do you really have to go, Papa? Mama hasn't been well, and with Alexei and Olga ill, and Anya too, I wonder if you shouldn't stay."

Anastasia interrupted her impatiently. "Papa, take me with you and old Mashka too. M. Gilliard is driving us mad at lessons and all our officers keep getting better and sent back to the front. We are crazy bored and I am so sick of sitting around reading to Olga and Baby. Anyway, Olga is horrible. All she ever says is, 'Oh read to me, Nastinka.' " She imitated Olga's rather whining voice, and we all laughed guiltily. "And then, when I do, she corrects me on my pronunciation. Alexei is no better because all he wants to do is play soldiers and I am far too old for that. I would rather go with you Papa and meet some real soldiers at the front."

Maria looked like she wanted to speak too, but Anastasia elbowed her into silence, whereupon Nicky raised an eyebrow and asked Maria, "What is it, my little Mashka? You look worried."

Maria glanced at me before replying. "Papa, what if Anya's measles mean that we all get them? I want so badly to go with you too, but wouldn't we give the poor soldiers at Stavka measles if we came with you?"

"Oh do shut up, Mashka," hissed Anastasia.

I shot her an admonishing look and she quietened down, glaring instead down at her soup plate.

Nicky smiled at her but addressed Dr. Federov instead of answering her.

"Dr. Federov, should it prove to be measles after all, do you not you agree that a convalescence in Livadia would be efficacious for all of them?"

Dr. Federov smiled back at Nicky and nodded his head.

"A stay in Livadia is good for anyone, Your Majesty."

Nicky's spirits rose.

"Let us hope that we all may one day see the beautiful Crimea again."

To which Dr. Federov added, "And let us pray that your young ones are not stricken by this devastating illness."

At that, Tatiana gave a little moan and put her hand to her face. We all looked at her. I said her name. Then, as her sweet head turned, she slid from her chair onto the floor.

Dr. Federov and Nicky were quickly at her side, Dr. Federov, placing his hand against her forehead and looking across her at Nicky.

"She's burning up, Your Majesty," he said.

As Count Fredericks called for assistance, I tried to stand to go to my girl, but found I was shaking too hard to do so.

I said, "Count Fredericks, order them to put her in the playroom with the other sick children. Dr. Federov, should we send Maria and Anastasia away? Would that keep them from falling ill?"

He shook his head, his attention on Tatiana.

"I cannot say, Your Majesty. There has been a great deal of exposure. I believe it is the measles."

He was interrupted by Nicky saying brusquely, "Well, as I have already told Botkin, I believe it is best to let this thing run its course and afterwards we will all go to Livadia." Then, refusing to meet my furious glare, he spoke reassuringly to Maria and Anastasia. "That will be nice, won't it, girls, going off to the Crimea?"

"Girls, go back to your classroom," I said, trying to stop them from answering him. "M. Gilliard and Mr. Gibbes will be wondering where you are."

"But, Mama, we don't have lessons in the afternoon now," Maria protested plaintively. "We go to visit the soldiers."

Dr. Federov shook his head warningly, so I said to Maria and a strangely quiet Anastasia, "Then go to your rooms and read. You will not visit the soldiers today."

Maria's eyes filled with tears but she stayed quiet and rose obediently behind her little sister. They waited until Dr. Federov had followed the footman carrying Tatiana, and then they and Count Fredericks both departed, leaving Nicky and me alone

He moved over to the window.

"Still snowing, I see. Well, I am sure it will clear by morning. I do not see it continuing overnight. My train should be able to leave on time."

"You are still going, then?" I asked incredulously.

He nodded without looking at me.

"Yes, I won't be gone long, just long enough to set things straight, then I will be back and we can all go to Livadia."

"Of course, Nicky," I said, rising shakily.

He turned at the sound of my scraping chair and moved towards me and I raised my hand to halt him.

"No, I shall see myself up. After all, I shall be seeing to everything else in your absence, shall I not? Oh, and Nicky," he looked at me hopefully, "could you sleep in your dressing room tonight? I imagine I shall have a late night with so many of the children sick now, and Anya too. I do not wish to be awoken that early in the morning. I wish you a safe trip and I shall write to you about the children."

I gave him my cold cheek to kiss and weakly made my way to the elevator.

As it happened, I was awake when he left, and I watched his small, lonely figure from the playroom window where I had spent a sleepless night. I saw him walk to the car, accompanied by Prince Dolgoruky, as he paused for a moment and looked up to the window where I stood, raising his hand to me.

I placed my palm against the cold glass, and he nodded and then vanished inside the car, which drove off into the swirl of snow.

I laid my hot cheek against the window and prayed for strength. All three of the sick children had passed a very troubled night, with high temperatures, terrible coughing, and head pains. Mercifully, they were all asleep now, although I knew Anya wouldn't be as I had just seen Dr. Botkin who told me she was "wide awake and bewailing."

I could not force my exhausted body to travel over to her side of the palace and so I remained where I was, eventually sinking into a chair and staring into the black, snowy morning.

It might have been hours later, or minutes, when Count Fredericks found me.

"Your Majesty, the Minister of the Interior, Mr. Protopopov is on the telephone for you. Shall I have the extension brought up or would you prefer to come downstairs? I have taken the liberty of ordering your morning tea as well. I only await your direction as to where to have it served."

I looked up at him, confused.

353

"Protopopov?"

"Yes, Your Majesty."

I rose so hesitantly that the ancient Count Fredericks took my arm and I looked at him gratefully and whispered, "We must be very quiet. I shall come downstairs and have my tea there. I shall take the call in … Where should I take the call, Count Fredericks?"

His old eyes softened.

"His Majesty's study might be the most comfortable for you, Your Majesty. I shall order a fire to be lit. You are shivering, Your Majesty."

His unexpected kindness brought easy tears, which I swiped away lest I embarrass him.

"Oh no, it is boiling in here. Dr. Botkin ordered that everyone be kept very warm. I am just very tired, I think."

Count Fredericks nodded and began to guide me out. At the elevator, he turned to leave me, but I gestured for him to join me.

"Neither of us are getting any younger, Count Fredericks."

He laughed to be polite, I think, and joined me in the elevator, which made a horrible, screeching, overburdened sound as it descended, shuddering mightily upon arrival downstairs.

As I turned towards Nicky's study, I said over my shoulder, "Count Fredericks, please order an engineer immediately to see to the elevator. I have no desire to fall to my death in that cage."

He said something but it was lost in the moment, and immediately I was speaking to a very agitated Minister of the Interior.

"Oh, Your Majesty, thank the Lord I have a chance to talk to you. We have very bad trouble in the capital and Count Fredericks told me His Majesty has left for Headquarters. I am greatly concerned about not being able to get in touch with him. The rioters are crossing into the heart of the city along the ice on the Neva, and the police are becoming overwhelmed by their sheer numbers."

"Please, Minister, calm down and explain what you mean by their crossing the ice. From where?"

"From the Vyborg district, Your Majesty."

"Where is the Vyborg district?" I asked.

"It is the factory district, Your Majesty. Bridges divide it from the rest of the city. The police have blocked the bridges but now they are coming along the ice."

"What is it they want, Minister?"

"They say they have no bread, so they want bread, but what am I to do about that?"

I squeezed my eyes shut and prayed for patience. Surely he was not so hopeless. Father Grigory had told me Mr. Protopopov was the only man who could save Russia. I had believed him and had Mr. Protopopov appointed to this key position to ensure the internal security of the country. I had fought Nicky tooth and nail to keep him. Now this!

"That is the very thing, Minister. You are the person responsible for doing something about this, and quickly. In the meantime, order some of the soldiers to block the rioters on the ice."

"The soldiers are not obeying our orders, Your Majesty. They won't come out of their barracks and I've received word that some of the Cossack regiments refuse to fire on civilians. I think His Majesty had better return right away to St. Petersburg before we have all-out anarchy in the capital."

"His Majesty is on a train in the middle of Russia, Minister. Can't you ask those idiots in the Duma what to do? I shall send a telegram to His Majesty. He will respond, I am certain, as soon as he receives it."

"*The Duma*, Your Majesty? May I remind you that His Majesty has dismissed the Duma?"

I drove my fingernails into my palms, which was becoming a common practice of mine. 'Nicky, how could you be gone now?' I thought desperately but only said, "When His Majesty is unavailable for whatever reason, you are the Head of the Government and I expect you to end these disorders at once."

His voice was shaking when he answered after so long a pause that I thought he had hung up on me.

"I am afraid that solution may lie well beyond my powers, Your Majesty."

'Oh, if only Nicky were here and not on the train,' I thought, but that was where Nicky was, on a train, and there he remained during the last week of the Empire, as our children sickened and nearly died, and as our autocratic power ended, as the only world we knew burned to ashes around us

Nicky was not here; he was on the train.

Chapter 36

Nicky first traveled to Stavka at Mogilev, Army Headquarters. Then, as soon as he arrived there, he received a telegram from poor Protopopov that assured him that, although there was much rioting in the capital, he had the situation well in hand. Apparently he knew enough to realize that when dealing with Nicky it was best not to worry him. However, within the hour, he also received one from Mikhail Rodzianko, the President of the disbanded Duma, which was very much more alarming, but Nicky was not unduly concerned as he had already been reassured by Protopopov's much more congenial report.

"Great, fat idiot!" he said of Rodzianko. "I dissolved the Duma so that I would not have to hear from him again. The man is a disgrace!"

Nicky had indeed ordered the closing of the Duma immediately before leaving Tsarskoe Selo, but given their sense of self-importance as the only possible saviors of Russia, its members had merely moved across the hall from one set of chambers to the next and carried on their proceedings there.

In Nicky's view, therefore, any communication from Rodzianko was of no consequence, however consequential the content of his telegram might have appeared:

> *Most humbly I report to Your Majesty that the popular disturbances which have begun in Petrograd are assuming a serious*

character and threatening proportions. The causes are a shortage of baked bread and an insufficient supply of flour, which is giving rise to panic. But most of all a complete lack of confidence in the leadership, which is incapable of leading the nation out of this difficult situation.

In such circumstances there will undoubtedly be an explosion of events, which it may be possible to contain temporarily at the cost of shedding the innocent blood of citizens but which it will be impossible to contain if they persist. The movement could spread to the railways and the life of the country will come to a standstill and at such a critical time. The factories, which are procuring armaments in Petrograd are coming to a halt due to lack of fuel and raw materials. The workers are without jobs and a hungry unemployed mass is being launched on the road to anarchy, elemental and uncontrollable.

Your government is completely paralyzed and totally incapable of restoring order where it has broken down. Your Majesty, save Russia, humiliation and disgrace threaten. The war cannot be brought to a victorious end in such circumstances as this ferment has already affected the army and threatens to spread, unless the authorities put an end to the anarchy and disorder.

Your Majesty, without delay summon a person whom the whole country trusts and charge him with forming a government in which the whole of the population can have confidence. Such a government will command the support of the whole of Russia, which will once more regain confidence in itself and in its leader.

In this hour, unprecedented in its terror and the horror of its consequences, there is no other way out and there can be no delay.

Nicky was outraged by the harrying tone of this telegram and forwarded it on to me with his letter:

Dearest Sunny, I received your telegram about the worrying strikes, but rest assured, my lovebird, that all is well in hand.

So there you are with three children and Anya lying with measles, how provoking for you! Do try and let Maria and Anastasia catch it too, it would be so much simpler for all of them and you also! I have again spoken with Dr. Federov and he finds it absolutely necessary for the children and Alexei especially to have a change of climate after their complete recovery. When I asked him which place he was thinking of he said the Crimea, which as you know was my very same thought! I must say I think the proposition an excellent one, and what a rest for you my darling!

Besides the rooms at Tsarskoe must be disinfected later and you would not care probably going to Peterhof so where is to live? We will think it over quietly when I come back which I hope won't take too long! My brain feels rested here – no shaking ministers and no fidgety questions to think over – I think it does me much good, but only the brain of course as the heart suffers from being separated. So difficult with the children ill, but what can one do?

I won't be long, Sunny, only to put all to rights and then my duty will be done.

Nicky

It was so late that night as I read these missives that I could not quite puzzle out what Nicky's last line had meant or whether he had read Rodzianko's terrifying telegram about the state of anarchy in the country.

What I knew was this: Today I had been visited by a panicked Protopopov, who looked as though he was being chased as he squealed in the high-pitched distress of a rat on a sinking ship. He told me that the army corps housed in Petersburg was joining the insurgents; then, nearly on his heels, my sweet little friend Lily Dehn arrived from town unexpectedly, saying she simply wanted to visit with me and see if she could be of help, but she also told me that the capital was an ominous place now.

"It is dead quiet where it shouldn't be. There are no trams running. Garbage is in piles everywhere. All the shops are either closed or on fire, but I hear that in other sections of the city there is a large amount of gunfire to be heard. Oh, Your Majesty, it is terrible. Is His Majesty coming back soon?"

I started to answer her, but was interrupted by a whimper. We both looked around the room in confusion, thinking we were alone, but then Lily shook her head and stood up, moved over to the curtains I had ordered closed to keep the room warm, and found Anastasia huddled behind there on the floor, holding her head.

As Lily dropped to her knees beside her, I ran over to her as well. My little one was on fire with fever and holding her head in pain. I moved over to the bell-push with difficulty and summoned a footman, thinking bitterly 'How pleased Nicky will be!' now that only Maria was yet to be stricken with this ghastly illness.

There was no more room in Baby's playroom, so I ordered Anastasia to be put into her bedroom and told a frightened Maria she should sleep with me.

I asked Lily to stay the night and it was as well that I did, for that night became long and cold and frightening. My elevator stopped working, then all the lights and steam heat cut out too.

I summoned Fredericks by shouting for him, as the bells were electric, and, shaking with exhaustion, asked what had happened.

Bundled up in a fur coat and looking more put out than frightened, he just shrugged.

"It appears that the lines to the palace have been cut, Your Majesty." He looked at Lili and shook his head. "I believe you will be obliged to be our guest for a while yet, Madam Dehn. You see, I have just heard that the rebels have taken over the train tracks leading into Tsarskoe Selo, so I fear that transportation will be impossible until His Majesty returns and sets things back to rights." Then, noticing my tears, his tone softened. "Please, Your Majesty, do not be concerned. We have plenty of fuel for the stoves and at any moment I expect a cable from His Majesty announcing his return. I am worried, however, about his bath."

I could only goggle at him. What a bizarre statement!

"*His bath*, Count Fredericks? I think you hardly need concern yourself with the complexities of drawing His Majesty's bath right now. At best, he will not be home for at least two days."

Count Fredericks scowled.

"I am referring, Your Majesty, to his bath having no heat. The entire pool will freeze within hours and that may well crack the tiles and the holding area. His Majesty will be most distressed about this."

"Count Fredericks, given that everything is falling apart around us, this is a most ridiculous concern. Have every stove in the palace brought to the rooms the children and I are in, particularly the children's rooms, and make sure there is a servant standing close by to keep them lit. They are terribly ill and the cold could finish them."

I collapsed into Lili's waiting arms while my Maria stood in the corner, a fist pressed to her mouth to keep her from screaming, I think.

"Fredericks," I shouted at his departing back, "tell them to keep the water boiling too. We need clean linens for my children." He returned to the doorway, and by the only light available, which was coming from the small fire, I saw that he was not annoyed but merely very, very old and frightened. "We will all manage somehow, Count Fredericks. After you have passed on my orders, go and try to rest. Make sure they put a stove in your room as well."

He bowed and I saw the tears on his old cheeks.

"Yes, Your Majesty. Thank you, Your Majesty."

There was a moan, followed by a faint scream that nevertheless echoed through our now-silent palace.

"Good God, it's Anya," I said. "She must be so frightened in the dark."

Maria straightened herself up and swallowed.

"I'll go to her, Mama. You must rest." She turned to Lili. "Can you go and check on the others, Lili? Poor Mama, I think she needs to lie down."

Lili, who was proving to be an angel in our midst, hugged Maria, kissed my cheek, and nodded cheerfully.

"It is true, beautiful girl, she does need to rest," and when I made a half-hearted attempt to rise to my feet, she added sternly, "You do need to rest! I'll see to the little ones, which still makes your Maria braver than me because Anya sounds beside herself."

She winced and put her hands over her ears, which miraculously made Maria and me giggle, and then they were both gone and I was left staring into the fire, wondering if Nicky could possibly understand any of this.

Chapter 37

Nicky, as it happened, had finally started for home, but he did not succeed in reaching us, because, late in the night and with only a hundred miles to go, he was told that the train tracks up ahead had already been seized by the rebels.

As it turned out, before Nicky had even begun his journey, he had received another telegram from Rodzianko, which said:

> The position is getting worse. Measures must be taken at once. Because tomorrow will be too late. The last hour has struck and the fate of the Fatherland and the dynasty is being decided.

I was told later by Nicky's companion, Prince Dolgoruky, that Nicky merely crumpled up the telegram and said, "That fat fool Rodzianko has sent me more nonsense to which I shall not bother to respond."

He did, however, apparently give orders for troops to march on Petrograd to "settle these disturbances, which will not be tolerated in a time of war," but unbeknownst to Nicky, his generals who had now decided he must go, countermanded his order.

Nicky, meantime, shrugged off the annoyance of rebels being on the tracks and ordered the train to Pskov, where the Ninth Army was headed by General Ruzsky, taking him hundreds of miles away from Tsarskoe Selo and us.

By the time he arrived in Pskov, the Duma, now calling itself the Provisional Government, had claimed to have taken charge of the country, and General Ruzsky who had been in correspondence with Rodzianko all along, had taken it upon himself to send a spate of telegrams to the other generals as he awaited Nicky's arrival. So, by the time Nicky finally reached Pskov, the traitorous general was ready to meet him clutching a batch of telegrams he had received back as he had asked each general in turn, including the ever-rancorous Grand Duke Nicholas, whether or not they thought Nicky should be required to abdicate.

These generals, who had spent the last two-and-a-half years agreeing on nothing, had finally something they could agree on – that Nicky had to go, and now.

Nicky, whose bravery could seldom be compared with that of a lion when confronted directly, folded like his dominoes, and, without a whimper, agreed to abdicate.

How fortunate for the Duma – 'the new government' – that General Ruzsky continued to keep in touch with it. "Now's the time!" he no doubt telegraphed to them. "Hurry up with those Articles of Abdication before he starts to realize that the Ninth Army could save him yet," or words to that effect.

The new government, all a-flutter with the scent of victory in its nostrils, ordered a fast train to be sent to Pskov, finding the railroad workers more helpful to them than they had been to their anointed sovereign, and by the time the Articles of Abdication had reached Nicky, he had decided that Baby should abdicate as well, a decision he had no legal right to make, made without a

366

word to me, as all communication between us had predictably been cut.

Instead, he proposed to hand the throne over to his brother Michael, but without consulting him either, of course. So, by the time the Articles arrived in Pskov, Nicky was positively eager to sign away his and Baby's God-given rights, and he proceeded to do so with an unaccustomed resolution in action, asking only that he be allowed to now back to Mogilev "to say goodbye to my beloved troops."

The deputies from the Duma, who had brought the Articles to him, were too surprised by his request to deny it, so they gave him permission to return to Mogilev, and off he went to Headquarters, where, to my forever shock, he remained for a further four days.

There he was visited by Minnie and by Sandro, who must have been so deeply gratified that his every dire prediction had come to pass, that he probably never gave a second thought as to what all of this meant for him, for his family, and for Russia.

Meanwhile, we who were barricaded together in Tsarskoe Selo were literally kept in the dark about this, and frozen out, you might say, of all understanding of what was happening around us, for Lili, Maria and I, and a dangerously exhausted Dr. Botkin, were trying frantically to keep our invalids alive as their fevers raged from between 102F and a terrifying 105F.

Olga developed encephalitis as a secondary infection and Tatiana developed abscesses in both ears that were so severe that she lost her hearing. Baby and Anastasia were delirious with spiking fevers that led to convulsions, and then, to cap it all off, Maria fell ill too and became the sickest of them all.

At this point, the Provisional Government, my new masters, although I did not yet know it, was more considerate than Nicky and kept in touch with developments at Tsarskoe Selo by telephone with Count Fredericks. They informed him of the abdication, and then the ever-solicitous Rodzianko told him to advise me and the children to flee without further delay.

I had not heard from Nicky for four days and was overcome with panic, believing him to be dead, the abdication to be but a rumor, and that we too were in mortal danger. Then Count Fredericks informed me that he had received a telegram from Nicky advising him that he would be home within two days and that we were not to run away or to do anything at all until his return.

Immediately after this, his Uncle Paul, the sole Romanov to be left in town – the others having wisely decamped to their estates in the Crimea and elsewhere – came to see me and told me that everything I was hearing was true. Nicky had indeed broken the vow he had made at his coronation and robbed my little boy of his crown at the same time as he had surrendered his own. It seemed, too, that poor Michael, fearing for his own life and that of his wife and child, had also abdicated almost instantly upon hearing the news that he was to be Tsar.

Thus ended three hundred years of Romanov rule.

Seeing Grand Duke Paul, or possibly former Grand Duke Paul, leave my boudoir, Count Fredericks came to see me to announce that he had just spoken to Rodzianko again and that a delegation would arrive at the palace in the morning to place us all under arrest.

The next morning, I went to the Maple Room, a beautiful but seldom-used grand parlor, filled with specially-built glass cases where I displayed my lovely Fabergé eggs, Nicky's gifts to me every Easter. I assumed there wouldn't be one this year, and then I wondered why I had not come here more often. Everything was so pretty, all pale green and white. It was a good room to be arrested in, I supposed.

The arrest was all completed with the least possible unkindness and at the same time managed to be the single most humiliating experience of my life.

The Provisional Government sent a very nice man named General Kornilov, who bowed and offered his hand, which I ignored, holding myself up with a strength of will that must have been sent by God alone, for how else can I explain my not breaking down in front of him?

"Your Majesty, I have been sent by the Provisional Government to place you and your family under arrest. This order will also apply to anyone inside the palace who chooses to remain here past the next forty-eight hours. All entrances will be sealed and guarded, and a commander, a Colonel Kobylinsky, will be put in charge of the security of the palace."

I swallowed, looked at a point above his head, and managed to say, "What does that mean, 'in charge of the security of the palace'?"

He sighed wistfully and I could see that he was not enjoying this assignment any more than I was, but what living person of honor could have done?

"He will be in charge of all packages and mail that arrive or leave the palace. He will either approve, or not, any visitors who may come. He will set the schedule for your family's daily activities."

"*Our daily activities*, Colonel? You are acting as though we will be prisoners in our own home. This is not acceptable. When the Tsar arrives tomorrow, he will have much to say to you, I can assure you."

"The former Tsar, Your Majesty, and, yes, you are now prisoners. That is what being arrested means, Your Majesty."

I felt tears start as the room tilted. Rallying my failing body and courage with difficulty, and not knowing what to ask him or to say in this startling and stark new world, I said stupidly, "Why do you call me that?"

"I beg your pardon, Your Majesty, I do not understand."

"*Your Majesty*," I said slowly. "If my husband is no longer the Tsar, if he is the former Tsar, as you have just said, then logically I am no longer a majesty either."

I waited for him to correct me, I wanted him to correct me, but above all I wanted him to make this all not so.

But he merely looked at me with pity and said, "That is true, Alexandra Feodorovna."

I swayed with shock. No one had called me that, not ever, except in the prayers of the Orthodox Church, but then it was always 'Her Imperial Majesty Alexandra Feodorovna.'

I gasped for air and swayed into a chair, no longer able to stand. He moved towards me in concern and I kicked out at him like a maddened child.

He jumped back, his expression tightening.

"I see you are distressed, Madame," he said, carefully choosing a less offensive mode of address, or so he presumed. "I will leave you, then. In a few days Alexander Kerensky will come to see you and the former Tsar. He has many questions to put to you."

"Keresnsky?" I spat out. "I told Nicky to hang him."

He smiled mirthlessly.

"As may be, but I assure you he is still very much alive and well, and now the Head of our new Democratic Government. It is possible that, with so many millions of dead from the war and your husband's daily reprisals, that he escaped through the cracks of random rifle fire. Well, I have much to do, as I am sure so do you, Madame. I have heard that your children are very sick and I am most sorry for that." He held out his hand again, and again I ignored it. With that he chuckled, "Ah, the Romanovs, gracious until the very end, it would seem."

He turned his back on me and stalked out of the room. It was then and only then that I noticed that our Abyssinian guards were no more, seemingly having fled along with nearly every other servant in the palace. They had opened the door for me on every occasion that I entered a room. Had I ever opened a door for myself? I could not recall.

I tried to stand. I needed to see to the children. I needed to go to Anya, whose nurses had run off along with all the others.

But I couldn't, not for hours. It was better here, with no one to pull at me, or to look at me and to ply me with unanswerable questions. I liked it here, and since there was no one to call to light the lamps and build me a fire, it grew cold and dark, for darkness comes so early in the winter and the winter goes on forever in Russia.

Russia, I hated it now, this land of my husband and the birthplace of my children. I think I always had. It had surely hated me from the beginning, and despite all my professions of love for it, they had never been the truth.

I wanted to go home, but where was home? Darmstadt, my beautiful little old home? The lilacs would be blooming there. Germany was not the land of endless winter, nor populated by a stupid savage people. It was a graceful place, my place, and I ached for it.

But there was no possibility of my going home. We were at war with Germany. It was the enemy, my husband's enemy, and I supposed my enemy too, or was that still true now that he was no longer the Tsar and I was no longer the Tsarina? And even if we could get there, Nicky would hate the very idea of Germany, and Nicky was still my husband, and I owed him my allegiance, for I had given it to him in glory, and so I must do so in destruction. Yes, loyalty I could still give him. But love, that I did not know about anymore.

I must still love him, I told myself fiercely. I had always loved him, Nicky the man, not the Tsar. That was true, I begged of myself, wasn't it? *Oh God help me, send me your strength, for I have none of my own. Help me to rise above every awful truth and at least show a grace I cannot feel. Help me, Father, help me!* I prayed with fervor, but I didn't feel him there, I didn't hear him there, and I wasn't comforted by him or warmed by him. In fact, I was freezing in this icy room.

Desperate for any sort of sign at all, I looked around, and above the cold marble fireplace I saw *her* gazing down at me amid the gloom, the doomed Queen in all her portrayed splendor, Marie Antoinette, captured in a painting which was one of my most prized possessions, a gift from the French during our trip there, long ago, when Olga had been a baby and I had been pregnant again with the child I knew would be a son. How they had shouted for us! *"Vive l'Empéreur. Vive l' Impératrice! Vive le bébé,"* but once they had shouted so admiringly at her too.

Yes, she would have understood me. How beautiful and young she had been, younger than I was now, and they had cut off her head, her own once-adoring subjects. When a queen's head is lighter of a crown, it becomes very vulnerable.

I stroked my neck. Would they kill us now? I thought they might. That would make me a martyr, a Queen in Heaven.

Then I heard a voice talking to me all the way from childhood, my little cousin Alice, now Queen of Greece, but then just a little girl, like me.

"Alicky, Alicky," she had said, "you always play at being sorrowful. What will ever happen if some real sorrow comes for you?"

"This marriage, I do not like it," said Grandmamma in reply.

I looked about frantically. I wanted her, but she was invisible to me, although I did hear her. That greatest of queens, that dearest of grandmothers! She must have been sad for me in heaven.

"The state of Russia is so foul, anything could happen," she had said. Yes, she had foreseen trouble ahead. Everyone had foreseen what I could not, or would not, recognize. Now they were all dead or too far away, and I could not tell them that they had been right.

I did not belong here. I never did. And they did not want me here. Nicky did this, he forced me here. He forced me upon his people too, all with his single-minded love and need for me. It had been the first and the last time in his life that Nicky had ever stubbornly held onto a belief, and now I could not leave.

Chapter 38

"His Majesty ... Oh, Your Majesty, His Majesty is back!" wheezed Count Fredericks, who had nearly killed himself trying to reach me to announce that Nicky was home.

I nodded.

"Thank you, Count Fredericks. I shall wait for him in here."

He looked at me with disappointment.

"But he is home. He is getting out of his car. Don't you want to greet him there?"

"No, I do not. I wish, if possible, to avoid any further encounters with the filthy rabble they have sent to guard us. Tell His Majesty that I shall wait for him here."

The "here" I was referring to was Baby's now deserted playroom. The enormous room had become impossible to heat, no matter how many stoves were brought in, and so I and my small ragtag bunch of nurses – which now comprised me, dear Lili, and Baby's two kindly sailors Derevenko and Nagorny, as well as my lovely Sophie Buxhoeveden, who had somehow made it back to my side from the hell that was Petersburg, together with the assistance of one remaining footman – had moved my sick darlings to other rooms.

Olga, who was better now, though terribly weak, had been put on a bed in the Red Room where Lili was sleeping. Baby had been moved back to his little bedroom, as had Tatiana. They, too, were getting better, although my pretty Tati was still as deaf as a post, but it amused Baby to act out things for her, so that was fine.

Sophie had valiantly moved into Anya's room to act as nurse and companion to her, to help give me time away from her as she was taking our newly reduced circumstances much worse than I. Anastasia and Maria were in their bedroom, and Anastasia, although very weak, was helping to care for Maria by holding oxygen to her face. My Mashka, having developed double pneumonia, was hovering near to death.

I had found comfort in that playroom, surrounded by all of Baby's little things, and had ordered up a cot to be brought in for me, because, with the elevator no longer in operation, I could not reach my children from our bedroom below.

I did not mind the cold. I didn't think I would ever be warm again. It was best to remain frozen. Any warmth would have shattered me, and then what would have become of us all?

"So you wish me to bring him in here?" Count Fredericks asked by way of startled clarification.

"Yes, here."

I heard Nicky coming only moments later. He was shuffling and staggering along the carpet in the corridor. 'My God, they have hurt him,' I thought, and steeled myself anew for fresh horrors.

Yet he wasn't wounded, although he was nearly unrecognizable, his skin tight across his face and as yellow as a Chinaman's. His eyes were tiny, sunken raisins, and when they met mine, his legs collapsed so that he fell to the floor and had to crawl across the carpet on all fours to reach me.

I shrunk back instinctively.

"Sunny, Sunny, Sunny, help me! Oh, Sunny, I'm so sorry!"

I sunk down to the carpet, more because I could not stand than to embrace him, but he was on me then, his arms clasping my waist and his hot head burrowing into my stomach as though he wished to crawl inside me.

I moaned and he moved even closer, knocking me onto my back.

It seemed forever before I could raise my hand to touch his wet face, but he didn't seem to notice as he rubbed his cheek back and forth against my icy palm. He stunk of fear and his skin was greasy against mine.

'He'll need a bath,' I thought vacantly, 'and we have so few to heat all the water and drag it up, but he must have one!'

I slid back away from him a little and sat up against the wall. Dislodged, he raised his head and stared at me through his death mask of a face.

"Sunny," hold me. "I need you. Oh, please!"

I shook my head wordlessly and, just like that, he regained control of himself, and a second later he was on his feet and holding out his hand to me. Warily, I took it, and he guided me over to a chair.

"Here, sit, Alix. Forgive me, I was not myself."

He lit a cigarette and turned towards the window. All was familiar then, although nothing was.

I spoke from a mouth filled with cotton.

"Why, Nicky?"

It was all I wanted from him now, an answer, a way to make sense of what he had just done to us and to Russia.

He made some noise. I could not tell what kind of noise it was, whether a mirthless chuckle or a sob, and I couldn't care.

"You of all the people in the world are the one person who has no right to ask me that," he said, indignant now, accusing, angry, bitter. "Mama, yes. Even Sandro. The children. My soldiers. A hundred million of my people. All of Russia. They all can ask me that, but not you, my darling."

Shaken from my paralysis, I asked haltingly, "What are you saying? Am I not the person, besides our son, whom you have robbed the most with your cowardice, Nicky?" I gestured around us. "Everything is gone, taken from me, and you dare to insist that I should not ask you why?"

His shrug cut me off and we stared at each other warily, waiting.

He broke the silence first.

"Our son is never going to have children of his own. If he lives another few years, it will be a miracle, and you too would know this if you weren't so stupidly and forever unable to face that truth. Oh no," he said more loudly, "not the fragile Empress Alexandra for whom all truth that is not hers is unpalatable, unspeakable, must not be spoken of. You brought that madman into our lives and smeared our family with filth, and destroyed the love for me of my subjects, all because the dangerously sick child you gave me was always going to die and that madman was the one person alive who could happily lie to you with impunity. So, yes, I abdicated the crown he was never going to wear, Alix."

I put my hands over my ears and squeezed my eyes shut.

"No, no, Nicky, stop!"

He walked over to me and pulled my hands down from my ears, gripping them in his own. His cigarette fell to the carpet and he stamped it out impatiently.

"You will listen this once, Alix. You will hear the truth and then do with it what you may." He fell silent for a moment and continued more softly. "I suppose we will go on. What else is there to do?"

"Nicky ..."

"No, Alix my wife, my heart's darling, my ex-Empress ... no, you will hear me now."

I turned on him as fierce as a lynx.

"Release me, you buffoon. You are mad. You are mad. You are mad with self-pity and failure. You reek of it."

He released my hands and bowed ironically, and for a moment I saw Felix Yusupov before me, and Sandro, and finally Grand Duke Nicholas. They were all bowing to me, disdainfully.

Nicky moved back towards the windows and lit another cigarette.

"As Your Majesty wishes." He gave me a horrible half-smile and I looked away. "That, I suppose, has always been my greatest failure, Alix, although I am sure you will disagree. My greatest failure, my most menial failure, has been my desire to grant your every wish. Do you know," he said abruptly, "how long ago I stopped seeing people, any people, even my own family ... anyone at all at court, because you didn't like them? You said ... oh, I forget all you said ... Do you know how many hundreds of reviews and receptions I attended alone, or later with our poor girls, because you were in bed, Alix, sick in bed? Do you know, my darling, that with very few exceptions you have now spent nearly twenty full years in bed?" He looked over at me to see if I would respond but I only glared at him. He laughed. "Still the tyrant, Sunny, even now. I wonder, my dear, why you feel you have lost a single thing by my abdication. Now take me for example, just for argument's sake ..." He gestured at his chest. "I seem to have lost my family, my army, my Russia." His voice broke on the last, but he swallowed and went on determinedly while I sat there paralyzed with hatred and fear. "But you, soul of my soul, your life will go on the same as always. You can lie in your boudoir and send us, your family, bulletins of whether your heart is number two or number three. And if that is too arduous for you, my darling, you can lie in bed, drugged on veronal and await our worshipful visits. You can make fun of Anya; I suppose we had better take her with us to England. You can send notes to the children and tell Botkin what is wrong with you so he can give us bulletins. And, all in all, your chosen realm will remain exactly the way it has always been since the day you decided, long ago, that everything, anything at all, was all too much for you."

I ignored his self-pitying attempt to blame me for his failures and addressed the sole interesting thing he had said.

"We are going to England?"

He smiled sadly.

"Yes, it has all being arranged. We will be sent there, at least until the end of the war, and then afterwards I am hoping we can return and live at Livadia. Does that please you, Alix?"

I shrugged.

"Why do you ask, Nicky? According to you, as long as I am reclining on a chaise somewhere, I will hardly notice."

His eyes filled with tears, his brief burst of bravado over as quickly as it had begun, as it always was.

"I didn't mean ... Alix, Sunny, you know I still love you. I have always loved you. That will never change, and as long as I have you and our dear children, what does anything else really matter?"

I looked beyond him out of the darkening windows, wishing everything would be over, without understanding exactly what that meant, and then met his hopeful eyes.

I held out my hand.

"Of course, Nicky, what else matters?"

CPSIA information can be obtained
at www.ICGtesting.com
Printed in the USA
LVHW082316140319
610743LV00022B/221/P